Whip of the Wild God

A Novel Of Tantra In Ancient India

MIRA PRABHU

"Whip of the Wild God is a magical novel, an exquisite work that lacks nothing, a wild ride into ancient India—enriching, heartening and inspiring. Richly sprinkled with spiritual gems, this is a lyrical saga which throws a clear light on the ancient practices of yoga, tantra and atma vichara (Self-investigation). And yet it will also drag you through the depths of despair, force you to confront your own darkness, enrage you with the heartless cruelty of man and the bitter fight for survival—then drench out the flames with love, truth and mercy. God, how I love this book!"

Jen Wilson, language teacher and yogini

"Mira Prabhu, artist/storyteller par excellence, plays on heartstrings, taking a reader through a profound primal experience reminiscent of the undying classics; yet this work is new and unique. Nothing is left out; one can experience life from full fall to transfiguration. It is a 'mover and shaker' read, a Great Book, one of the best I've ever read, and it will make a fantastic motion picture."

Joneve McCormick, creative writing guru, poet and writer

"Imagine my delight to find Whip of the Wild God to be both a page-turning adventure as well as a book of profound spiritual wisdom! I savored every single page—the craft of the writing and the author's depth of understanding—and yet I couldn't wait to get to the next page. Mira Prabhu has produced a rare gem!"

Swami Asokananda, President, Integral Yoga Institute of New York

"The story winds down beautifully, and the final encounter is brilliant. I couldn't help but feel tremendously inspired at a deep level...all the mysticism is presented with pin-point accuracy."

Raj Acharya, software programmer

AUTHOR'S NOTE

Whip of the Wild God is a work of visionary fiction inspired by the author's passion for eastern mysticism and ancient India. Set in a mythical civilization evocative of the sophisticated urban societies of the Indus Valley Civilization (circa 3300–1300 BCE), this novel weaves together the doctrines of *Karma*, Reincarnation, certain approaches to *Kundalini-Tantra*, and enlightenment. Given the many conflicting views of that time, the author makes no claims to historical or scholarly accuracy.

Melukhha...

Many thousands of years ago, an urban civilization of singular caliber arose along the fecund banks of the Indus and Sarasvati Rivers. Growing rich on maritime trade, Melukhha steadily expanded until it covered a quarter of a million square miles, twice the geographical area of the contemporary kingdoms of Egypt and Mesopotamia.

Then, after impressive epochs of peace and prosperity, and well before the consciousness of the Sakya Prince Gautama rose into enlightenment in the sixth century B.C.E., this jewel of the ancient world simply vanished.

Archaeologists have uncovered the remnants of Melukhha in territory now controlled by both India and Pakistan. The ruins point to a civilization that had reached an extraordinary level of material, scientific and spiritual evolution, where momentous events flowered before fading away, in the manner of all transient things.

Who or what destroyed this thriving river metropolis? A cataclysmic yoking of elemental forces? Barbarians who scaled high mountains to raze her to the ground? Or was it Rudra, the Wild God himself, who obliterated her, incensed with her rulers for misusing the serpent fire?

And so the mystery of Melukhha remains, still haunting curious minds.

Oh Mother!
From untruth, lead me to truth,
From darkness, lead me to light,
From death, lead me to eternal life!

Brihadaranyaka Upanishad

TABLE OF CONTENTS

CAST OF CHARACTERS

<u>*DIVINE CHARACTERS*</u>
Mahadevi/Shakti (*Great Goddess*) goddess of the Unmanifest
Rudra (*the howler*), Wild God, lord of the Unmanifest;
Shiva/Ishvara
Apsara (*elegant*), celestial nymph
Gods & Demons: rulers of higher and lower realms of
consciousness respectively
<u>*MAJOR MORTAL CHARACTERS (IN ORDER OF APPEARANCE)*</u>
Ishvari (*consort of Ishvara*), girl of Devikota village
Sumangali (*she who is auspicious*), mother of Ishvari
Hiranya (*golden one*), father of Ishvari, husband of Sumangali
Obalesh (*Lord Shiva*), brother of Ishvari
Ghora (*agitated*), priest of Devikota village
Andhaka (*blind),* headman of Devikota village
Kushal (*clever*), royal envoy of Takshak, maharajah of Melukhha
Devadas (*servant of the gods*), royal astrologer
Takshak (*cobra*), maharajah of Melukhha
Nartaka (*dancer*), sadhu of the sacred valley of Devikota
Atulya (*unequalled*), head acharya or guru of Rudralaya Ashram
Hariaksa (*Lord Shiva*), senior acharya at Rudralaya
<u>*ASPIRANTS*</u>: tantrikas-in-training at Rudralaya
Archini (*ray of light*)
Brijabala (*daughter of nature*)
Charusheela (*beautiful jewel*)
Dalaja (*honey*)
Gitali (*melodious*)
Gandhali (*sweet scent*)
Ikshula (*holy river*)
Ishvari (*consort of Ishvara*)
Kairavi (*moonlight*)
Makshi (*honeybee*)
Tilotamma (*celestial dancer*)
Urmila (*enchantress*)

Maruti (*incarnation of Lord Shiva*), leader of the monkey tribe at Rudralaya

Inanna Sumerian for goddess of sexual love, fertility and warfare; ex-high tantrika of Melukhha

Vikranth (*powerful*), a monk residing at Rudralaya; Atulya's assistant

Shaardul (*tiger*), father of Takshak

Alatu: Sumerian for goddess of the underworld; black magician and Takshak's mistress

Daruka (*deodar tree*), chief of Takshak's Royal Guardsmen

Ketaki (*flower of Ketaka tree*), personal advisor to the high tantrika

Mandakini (*gently flowing*), personal maid to the high tantrika and later housekeeper

Vasudeva (*bright, excellent*), head gardener and husband of Mandakini

Abhilasha (*desire*), wife of Shaardul and mother of Takshak

Eshanika (*one who fulfils desire*), deceased wife of Takshak

Vegavat (*swift*), leopard of the sacred valley of Devikota

Kharanshu (*sun*), ex-member of the Melukhhan Council, now disguised as a ferryman

Gaurika (*pretty girl*), crippled girl of Devikota village

Skanda (*spurting*), first supplicant of the healer of the valley

Harshal (*happiness*), blind son of Skanda

Kusagra (*king*), chief of the Kirata jungle tribe

(Sanskrit translations in parentheses, beside names of characters)

I do not know what I truly am
I roam about, mysteriously fettered by my mind
    —*Rig Veda*

DEVIKOTA VILLAGE: 1839 BCE

A drongo bird shrieked a raucous warning from the *devadaru* tree as Ishvari turned the corner of the narrow path leading out of the valley. She skidded to an abrupt halt, sucking in her breath at the sight of the yellow-banded coils of a king cobra lying before her on the sunwarmed path.

The king cobra was belligerent, its venom capable of killing an elephant! Fast as lightning, Ishvari clambered sideways on to the rocks bordering the trail, hoping the serpent was too sluggish to give chase. When she glanced back fearfully moments later, the cobra had only raised its painted hood in her direction, its tongue a forked, flickering earthworm.

She resumed her zigzag flight along the regular pathway, her long, black braid bouncing against her skinny buttocks. Again she sensed the presence of a benevolent entity: *had this power prompted the drongo to shriek its timely warning?* And why did she feel its hovering warmth most intensely in the quiet of the forbidden valley, where the fog of sadness enshrouding her since her father's callous murder nine moons ago always seemed to temporarily dissolve?

Despite the valley's abundance of fruit, herbs and berries rendered more valuable than ever by impending famine, the superstitious Devikotans kept away from it for fear of ghosts. So Ishvari had been free to explore its lush beauty in peace, gorging on its bounty, and drinking from a spring so clear it reflected not just her thin face, but the glory of the sun. Best of all, she always returned home with her frayed shoulder bag bursting with rare herbs her mother could barter for staples at the weekly village market.

A vision of the riverside cave she'd stumbled upon today arose in her mind's eye as she raced homeward. The cave had been veiled by a thick tangle of tall reeds, and on the crystalline surface of the water below, a white lotus had reigned. Amazed, she had watched a leopard emerge from its gloom and slip down to the riverbank, scanning his surroundings with liquid eyes before extending his neck to lap at the cool water.

The big cat had raced up a slope and into the stone temple perched on the valley's rocky outcrop. Padding right up to a *sadhu* meditating within, the beast had placed his tawny head on the man's lap, as if in some primal form of worship. And even from afar, the sadhu's copper-skinned beauty and regal air had enthralled her: if he was guardian of the valley, she wondered now, why was he allowing *her* to roam its length and breadth when the few Devikotans who'd ventured there could only stammer about chilling experiences that served to keep others away?

Mica-flecked piles of rock lining the edges of the trail caught shafts of dying sun, bringing her back to the present as they sparkled like stardust; even at its most bitter, life had its precious moments. But, as she cut through the fruit orchard that spread behind the cottage she'd been banished to with her mother and baby brother after her father's murder, she sensed something was horribly wrong.

Stealing up to its back wall, she peered in through an open window. Her fist shot to her mouth to stifle a scream—Ghora, the village priest, knelt naked on the earthen floor, his thick-fingered hands grasping the waist of her equally naked mother from behind. The squat priest was uttering ugly cries as he bucked crazily against her mother, the juttu of hair proclaiming his high status bobbing on the crown of his shaven head, the sacred thread worn across the chest by the high-born looped conveniently over his left ear. In a corner, her baby brother, Obalesh, lay placidly on a kusha mat, a trickle of milk oozing out the side of his rosebud mouth.

Ghora's body vibrated with a weird energy, his frenzied movements suggesting mingled pleasure and pain. But what of her mother? Could Sumangali possibly be enjoying *this*? She crept towards a second window for a better view. Ghora's small eyes had rolled upwards in obscene gratification, but her mother's lovely face was contorted with loathing.

Grabbing a sharp-edged stone, Ishvari stole back to the first window. Tucking it into the leather pad of the slingshot she used to chase monkeys away from the orchard, she aimed at the cleft of Ghora's plump buttocks and let fly, praying to the gods for a perfect shot. Then she turned and fled through the approaching darkness, racing back along the tortuous path until she reached the giant rock throwing its oblong shadow across the base of the valley. Only then did she release her anguish in a piercing wail, dashing her forehead against the rock and welcoming the agony of tender skin splitting open.

Thunder rumbled ominously. Startled, Ishvari looked up to see the sky turn a violent maroon as a mass of storm clouds scudded rapidly past, leaving the sky clear again. *So the Little Goddess attempts to force open her third eye but only succeeds in doing violence to herself!* a great voice roared through the silence.

Little Goddess? Had the pain crashing through her head driven her insane? Or was Ghora playing a trick on her? Impossible! The stout priest could never have chased her all the way here in so short a time...besides, this mighty voice sounded nothing like Ghora's plaintive whine.

Warily she opened her eyes and beheld a gigantic being, shining like the sun, straddling the valley. The black and gold striped skin of a tiger covered his *lingam* and the velvet hide of an antelope draped itself across his massive chest. Knots of cobras writhed about the peacock-blue column of his neck and a crescent moon, luminous and delicate, hovered above his matted coils of hair. The god raised an enormous hand from which light streamed forth to enter her forehead.

Harness your rage, O Ishvari! the cosmic apparition thundered. *Anger weakens the spirit and attracts the attention of demons. I come to grant you great gifts, earned over a thousand past lifetimes. Abuse them and I shall whip you until you beg for oblivion.* The awesome face visibly softened at her terror. *Now, take heart! Your marksmanship has sent the false priest scuttling. Be kind to your mother tonight, for soon, Devikota will exist only in memory.*

Ishvari touched her wound with tremulous fingers—still wet with blood, but the pain was miraculously gone. Then she was alone again in the shimmering valley. Stumbling home in an incredulous daze, she found Sumangali seated on the stoop, cradling Obalesh as she fretfully scanned the horizon with kohl-smudged eyes.

"Why so late?" Sumangali demanded as Ishvari silently set the bag of herbs down by her feet. She grabbed Ishvari's arm and drew her close to examine the discoloration on her forehead. "What happened?" she demanded, her anger changing to concern.

"Tripped," Ishvari mumbled. "Hit my head on a rock."

"Get inside this minute!" Sumangali ordered shrilly. "When will you ever learn?"

And when will you? Ishvari thought angrily. Inside the one-roomed cottage, she rocked her drowsy brother in her arms while Sumangali ground healing herbs for a poultice on a pock-marked grinding stone. She dared not speak of her outlandish experience in the valley—how would Sumangali react to the god's cryptic words? Then her eyes fell on a straw basket of vegetables and a sack of rice standing next to the doorway and rage flared again—so *this* was Ghora's pay for using her mother's body!

Obalesh whimpered restlessly in her arms as Sumangali applied the ground herbs to her bruise. "A rock flew in through the window while you were gone," her mother announced tersely, tying a piece of muslin around Ishvari's forehead to keep the poultice in place.

"Really, maa?" Ishvari asked, her eyes widening mock innocently. "Was it a monkey, do you think? They hurl stones at me, you know, when I chase them away from the orchard. Except for Ghora," she added slyly, "no Devikotan would dare to come this close to the valley."

Suspicion alternated with guilt on Sumangali's expressive face.

"Did the stone strike you?" Ishvari persisted.

"If it had, idiot," Sumangali retorted. "I'd be bleeding."

Ishvari hid a satisfied smirk as Sumangali served her a clay bowl of rice gruel and greens; so the god had spoken true—Ghora would think at least twice before coming here again!

"Sleep well, child," Sumangali said, her face pinched and weary as she picked up Obalesh to give him her breast. "Ghora came by to say that a royal envoy arrives from Melukhha tomorrow early morning to address all of Devikota." Bitterness flashed across her face. "The occasion is so important even *pariahs* like us must attend."

Ishvari's spirits plummeted. "But what's this got to do with *us*?"

"We'll find out soon enough," Sumangali muttered. Then her voice rose, indicating her constant state of tension. "I beg you—do *not* follow your father's example! It's dangerous to provoke even the *lowest* of them! Swear to me by Mahadevi you'll keep your mouth shut?"

Ishvari nodded a sullen assent. The wound on her forehead throbbed faintly, but the rawness of the pain was truly gone. "Rest now," Sumangali coaxed, placing sleeping Obalesh on the kusha mat beside Ishvari. "Your dreams will be sweet if you obey me."

She lay down beside Obalesh as Sumangali tidied up the kitchen area. The image of Ghora slamming himself against her mother's willowy body forced a sharp cry from her, which she managed to disguise as a cough. Sumangali half-turned before resuming her work, and Ishvari glimpsed the stark misery on her face. Her mother hated Ghora, she reminded herself sternly; the only reason she could have submitted to the lecherous rascal was for the food he brought.

Ishvari stared up at the cracked ceiling, her thoughts a confused jumble as she considered her mother's recent ramblings. Sumangali had traced the onset of their current troubles in Devikota to her mother-in-law's death four years ago, when a pestilence had raged through the village and stolen over a hundred lives. Soon after, her father-in-law too had sickened and died, and Hiranya had begun drowning his sorrows in liquor.

That wealthy Hiranya had been hit hard by the death of both his parents in such quick succession had reached the wrong ears: Andhaka, village headman, had joined with Ghora to circle around him like birds of prey. Soon, vicious rumors concerning his parents' consecutive deaths were floating around Devikota.

Possessed by a reckless god, or more likely demon, Hiranya had retaliated by making public speeches denouncing the powerful headman and his main accomplice, the priest. Fuelled by shots of rice liquor, his eloquence had soon attracted a swelling crowd; whereupon the demon of drink had tightened the noose over his foolhardy neck and led him toward a humiliating death.

Sumangali's dismal version of events continued to disturb Ishvari; was there really a curse on her mother as Ghora had publicly claimed? Like Hiranya, Sumangali too was an only child, orphaned by cruel circumstance. Born in the seaside village of Parushni, her mother had lived a carefree life until the night her merchant father had been struck dead by lightning. Parushni's spiteful necromancer had warned Sumangali's mother that her daughter's beauty had provoked a jealous demoness into killing her father—unless Sumangali was cast out of Parushni, the hag swore, this malevolent entity would prey on its men, one after the other, ravaging the village. Believing the necromancer, her mother had thrown Sumangali out into the streets, then, in a frenzy of grief, drowned herself in the raging Parushni River.

A childless widower had offered Sumangali shelter. Fearing for her safety in the seething village, he'd immediately sent a message to his nephew in Devikota—a nephew who just happened to be Hiranya's father. Stressing Sumangali's suitability as a bride for Hiranya, he'd even offered a small dowry in precious stones.

Fortunately Hiranya's parents had accepted his offer, and the kindly fellow had personally escorted the nervous teenager by bullock cart all the way to Devikota. Sumangali had fallen in love with her silver-tongued husband; producing Ishvari, she'd blossomed into womanhood. Then disaster had struck yet again.

Ishvari sucked on her thumb for comfort, feeling no older than Obalesh. How long before Sumangali broke down from the strain of keeping them alive in this wilderness? Would they survive the coming winter without a single kinsman to cushion their exile?

On the other side of the room, Sumangali prostrated before a stone deity of Mahadevi, adorned with stripes of vermilion and a few wilting marigolds. Tears streamed down her gaunt cheeks as she gazed at the image. "Where is your protection, Goddess Mother?" she sobbed. "Do you not love us any more?" Her beautiful face twisted with torment. "Allow him to defile this body just one more time," she cried softly, "and I shall end my pain forever."

Ishvari shivered under the thin quilt: could a good mother really abandon her children to such an unfriendly world? And why was Sumangali so *spineless*? Her hatred for Ghora intensified; at least, she consoled herself as sleep dragged her down into the underworld, her mother had not willingly joined with the bestial priest.

When the Supreme Shakti
Of her own will assumes every form in the universe,
In that one quivering instant the Chakra comes into being.
　　　—*Yogini-hrdaya*

LORD KUSHAL, ROYAL ENVOY

Sun beat down on the village square, scorching Ishvari so callously that she stamped her feet in a furious dance. The surrounding throng of Devikotans sent hostile looks and muttered curses her way, but she did not care—hours of waiting in this pitiless heat and still the grand envoy from Melukhha had not deigned to appear!

"Behave!" Sumangali snapped, rocking Obalesh in her thin arms. "You know how easy it is to provoke...."

"Why did you hide my slingshot then?" Ishvari cut her off rudely. "I'd shoot the eyes out of the first...."

"You promised to shut your mouth, demonspawn!" Sumangali hissed, twisting Ishvari's ear, her voice hoarsened by heat, dust and rising anxiety.

Ishvari rubbed her smarting ear, fighting back tears. *Demonspawn!* Ghora's vile name for her! Ever since his intrusion into their lives, her mother had turned into a jittery wreck.

Turning her back on Sumangali, she furtively surveyed the villagers. By the gods, the entire population of Devikota seemed to have assembled in the square, all waiting for this cursed envoy!

Ghora and the moribund Council of Elders stood at the head of the community, females congregated behind, while males lounged alongside the baked mud wall edging the square's north end. Only she and Sumangali stood apart, as was customary for those declared pariahs.

Hanging her head in frustration, Ishvari thought of their own little orchard: the instant this ridiculous gathering dispersed, she'd race home to pick the ripening fruit before birds and monkeys got them all. Her toe dug into the dry earth to trace a rough circle. She added small eyes—like those of the grunting pigs kept by the barber's new mistress—then a wide slash of a mouth and a tongue hanging out. Looks like Ghora, she thought, gratified—only, not so ugly.

Muffled laughter rose from the dense ranks ahead of her. Village belles, kohl-rimmed eyes glittering with expectation, exchanged whispers under the hawkish scrutiny of their elders— heat had not dampened their spirits, nor affected the richness of their garments. She noticed that the twin daughters of the spice and incense merchant were dressed in scarlet and blue tunics edged with gold, while the sulky, double-chinned daughter of Devikota's jeweler sweated in a tunic fashioned out of turquoise linen. In contrast, she and Sumangali were garbed in the plain white homespun pariahs were enjoined to wear for all public occasions.

Her eyes met those of Anasuya, the good-natured daughter of the village goldsmith. Anasuya flashed her a shy smile, whereupon her shrewish mother hit her daughter sharply on the head. Ishvari flinched, as if she herself had been struck; not that long ago, she'd played Seven Tiles and Snakes-On-The-Roof with the rich village girls. Blinking back tears, she recalled the necklace of seashells Anasuya had once gifted her—Sumangali had recently bartered it for herbs she hoped would strengthen her shattered nerves.

The crowd parted to let Andhaka through. Ishvari watched him stride to the front of the square and fall into agitated discourse with Ghora. Her throat constricted with renewed fury: was it only nine moons ago that these fiends had arrived at the gate of their ancestral home at twilight, accompanied by a couple of louts pushing a hand cart? Andhaka had yelled out for Sumangali, who'd hurried out, sleeping Obalesh in her arms, Ishvari tagging behind. Ghora had pointed to Hiranya's body, splayed over a hill of dung at the back of the cart, his feet sticking out into mid-air. "Dead of snakebite," he'd announced, the tic beneath his left eye jumping crazily. "A fitting end for a loose-lipped scoundrel, eh?"

Ghora had turned to the grinning men, whom Ishvari recognized as kinsmen of Andhaka. "Burn the corpse quickly, fellows, lest it further pollute Devikota. And don't forget to bathe right afterward, and light incense to appease the gods, *plenty* of it!"

Sumangali's slender body had swayed like a lily in a strong breeze. Obalesh had awoken and begun to wail. Ishvari had made to run after the cart, whereupon Andhaka had lunged forward and struck her so viciously she'd skidded backward to hit a devadaru tree. Andhaka had ordered them back inside, then stalked off with the smirking priest.

Before daybreak, Ghora had returned with the same men, pushing the same filthy cart. Eyes glittering with lust each time they fell on her frightened mother, the priest had ordered his accomplices to toss their essentials into the cart. Then he had force-marched them to the stone cottage at the base of the haunted valley, abandoned by its sheep-herding owner who'd sworn that peals of laughter rolling across the deserted region at night had driven him near insane.

Next morning, Ghora was back with more black news: by unanimous order of the elders, their home, orchards and wheat acreage had been sold to the merchants' guild to pay off Hiranya's debts. Moreover, the elders had declared the three of them to be pariahs. "Be grateful, woman," Ghora had leered. "If not for *my* intervention, you and your litter would have been burned alive."

Paralyzed by the ruthless events that had overnight deprived her of husband, assets and reputation, Sumangali had fallen into a near-catatonic state. But Ishvari's own anger against the influential bullies had risen to fever-pitch. Doubtless, her father had gradually turned into a violent drunk. Truth be told, mere weeks after Obalesh had emerged into the world, Hiranya had thrashed Sumangali near senseless for begging him to stop antagonizing Devikota's administrators. Then he'd stumbled back to the tavern, muttering about an insatiable demon that had cast its spell over him. Soon after, Devikota's rogues had murdered him.

Sumangali blamed Hiranya's liquor-loosened tongue for their troubles. "Guard your own tongue from here on, child," she'd begged Ishvari, her eyes swollen with weeping. "We women are defenseless against such evil." But Ishvari's spirit was only temporarily quelled; soon she was conjuring up fantasies of revenge.

Now, hot winds from the encroaching desert buffeted the square, sweeping grains of sand into her eyes. Ishvari rubbed them with grimy fists. A sob escaped her, causing Labuki, eldest daughter of the headman, to swivel around and shoot her a derisive look.

"Thhhhu!" Ishvari spat like a wild cat, unable to hold back her own contempt.

"What is *wrong* with you?" her mother cried. Obalesh stirred in the cloth pouch hanging around Sumangali's waist, disturbed by the mounting tension. "Calm yourself!" she ordered, gripping Ishvari's hand. "See? Over there! Lord Kushal has arrived!"

Ishvari saw the envoy descend from a semi-enclosed traveling coach drawn by four snorting, jet black stallions. The driver sat on a red seat, while the coach blazed in stripes of gold, green, crimson and saffron, colors of the royal elite. A phalanx of guardsmen formed a protective shield around the nobleman, who, despite his jeweled headdress and sumptuous attire, seemed quite ordinary—except for his eyes, which gleamed with cold intelligence.

Men jumped off the walls as Lord Kushal climbed onto the mud-packed dais, his keen eyes sweeping over the sea of upturned faces. "Salutations from Takshak, Maharajah of Melukhha!" he began—with such sure authority that the restive crowd grew quiet. "In celebration of the trade treaty between Melukhha and Sumeria, your maharajah has instructed his engineers to divert the Sarasvati River into the lowlands. Soon Devikota will be fertile again!"

"Come, Kushal, don't we deserve a little honesty?" a man shouted. "Takshak concocts these so-called treaties to appease the masses. Why not spit out what you're *really* here for?"

Dead silence followed these incendiary words. Lord Kushal's eyes darted fiercely from face to face, looking for the source. The stranger laughed, his voice now coming from a different angle, confounding both the envoy and the edgy mass of Devikotans. "Your loyalty to a corrupt king baffles me, Kushal. If you truly love Melukhha, inform Takshak that to seek new *tantrikas*—even as he abuses the old—only serves to further enrage Rudra!"

"Who speaks?" Lord Kushal demanded, even as the guards' hands flew to their scabbards—which villager would address a royal envoy with such easy familiarity? Ishvari peered through the gaps in the surging multitude until she spied a tall stranger, standing at the far edge of the square. His chiseled face shone like burnished gold, while his body, clad only in a red loincloth, stood as sure as an unsheathed sword. A wide grin of recognition broke the gloom of her expression—why, here was the sadhu of the valley himself!

"Speak up, if you dare!" Lord Kushal roared. "Who insults our maharajah?"

Ishvari looked to see what the sadhu would do, but he'd simply vanished!

"Not a Devikotan for sure, sire," Andhaka offered fearfully. "Rest assured, he does not speak for anyone of significance...."

"Mahadevi showers us with prosperity," Ghora broke in frantically. "May the benevolent Takshak live forever in the hearts of his people!"

Lord Kushal summoned up a disdainful smile. "Madmen pop up in the oddest places," he remarked languidly. "And now permit me to explain my presence in Devikota: our royal astrologer has chosen twelve—out of the three thousand villages surrounding Melukhha—for a signal honor. Devikota, I'm happy to inform you, ranks first among them."

A burst of surprised cheering broke out.

"Today," Lord Kushal continued gravely, "I shall select one single virgin from among you. Tomorrow, she will leave with me to be trained—along with eleven aspirants from other villages—by Melukhha's most venerated Tantric monks. All twelve shall later serve our nobles, but only *one* among them shall be elected high tantrika—potentially the most revered female role in all of Melukhha." The envoy's lips widened into a broad smile. "Who can predict the play of the gods? This fortunate woman may well turn out to be Devikotan!"

Ghora rushed up to the dais eagerly, his juttu of hair bobbing atop his freshly shaved dome of a head. "Tell us more, my lord," he urged. "Provide every detail so we may better serve our maharajah!"

Lord Kushal ignored the fawning priest, and for this reason alone, Ishvari began to warm to him. "Yes indeed," he continued, "a high tantrika may evolve into the most influential woman in Melukhha, which is why my choice today shall not be arbitrary. Indeed, our astrologer has given me psychic and physical signs to guide me unerringly to the right aspirant." His gaze swept over the hushed assembly. "I trust you will all cooperate."

Puzzled, Ishvari scratched her dry head, which Sumangali had not inspected for nits since Hiranya's death. What in the name of *karma* was this fellow going on about? And why were these over-dressed girls vying so brazenly for his attention?

Lord Kushal stepped down to stroll between rows of nervous women. The crowd held its collective breath as he stopped before Labuki, Andhaka's teenage daughter, considered the prettiest girl in Devikota. He studied Labuki's slender ankles, raised his practiced gaze to her jewel-studded silver waist belt, and examined her sloe eyes. The girl thrust her full breasts forward, a seductive smile curved her lips. In time, Ishvari thought disdainfully, her breasts would hang low and dry, like those of her querulous mother, first wife of the brutal headman.

Suddenly he whipped around to face Ishvari. "You, in the white tunic!" he called. Sumangali nudged her sharply and Ishvari gawked at him, petrified by his approach. Lord Kushal reached forward to cup her chin with cool fingers. "Your name, child," he ordered.

"Ishvari," she whispered. A trickle of urine ran down her thighs.

"Ish-vah-ree," Lord Kushal repeated, breaking her name into its three syllables. A glimmer of a smile crossed his face as he inspected her even more meticulously than he had Labuki, taking in the homespun shift, the skinny limbs and the black eyes that dominated her oval face. "Ishvari," he repeated, rolling her name around his tongue like honey. Unnerved, she ducked behind Sumangali. The envoy chuckled. "Ah, so the dirty Little Goddess hides behind her mother's skirts," he drawled. "Do you know what your name means?"

'Little Goddess' again? Panicked, Ishvari clutched at Sumangali's garment and the fabric ripped. Losing her balance, she fell flat on the dusty ground. A ripple of nervous laughter broke out as she scrambled to her feet, scarlet with shame, raking her eyes over the prettified girls.

"By Rudra's whip!" the envoy exclaimed. "Fire animates this child!" He caught Ishvari by the shoulder and drew her towards him. "Ishvari means *goddess*," he explained kindly, "feminine form of Rudra, Wild God, master of life and death in the Triple World. Your fierceness doesn't surprise me, little one—all those chosen to serve our God shine as brilliantly as Melukhha's midday sun."

Lord Kushal gazed steadily into her frightened eyes. "Many honor the Wild God as Rudra, the Howler, while to others he's Ishvara, or Shiva the Destroyer. Whatever his name, our God encompasses everyone and everything, for he is the source of both darkness and light, as well as the fount of all contradictions." Bending low, he whispered into her ear: "Take care never to displease Rudra, Ishvari—the misery inflicted by his whip humbles the proudest soul!" Then he noticed the bruise on her forehead and his eyes narrowed into slits. He turned to her mother. "Your name, if you please," he ordered frostily.

"Sumangali," she whispered, her almond eyes widening in her pale face.

Lord Kushal pointed to Ishvari's forehead. "Are *you* responsible for this?"

Sumangali shook her head, too intimidated to speak. She clutched Obalesh to her breast, her demeanor reminding Ishvari of the sacrificial goat the butcher had tied outside his door on the night of the last full moon.

"I fell, my lord, while running," Ishvari cut in quickly. "Hit my head on a rock."

"And just *who*," Lord Kushal demanded, moving forward again to grasp her chin and pin her with his eagle eyes, "were you running from?"

"Ghora, our priest," Ishvari blurted, her heart beating so fast she worried about falling dead at his elegantly shod feet. "He was hurting my mother with his body."

A cry of horror escaped Sumangali; she shielded her eyes from the startled stares of the mob surging about them with her free hand.

"The girl's lying!" Ghora shrieked, darting Ishvari a searing look in which she caught a flash of naked fear. "Ask anyone here, they'll tell you—"

"Quiet!" Lord Kushal barked. Ghora's face flushed an ugly red, though he subsided instantly. The envoy turned to Ishvari, stroking his beard thoughtfully. "Are you sure your mother does not invite this...this unappetising fellow to sport with her? Coupling is permitted if both parties are willing, you know."

"My mother's *not* willing, sire," Ishvari cried, her skinny body trembling with rage. "She does it for vegetables and rice—or we might starve!"

Lord Kushal's face expressed fastidious disgust. He cast a withering look at Ghora before addressing the restless crowd. "Where is Ishvari's father?"

"Sumangali's a widow, great sire," Vamadeva, Andhaka's cousin, and Devikota's tavern keeper, shouted hoarsely. "Her man died in debt—after poisoning his *own* parents at his wife's urging...we found his body in the Field of Cobras...only drunkards blunder there at night."

"A dreamy stargazer who lived for his liquor," Labuki's mother offered in a quavering voice. "Sold his soul to a witch and got everything he deserved!"

Ishvari wanted to scream that *they* were all liars and thieves, but Lord Kushal was raising a hand for silence. He turned to her shaken mother. "Answer me truthfully, O Sumangali—was the name Ishvari your choice?"

Why was he changing the subject at this critical point? Ishvari frowned.

Wiping her face with the edge of her garment, Sumangali shook her head shyly even as she jiggled the restless baby in her arms. "It was her father's notion, sire," she said hesitantly. "He swore a voice too sweet to be human breathed it into his ear."

A faint smile hovered about the envoy's mouth. "What was the exact time of her birth?"

"Ishvari slipped out of my womb at dusk," Sumangali whispered, forcing the envoy to bend to catch her words. "My husband urged me to look out of the window, and I saw the moon, hanging silver radiant in the sky. As we both watched, transfixed, the sun, already sinking into other worlds, rose high again to blaze forth on Devikota." Her eyes blurred with tears. "I'm no sorceress, my lord, and my Hiranya was the finest man in all Devikota. It was the sudden death of both his parents that led him to drink...."

Lord Kushal halted her rush of words with a raised hand. He pointed toward Vamadeva and Labuki's mother, the diamonds on his manicured ring finger flashing. "Such conflicting statements to make," he tut-tutted. "Does a dreamy stargazer murder his own parents? Your scurrilous lying may get the both of you executed—and for no less than murder!"

Ishvari stifled hysterical giggles at the impotent fury on Vamadeva's face. Her eyes darted back to the envoy, now addressing her mother for all to hear. "I've circled the civilized world and learned much about our universe, O Sumangali. I'd wager my stallions you're the furthest thing from a sorceress. By the power our monarch has vested in me, I hereby guarantee your safety. Now, if you please, kindly complete the recounting of your daughter's birth."

Sumangali's voice was choked with emotion. "My...my husband...he claimed the sun's unusual ascent that evening was due to the gods pouring fresh fuel on that shining orb. Hiranya enjoyed playing with language and ideas, my lord...he said it was a sure omen that our daughter was destined for *moksha*, for full liberation."

Ishvari's eyes grew big—*why on blessed earth had Sumangali kept this from her?*

Lord Kushal nodded with satisfaction, seemingly impressed by Sumangali's surprising eloquence. He drew a clay tablet from the folds of his inner garment and scanned its markings. "Devadas predicted the girl would be born when both sun and moon were in the sky," he muttered. He turned to Sumangali: "How did your husband die?"

Andhaka shoved Ghora forward. "Of...of snakebite, sire," the priest stuttered. "A terrible omen, if one refers to the teachings of our *rishis*—"

"Fascinating," Lord Kushal remarked, cutting him off in mid-flow. "A boor who violates defenseless widows claims intimate knowledge of our wisest men!"

Ghora's cheeks flamed. Bowing clumsily, he backed into the crowd. Again Ishvari suppressed giggles—if the priest dared approach the cottage again, she'd aim for his eyes!

The envoy swiveled around to face her. "How many years do you have?"

"Twelve," Sumangali answered for her. The envoy took Ishvari's right hand, clucking reprovingly at the dirt embedded in her broken nails before turning it over to study the lines on her palm. She pressed her lean thighs together, hoping he would not smell her drying urine. He reached into the folds of his tunic and withdrew a transparent disc with a golden stem which he held over her palm, squinting at the network of creases that covered the work-toughened mounds—it was a magical device, Ishvari marveled, one that made things appear larger!

Lord Kushal turned to Sumangali, observing her weary beauty. Drawing a leather pouch out of the pocket of his robe, he handed it to her with a formal bow. "Compensation for your loss, my good woman. Kindly prepare your daughter to leave with me at first light tomorrow."

Sumangali's hand dropped with the weight of the purse. She cast an anguished look at Ishvari, whose legs had begun to shake uncontrollably: was her mother planning to *sell* her to this man? "Your husband was correct," Lord Kushal murmured reassuringly. "Ishvari's lines reveal extraordinary intelligence and depth, while the crescent in the corner of her palm indicates Mahadevi's direct protection—it would take great crimes to negate this spiritual benefaction."

Slowly, Ishvari returned to the scene around her. The sun still burned her body, and the surrounding crowd was now as ominously hushed as was the earth before the quake that had recently hit Devikota. "Hey, Andhaka!" a woman yelled. "Does the envoy know about the curse on the girl's mother? Tell him Sumangali's a witch, and all three of them pariahs!"

Then the voice of Andhaka himself, raised high in outrage— "Lord Kushal *must* reconsider! A disgrace for Devikota—choosing a pariah over my own daughter! Huh!"

The envoy confronted the hulking headman. "Could it be," he said, enunciating each word clearly, "could it possibly be you've forgotten whose authority you question?" He took a step forward. "Lording over this insignificant little village may well have addled your brains, assuming you had some to begin with." He paused to adjust his headdress. "In fact, my dear fellow, it's almost as if you harbor a death wish."

Andhaka made to turn away, but Lord Kushal held up a restraining hand. "I've selected aspirants for twenty-one years, you should know, and many consider me an expert in the area of aesthetics." He flicked a spot of dust off his embroidered jacket. "Your daughter, while pretty enough, lacks the depth of character that flowers into classic beauty. On the other hand, I predict that seven years from now, Ishvari will dazzle Takshak himself." He wagged a playful finger at Andhaka. "Don't you go blaming your daughter now…shallowness is often an inherited trait."

As the headman backed away from the dapper envoy, Ishvari began to comprehend the meaning of royal power: if even influential Andhaka quailed at the words of this aristocrat, she could only imagine the might of the maharajah! Lord Kushal leapt nimbly back onto the dais. "People of Devikota!" he cried. "Be assured—the girl Ishvari has all the signs I was directed to look for!"

A stone flew out and struck Sumangali on the shoulder. The head of the guardsmen, a burly man with expressionless eyes, stepped forward. Lord Kushal waved him back. "Had that stone struck Ishvari," he said calmly, "I'd find and execute the culprit—right now! Now hear me well! Should *any* of you, high or low—" and here he stared directly at Ghora—"misbehave towards Ishvari's family in the slightest, your punishment shall be swift and severe. Ishvari is now the personal property of the maharajah. By sacred law, all her kinfolk fall under royal protection and are no longer pariahs. Never forget—Takshak has eyes *everywhere!*"

The jealousy of the crowd hit Ishvari like a palpable wave. A mantle of perverse pride fell over her as Lord Kushal returned to her side. It was followed by a steady drizzle of fear. This is *real,* she told herself, rubbing her arms with sweating palms. Tomorrow, she'd be packed off with this intimidating nobleman, sold, like a sack of grain. The lump in her throat grew as big as the rock that stood at the foot of the valley. Dazed, she scratched her scalp again as the god of the valley's prophetic words echoed eerily in her head.

Lord Kushal took a lock of her hair in his hands and gingerly separated the strands between his fingers. She'd left it long and loose this morning, too vexed to even braid it. "Nits!" he cried, appalled. "Is there a barber among you?" he called to the crowd.

Kutsa came bustling forward.

Lord Kushal pointed to Ishvari. "Shave this child's head clean," he ordered.

Kutsa gaped, taken aback.

"The fool thought the envoy needed a trim," a woman chuckled. Ishvari recognized the voice of the barber's rejected mistress. Sniggers erupted—the liquor-addicted Kutsa was not popular. "Watch out, Kutsa," the herb merchant sneered. "The girl bites."

"Catching flies, are you?" Lord Kushal barked at the barber. "Go on now, get your implements and be quick about it."

Kutsa lumbered away and Ishvari's spirits sank into the earth—of all the awful things she could have envisioned, this had to be the worst. The barber returned with a worn leather bag and a wooden stool. Seizing Ishvari roughly, he deposited her on the stool and proceeded to hack off her long hair before shaving her skull clean with his razor.

"*All* of it," Lord Kushal ordered, pointing to a spot he'd missed. Kutsa obeyed with alacrity. The envoy stepped back to view her properly. "A perfectly shaped head," he murmured, pleased, dropping a gold coin into Kutsa's waiting palm. He swung around to face the crowd. "The spectacle's over. Leave—you two, as well," he ordered, pointing at Andhaka and Ghora who stood huddled together. As the Devikotans dispersed in grumbling waves, Andhaka strode toward Labuki to enfold her in hairy arms. Given his violent cunning with anyone who posed the slightest threat to his position, his genuine concern for his daughter baffled Ishvari. With a malevolent glance at Ishvari, Andhaka too left the square, his arm encircling a pale Labuki.

Then there were just the four of them and the guardsmen. Leading Sumangali a few feet away, Lord Kushal spoke to her in low tones. Ishvari caught the tremor in her mother's responses. Sumangali walked back to Ishvari, rubbing her bruised shoulder with her free hand. Grasping Ishvari's arm, she led her homeward in bleak silence, Obalesh napping all the way.

Ishvari sat on the stoop, unwilling to enter the cottage. "Come inside," Sumangali called from within, her voice immeasurably sad. "We've so much to do tonight."

In dramatic response, Ishvari jabbed her nails into her skull; bile shot up into the scrawny column of her throat and she vomited bright yellow bitter stuff all over the stoop.

Sumangali rushed out, Obalesh tucked under her arm, squalling loudly. "This is the result of too much heat!" she cried, dragging Ishvari inside. She set the baby on the mat in the corner and gestured for Ishvari to lie down beside him. Then she placed the urn of spring water next to the mat and proceeded to bathe Ishvari's feverish body with a moist cloth.

"Breathe deep and slow, child," she instructed gently. "Your heart beats too loud."

It was true; Ishvari thought, her heart beat as loudly as the drum she sometimes heard in the middle of the night. Rigid as a corpse, she watched Sumangali make space for her purse behind a loose stone in the wall. It was clear why her mother had accepted the envoy's selection; this much gold would buy much more than just food, clothes and luxuries they'd almost forgotten. And after the envoy's warning, Sumangali could reject Ghora and live with dignity.

Trapped alone in a chasm between discordant worlds, Ishvari fell asleep. In the dream that came to her, she lay in a clearing beside the sparkling river that snaked its lazy way through the valley. The leopard of the valley sprang upon her, tearing the heart out of her chest. Rearing up on sinewy hind legs, the wild cat held the mass of still-pumping flesh high in his bloody jaws. She screamed, so vivid was the vision.

"What is it?" Her mother came rushing to her. "What is it, my precious love?"

Ishvari turned her back on her mother and curled into a fetal ball. Only this morning, Sumangali had cursed her with 'demonspawn', now she was her 'precious love'. *Could a purse of gold really alter a person's attitude so easily?*

"Eat this, please," Sumangali begged, returning with a bowl of watery gruel she attempted to spoon into Ishvari's parched mouth. Ishvari pushed her mother away, refusing the food. Sumangali gave up with a sigh and sat on the floor beside her mat. "Then go to sleep," she coaxed sadly. "You must look well tomorrow."

"Give his gold back, maa," Ishvari moaned desperately, drawing her legs up to her chest. "I promise I'll work harder. We'll have better food, warmer clothes...."

Obalesh chose that moment to howl. "All will be well," her mother consoled dully, putting the baby to her breast. "Remember what Lord Kushal said? Mahadevi herself protects you...soon you'll have plenty of nourishment for body and mind, and the monks will gladly answer all those questions you keep throwing at me. Here in Devikota, nothing but drudgery and shame await you." She reached forward and kissed Ishvari's perspiring forehead. "One day, beloved child," she whispered, her eyes streaming with tears, "you will understand."

But Ishvari turned away, numb with despair, hugging her bony knees to her chest.

Know that the Self is the lord of a chariot,
And the body is that chariot.
Reason is the driver and mind the reins.
The horses, it is said, are the senses.

    —*Katha Upanishad*

RUDRALAYA

Bands of pale sun gold illuminated the flaking whitewashed walls of the cottage as Ishvari came grudgingly to her senses a little past dawn. Sapped by feverish dreams, she raised a hand to feel the strange smoothness of her skull, realizing that the god of the valley had indeed spoken true.

On the other side of the room, Sumangali sat before her altar, tears coursing down her cheeks as she gazed beseechingly at her precious Mahadevi. Ishvari inhaled the essence of her mother's misery, but instead of softening her heart, seeds of resentment rooted firmly within.

Footsteps sounded on the roughly paved path outside their door. Sumangali mopped her tears with her garment and stumbled anxiously forward, but Ishvari already knew it was Ghora, from a cloying blend of hina and patchouli he wore on special occasions. The priest flung the door open and stormed in. "Not ready yet?" he chided, pudgy face ruddy with exertion. "Nobles don't wait for pariahs, you know." He glowered down at Ishvari. "Get dressed, *now*, demonspawn, or I'll give you the farewell whipping you richly deserve!"

Ghora's contempt stung Ishvari like a swarm of hornets; feeling too vulnerable to defend herself, she pulled the quilt right over her face. Ghora aimed a kick at the worn kusha mat. "Rise this instant!" he shrieked. "You're not tantrika yet, nor will you ever be!"

So the events of the previous day had really shaken this thick-skinned bully! Knowing she'd humiliated him before all Devikota infused Ishvari with fresh spirit—throwing the quilt off her body, she leapt to her feet, crossing her eyes and sticking her tongue out at him.

"*Pariah to the end!*" Ghora roared. He spat a wad of phlegm on to the earthen floor, his eyes glittering with such malice that Ishvari shrank back in terror. "Be assured, slut," he smiled mockingly. "No matter how high you fly, one day I shall expose your base origins!"

Like the furious desert wind that raged through Devikota every summer, Sumangali darted across and slapped the priest's face so hard that he rocked right back on his heels. Ishvari gasped—her timid mother defending her against *Ghora*? "*Base origins?*" Sumangali hissed. "We were made pariahs only by decree of the corrupt—and the envoy erased that wrongful taint in the presence of all! And even if we *were* pariahs, my daughter would still rank higher than a false priest." Her slender body trembled as she faced the dumbstruck priest. "Come here just *one* more time, lecher, and you'll be *very* sorry!"

Ghora massaged the red mark on his cheek, his other hand clenched into a fist. Ishvari stiffened, ready to spring to her mother's aid, but there was no need—perhaps those who challenged royal authority were as good as dead, for Ghora did nothing. Sumangali pointed a trembling finger at the priest. "Wait outside!" she ordered. "And never again pollute my home!"

A savage energy pulsed through Ishvari as Ghora slunk out of the cottage. Yet she knew that the battle was far from over—the priest was a vengeful rogue who would bide his time; Sumangali would have to be on high alert from here on. Wriggling out of her threadbare tunic, Ishvari marched naked to the clay basin to splash her face with water—there was no time to bathe or eat. Sumangali patted her dry and slipped a fresh tunic over her head. Obalesh awakened with a loud wail. Impulsively, she ran across to kiss his little mouth, fighting back tears as she tasted the sour mother's milk that had collected at its corners.

"Go with my blessings, child," Sumangali whispered, planting tremulous lips on Ishvari's forehead. "I shall light oil lamps and pray to Mahadevi every single day for your wellbeing." She waited nervously for Ishvari to bid her farewell, but Ishvari spun around and dashed into the courtyard, right past the livid priest.

"Slow down," Ghora barked, grabbing at her arm. "It's my duty to instruct you on how to bow before the envoy, how to prostrate before the monks…."

"First teach a goat how to fart, Ghora-pora," Ishvari retorted, giggling madly at his flabbergasted expression. Exhilarated by her own daring, she raced ahead on the winding path she knew so well. Much too soon, the village square loomed. Only then did she permit the panting priest to close the distance between them.

Lord Kushal's chariot thundered into the square, flanked on both sides by the royal guard. Atop the chariot, the Melukhhan royal flag flew proudly in the morning breeze, a rare remarkable sight for the inhabitants of Devikota. Propelling Ishvari before him, Ghora threw himself at the foot of the chariot door, making her wish fervently she'd saved some of the bile she'd spewed the night before to desecrate his white garments. Ignoring both the priest, as well as the sullen headman, Lord Kushal stepped down and lifted Ishvari into the chariot. The chief guard approached him. "No need to accompany us, Daruka," Lord Kushal said. "*I* shall escort the aspirant to Rudralaya."

"Bandits abound in these parts, my lord," Daruka cautioned.

"No bandit could attack a chariot traveling at lightning speed," the envoy retorted complacently. "And you're far too conscientious for such a spectacular morning." He winked conspiratorially at the giant guard. "Why not stop off at Alamkar? Ravishing adepts of love reside there, I hear, ready to please royal warriors." He drew a couple of gold coins out of his pocket and handed them to Daruka. "Go rejuvenate your spirits, my friend," he encouraged with a broad smile. "Consider it a fair reward for your unstinting devotion to Melukhha."

With a curt nod to the assembled villagers, a few too irate to hide their displeasure even from such a grand personage, Lord Kushal leapt back into the chariot and signaled for the driver to proceed. As they rode out of Devikota, Ishvari turned around for a final look—the mounted guardsmen appeared as part of a glorious painting, and, as the chariot gained speed, the throng of Devikotans began to shrink to the size of wooden figurines. Only Ghora's face stood out, his expression so venomous that she shivered, causing Lord Kushal to cast his cloak over her.

"You're the twelfth aspirant to be selected, Little Goddess," Lord Kushal informed her courteously, as the chariot shot along a narrow country road and onto a tree-lined highway. "And *you* alone have merited a royal envoy as escort."

Ishvari swallowed drily; she longed to ask just *why* he called her 'Little Goddess,' and whether he was in league with the omniscient god of the valley, but his proximity paralyzed her tongue. Lord Kushal studied her wretched face with wry amusement. "Take my advice," he said, patting her skinny thigh. "Leave the past where it belongs. Brooding drains vital energy, and you'll need every atom you've been blessed with for the challenges ahead."

She stared down at her dusty feet, the hellishness of recent times coming up in a sudden rush of feeling. Ashamed to let him see her cry, she buried her face in his cloak.

"Sometimes just being alive hurts," Lord Kushal remarked crisply, turning her chin towards him. "You've endured much, Ishvari, and only the gods know what is yet to come for us all. And yet it's suffering that blasts open the doors of the spiritual heart." He patted her hand consolingly, and a tantalizing blend of sandalwood and musk wafted into her nostrils. "Let me assure you—your fury will fade once you meet the noble tantriks destined to be your guides. It won't be long before you're thanking your mother for setting you free."

Oh, but he was so wrong! True, her mother had sprung to her defense against Ghora that morning, but could anything compensate for selling one's own flesh and blood?

"Dry your tears," Lord Kushal ordered, handing her a kerchief. But her face was so contorted with hurt that he reached into a metal chest clamped to the floor of the chariot and drew out a clay amphora and a copper cup. "Drink every drop," he urged, pouring out a green liquid and handing it to her. "This is bhang, prepared by our royal astrologer himself from the buds of his very own ganja plants." He watched indulgently as she drained the cup. "Trust a stargazer to know I'd be escorting a *very* upset girl to Rudralaya! I myself avoid intoxicants, except for the occasional tankard of Egyptian beer, or that Laodicean wine Takshak hoards in his cellars, but I'm told Devadas's recipe for bhang deeply relaxes body and mind."

The liquid was sweet and milky with an agreeable herbal aftertaste. As it coursed down her throat, Ishvari felt a strange sense of comfort. She turned her attention to the vista of rolling hills and emerald valleys splotched with vivid colors, her mood lightening as a pretty doe flapped its ears at her from a rocky outcrop.

"Can you tell me something about Rudralaya?" she asked timidly.

"Ah, well," the envoy said, flashing her a broad smile. "Rudralaya is perhaps the most charged spot on earth, for it's where the Wild God appeared quite frequently to our rishis. Many consider it the perfect place to unite spirit with body and mind in service of Rudra, which I too believe is our *highest* duty as Melukhhans. And certainly it does not pay to displease our God—the agony of his psychic whip has driven many to insanity, even death." The envoy smiled. "He has many faces, this god of ours, and many things to do. Only a fool would tax him further."

"What things must a god do?" she asked, forgetting for a moment her own misery.

"Oh, well, let's see....first Rudra aids his brother god to create—not just humans, animals and plants, but also the patterning of the heavens, earth and the netherworlds, second, he must preserve his multitudinous creations, and third, he destroys everything, just so the cosmic cycle can begin all over again."

"But why would a god destroy his own work?" she asked, mystified.

"Now *that's* a question you must put to your gurus—for only the enlightened see the whole picture." The envoy smiled down at her. "What *I* can tell you, however, is that Rudra is at his most seductive when he destroys...even the wives of great rishis have grown besotted with this haunter of cremation grounds. And finally, Rudra's fourth task is to obscure. Here, he colludes with *Maya*, the feminine power of delusion that veils our perception of the truth...and if I'm deluding myself that you've absorbed much of what I've just said, little one," he added with a laugh, "will you at least keep in mind that Rudra's grace alone can liberate one from suffering?"

Ishvari nodded gravely, thinking of the god of the valley. "What does Rudra look like?"

"Oh, our God's form can span earth and sky, or he can come in the guise of a naked wanderer carrying a begging bowl. Yet no matter how he manifests, our God always inspires the most terrible awe." The envoy laughed. "I recall my dear wife Sarahi claiming that one particular rishi was so staggered by the sight of him that his hair instantly grew from white to black!"

Sumangali's clay figurine with its fan-shaped dress and girdled loins came to mind. It was her mother's prized possession, along with a *linga*, a rounded, vertical shaft of stone implanted in a circular base, for both were marriage gifts from the widower who'd saved her life in Parushni. Sumangali claimed the linga represented the Great Gods, Shiva and Shakti, in union, Shakti being simply another aspect of Mahadevi, while Shiva had emerged from Rudra, the Wild God. The linga was therefore worshipped as a symbol of the whole universe.

"What of Mahadevi?" Ishvari asked drowsily. "Does she too come in a thousand forms?"

The envoy's smile deepened as he studied her sleepy face. "I think we've spoken enough for now," he murmured kindly. "Why not relax and enjoy Devadas's potion for a while?"

Impulsively she reached for his hand and gave it a grateful squeeze, before turning to gaze out of the window. Soon, languor wrapped its arms around her slight body and all her hardships drifted away like summer clouds. She giggled as a flock of parrots, nesting in a banyan tree, shot over the chariot in a blaze of bright green and flashing red. Again, she turned her adoring gaze upon the envoy, provider of this ecstasy-producing nectar, now engaged in inscribing careful marks on a soapstone tablet. Moments later, her eyes began to swim and her head fell towards her chest.

"Sleep deep, wonderful child," Lord Kushal said softly, propping up her head with a pillow. "I'll wake you when we get to Rudralaya."

As she sank into a magical sleep, the leopard of the valley molded his sinewy length to her body. Ishvari placed her throbbing forehead on his, feeling a silken growl rise up his throat and into his headspace. The handsome sadhu smiled down on their entwined figures.

The envoy's frantic shouting broke into her dream. "Faster, man, faster!" he was yelling at the driver as the chariot hurtled down the highway. "Whip the beasts harder, I say, *whip* them!"

Lord Kushal was staring out of the carriage window in disbelief. Following his gaze, Ishvari cried out in delighted surprise—the sadhu of the valley was racing barefoot alongside the chariot! "Even *your* steeds won't win this race, O Kushal," the sadhu laughed, his fine head adorned with its matted coils bobbing alongside the chariot window. The envoy recoiled. "I come to ask a favor," the sadhu said gently, his dark eyes shining.

The envoy cocked his head, motionless though alert.

"I'm told Takshak honors your counsel, and that you rank highest among the few who seek Melukhha's good," the sadhu continued. "If this is true, advise the maharajah to annul all laws that contradict the code of the sages. Tell him his royal brother is concerned about his fate—should Rudra withdraw his love, Melukhha will perish!" Then, in a moment Ishvari was never able to forget, the sadhu turned his deep gaze on her. "Fare you well, Little Goddess!" His dazzling smile pierced to the core of her heart. "The valley awaits your return." Then he turned away and simply disappeared.

"The dissenter at the village square!" the envoy cried. "I recognize the voice!"

Ishvari nodded, stars in her eyes. "Yes, *that* was the sadhu of the valley."

"*What?* You know this fellow?" Lord Kushal's tone was suspicious.

She nodded again, suffused with the pleasure of the drug. "I spotted him once, in the valley that lies beyond Devikota. Hark to his counsel, my lord—even the wild leopard adores him."

Lord Kushal's brow furrowed. "He appears highbred, despite his near-naked state," he muttered. "And he's far too impressive to be a common sadhu." He took Ishvari's hands in his, absently rubbing warmth into them. "Didn't he say he was Takshak's royal brother? Perhaps he meant *tantric* brother? As I recall, Takshak's gurus had many fine students." His eyes gleamed with excitement. "Perhaps he was Rudra himself, in one of his infinite disguises?"

"Oh, but this man is no god, my lord," Ishvari said, recalling the gigantic luminous being who had straddled the valley. "Just a sadhu of much power."

He looked down at her tenderly. "Perhaps we're all lost in some fantastic dream…for how could *any* human outrace my steeds without even breaking a sweat? The dealer who drove them down from Khotan swore I'd not find faster stallions…then he called you 'Little Goddess,' which is *my* name for you…and did he not say 'the valley awaits your return'?" Suddenly the envoy's eyebrows came together in so distrustful a frown that she did not dare share with him that he was not first to address her as 'Little Goddess'. "By Rudra's whip, child!" he cried. *"Do you intend to escape the monks?"*

Instinct warned her sharply that it would be unwise to speak of her mystical experiences in the valley to *anyone*, not even to this kind nobleman. "How could I have made any such plans when you chose me just yesterday?" she asked, smiling innocently up at him. "The powers of holy men come from the gods, my father used to say. Ordinary folk can only marvel at them."

He patted her hand even as he continued to brood. "I truly cannot conceive of any rustic sadhu knowing the inner workings of the Melukhhan Council...and even more curious was the force of his spirit....it drew me strongly to him, Ishvari, moth to flame." He turned eagerly to her. "Did you feel it too? *Yes?* Come to think of it, I could barely resist reaching out to touch his face, just to make sure he wasn't some uncanny trick of the light." He smiled buoyantly at her. "I'm convinced he came for *you* as well, Ishvari. Devadas is right—I do believe you were born with the potential to transform our errant king. And perhaps it *is* indeed a good thing that Takshak's going wild now—in seven years, I wager he'll be disillusioned enough to welcome a *real* goddess into his arms."

Lord Kushal pointed to a vast clearing faintly visible through the surrounding jungle. "Ah! Here comes Rudralaya." The driver expertly brought the steeds to a halt and jumped down to unlatch a wooden gate etched with curious symbols. Then he climbed up to his seat again, and the stallions took off, cantering down a cobbled road and into a courtyard; in the fractured gold and orange of twilight, a rambling brick building began to take shape.

Ishvari sat upright as two monks in saffron robes appeared at the doorway. The taller man stepped forward as the chariot rolled to a halt. Lord Kushal stepped down, bowing low before the unsmiling monk before turning to lift her out of her seat. "This is Ishvari of Devikota, our twelfth aspirant," he announced. "Child, meet Atulya, head monk of Rudralaya." The force of Atulya's aura struck Ishvari, still reeling under the spell of the bhang. She blinked, awed—no comparison was possible between this commanding ascetic and Devikota's mean apology for a priest!

Then the second monk came forward and she was enveloped by the love blazing from his eyes. "Welcome, Ishvari. I'm Hariaksa, the second of your tutors." He inspected her face with warm concern, and she stared bravely back, appreciating his stout homeliness. Placing his hands on his hips, Hariaksa bent low in order to gaze directly into her eyes. Ishvari giggled—the adult world seemed to be taking her very seriously ever since the god of the valley had spoken.

"So your tryst with the big cat went well, eh?" Hariaksa inquired softly. "And then the sadhu came to bid you farewell, did he not?" He grinned at her bemusement. "Now come, say farewell to Lord Kushal—you won't be seeing him for a long time to come."

Before she could obey, Lord Kushal was grasping her scrawny shoulders. "Excel in all you learn here, Little Goddess," he urged in an intense whisper, touching his forehead to hers in blessing. "If that sadhu spoke true, our maharajah will soon be in urgent need of your healing fire." Then he leapt into his waiting chariot, ordered the driver onward to Melukhha, and was off.

Ishvari reached for Hariaksa's hand as he led her to one of the smaller buildings, a dormitory divided into cells. She followed him through a corridor, past a communal bathroom, with cubicles for private use. A burnished sheet of copper hung against its far wall, serving as a mirror. She stopped to admire her skinny reflection. Smiling at her delight, Hariaksa beckoned for her to follow him to the furthest cell. He threw open the door with a grand flourish. "Your palace for the next seven years, your Majesty," he announced, standing on tiptoe and turning up his nose.

She cast happy eyes about the clean space, enjoying the sight of the swaying *arka* trees growing right outside her window. Beside the window was a sleeping mat, upon which had been set a pile of new garments. On a shelf above the mat she spied an open lacquer box containing a string of rudraksha meditation beads. A low desk stood at the other end of the room, complete with clay tablets and a stylus. Taken aback by the simple splendor of the dwelling, she uttered the first thought that came to mind—"But I cannot write, O acharya!"

Hariaksa chuckled. "I wager you'll soon be doing a lot more than just writing." He selected a white tunic from the pile on her bed and tossed it at her. "Now wash up and change—I'll be waiting for you right outside, ready to escort your Majesty to the dining hall."

Ishvari followed him into a dining hall attached to the main building, her stomach growling—she'd eaten nothing all day, and the bhang had intensified her hunger. A group of extraordinarily pretty girls sat on kusha mats around a low, rectangular table. Three clay jugs of spiced yogurt garnished with sprigs of fragrant herbs stood in the center of the table. Earthenware bowls filled with steaming mounds of rice, lentils and vegetables were placed before each girl. As eleven curious faces turned to get a better look at her, she quailed.

"Meet Ishvari, ladies, Devikota's contribution to Melukhha," Hariaksa announced. "This is all new to her, so be kind, be kind."

He led her around the table. "This is Dalaja, the giggler." Dalaja pointed at Ishvari's shaven head and tittered. Ishvari cringed as others joined in. Hariaksa tugged hard at Dalaja's long braid and she yelped. "You be careful," he warned. "I'll chop this right off if you tease any of your sisters, understand?" The laughter subsided, and Ishvari squeezed his hand to indicate her gratitude. Hariaksa moved on to the next aspirant. "This is Charusheela, a sparkling creature, but only when she chooses to be. And here sits Archini, of the jeweled eyes." Archini looked up, smiling sweetly, and Ishvari's heart brightened instantly—the fragility of the girl aroused the same rush of protective love she had felt for her baby brother.

Hariaksa patted the cheek of the next girl. "Behold Makshi, the mischief-maker, and Brijabala, the tongue-tied, who seems to consider speech an unnecessary art. Now, the inseparables—Urmila and Tilotamma, cousins from Ghotphal village." Urmila glared at her and Ishvari flinched, unnerved by the girl's blatant hostility. Clutching at Hariaksa's hand, she followed him, closer than his shadow, as he moved around the table.

"Meet Gitali, of the cow-eyes, who spends every spare moment gazing into space." Gitali blushed as Hariaksa pinched her rosy cheek. "Here's Ikshula, perhaps the only lady in our midst, for she knows when to seal her lips, and solemn Kairavi, who enjoys her own company best of all. Finally, meet Gandhali, who already questions every syllable I utter."

Dalaja giggled again, inspiring an outburst of laughter that took the edge off Ishvari's nervousness. Hariaksa pointed to a cushion beside Gandhali, in front of which stood a waiting earthenware bowl. "Sit and eat, Ishvari," he invited. "Plenty more where that came from. Chew every mouthful thirty times on each side or your digestion will suffer."

If a thousand suns were to rise
And stand in the noon sky, blazing,
Such brilliance would be like the fierce
Brilliance of that mighty Self.
　　—Bhagavad Gita

HARIAKSA

Hariaksa began their first class by scrutinizing a rectangular clay tablet marked with the Melukhhan seal. He surveyed the girls seated on kusha mats in a semicircle before him, his wise eyes alighting benevolently on each of them in turn. "Our records show that your ages range from nine to thirteen," he announced, his chubby face unusually solemn. "You'll train here for seven years before moving on to Melukhha to serve as tantrikas." He struck a brass gong three times. "Be alert!" he growled dramatically, startling them into nervous laughter. "The process of dissolving every trace of ignorance blocking your evolution into tantrikas has begun!

"When do we start learning *hatha yoga*, O acharya?" Charusheela asked earnestly, her habitual scowl absent. "Already I can arch like a bow and stand on my head...."

"After you master the *asana* known as 'sealing the lips,'" Hariaksa teased, provoking more laughter. He raised a hand to quiet the room. "Before this moon wanes," he continued, "Atulya will teach you asanas revealed by Rudra himself. But first, he will instruct you in the *shatkarmas*."

"Shatkarmas, acharya?" Gitali inquired with a frown. "What are they?"

"Cleansing rituals designed to remove wastes from the body, in order to free the spirit within," Hariaksa explained. "Atulya performs six, but I myself use only three. Before dawn, I wash out my nostrils and stomach, and every seventh morning, I flush out my intestines. I perform all three with warm water and salt from the sea."

"Foul!" Gitali blurted. "And we must do this too?"

"Don't make big eyes at me, Gitali. You weren't brought here to relax." Hariaksa wagged a stubby finger at her. "If you don't clean out your insides—and here, I include emotional waste—the fire goddess will adamantly refuse to rise. Acharya Atulya will teach you shatkarmas corresponding to your individual needs, and you must perform them assiduously, even after you leave Rudralaya. Seven years will fly by, you'll see. Now be quiet and watch your breath while I scan your astrological charts. I won't have you frittering away your energy in gossip."

Ishvari had already fallen in love with Rudralaya. Set like a rough jewel in an expanse of virgin jungle, the ashram was managed by an order of celibate Tantric monks under the austere rule of Atulya. Some monks tended fruit orchards, and gardens of greens, vegetables and sweet-smelling herbs. Others swept and mopped the buildings, cooked communal meals, and milked goats and cows to make sweet yogurt and creamy cheese. The rest fashioned robes, shawls and sandals for ashram residents. As for the aspirants, their only physical chore was to clean their rooms and common areas of the dormitory—their prime duty at

Rudralaya, as Atulya informed them, was to grow harmoniously in body, mind and spirit.

Atulya taught asana, *pranayama* and royal protocol, while Hariaksa's unique talent lay in transmitting to them the essence of Tantric art, science and philosophy. Her gurus were perhaps the oldest men Ishvari had ever encountered, yet their energy appeared boundless. Both were active well before the aspirants awoke, and rumor had it they often meditated right through the night, in the small caves dotting the wilderness above the meandering river.

Charusheela—whose garrulous father had risen to become the maharajah's chief elephant trainer, and was therefore privy to much information—revealed that Hariaksa had once owned a sweetshop in a distant township. Rumor had it that Rudra had appeared to the young merchant in a vision and ordered him to redirect his energies to realizing his true Self. As for Atulya, he'd been born a prince of a southern kingdom, but had escaped to Melukhha to pursue an esoteric path denied to the aristocracy of his race.

When the gong struck seven times at dawn, the girls rose to perform the shatkarmas. After bathing and dressing, they walked to the open courtyard where Atulya coached them in hatha yoga. Beginning with a series of sun salutations enhanced with mantras for each of the twelve positions, they moved into a series of asanas to stretch and align their supple bodies, and ended with deep relaxation.

Atulya went on to guide them in the science of breath control known as pranayama. Control of breath, the sage taught, was a way to control the mind. A combination of these simple though deep practices could propel a genuine seeker toward freedom from desire and fear—to a state of enlightenment known as moksha or Self-realization. Finally, seated in lotus position, the girls meditated in a circle with both their acharyas. Only then did they break fast, heading to the dining room where silent monks set bowls of rice gruel, fruit, honey and yogurt before them.

Ishvari soon began to find the strict routine satisfying. She enjoyed learning about diverse things she'd never dreamed of, from the significance of the beneficent cow to the perplexing customs of royalty. As Atulya had promised during their introductory class, the practice of hatha yoga loosened the grip of fear over her mind and heart. Under the dynamic influence of asanas—a practice designed by sages to unify male and female elements within the body—she often experienced a relaxation so deep she felt like a cloud floating freely in the vastness of space.

In the moons that followed, she struggled to find a niche within the tight band of aspirants. Awkward in groups, she began a quest for a special friend. Her first impulse was to seek out Archini, but it was hard to break through the timid girl's reserve. Then she considered Kairavi, whose quiet personality intrigued her. To her chagrin, she discovered that Kairavi liked to roam the riverside paths alone during their free time, and tended to rebuff all overtures.

Charusheela was next in line, but, as Hariaksa had already indicated, the girl was given to sharp mood swings—a trait inimical to close friendship. After a few half-hearted attempts to win her over, Ishvari concluded glumly that loneliness was preferable to being rejected.

Then, late one evening, she heard Archini whimpering in the herb garden behind the kitchen, possibly homesick. Ishvari slipped into the fragrant patch and perched quietly beside the petite girl until she was calm. Archini smiled so gratefully at her that tears blurred Ishvari's eyes; despite closing her heart to Sumangali, she still yearned for the warmth of family.

Holding hands like long-lost sisters, the girls walked down to the river to watch the gold of sunset surrender to the silver of moonlight. From that night on, a comfort Ishvari believed could exist only between soul mates marked their friendship. Classes, meditation and asana practice took up six days of the week but, on the seventh day, left free for the aspirants to do as they pleased, the pair would wander off to pick berries and the tart mangoes that grew wild on the fringes of the jungle. Later they would find the perfect spot to bask beside the lazy river, listening to its song as they stained their mouths with the juicy fruit.

Three moons from the day the twelve aspirants had arrived at Rudralaya, Hariaksa introduced them to the concepts of rebirth, karma and maya. "Let's assume life originates from one single source we shall call the Divine." And so began his course in philosophy, igniting an instant interest in Ishvari. "Each of us emanates from this source as a spark of consciousness. We call this spark a jiva, soul, or spirit. Set loose into the world, the jiva's initial desire is to return to the bliss of the Unmanifest. But, dazzled by Maya, the goddess of illusion, it forgets that this world is only a school and begins a vicious cycle of identifying solely with mind and body."

Hariaksa eyed them somberly. "This cycle of involuntary birth and death can continue for eons and is characterized by alternating periods of pleasure and pain. Most often, it is emotional pain that whips one on into becoming a *genuine* seeker—by which I mean one determined to put a permanent end to suffering."

"Is it a sin to forget our origins, O acharya?" Gandhali asked with a frown.

"But what is sin?" Hariaksa countered. "Often just a word used by dishonest priests to milk the rich and keep the poor in line. All the same," he added, "one pays a heavy price for disconnecting from the Divine."

"You say our spirit is immortal, O acharya," Ishvari spoke up. "Why then do we age? Or is it just our minds and bodies that die, leaving Spirit free to take another form?"

"Your second arrow strikes the target." Hariaksa beamed at his star pupil, but his joy was mixed with sorrow, for his third eye saw the stony encrustation of bitterness covering her heart chakra. He could only hope it would dissolve well before she left Rudralaya. "Body and mind are ephemeral, bound to be destroyed sooner or later," he said firmly. "But Spirit is eternal—it cannot die."

"What must I do to become enlightened?" Ishvari asked simply.

Hariaksa studied her for a long moment, observing with satisfaction that nourishing food and freedom from constant fear were already drawing out her striking beauty. Though he tried to treat all his students alike—for jealous rivalries never failed to disrupt the flow of learning—he could not hide his special fondness for this particular girl. And who could really blame him? Was it not rare for a girl from an obscure village to see herself becoming enlightened?

"That's the ultimate question, my dear, and I'm glad you're asking it," he said, well aware that most of what he taught only served to baffle most of his students. Nevertheless, tiny seeds grew into towering trees. He sent up a prayer that at least a few of the seeds he was planting would—in this lifetime or another—grow into enlightenment. "As a basis for your future growth, ladies, let me explain what our seers referred to as the *two truths*—the realms of Absolute and Relative consciousness, also known as *nirvana* and *samsara*." He gave the girls time to digest his words. "The Absolute is that which does not change; it exists within each and every one of us and is 'real', in the sense that it is permanent and lasting.

When a seeker merges with the Absolute within—which is her true nature—bliss erupts from the spiritual heart.

"As for the Relative," Hariaksa went on, "it encompasses everything connected with our body and mind, as well as the energy that runs it—which we shall call ego or *ahamkara*. Let's define the ego as the identity each of us begins to fabricate from the moment of our birth—an identity shaped by the predilections of past lifetimes. Be clear, however, that the Relative is considered 'unreal' *only* in the sense that it is neither permanent nor lasting. So while our bodies, minds and emotions *do* exist, a seeker considers them "unreal" since they are in a state of constant flux. If you truly wish to become enlightened, my dear," he said, looking directly at Ishvari, "strive to realize the Absolute within your own body and mind—only then can your inner journey to moksha begin!"

"How can I practice this in every moment?" Ishvari asked, her voice thick with emotion.

"Start by behaving as if each act you perform could be your last," he advised softly. "Actions prompted by anger, fear, hate or jealousy create bad karma, while those inspired by love awaken the indwelling spirit. Once the gods are convinced you are that rare human who seeks more than ordinary pleasures, the doors to higher knowledge will fly open. You will see!"

"Explain karma, O acharya," Ishvari demanded, disregarding her classmates' exasperation. It truly surprised her that only a few simmered with eager questions; perhaps, as Sumangali claimed, she had inherited the young Hiranya's hunger to investigate deeper truth.

"Karma means that even the most trivial thought, word or act has a consequence," Hariaksa replied. "We sow karmic seeds every time we think, speak and act, and these seeds germinate and ripen across lifetimes, crafting our different realities. Remember—a drop of venom can kill, while a tiny seed holds the potential to grow into a towering tree. Only the deliberate purification of our misdeeds lightens karmic consequences. What our sages say is true—we reap what we sow." He grinned impishly at the dissimilar reactions to this critical teaching. "Have any of you, perchance, encountered a fig tree that produces mangoes?

An image of Ghora's mean face flashed before Ishvari's eyes. It was followed by a memory of Andhaka's sprawling home and his thriving enterprises, rendered obscene by the destitution of Devikota's poorest. She shivered, wrapping her cotton shawl tighter around her body. "If karma's so accurate, O acharya," she asked quietly, "why do the wicked prosper?"

"You forget the reality of rebirth, Ishvari. Karmic law is like a pendulum which always returns, sooner or later. A murderer may live and die in great comfort, seemingly honored by all. One may ignorantly think—'Hah! So much for karma! Why don't *I* kill someone and prosper?'"

Ishvari sucked in her breath—was Hariaksa plucking thoughts out of her head?

"But the spirit of this murderer survives the death of his physical body," he added. "And as surely as dawn follows night, his destructive behavior must eventually destroy him, in this lifetime or another."

"Have we known each other in past lives?" Urmila broke the silence, glancing meaningfully at her cousin Tilotamma.

"More will be revealed along this path," Hariaksa replied lightly. "Meanwhile, remember that while we humans share a common karma, it's our personal karma that compels us to perceive the same reality so differently. As Atulya says, the seeker who evolves *despite* the mesmerizing drama produced by the senses is as rare as a star glimpsed at noon."

Again he surveyed the varied effects of his words on his pupils. "Observe, ladies," he said drily. "I give you truths that can liberate you from the cycle of rebirth, and what's the response? Fascination on a few faces, tepid interest on others, and downright boredom on the rest. In fact, I hear Brijabala snoring, but don't wake her, don't wake her."

The girls giggled, sneaking peeks at Brijabala who was indeed fast asleep, her head hanging over her chest. Hariaksa's humor was one of the nicest things about him—and yet it could quickly turn into a dry sarcasm, the memory of which could sting for days.

The gong rang three times to signal the end of morning class and the aspirants began to leave the room. Brijabala awoke with a start, stuttering an apology. Hariaksa waved her away with an indulgent smile, bending to knead his cramped feet. Ishvari was last to leave. She gazed at him with worshipful eyes as the other girls filed out, confident that this bright guru had been brought into her life by the gods themselves. Never before had her mind felt so spacious.

That night, lying on her sleeping mat, she imagined her fate had Lord Kushal not selected her. Now, the very thought of Devikota filled her with repugnance. Much had already changed within her since coming to Rudralaya; only the resentment she still harbored against Sumangali seemed to grow in the dark, like a poisonous weed. Contrary as it was to the ancient wisdom she was receiving, it had grown so devilishly that she beseeched Mahadevi to completely obliterate Sumangali from her memory.

To distract herself, Ishvari related the theories of rebirth and karma to the events of her own life. Ghora had attributed her father's death to bad karma; then, she'd dismissed his glib explanation, but now she was not so sure. If Hariaksa spoke true, all seeming injustices were part of a magnificent cosmic tapestry that ordinary human eyes were incapable of envisioning. She blinked sleepily at the enticing slice of moon visible through her window, thankful that existence as a whole was beginning to make more sense. *One day,* she promised herself out loud before drifting into sleep, *I shall know everything.*

Man sees woman as goddess.
Woman sees man as god.
By joining diamond scepter and lotus,
They offer themselves to each other.
There is no other worship than this.

— *Chandamaharosana Tantra*

RED TANTRA

The early years at Rudralaya flashed by, the challenging academic curriculum—interspersed with a rigorous schedule of physical cleansing, hatha yoga and meditation—leaving the aspirants with scant energy for frivolous pursuits.

Ishvari blossomed under this regime; with almond eyes disconcerting in their intelligence, high breasts, a narrow waist, and hair—shaved off by Kutsa on that afternoon of mingled humiliation and liberation now rippling down to her waist—she blazed like a rare jewel, even in contrast to her pretty classmates. And yet it infuriated her that—right down to a mole on the left of her lower lip—she resembled the woman who'd sold her to Lord Kushal for a bag of gold.

It was no secret that both acharyas favored her for high tantrika. Hariaksa once attributed her success to an outstanding ability to grasp and apply concepts, but his innocent praise sparked a furious wave of jealousy—Urmila began to make lewd jokes about Ishvari's closeness with the old monk, and others followed suit, unnerving Ishvari with their sniggers and perverse comments.

Things got so bad that Hariaksa was forced to approach Atulya for help.

Atulya began his next class by drawing a vivid picture of a straw basket of sea crabs destined for the cooking pot, uniting to pull down any intrepid crab who dared climb out of their prison. Were tantrikas-to-be no better than these brainless creatures, condemned by nature to operate on pure instinct? The gods had carried them to Rudralaya to be refined in body, mind and spirit; petty jealousies would only tarnish this high goal. One more complaint that any aspirant was being harassed, he concluded sternly, and troublemakers would be summarily expelled. And since no one doubted the senior acharya would keep his word, his classic tactic of mixing metaphor with good counsel and a believable threat put an end to the cruel baiting.

On the cusp of their fifth anniversary at Rudralaya, Hariaksa announced that instruction in *Red Tantra* would begin the next morning. Excitement gripped Ishvari as she entered the terracotta-tiled classroom. "So far we've covered preliminary techniques to awaken your indwelling spirits," Hariaksa began, drawing his ochre shawl close to protect himself against the chill breeze gusting in through the windows. "Hatha yoga has initiated the process of uniting male and female within, and, as this unified energy has risen upward, your spirits have evolved.

"From hereon you will learn to cultivate the mysterious energy which lies coiled at the base of the spine. We call this primal force 'kundalini' or *serpent fire*. And let me warn you that if this fire does *not* awaken, your practice of Red Tantra will degenerate into farce, and moksha, or enlightenment, will remain an unattainable fantasy!" He paused to give them time to digest his words. "Looping kundalini upward through the *chakras* is a sure way to generate the fire you will share with your partners. If your heart is pure, kundalini will rise fully to burn away all the predispositions or *vasanas* that hold you to the material realm. If not...."

A black-and-gold striped wasp buzzed around his head, perching daintily on the tip of his right ear. Hariaksa captured it carefully, opening his hand to reveal the insect vibrating in the center of his palm. "And why do we insist you meditate?" he asked, his intense gaze pinning the wasp down until it grew still. "Because our Self—as opposed to the body-mind system with which we mistakenly identify—is nothing less than existence itself! When we become aware of this truth, bliss erupts from the heartspace and floods one's entire being. And it's meditation alone—which I define as a persistent inquiry into our true nature—that stops the incessant whirling of thoughts, allowing us to sink into an inner ocean of peace and joy."

The wasp lifted off his palm, spiraling gracefully into the crisp morning air. Hariaksa scanned their mostly bemused expressions; moksha was given only to those who craved it as desperately as a drowning man craved air, but no thanks to Takshak's amendment to sacred law restricting the selection of aspirants to rural areas, the overall caliber of Rudralaya's students had fallen drastically. Not that rural folk were any less capable of brilliance; he himself had been born and raised in a village. But with Takshak and his cabal in charge, rising poverty and corruption in outlying villages were making increasing nonsense of Melukhha's old values.

"I can see why I'm not just my body," Urmila mused, her cat-like eyes narrowing with doubt. "But how, O acharya, can I not be my mind?"

"What were you *before* you entered your mother's womb?" Hariaksa demanded. "Pure consciousness and nothing else! Mind and body began to take concrete shape only *after* you began to grow in your mother's womb...where I wager you learned to wriggle and twist in that incomparably feline manner."

The classroom erupted into titters. Hariaksa often used doses of quick humor to lighten profound subjects. Knowing his heart to be as vast as the universe, the girls had learned not to take offence. It was Atulya—never known to smile or crack a joke—who intimidated them.

"As for the mind, it is an awe-inspiring power which originates from the Self and dissolves back into it when the body dies," Hariaksa added. "Our spirit is pure consciousness infused by bliss, and the only obstacle to realizing this is the untamed egoic-mind."

"But *my* mind appears to be in charge of *everything!*" Gandhali cried, her red lips melting into a practiced pout. "It's hard to believe what you say, O acharya."

"Then suffer the consequences of your ignorance!" Hariaksa retorted. Gandhali came from a farming community that cultivated peas, sesame and dates; now he wondered bleakly whether she would not have been better off caring for a peasant husband and a hungry brood. But no, he would not give up so easily! "Why not ask Atulya for clarification?" he suggested slyly, knowing she feared the senior acharya. Gandhali shook her pretty head fiercely. "Higher truth is subtle, my dear," he added gently. "Take the trouble to really digest these teachings, and you'll find the rewards to be inconceivably rich."

Then his eyes fell on Ishvari sitting at the edge of the semi-circle. Praise Mahadevi! Here was a lotus plucked out of the muck of ignorance, an aspirant who justified his dedication to spreading the wisdom of Tantra. *She* would certainly make a fine tantrika;

perhaps, someday, she would follow the non-dual path that Atulya and he had been so fortunate to come upon.

"Could you say more about the in-dwelling spirit?" Ishvari cut into his thoughts.

"All right," Hariaksa said, clapping his hands for attention. "I want you all to picture a chariot driver, an arrogant fellow who believes he's heaven's gift to the world. One evening he tosses down some potent *arak*, leaps into the driver's seat and whips his horses forward. Soon his head starts to spin and he loses control of his beasts, which drag him forward through exciting terrain and many adventures. When they finally come to a halt, our man is drained, disoriented and confronted by a knot of crossroads in the fast fading light."

Hariaksa's voice rose like a rumble from his belly. "Our lad hears the thunder of horses, raucous laughter, the screams of women—his stallions have carried him to a perilous crossing ruled by a band of dacoits who worship the Black Goddess! But which of the three roads should be take to escape? Panicked, he hears a voice speaking to him from the interior of his own chariot—if he takes the middle road, it promises, it will lead him to the great highway."

He was a master storyteller, the quality of his tales eclipsed only by the almond-honey sweets and crescents of crystallized mango he prepared as a treat on full moon days. Eagerly, the women awaited a stunning conclusion. "*You* tell me," Hariaksa said, grateful that a ripping good tale could always capture their fancy. "Will our imaginary friend obey or not?"

The girls broke into disappointed murmurs.

"Aha! So you lazy chits thought this was just another yarn, eh?" Hariaksa shielded his face comically, as if to ward off their blows. "Tonight you will each ponder the meaning of this parable in your life. I'll be asking for your conclusions tomorrow, so take this seriously, hear?"

"Acharya Atulya spoke about this too," Urmila remarked in the blasé drawl she'd recently begun to affect. "Truth is," she added, a smirk marring her attractive features. "I didn't get *his* point either."

"So it's a well-used metaphor—which makes it all the more valuable for a thickhead like you. Now listen carefully: each of us is, or has been, that arrogant driver. What does he represent? Ordinary mind. The horses are his untamed senses; the dacoits, the pleasures of this world that leech *prana*. Then there's the immortal Self, ready to provide wisdom when one is ready. The highway, of course, is one's specific path to enlightenment." He cocked his head at them: "Enough to start you off, I hope?"

Ikshula scrunched up her lovely face. "But what's all this got to do with Tantra?"

"*Everything,*" Hariaksa rejoined calmly. "The goal of both celibate and sexual Tantra is to transform oneself into a magnificent being of awareness...but in order to begin this great task, one must understand the interaction between body, mind and spirit. Even the grandest palace must soon fall to dust without a solid foundation."

"Would you define Tantra for us again?" Brijabala asked quietly.

Hariaksa's seamed face cracked into a grin. "Ah, Brijabala, a thousand tantriks would answer your question in a thousand different ways. The blind bard who sings hymns outside Melukhha's Great Bath swears Tantra is a mystical birthcord that links him to Mahadevi. As for me, I think of it simply as the transmutation of consciousness, from darkness to light. How this task is accomplished is, of course, up to each one of us. Atulya and

I use the techniques of gnosis, which we call jnana, or the path of wisdom. We too raise the fire, but without a partner."

He picked up a spindly red ant racing up his arm and placed it on the floor. "As tantrikas, however, you'll focus on Red Tantra—which is sexual alchemy practiced with a mate. This involves the channeling of energy up the center of the spine and into the heart, brain and beyond. And when your seven-year terms in Melukhha are done, you'll each be free to explore an advanced path of your own choosing. Yes, my dear?" he asked Kairavi, who had raised her hand.

"Is yoga part of Tantra, acharya, or is it the other way around?"

Uncrossing stubby legs, Hariaksa rose and walked to a wooden chest in a corner of the airy classroom. A silver and black langur monkey with bright inquisitive eyes leapt off a pipal tree and on to the broad window sill above the chest. Landing lightly on Hariaksa's back, the monkey flung sinewy arms around his wattled neck. "Steady on, Maruti, you rascal," Hariaksa crooned, reaching behind to pat the animal's head. "Must you disrupt my classes?"

Ishvari winked at the monkey, whereupon Maruti vaulted on to her back. Tillottamma sniggered at Ishvari's startled gasp, and the langur stared at her with his fathomless eyes, silver-tipped black tail arching tautly, before making a giant leap back onto the pipal tree.

Hariaksa returned to his seat to display a hand-drawn parchment chart which depicted the seven major chakras of the human body, each marked by a vivid, differently-colored blossom. "Here's your answer, Kairavi: these are chakras, major points in the psychic body where energy, matter and consciousness meet. The yogi focuses on higher centers, but what does a tantrika do?" He pointed to the lowest blossom. "Taps *this* center—which controls primal drives—in order to liberate energy which she then channels upward. Some determine to reach enlightenment quickly—and their extreme techniques comprise *Aghora*, or the left-hand path, reputed to be fast, terrible and intense. But don't you worry now...all *you* girls have to concern yourselves with is the practice of *maithuna*."

"And what, dear acharya," Makshi asked, fluttering her eyelashes, "is Maithuna?"

"Tantric love-making," Hariaksa replied. "As I said just moments ago, it involves partners channeling energy up through the chakras—whose invisible locations in the body I shall now demonstrate." He pointed to the bottom of his spine. "*Muladhara*," he announced. "Root chakra, located between *yoni* and anus, source of raw sexuality and survival in this oh-so-cruel world." He waggled his eyebrows at Dalaja, whose hand flew to her mouth to suppress laughter, then pointed to the middle of his lower belly. "*Svadhistana*, governor of senses and emotions." He moved up to the region around his navel. "*Manipura*," he announced in a high treble that sent Dalaja, Kairavi and Makshi into gales of laughter. "Key to personal power."

Coming to his heart, he intoned—"*Anahata*, font of compassion and upon whose energy I'm forced to draw in order to deal with certain unruly monsters." He touched the centre of his throat—"*Vishudhi*, for unfettered creative expression." Then he tapped the mid-point between his eyebrows. "*Ajna*, or the third eye, associated with inner space, light and heightened perception. And finally," he said, patting the crown of his head, "*sahasrara*, which erases all sense of separation." He beamed at them. "Any questions?"

"Atulya's taught us quite a bit about the chakras too," Ikshula said. "But I'm curious about Aghora...can it really be that dangerous?"

Hariaksa turned to gaze at a group of monks cutting through the devadaru grove, shouldering sickles and chanting softly. "Some say walking on swords is child's play in comparison," he remarked as he turned back to them. "Which is why so few dare experiment with their complex rites of wizardry, drugs and copulation." He wagged a finger at Ikshula. "Stick with Red Tantra, my dear—it's safer and far more pleasurable."

"Why does Atulya call Tantra 'the highway to the gods'?" Gitali asked.

"Because, when the fire reaches the thousand-petalled lotus that hovers slightly above the crown, you'll know yourself to be blissful and immortal."

"Can you tell us where the ego originates?" Ishvari asked. Her own ego operated differently from her classmates, who were already competing fiercely in the areas of physical beauty, witty banter and other such trivialities. She'd long since taken her extraordinary gifts for granted; as Atulya had once quipped, in the kingdom of the blind, the one-eyed woman is queen. Now she awaited Hariaksa's answer, aware that her greatest battle would be that between her equally-matched ego and spirit.

"That's a matter each of us must investigate," Hariaksa said, his plain face glowing with love for his star pupil. "The ego is the biggest, as well as the *subtlest*, block to enlightenment. It's a potent entity in its own right, capable of causing agony as well as joy. The trick is to coax it to serve your spirit. Succeed in this, my dear, and you'll never again be *forced* to take birth."

"My ego causes me to suffer terribly," Kairavi blurted. "My father's a priest, as you know, acharya, but even *he* couldn't teach me how to soothe my emotions."

Hariaksa settled his dumpy figure into a lotus. "Here's a simple but powerful tool you can perfect, Kairavi…any time you suffer, dig beneath the surface and locate the particular mask your ego is wearing. Shine the light of awareness on it and all pain dissolves. Try it and see!"

Kairavi nodded; like Ishvari, she too was quick to comprehend subtleties.

"It's like lighting a lamp in a room that's been dark for a thousand years," Hariaksa explained. "The light of awareness banishes all darkness." He took a draught of tulsi tea from his copper cup. "So, Kairavi, did your father happen to instruct you on the nature of the ego?"

"He did, and I think I can recall his exact words," Kairavi said, screwing up her pretty face with the effort. "The ego is driven by power, self-gratification, fame.…"

"And he was right," Hariaksa cut her off. "The ego is a necessary evil; no matter what path you eventually choose, you'll find it to be your most powerful obstacle."

"Why so discouraging, acharya?" Charusheela grumbled. "How can the ego stand in the way of moksha?"

"Because, Charu," Hariaksa explained patiently, "the ego manifests as the desire to be special, and this fosters a sense of separation—of 'I', 'me', 'mine'. Meanwhile the whole purpose of spiritual evolution is to dissolve the 'I', to melt into oneness.…does this somewhat clarify the point?"

Charusheela nodded, chewing on her lower lip. "How do *you* deal with your ego, acharya?" she asked. "Only hatha calms me for a while, but I can't be standing on my head all day long now, can I?" She glared at the old monk as if *he* was the source of all her problems.

Hariaksa's eyes twinkled. "Praise hatha then, for I fear you'd have killed us all without its benefic influence." His lips twitched. "I should kiss the hem of your tunic, dear Charu. Every time dark clouds obscure your beauty, I'm grateful for my celibacy."

Charusheela scowled, but did not say a word. The Ghotpal cousins exchanged winks and others smirked cautiously, but no one dared laugh. Despite Atulya's strict law against violence, Charusheela had once lunged at Dalaja and bitten her on the arm for some slight, real or imagined. The wound had warranted the healer's care. Fortunately for Charusheela, Atulya had been away from Rudralaya during that time, and the matter was deliberately forgotten.

"One must seduce the ego in order to channel its power, a difficult thing no doubt, because, until the fire burns it to ashes, it will seek to control you." Hariaksa's eyes softened. "Better to tame your temper *now*, Charu. I've warned you many a time that our current crop of aristocrats won't be bullied by a woman of humble birth, no matter her title."

A tear rolled down Charusheela's cheek, but Hariaksa did not regret his directness. It was unfair *not* to warn these innocents of the perils ahead. The apsirants fidgeted, except for Ishvari, who sat quietly, and Charusheela, now staring fixedly out the window. It was a mean reality Hariaksa was painting. Here at the ashram they were safe and cherished. While Atulya was often grim, clearly he wished them to flower into superb tantrikas. And how could Hariaksa's love for them be denied, no matter his trenchant insights and sly humor? *But what would happen once they left Rudralaya?*

"Hah! I don't believe it!" Hariaksa declared, breaking the uneasy spell. "Run out of questions, have we?"

"Not so quick, acharya," Ikshula raised a hand. "Tell me, is the intellect distinct from the ego, or are these different names for the same thing?"

"The intellect is an inner voice," Hariaksa replied, massaging his left foot. "Its job is to analyze, judge, warn and predict...."

"Goddess!" Makshi interrupted him, grasping her head as if it were going to burst. "No more mindstuff for today, dear acharya! What *I'd* like to know is whether Tantric lovers really experience great bliss—"

"But naturally, my dear, or why bother?" Hariaksa shot back. "Tantric lovers seek more than the fleeting pleasure of a genital orgasm which, I suppose, even a water buffalo could experience." Dalaja laughed shrilly. "A Tantric orgasm is an altered state of consciousness, caused by an upward explosion through the chakras. But don't imagine we celibates miss out on this rapture— our path just takes extraordinary discipline and can be lonely in the initial stages."

"Our priest related such bizarre tales about kundalini that I'm thoroughly confused," Gitali broke in, her smooth forehead creasing. "Does a fire-breathing serpent really live inside me?"

"By the gods, Gitali," Hariaksa chortled, "no monster's lurking beneath your yoni, waiting to bite! That's just the way kundalini energy appeared to our sages—like a radiant serpent coiled three-and-a-half times at the base of the spine."

The girls were quiet, their usual concerns usurped by deeper ones. Usually it was Ishvari, Ikshula, Gitali and Brijabala who really listened, but now it was clear to *all* that the work ahead was capable of smashing them to atoms, or blessing them with the grace of inscrutable gods.

"Are *you* going to teach us maithuna?" Brijabala asked Hariaksa nervously.

"Wish I could, sweetness, wish I could," Hariaksa teased, mimicking a lascivious leer to lighten the collective mood. "But since we monks are celibate, you'll practice the *theory* of maithuna here, while your physical experience will only begin in the sacred city. Don't forget you must be virgin to get to Melukhha."

"Is…is maithuna easy?" Archini stammered timidly.

"Simple, but far from easy. Nothing that leads to bliss is painless."

"What…what would a noble expect of a tantrika?" Archini persisted, pale with anxiety.

"A fine question," Hariaksa said, glad to hear her speak up. Archini's parents had died of the plague, and she'd been reared by a dour widowed aunt, which could at least partially account for her extreme insecurity. As an orphan himself, Hariaksa empathized with her fragility, though it continued to baffle him that Lord Kushal had chosen her for so challenging a task.

"Here's a quick sketch of maithuna, Archini: lovers begin by raising sexual energy almost to the point of orgasm, but instead of allowing the energy to leave through their genitals, they direct it up the spine, to flood the heart. When the heart center opens, love erupts like a volcano. This is why you twelve are being groomed to teach our nobles the art of true loving; from regular maithuna springs right thought, speech and action, which in turn result in a realm of vibrant and contented people."

"So," Makshi asked coyly, "will you teach us how to dazzle those snooty aristocrats?"

"That's all you modern girls want, a nice bag of tricks," Hariaksa said, trying to hide his disappointment. "But Tantra's not trickery—it's a sure way to enlightenment! One day you could truly *see* your mate as divine, while he could see you as the goddess."

"O acharya, now you've got me wondering about this feeling we call *love*," Dalaja grumbled. "I love sweets, we say, I love jungle berries and fresh goats' cheese and diamond nose-pins, or whatever. How should a tantrika view love?"

Hariaksa beamed; was he wrong in assuming most of these young women were incorrigibly shallow? "First, Tantra teaches us that our deepest hunger is for the Divine, then it shows us that loving another is the relative experience closest to God-realization. If you can't love generously, Dalaja, you can bid farewell to higher consciousness."

"Why did the institution of tantrika come into being, acharya?" Tilotamma asked.

"You've heard of women who sell their bodies, have you not? Whores, prostitutes, hetaeras, courtesans—different labels for the world's oldest professionals. You see, when a man fears intimacy with a woman, he alienates Mahadevi, for her essence is in *all* women. Well, our sages believed that women trained in the arts of tantra could raise the consciousness of our nobles much more effectively than paid prostitutes, which is why you are all here."

"When was her role formalized?" Ishvari asked.

"Around the time our people began to grow rich from maritime trade," Hariaksa replied.

"And how does this system work to change consciousness?" Brijabala demanded.

"Let me put it this way…when an ordinary man mates, he ejects seminal fluid. The more he ejaculates, the more his body is forced to produce. Now, sperm's a rich substance, created by fusing elements extracted from heart, kidney, liver and the brain. A single drop contains such immense prana that if a man mates indiscriminately, his body goes into decline. A tantrik reverses this cycle—he retains his seed and drives it upward through the chakras, whereupon something precious called *ojas* rises from the sexual center to the brain, harmonizing lower urges with higher, and leading to balance. Retention isn't just for men, you know," he added warningly. "Women too must transmute sexual fluids."

"Is this easy?" Ishvari asked.

"Use the techniques of Tantra as a pump, and you can drive sexual energy all the way from the yoni or lingam up to the brain," Hariaksa replied. "The result is so blissful you'll never wish to return to ordinary mating."

"By the gods, acharya," Dalaja tittered. "How you do complicate things!"

Hariaksa shrugged. "This is as simple as it gets, Dalaja. Either you ride sexual energy to the sky, or it will drive you down to hell, which is why it's best to learn as much as you can about it while you still have the opportunity. Yes, Ikshula?"

Ikshula blushed. "Could you paint a more vivid picture of maithuna for us please?"

Hariaksa nodded; absorbing theory without practical experience was inevitably a frustrating experience for his pupils, but what could he do about that? "Think of maithuna this way: while ordinary lovers race toward climax, Tantrics relax into an embrace that can last for hours, allowing their energies to melt into each other. Tantric lovers cherish the upward-rising orgasm, for it's when the mind stops and one experiences pure consciousness. So loop the fire, ladies, and assist our aristocrats in opening their hearts—*this*, in a nutshell, is your sacred task."

"Dalaja's right, acharya," Archini spoke in a worried squeak. "It's…it's all too complicated. I'll *never* be a tantrika at this rate."

"I promise you, child," Hariaksa said, "you wouldn't be here if you were not capable."

Archini bowed her head, and Ishvari felt a rush of compassion for her; it wasn't that her friend lacked intelligence; it was primal fear that prevented her from absorbing all this richness.

"Don't you fret," Hariaksa reassured Archini. "Twenty-four full moons must pass before you enter Melukhha, and by then, you'll know enough to face *any* lover with equanimity."

"Why is our training entrusted to celibates, O acharya?" Makshi asked.

"Because Tantrikas must go to Melukhha untouched. Can you imagine a virile guru unbound by vows of celibacy not wanting to entice you into his bed? Still, I admit, it's a precarious situation—faced by the maharajah himself, a virgin may panic. In the end, ladies, it is control, courage and commitment to the path that raises the fire. The final kiss is grace, of course, which comes unbidden, from the gods themselves."

"And if the high tantrika should fail?" Ishvari asked.

Hariaksa struck his palms together. "*What have I been telling you all these years?* Melukhha herself would decay and fall, for a ruler who does not transform his warrior energy sinks into the quicksand of gratification, while his administration disintegrates!" He eyed them sternly. "*Now* do you appreciate your crucial role?" He scanned their faces rapidly. "Why so timid?" he demanded. "Upon your very first physical encounter, theory *will* transmute into practice. Take heart, ladies, we've yet to send a coward onward to Melukhha."

He turned to Archini again. "Why so pale, dear? You're to be a cherished tantrika! Not a rootless renunciate at the mercy of wind, rain and ravenous beasts...." The sage stopped speaking suddenly. He stared blindly at Archini, the blood draining from his face. Ishvari shuddered—*what had he seen?* Kairavi broke the spell. "If semen's drawn upward, O acharya," she asked curiously, "how are children born?"

"Last question for today," he grumbled, recovering his composure. "Now listen carefully: ejaculation's essential only for those who wish to procreate. Men who discharge seed heedlessly lose strength, while their spirits shrink. However, if semen is reserved and energy channeled upward, vigor is retained until one's final breath."

Adorned with ashes, garlanded with snakes and human skulls.
Three-eyed Lord of the Triple-World.
Trident in one hand, in the other, blessing.
Embodiment of Gnosis, giver of Nirvana.
Everlasting; pure; flawless; amiable; benefactor of all that lives,
God of Gods.
    —Mahanirvana Tantra

BURNING GROUNDS

Ishvari strode back to the dormitory after the evening meal, Archini trailing behind her like a lost sheep. Most of the other aspirants were already on their way down to the river to watch the sun set in a blaze of iridescent colors over the distant mountains, but she was eager to use this quiet time in the dormitory to study the fascinating new scroll Hariaksa had lent her.

Recently Archini had been complaining of attacks of panic that drained her, accompanied by a tremor that ran up her spine like a live thing. The healer's remedies had only managed to alleviate these acute symptoms. As soon as they entered the open dormitory door, Archini flew down the long corridor and into her room, slamming the door shut behind her—as if some malevolent entity was in hot pursuit!

Questions buzzed like angry hornets in Ishvari's head as she entered her own room: *just what had Hariaksa seen that afternoon in class?* And how could their acharyas even *consider* graduating such a tormented girl? She sat on her kusha mattress with her back against the wall and calmed herself with some pranayama before picking up Hariaksa's scroll on the nature of moksha. While the subject was not on the Rudralaya curriculum, snippets Hariaksa had let drop to her about this mysterious state reputed to permanently erase suffering had intrigued her.

She was already convinced that Hariaksa himself was close to full enlightenment—a conviction based on her own experience of his supersensory powers or *siddhis*. Hariaksa had warned her not to be dazzled by his paranormal abilities; he had added enigmatically that if the fire ever blessed *her* with siddhis, she was to use them wisely. Then he had introduced her to his 'mountain analogy'—the mountain being a metaphor for higher consciousness.

On the tortuous way up this mystical mountain, some humans collapsed, languished or got lost; many forgot why they were scaling it in the first place; others were dragged all the way back down into the material world by their ravenous senses. Few were aware that Maya the Enchantress was their invisible companion, determined not to let seekers reach the top without a fight to the death. "Whose death?" Ishvari had quipped. "Why, that of the ego," Hariaksa had retorted, "which dissolves back into the Self when one shines permanently with light."

The old monk had entranced her with his fluent description of the various stages of enlightenment. Sensual pleasures were like licking the honey off a razor's edge, he'd explained; in the world of duality, pleasure is inevitably followed by pain, and vice versa, which is why gnostics aim to transcend both mind and senses by focusing on the bliss of the Self.

"It's a tricky mountain," he had concluded his fascinating little sermon. "Some of its flanks are even fashioned out of sheer diamond. But she who ascends to the peak *knows* her true nature to be the essence of existence itself; bliss erupts from the lotus of her heart, liberating her from all desire and fear. Such a blessed one has attained moksha, and is never again forced to suffer the pains of birth and death."

"Are you holding forth from the peak right now, acharya?" she'd teased.

"If you *really* want to know, sweetling," he'd retorted with a lopsided grin, "fulfil your dharma in Melukhha and aim to reach the peak yourself."

The chatter of girls returning to the dormitory broke through her reverie. Most would soon retire for the night, but she was too edgy to sleep. Slipping out, Ishvari made for the river, hoping to find Hariaksa at his favorite spot.

"Hey Ishvari! Look up here, it's me!" Startled, she obeyed to see Archini perched like a ghost on the wall separating their dormitory from the rest of the ashram.

"What in heaven's name are you doing up there?" Ishvari cried, striding up to the wall. "I thought you'd be dreaming by now." She hopped up on to a rectangular block of granite placed beside the wall to see Archini better. In the silvery moonlight, her friend's face appeared white.

"I *did* go to bed," Archini replied in her timid fluting voice. "But Makshi hammered on my door and we came outside to talk. Then I climbed up here to watch the moon in peace." Archini patted the wall beside her. "Sit with me for a bit, Ishvari, it's so nice up here," she pleaded.

Ishvari shook her head, impatient to get to Hariaksa. "So you let that cretin bother you again…why didn't you just let loose a big snore and let her think you were fast asleep?"

Archini's inability to say 'no' tended to draw bolder girls into trusting her with secrets they wouldn't dare spill to others. Makshi, in particular, couldn't care less about the damage the dumping of her murky secrets inflicted on Archini's nervous system. But Archini's lower lip was quivering at her sharp tone. "So tell me, jewel face," Ishvari asked more gently. "What did that selfish creature say to disturb you?"

"Oh, she gabbled on and on about that monk with the smoldering eyes—the same fellow who crafted your sandals…the one who kept staring at your breasts, remember?" Archini dangled her feet over the wall like a disconsolate child, "Makshi's planning to go into the jungle with him tonight…wants to practice Red Tantra, she says. I said she'd be sinning—"

"And what did she have to say to that?" Ishvari interrupted sharply.

"Oh, well, only that she didn't know why she bothered to share her secrets with such a ninny." Archini dabbed at her eyes with her shawl. "So I threatened to tell Atulya everything."

"And?" Ishvari nudged her on.

"She hooted loudly—*everyone* knows how terrified I am of Atulya." Archini's little face crumpled. "Except for you, Ishvari, the others just tease or use me. I'll never be able to face those nobles in Melukhha…I'll wager they're worse than Makshi, and that sneaky Urmila." She pulled her shawl even tighter across her hunched shoulders.

"Makshi said worse, didn't she, sweetling?" Ishvari probed. The girl had a talent for taking care of herself, even while getting others into hot water. If she *did* sport with the monk, Makshi was wily enough to ensure *she* wouldn't get caught.

Archini released a weary sigh. "She said that if I *ever* got to Melukhha, I'd learn that the *real* world's nothing like Rudralaya. And she's right—*everything's* going to change…you'll be high tantrika and won't be able to see me.…" Archini began to wring her thin hands. "Won't Makshi be punished for losing her virgin shield? We've got to stop her, Ishvari.…"

"*We* are going to do nothing," Ishvari declared, wanting to slap the teeth right out of Makshi's smug mouth. Balancing on the block of granite, she reached up to grasp Archini's cold hands. "Makshi leaps about like a brainless frog. If it's not this mischief, it's another. And as you well know, some monks are not as pure as our acharyas, so why such an unholy fuss?"

Archini fell into a brooding silence. "Tell you what," Ishvari said. "I'll get Hariaksa to make sure that Lord Devadas arranges for us to stay close to each other in Melukhha." A tear rolled down Archini's cheek. "I swear I *won't* abandon you, sweetling," Ishvari promised, tightening her grip on the cold hand. "And once we're done with the city, you and I shall move out to the country…can't you see us as two happy old women, chatting by the river as we gorge on mangos and berries?"

Archini's face brightened for a moment, then dimmed again.

"Any wonder you get sick?" Ishvari grumbled. "Up and down you go, fretting about everyone and everything…one day you'll just explode with worry, poof, and then what will I do?" Releasing Archini's hand, she stepped back on to the ground.

Archini looked down at her mournfully in the moonlight. "It's not just Makshi I worry about," she whispered. "Atulya will punish us *all* if Makshi gets caught. You won't tell Hariaksa what she's planning to do, will you? If Atulya finds out, he'll pack her right back to Ghaggar Village."

"Which would be a splendid thing for us all," Ishvari retorted. Archini whimpered so she added quickly—"All right, all right, I promise not to tell him if you promise not to listen to any more drivel. Is that a bargain?"

"I'll try," Archini said, jumping off the wall to land right beside her friend.

"You smell like a flower," Ishvari said, dropping a kiss on her perspiring forehead. She drew her petite friend close, hoping to infuse her with her own strength. "Now straight to bed!"

As Ishvari hurried along the path to the river, she heard noises coming from a seldom-used washroom. She stopped and carefully pushed the door open a fraction. An oil lamp burned on the windowsill. In its flickering glow she saw two women, tunics falling about their knees as they explored each other's bodies, their bare flesh gleaming copper in the soft light. She caught tantalizing glimpses of fingers caressing breasts, nipples rising as a hand slipped downwards to explore the petals of a yoni, the surreal scene punctuated by fractured breathing and gasps of pleasure. Like a blow to her gut, the image of Ghora violating her mother flashed— just as she recognized the women to be Urmila and Tilotamma, the inseparable cousins from Ghotphal.

"Someone's watching us," she heard Tilotamma's panicked whisper. Before she could flee, Urmila had raised the lamp. "It's that cursed Ishvari!" she exclaimed. "The rat is spying on us!"

Paralyzed by her own churning emotions, Ishvari gaped at the cousins hastily pulling on their tunics. Tilottamma rushed forward, joining her palms in supplication. "It was…it was all that talk about Red Tantra, Ishvari," she stuttered. "We wanted to see whether women lovers could also…well…you know, experience the Tantric orgasm, I suppose." She threw herself at Ishvari's feet. "Promise you won't tell Hariaksa? He's bound to tell Atulya."

Urmila pulled her cousin up with surprising strength. *"Don't beg!"* she snapped. She raked her eyes over Ishvari. "Maybe you were hoping to join us? Or are you saving your precious body for Takshak, who deflowers virgins only when he has no other choice?" She tightened her hold on her weeping cousin. "The rest of the time, we hear our great maharajah prefers professionals."

It was hard not to punch Urmila right in her mocking mouth. Takshak was a tantrik, and tantriks practiced maithuna! "Better play your games in the jungle next time," Ishvari warned angrily. "Or it might be Atulya who catches you next!" The senior acharya would deem aspirants pleasuring each other to be aberrant behavior; the cousins would be severely punished.

Tilottamma was still weeping—it was Urmila who appeared to instigate their mischief. "Have no fear on my account," Ishvari assured Tilottamma in a stronger voice before fleeing.

Hariaksa was seated at his usual spot, where the jungle gave way to the murmuring water. She sank on to her haunches and watched him from a distance. Their bond had strengthened over the years, provoking more jealous grumbling from her mates, though they did not dare attack her blatantly. Should she tell him what she'd just seen, despite giving her word to Tilottamma?

"Come here, child," Hariaksa called, startling her, for he had his back to her. "The river sings loud for us tonight." She moved forward to crouch beside him. "Maya blinds us with her dramas," he murmured, "and yet all we experience is merely a dream. Learn to take life lightly, and all the pieces of the puzzle will gradually fall into place."

Hariaksa's third eye told him most everything; could he be aware of the love scene she'd just witnessed? She wanted to spill *everything* to him—her fury about Archini's degenerating health, Makshi's planned jungle tryst, the Ghotphal cousins' sensual madness…but she had given her word not to talk. "I'm frightened, acharya," she whimpered suddenly.

"Life was hard for me too, at your age," Hariaksa said, patting her knee consolingly. "Then, in one master stroke, everything changed."

"Tell me," she invited.

"It's a long story," Hariaksa said. "Can you stay quiet that long?"

"I can listen to you forever!" she declared passionately.

"How obsequious of you," he chuckled. "Well then, I must return to Lohumjudaro when I was but seven, the only child of loving parents. Then a craft carrying my father and mother home from market capsized, and in a flash I was an orphan. The childless sweet-maker in our village took me in and put me to work right away, teaching me how to keep fresh goats' milk from sticking to the bottom of his vats as it boiled down into scrumptious khoa." Hariaksa threw her a lopsided grin. "And doesn't everything happen for the best, sweetling? You see, it was in that smoky kitchen, with its cauldrons of bubbling milk, golden honey, nuts, ghee and a multitude of other delectable flavorings, that I learnt to rustle up the sweets you girls devour."

"What were you like then?" she asked curiously.

"Just as short and round as I am now," Hariaksa chortled, "though my face was bedeviled by eruptions of pus-filled hillocks. Soon after I turned eighteen, my stepfather died—he'd grown obese from sampling his own sweets. One day, his heart stopped beating—it had taken enough abuse and opted for permanent retirement."

Ishvari giggled; Hariaksa could make even *death* sound funny.

"I was well-off, now, but still deeply unhappy. Perhaps a wife would bring me joy, I thought, so I asked my stepmother to find me a bride." He laughed. "Wouldn't you know it? Despite the business I'd inherited, even the plainest of local girls refused my suit!

"In abject despair, I trudged up the sacred mountain behind Lohumjudaro, where it was rumored that the Wild God had appeared to one of our rishis. I was drumming up the courage to fling myself into oblivion when this crazy sadhu with burning eyes materialized before me. *Rudra destroys all obstacles,* he said—as if I'd asked for his advice—and promptly vanished.

"So I parked my bottom on that mountain top till the sun went down: if you don't do something quickly, I threatened Rudra, shaking my fist at the heavens, you'll be sorry." Hariaksa grinned. "I must have scared our God, Ishvari, because next morning a matchmaker came by to say that a farmer's daughter with a misshapen foot but a decent dowry had agreed to marry me."

Ishvari gawked at him—Hariaksa *married*?

"But soon after the marriage feast, my bride became ill. Others too began to suffer dizziness and vomiting. A runner from the next village arrived, panting like a wild dog. "It's the plague!" he shrieked. "Camp in the jungle till the danger passes!" But it was too late—by nightfall the next day, seventy villagers were dead, along with my virgin bride."

"Sweet gods, but that's awful, acharya!" she exclaimed. "What did you do?"

Hariaksa's eyes sparkled in the gloom. "Oh, I joined the corpse bearers on their march to the burning grounds and stayed behind after they left, cursing Rudra more fiercely than ever. I stared into the fire, nauseated by the stench of burning flesh, until I fell into a dead sleep."

A slim green snake patterned with black diamonds slithered up Hariaksa's bare leg and settled into a coil on his lap. He stroked it, ignoring Ishvari's grimace—for snakes both frightened and fascinated her—then picked it up and draped it around a knot of river reeds, his eyes taking on a faraway look. "I awoke to see a naked ascetic fishing around the smoldering pyres for slivers of flesh, which he then tossed into his mouth as if they were appetizing treats."

"Did you scream?" she whispered.

"Why? I wasn't scared, you know, merely outraged. I prepared to berate this unholy fellow when, to my amazement, he transformed into the Wild God, covered in the gleaming skins of giant animals, with cobras writhing around his blue throat, third eye blazing like crimson fire in the center of his forehead. Rudra spoke to me then," Hariaksa murmured. *"My beloved heart-son,* he said, so tenderly that a fountain of ecstasy erupted from my heart. I began to weep as I'd never wept before. He told me my parents had long since been reborn into better circumstances, and that my own soul had united in many past lives with the soul of my bride. I took his final words seriously. *O Hariaksa,* he said, *both birth and death are mere illusion. Know you are the eternal Self and dissolve into the bliss of your true nature."*

Ishvari watched her guru's aura brightening in the dusk. "Rudra opened his mouth wide then, Ishvari, and I saw his teeth glittering like diamonds, even as the entire cosmos appeared before me in all its awesome shimmering glory." He laughed. "You can imagine what a great daze I was in by the time I finally got home. Before my foster mother's pet rooster could begin his obnoxious crowing, I woke my cousin to say I was leaving. His shout of delight when I told him I was giving him the family business woke my stepmother, and when *she* heard I was leaving to become a monk in a far-off place, she tugged at her hair like a madwoman and swore my bride's death had shattered my mind. Despite her entreaties, I started the three hundred *ko* trek to Rudralaya, determined to beg initiation from a southern monk I'd heard good things about." He nodded. "Yes, Ishvari, I speak of Atulya, then a recent immigrant to Melukhha, and younger than I, but already a renunciate of much power."

The image of the shining being of the valley danced before her eyes. So it *had* been Rudra who had appeared to her! The vision was so precious she'd kept it even from Hariaksa, and yet, what he'd just recounted explained just why the bond between the two of them was so pure—Rudra had appeared to *both* of them in their time of need, and transformed their lives. Unaccountably her thoughts strayed to Sumangali; despite the wisdom she'd acquired since leaving Devikota, Ishvari still had not forgiven her. "Unlike you, O acharya," she confessed, "so much floods my restless mind that I often confuse true and false."

Moonlight rippled upon the surface of the lake. "You whip yourself too hard, Ishvari, and for this reason you whip others too," Hariaksa said, plucking the thoughts out of her head. "Someday, serpent fire will rise within you too, gifting you with powers most humans only dream about. Now go, surrender your pain to higher powers and sleep sound."

Back in her room, bemused by the troubling events of the evening, but especially by Hariaksa's prophetic words about her future, she prepared to sleep. Somewhere in the dormitory a girl moaned. Was it Archini? Worry grew within her like a canker. True, Hariaksa had advised her to take life lightly and yet, he himself had grown pale at what he'd seen that day in class.

Her thoughts turned to Makshi; was the fool sporting with that monk in some moonlit glade? Practice Red Tantra indeed! An aspirant could not be touched without the express permission of the maharaja himself! Archini was right to be scared—if discovered, Atulya could pack Makshi back to Ghaggar, where her own clan could lawfully kill her for bringing them dishonor. As for the monk, according to sacred law, he'd be castrated, bound, and thrown into deep jungle to be devoured by wild beasts.

What was this impetuous urge that drove humans to risk their very lives? Ishvari wondered as she tossed and turned. When the same monk had recently crafted new sandals for her, the force of his energy as he'd deliberately prolonged measuring her feet had caused a tumult in her lower regions. Though she'd complained about him later to Archini, in truth it had been hard to turn away from the desire burning in his eyes.

Images of the Ghotphal cousins loving each other arose; the inseparables had been so lost in pleasure they'd been oblivious to a dangerous world outside the door. Lust smote her again. Aghast at her weakness, she tried to recall Hariaksa's words of advice, but a disturbing mixture of feelings struck again with even greater force. "Mahadevi forgive me!" she cried softly as she slid her fingers downward.

Out of the ashes of her surrender rose a man standing naked and proud on a mountain peak. Tendrils of light played about the breadth of his shoulders and accentuated his muscled torso. The radiance emanating from his third eye blinded her. A burst of energy shot up her spine as the tempo of movement of her fingers increased until wave after wave of liquid gold swept over her, awakening her chakras and melting her mind so she became the rising moan warbling forth from her own throat. She lay in bed, stunned, as jungle winds buffeted the walls of her cell. Had she just been given a foretaste of kundalini? If so, her acharyas were right— it was dangerous to flirt with this mystifying force, like a child fanning a flame that could easily turn into a raging inferno.

Women are heaven.
Women are dharma.
Women are the highest sacrament.
  —*Chandamaharosana Tantra*

INANNA

On the seventh day of the week given to rest and recreation, Ishvari found Archini in her room, curled fetus-like beneath her quilt despite the rising afternoon heat. As she stared down at the frail body lying on the narrow cot like a broken doll, it struck her like a blow to the gut that her friend had fully surrendered to the malaise inexorably strangling her spirit.

"Hey, lazybones!" she called, pulling the quilt right off Archini's slight body. "Get up, it's only me!" Archini's eyes fluttered open and she conjured up a watery smile—like a sickly child brightening at the sight of her mother—before curling back into fetal position. "I swear I'd beat you to death if you weren't already half there!" Ishvari cried, overcome by fury at the pathetic sight. "You're walking down to the river with me right now, and that's that!" She hauled Archini up and deftly laced leather sandals onto her small feet. Tonight, she decided, clenching her jaw as she marched her timid friend along the narrow path leading down to the river, she'd ask Hariaksa just *why* Archini's illness was not being given due consideration.

When they got to the riverbank, Archini asked hesitantly if they could walk farther into the jungle. Could this be a *small* sign her friend was willing herself to recover? With fresh hope, Ishvari drew her down a winding trail shaded by devadaru trees; and sure enough, Archini's gait grew noticeably lighter as the dim interior of the jungle enfolded them in febrile shadow.

A colony of red-bottomed monkeys, including mothers with wrinkled babies clinging to their underbellies, leapt from tree to tree, gibbering at each other. Deer flashed by on their slender legs, on their way down to the river. A herd of elephants milled about in a clearing, nudging tillai trees with ivory tusks as they foraged for food.

Archini halted abruptly and gestured in fear toward a nearby grove. At the base of a gnarled and ancient tree, a cobra spread its hood before a belligerent, silver-and-black furred mongoose with red eyes and a long, bushy tail. The mongoose broke into a lithe dance, drawing the serpent into a swaying defense. With a hiss, the serpent struck. The mongoose backed away just in time, and the serpent hit the ground with an audible thud. A startled drongo bird rose from the lower boughs of the tree, venting a high-pitched cry. Its forked tail struck the honeysuckle covered branches of the tree and a spray of ivory flowers showered down from it, distracting the mongoose. Quick as lightning, the cobra struck again—this time with lethal accuracy.

Loathe to watch the death struggle, Ishvari turned, pulling Archini with her back along the path leading to Rudralaya. As they approached the ashram, she was astonished to see a closed chariot—decorated with mystical signs and drawn by two massive horses—parked by the main entrance. Hariaksa was speaking to the driver, a strikingly beautiful older woman whose skin shone like burnished mahogany against the white of her cotton robe, and whose silver ropes of hair fell to almost half-a-foot below her slender hips. A cluster of aspirants milled excitedly about the gate, behind their portly guru.

Since Archini was panting heavily, Ishvari led the tired girl directly to her room and arranged the cotton quilt tenderly over her body, alarmed afresh by her pallor. "Rest now, sweetling," she murmured. "I'll be back later with warm goat's milk to help you sleep."

Flying back out into the courtyard, Ishvari saw the stranger striding toward the dining hall, holding a whip whose knout gleamed with emeralds and rubies set in heavy gold. She was followed into the hall by both the acharyas and the other aspirants. Hariaksa caught sight of Ishvari, and beckoned for her to join him. Cutting through the line of whispering aspirants, Ishvari walked into the dining hall with Hariaksa to see their guest already seated beside an unsmiling Atulya.

With a nod, Hariaksa indicated for Ishvari to sit beside him. The other women huddled on the opposite side of the hall, continuing to speak in whispers as they stared at their resplendent visitor. Ishvari perched next to Hariaksa, embarrassed by this special treatment. Across from the two of them, their visitor was speaking to Atulya in an undertone. A monk set a copper tumbler of tulsi tea before her. Draining it in one go, the woman turned to Ishvari, who held her breath as eyes the color of amethyst bored straight into her.

"Meet Inanna, former consort of Maharajah Shaardul," Atulya addressed Ishvari. Awed, Ishvari could only bow her head: so *this* was Inanna, only daughter of a high priest of Sumeria and a tribal princess native to the mountainous region surrounding Melukhha! This was the fiery beauty who'd won the heart of Shaardul, father of Takshak, the priestess who had persuaded her lord to revise the spiritual code of Melukhha and thumbed her nose at the Council after his death. Hariaksa had once mentioned that *all* aspirants owed Inanna a great debt for coaxing Shaardul into outlawing the triennial sacrifice of a tantrika to the Wild God.

"Takshak has forbidden you to interact with our aspirants without his permission, Inanna," Atulya said coldly. "I'm afraid you must leave Rudralaya as soon as you're rested."

Inanna threw back her head and guffawed, revealing a choker of seven entwined golden serpents that grasped the long column of her neck. "Eh, Atulya, taken to comedy to brighten your old age, have you? Can you see me begging permission from a miscreant to do my sacred work?" She flicked her thigh with her whip. "Oh, and given your great regard for the law, let me remind you of Shaardul's final promulgation: my person is inviolate, which means I'm free to come, go and act as I please, sharing my wisdom with even your *cows*, if I so desire."

"Yet it's Takshak who now rules," Atulya broke in tersely, his lean face flushed. "Convert our cattle, if you've a mind to, but stay away from the aspirants. Royal protocol...."

"Be damned!" Inanna finished for him, her balled fist striking the table violently. She glowered at Atulya. "*You* know how abysmally low our monarch has sunk, and yet you defend him...do you want the curse of these innocents to fall upon you when they learn the truth?"

Atulya was quiet—which, Ishvari realized, could only mean one thing: *Inanna was speaking the truth!*

"Did you know Inanna served Shaardul long past her seven-year term?" Hariaksa asked Ishvari calmly. She nodded, unnerved by the heated exchange. "Once you get to Melukhha," he added, "you'll hear *many* stories about our priestess. But few know that after Shaardul's death she joined Atulya and myself in the practice of gnosis." Hariaksa's cherubic face glowed with admiration as he turned to Inanna. "I hear you seldom grace the outside world these days, Inanna—which makes your visit to Rudralaya an even greater honor."

Atulya frowned at Hariaksa, but the older monk studiously avoided his gaze. Ishvari felt a frisson of fresh excitement at the memory of certain snippets Charu had dropped, courtesy of her garrulous father: Takshak hated Inanna for her blunt attacks against his regime, and only an influential faction had saved her from his spiralling wrath. After the maharajah's third assassination attempt, Inanna had vanished overnight from her city residence, though the bold priestess would *still* drive her chariot right through the palace gates from time to time, shoving past flustered guards and into Takshak's private quarters to castigate him, as if he were a wayward lad and not a mighty king. Then she would disappear indefinitely, confounding all those who tried to discover her whereabouts.

Inanna acknowledged Hariaksa's praise with a nod and a smile, then turned to Atulya. "I'm not here to wage war, dear one— had the fire not urged me to share a vision with the aspirants, I'd care a fig for the mess Takshak's been making. But you and Hariaksa of all beings must know that everything we've done to keep Melukhha holy and vibrant is now at stake." She swung around on Hariaksa. "Prove to me you serve the gods and not an errant king, Hari, my dear...there's a mahaseer fish and other delicacies in my carriage, smuggled with a bit of inside help from the royal kitchens." She snorted with wicked laughter. "Do instruct your monks to prepare a feast for these women tonight, Hari...and don't forget the vegetarian delights I packed for you monks, with my very own hands, mind you." She cracked her whip lightly against the terracotta tiles, giggling like a child. "Oh ho, ho, how I'd love to be a fly on the wall when that snout-in-the-air chef discovers his crowning dish has vanished!"

Hariaksa's round face broke into a broad smile, but Atulya was scowling ferociously—he tolerated the consumption of flesh at Rudralaya *only* for ritual purposes, and surely Inanna must have known this. Besides, she'd stolen the food right out of Takshak's mouth! Ishvari could barely stifle her own giggles.

"Blazing Heavens, my dear Atulya!" Inanna exclaimed. "How tragic that you've gone and lost your sense of the absurd!" She placed a sunburned hand lightly on his arm. "Was it not you who advised me not to take samsara too seriously? And don't we gnostics owe first allegiance to the Divine?" With a dramatic sigh, she drew away from him. "Remember my handmaid Zakiti? Well, after decades of soul-searching, I've come to believe she was almost always right in her counsel. For one thing, I should have first joined Shaardul in his hunt for pleasure before trying to steer him on to the higher path." Her eyes beseeched the senior acharya. "Soon your aspirants will be mating with men who scorn the simple living and high thinking of our ancestors...won't you escort your monks to the jungle for a few hours so I can counsel them in private? I would so hate for them to make the same mistakes I did...."

Bracing his shoulders, Atulya rose to his feet. "Your irreverence has always cast a pall on your brilliance, Inanna...and yet the fire tells me it is the gods themselves who've sent you here tonight." He turned to Hariaksa. "I'll round up our monks and escort them to the jungle hermitage. Arrange for the meal and follow us, brother."

The priestess' face broke into a brilliant smile. "Swear your monks to secrecy while I command the womens' silence, Atulya." She lowered her voice. "And return the instant you hear my chariot leave…as you must know by now, demons roam freely throughout the land. It would be *most* unwise to leave the aspirants unprotected in the hours of darkness."

Ishvari stiffened—*demons here at holy Rudralaya?*

Beckoning to the aspirants to follow her, Inanna stepped outside. Two monks were brushing her horses down, while a third fed and watered the great beasts. Inanna summoned the aspirants to her and counted their glossy heads. "Where's the twelfth?" she asked.

"Archini rests, my lady," Ishvari offered, her throat swelling with anxiety. "She's ill."

"Ah, yes, I'd forgotten the sick woman. Lead me to her." Inanna took Ishvari firmly by the elbow and strode toward the dormitory. Halfway there, she wheeled around on the chattering girls. "Soon you'll have something of *real* substance to prattle about!"

Archini's eyes flickered in disbelief as she took in Inanna's splendid figure. Smiling reassuringly, Inanna laid her right palm on the girl's forehead and pressed down. In moments, Archini was asleep! Reciting mantras unfamiliar to Ishvari, Inanna moved her hands rapidly over Archini's sleeping form, three times, from toes to crown. Then she sat beside the sleeping woman and sank into meditation.

Staring out the cell's small window, Ishvari realized that next to Hariaksa, there was no human she loved more than this child-like friend, so prone to nameless dread. In the distance, she spied Atulya's gaunt figure leading a group of monks in saffron robes past the devadaru grove and into the jungle. Not long after, Hariaksa and the monks assigned to kitchen duty followed. Then Inanna was patting Ishvari on the shoulder, indicating it was time to leave.

Back in the courtyard, Inanna summoned the aspirants. "Travel never fails to make my stomach growl," she announced, ropes of hair dancing around her luminous face as she led them back into the dining hall. On its central table, a whole peacock— prepared by the ingenious palace chef and still wearing its iridescent, multi-hued tail feathers—rested on a clay platter in a pool of savory sauce. Beside it lay a massive mahaseer fish garnished with cumin, tulsi and other fragrant herbs. On the adjoining table sat a wicker basket of Mesopotamian dates, each split in the center and stuffed with a concoction of thickened, sweet milk and chopped nuts.

Only three times in the past seven years had the aspirants tasted flesh—on the eve of auspicious fortnights in their fifth, sixth and seventh years, when they had studied maithuna, the Great Rite. Now Inanna served each of them slices of crusty flatbread flavored with aromatic greens, accompanied by generous portions of the meat and fish, while she herself ate only bread and greens. As they ate, she treated them to tales of old Melukhha, and they responded with excited oohs, aahs and gales of excited laughter. Then, as the descending sun set the trees ablaze, Inanna walked them briskly to an airy classroom. "Gather close," she invited, gesturing for them to be seated. "I've much to say to you tonight."

Never had either of their acharyas commanded such rapt attention! Makshi settled in between Brijabala and Dalaja, for once minus her infectious giggle. Urmila leaned against Tilotamma, and Gitali perched beside dainty Ikshula at the edge of the semicircle, her thickly-lashed eyes thoughtful. Ishvari sat close to Charusheela, Kairavi and Gandhali, whose stubborn skepticism had amazingly given way to a desire to penetrate the mystery represented by the gods.

"We're one short, for Archini's spirit is ailing," Inanna began, fastening her gaze on Ishvari. "To rise into light, we must apply the teachings to the vagaries of earthly life. And how does this apply to the physical realm? To accept, first and foremost, that all things born must one day return to the source!"

Ishvari fought the urge to race back to the dormitory to check on Archini. "Seven years ago," the priestess continued, "signs from the gods led you here—an honor far outweighing noble birth! Today, your instruction at the hands of Melukhha's wisest marks you with rare distinction." Her melodic voice rose and fell, deepening her spell over the aspirants. "Knowledge of yantra, mantra, japa, nyasa, puja, pranayama, asana, bandha, kundalini and the chakras has been transmitted to you—so that, when you enter the capital, you'll each be as prepared for the rites of love as any virgin can be. And yet you've not been trained merely to provide pleasure to our rulers! The true intent of our sages was far greater!"

Twilight splashed gold on Inanna's slanting cheekbones. "Now hark to my own story! At eighteen, I was escorted to the capital from Rudralaya, overly proud despite the warnings of my gurus. You see, I was the *first* half-foreign woman to be elected high tantrika in the history of Melukhha—given the role espionage played even then, no alien was allowed this training. But my mother presented such a compelling case before the Council that I was grudgingly admitted into Rudralaya."

Inanna smiled faintly. "Of course it helped that my mother's lover was Lord Nikunja, royal astrologer at the time. Believe it or not, their alliance was arranged by my *own* father, who ranked as high priest of Sumeria's Temple of Eshnunna. You see, at the time he married her, my father had sworn to return with my mother to her precious mountains the year I turned nine. But when that time finally came, he found he could not leave his sacred post. It was to ensure our protection that he mated my willing mother to Lord Nikunja.

"At Rudralaya," Inanna continued, "I found it easy to dazzle the acharyas with my hybrid beauty and ability to absorb complex concepts. Soon I grew cocky and difficult." The silver in her braids caught rays of dying sun. "But karmic law is both infallible and humorous, my dears—it waited patiently until *after* I rode to Melukhha before it began to punish me for my many follies."

The aspirants were quiet, trapped in the web the glamorous priestess was spinning. "As you must know by now," Inanna said, "ancient Melukkhans were a practical and compassionate people who honored the living over the dead. Unlike Egyptian royals— who sacrificed thousands to secure a dubious comfort in the afterlife—we sent our dead away empty-handed. We were governed by an elected Council of both men and women under the *guidance* of a priest-king, for we had not yet disregarded the mandate of our sages—which was *never* to grant absolute power to he who was both our monarch and chief priest.

"But by the time I arrived in Melukhha, that old form of government had long given way to the autocratic rule of a priest-king. In some ways this change was good, for a single powerful king is able to accomplish far more than a group of squabbling nobles. Indeed, Shaardul's bold strategies had shaped us into a maritime force far greater than those of Egypt, Mesopotamia and Crete. Our trading ships carried an abundance of riches to cities clustered around the Tigris and the Euphrates, and goods flooded into Melukhha as well—emeralds from Egypt, glassware from Tyre, Alexandria, and Sidon, wine from Arabia, Laodicea and Persia, marvelous items from Bactria and Kapisa...I recall Sargon of Akkadia begging Shaardul for more of our best cotton.

"Indeed, our weavers, potters and copper smiths were the world's finest, while our craftsmen carved seals with ivory and terra cotta. Shaardul began to pour gold into the cultivation of millet—a new grain at the time, even as he developed new markets for hardwoods, tin, lead, copper, gold, silver shell, pearls and ivory. And for the first time in centuries, the mountain tribes became his willing vassals. All this success went to his head; Shaardul's warrior energy began to run so wild that soon he was scorning sacred law."

"You suffered greatly before the fire rose, didn't you?" Makshi asked breathlessly, her kohl-rimmed eyes riveted on the fascinating woman.

"Everyone does," Inanna retorted tartly. "In my case, what hurt most was to discover that Shaardul had scant reverence for my role. When I advised him to practice regular maithuna in order to balance his energies and re-direct his kundalini, he retaliated by shunning me. Soon the Council was paying foreign courtesans to satiate his lust, and I was in utter torment….you see, ladies, I'd made the mistake of falling in love with that imperious fool!"

"So how did you raise the fire?" Ishvari asked, impressed by Inanna's honesty.

"Well, it was less than six moons after my triumphal entry into Melukhha that Shaardul was sporting with a Cretan beauty and I was contemplating suicide. Fortunately my father knew what was happening. He sent to me Zakiti, a trained handmaid of the gods, and she was truly a gift of the gods. I had two choices, Zakiti informed me starkly: life or death. Of course I chose to live. I recommitted myself to tantra and soon the fire rose, transforming my inner world into a haven of light.

"So my dears, can you not see how the gods work to remove our defects?" She cracked her whip against her thigh and grinned at their spellbound faces. "By mating me with the haughtiest of men, they forced me to confront my *own* awful flaws!"

"How did you persuade Shaardul to outlaw human sacrifice?" Ikshula asked.

Inanna's amethyst eyes glowed "Not just human sacrifice, my dear, but also the burning of a tantrika every thirty-sixth moon—which the Council had dared to consecrate as a day of public celebration. The noble who'd pushed that bestial law through generations ago loathed our kind—the tantrika he'd panted after left him for a chariot driver after her seven-year term and the small-minded jackal never forgave her. Although the high tantrika was exempt from that ghastly lottery, I fought for the sake of my sisters, and for the fire teachings themselves, using every atom of my influence with Shaardul to have that inhumane law annulled. Praise the gods I succeeded! Had I failed, those rogues in the Council would have had *me* sacrificed."

Every one of the aspirants was silent now, stunned by her revelations.

"Now let me speak of *your* future in Melukhha." Inanna's tall pacing figure threw gigantic shadows on the walls. "Each of you was selected from a village, but it was not out of a desire to provide opportunities for his less fortunate citizens that Takshak passed that law—he intends to have you *right* where he wants you, which is at a social and economic disadvantage. The true test of your caliber will come when you first face an unknown lover, naked and alone—*will you raise the fire or will you fail?*

Her intensity permeated the space. "I came here to warn you that while you fantasize about your coming glory in Melukhha, our maharajah surrounds himself with debauchees who desire *whores,* and not tantrikas!" She paused, allowing her words to sink in. "Coaxing our nobles back to the dharma is up to each one of you.

Neglect your spiritual work and—" she cracked her whip hard against the floor, causing Ikshula to cry out, "I swear, by Rudra's whip, these men will drag you down to the level of the harlot plying her trade in Melukhha's alleys!"

"Wasn't the Council created to temper royal excess?" Ishvari broke the taut silence.

"Certainly that was their original aim," Inanna replied. "But now Takshak and his coterie are systematically emasculating our Council. Our finest have fled, leaving mainly dregs in control. Charaka—who heads our Council—occasionally bestirs himself to dazzle the masses by hosting so-called 'sacred' ceremonies, but that's the extent of his reverence for our holy origins."

Inanna laughed harshly, the sound grating on Ishvari's stretched nerves. Dalaja half-stood, her face reflecting uncertain incredulity, Charu broke into wild sobs, Kairavi and Gitali wept softly, while Tilotamma clung to Urmila like a broken child. Ishvari's own head was spinning as her mind fought against Inanna's words: could the monarch she was so zealously preparing to serve a lowly beast of no conscience? *It just couldn't be!*

Inanna closed her eyes and began to sway before them, as if in a trance. "Last night the fire threw up a vision," she said in a deep voice. "Earth opened her jaws and swallowed entire cities. The waters of the Sarasvati rose higher until they dwarfed our mountains. My spirit moved to an age far in the future…I saw pale-faced men standing on the ruins of Melukhha, exclaiming over skeletons uncovered by sweating laborers. The Great Bath appeared stark and forlorn, and fragments of our citadel were scattered all over the site…*"Mohen-jo-daro!"* I heard a man exclaim. *"That's what the locals call it."*

"What does it mean?" another cut in,

"Mound of the Dead," the first replied.

"*But Melukhha was refulgent in her prime!* I cried. *If only you knew of our passion for the Divine!* But they could not hear me, for I belonged to the past." She sank down on to her haunches before them. "Then Rudra and Mahadevi appeared before me. Mahadevi spoke: *Share this vision with your sisters. Let them know the fate of Melukhha should the desecration of our old ways persists.*"

A tiger roared outside, the savage sound reverberating through Rudralaya. It was rare for such a beast to come so close to the ashram. Ishvari shivered—*was this an omen of worse to come?* The aspirants clung to one another in rising fear. Only a few seemed to grasp the import of what Inanna was risking her life to share with them; the rest would not allow for the ruthless demolition of their fancies. Ishvari was glad Archini slept—these brutal revelations would surely have pushed her over the edge.

"Will none of you take up the challenge to transform these fallen men?" Inanna cried. "Not *one?*" But she'd already lost them. "Well then, if all Melukhha has in her favor is a bunch of vapid cowards masquerading as tantrikas," she spat furiously, "we're in even *worse* trouble than I thought." And wheeling around, Inanna marched straight out of the room.

In a daze, Ishvari rose and followed her. Inanna was sitting on the granite bench beneath the deodar trees in the moonlit courtyard, patting the space beside her. "Contrary to appearances, sweetling," she giggled softly as Ishvari joined her, "I'm far from mad. I wanted to stir you up, force you to *think!* You are all so young… how could you possibly know what's at stake here? If even a fraction of my warning takes root, this night will not have been in vain."

She patted Ishvari's hand. "Take heart, my lovely— Melukhha still has great beings on her side…like Lord Kushal, who happens to be most fond of you. D'you know he's one of the few who fought Takshak's decree to elect aspirants from villages?"

"But why would such a ridiculous law be forced through?" Ishvari broke in excitedly. "If tantrikas are the backbone of Melukhha, should they not be selected regardless of birth?"

Inanna uttered a deep sigh "What a pity that divulging the dirty secrets of our elite is not on Rudralaya's curriculum…much is hidden from you, sweetling, lest you lose heart before the real game begins. Think for a moment…if Takshak or his cronies were to unjustly punish you, who would rush to your defence?"

"Are things really so awful?" Ishvari whispered.

"I'm afraid so," Inanna whispered back, enveloping Ishvari's hands in her own warm ones. "But oh, you cannot imagine my relief that my performance was not entirely wasted!"

The eerie somberness of her tone was back. "Events will arise, work themselves out and disappear…your stars predict a treacherous path, cast as it is by old links with the gods. Already demons hover, for it's in their nature to feed off the pure. Yet all you need do is dwell constantly on the Divine and never succumb to fear."

A storm of questions whirled through Ishvari's head. Before she could begin to articulate them, the priestess rose to her feet and gazed up at the star-speckled sky, as if looking for a sign. "I must be off," she announced, bending low to place her forehead against Ishvari's in blessing. Mounting her chariot with amazing agility, she whipped her steeds through the open gate and on to the moonlit highway.

I am death, shatterer of worlds,
Annihilating all things.
　　—Bhagavad Gita

ISHVARI

That night she dreamed of the sadhu of the valley and Inanna, dancing wildly around the blazing figure of a man she discerned to be the maharajah. With an ugly cry that rent the skies, Takshak dissolved into thick spirals of smoke, whereupon Inanna jubilantly drew the sadhu into her arms, inviting him to suckle at her milk-swollen breasts. Wide awake now, Ishvari replayed the dream sequence several times in her mind's eye. Unable to make any sense of it, she finally drew the quilt over her head and slept until the chanting of the monks wafted into her room at daybreak.

She had to force herself out of bed: Inanna had stripped away Melukhha's sparkling veneer, leaving her with little choice but to prepare for a menacing new world. Quickly she bathed and dressed in a sky-blue tunic, then rushed off to wake Archini, hoping her friend had benefited from Inanna's miraculous energy and was on the mend. But Archini's door swung open to reveal an empty room.

Archini *never* left the dormitory without her! Panicking, Ishvari raced back to the washroom. "Seen Archini?" she asked Urmila, engaged in braiding her glossy mane before the mirror. Tilotamma stood beside her cousin, frowning as she examined a red spot on her chin. Urmila shook her head. Dalaja and Makshi were drying their hair in a corner, but ignored her. So she was being punished for the special attention shown to her last night! Inanna was right—her courageous advice had most likely been wasted on these petty women!

Sprinting outside, Ishvari found Hariaksa in the jasmine arbor beside the courtyard, peering into the jungle. Why was he not breaking fast with the other monks? "O acharya," she cried, intuiting that something was grievously wrong. "Have you seen Archini?"

Hariaksa turned to her, his eyes brimming with sympathy. "Be strong now, sweetling," he muttered, pointing toward the jungle. Ishvari saw Atulya's spare figure striding up the path, followed by Vikranth, his burly assistant, hefting an inert female body across his shoulders. She stared at the bizarre tableau, trying to catch a glimpse of the face hidden by the streaming hair. Then she recognized the small feet dangling from the body—Archini was dead.

A protracted howl of anguish loosed itself from her throat. A howl that brought both aspirants and monks running toward the courtyard. Ishvari bolted back to her room and dived beneath her bedcovers. Much later, Hariaksa entered and set himself down on the floor beside her. Ishvari reached for his hand. "How did she die?" she whispered, looking up at him.

Tears sprang into Hariaksa's eyes. "Two monks milking cows spied her slipping into the jungle before dawn," he said gruffly. "The poor girl was in a trance, they say—her eyes were open, and her steps as deliberate as if a voice was guiding her. One tried to ask where she was headed so early in the morning, but he swears his tongue froze."

"How did Atulya find her so quickly?" she cut in. Rudralaya's buildings had been artfully constructed in the approximate center of a vast jungle, much of it not easy to traverse.

Hariaksa dabbed at his eyes with the back of his hand. "They came to me first, child, but since I lack Atulya's tracking skills, I sent Vikranth to find Atulya." His eyes filled with fresh tears. "They found her in the coils of a python."

Ishvari grabbed at her stomach, as if she'd been viciously punched.

"Can you hear more now?" Hariaksa asked gently.

She could only nod, as a monstrous sadness took hold of her.

"Vikranth believes the very sight of the serpent stopped her fragile heart…a drongo bird led them to her, fluttering over their heads and uttering sharp cries if they took a wrong turn, Vikranth reports. They would never have found her otherwise—pythons swallow prey whole."

The drongo's warning cry on that distant evening in the valley echoed faintly in her ears. Another drongo's eerie call had allowed the cobra to strike at the mongoose only the day before. Why did these strange birds and snakes of death entwine themselves in her life? "Did they have to kill it to free Archini?" she managed to whisper painfully.

"Gnostics do not kill, Ishvari, not unless human life is at risk. And serpents represent kundalini. Atulya knows the mantra for commanding these creatures. He uttered it three times and the snake released her and slithered away."

"You *saw* what was going to happen, didn't you?" she accused him. Hariaksa did not attempt to defend himself; instead, seeing fury take birth in her eyes, he left the room.

Ishvari did not attend the cremation. Makshi carried a bowl of vegetable broth to her much later, but she could not eat. As monks beat drums all through that first night in order to free Archini's spirit from the invisible chains of the relative realm, she cowered under her quilt.

Brijabala and Gitali came by with the news that Atulya had announced the temporary suspension of classes; Rudralaya had plunged into mourning and they would fast all day tomorrow. However, tulsi tea would be available at any time in the dining hall. Did she want anything? After hovering briefly at the door, they left. Tilottamma poked her pretty head in then, followed by Dalaja, Charusheela, Kairavi and Gandhali. Archini's sudden death seemed to have erased the hostility most of the aspirants usually directed her way. Most had been genuinely fond of the delicate girl, known to shy away from harming even the peskiest of flies.

The women stood by her door, sniffling and glancing uncertainly at each other, but Ishvari lay curled up on her mattress, unable to speak. She hid in her room throughout the next day as well. Once she heard Atulya asking her to open the door, but she stuck her fingers in her ears until there was silence again. Memories of Archini rose—her innocent face breaking into a shy smile, snatches of their conversations down by the river, the happiness in her eyes as, arm-in-arm, they'd explored the jungle on holidays, giggling at each other's berry-stained mouths.

Around twilight, a loathsome whispering began in her left ear. At first, Ishvari thought someone had managed to break into her room, but when she opened her eyes, she was alone. The moment she shut her eyes, the whispering started up again—a rasping voice uttering the same string of indecipherable words over and over in a foul and incomprehensible argot.

Outside the moon was rising. She leapt out of bed and shot out of the quiet dormitory, racing down a moonlit side path until she arrived at the cottage of Rudralaya's healer. The monk was seated on the terracotta porch encircling his cottage, strewn with wooden trays containing herbs and dried fruit, using a mortar and pestle to powder ingredients.

Ishvari stood before him, panting like a dog after a hard run. Rage flared up within her against this man too, for not healing her friend. "Give me your *strongest* sleeping potion!" she demanded. The monk must have recognized her, for he quietly entered the cottage and returned with a corked glass vial. "Three drops in water before sleep," he said. "To last you two or more moons."

Grabbing the vial, she raced back to her room and sat on her mattress, shuddering like a leaf in a storm. She fought the urge to toss the entire contents down her throat; the pain was agonizing, and yet something unsullied within her denied her a coward's oblivion. She added *four* drops of tincture to a glass of water and tossed it down. The mixture was bitter on her tongue. She lay back and waited for it to take effect as she digested the hard truth that she'd lost her only friend among the aspirants: Archini had shown no jealousy of her bond with Hariaksa or of her many gifts. In her company, Ishvari had felt free to shine, to be herself, to drop defenses that instinctively shot up around the others.

Atulya temporarily excused her from classes. She spent the next few days and nights sleeping like the dead with the aid of the healer's potent draught, occasionally picking at whatever food was left outside her door. Hariaksa visited her as she lay on her mat one sultry afternoon, but she turned away and faced the wall until he left, unable to forgive him.

As her body got used to the potion, sleep became elusive. She began to sneak out of the dormitory to roam the jungle, trying to make some sense of her loss. Serpents represented both the torment and the wisdom granted by the rising of the kundalini; these slithering killers had destroyed two beings she had loved; both Hiranya and Archini had stolen her heart, and her bond with each had been bitter-sweet. Had the gods embedded a message for her in these brutal losses? Was she, Ishvari, the common factor, the *jinx*?

Meanwhile her resentment against Hariaksa rose to the point that the mere thought of him sitting peacefully by the river made her queasy. At night, nightmares plagued her. Often, she would see the python sucking the prana out of Archini's slight body. Awakening, she'd muffle her rising scream with a pillow, lest she rouse the sleeping women.

When Atulya finally ordered her to return to class, Hariaksa welcomed her back warmly, but did nothing to alter her stony anger against him. Though she ached for the solace only *he* could provide, she was too proud to seek it; no longer could she hide from knowing it was her own ego that blocked her from receiving the love she craved.

Four moons before the election of the high tantrika, Ishvari was bathing with the other women in a communal pool set in the midst of flame-of-the-forest trees in glorious bloom. Urmila began to mock Hariaksa, hobbling along the rim of the pool in mimicry of his gait, her feline face set in his lopsided smile. Women gathered around her, some remarking on how clever a mimic she was, others giggling in embarrassment, for Hariaksa was much loved.

Despite her own stubborn refusal to make peace with Hariaksa, Ishvari was enraged by Urmila's irreverence. She grabbed

Urmila off the edge and shoved her underwater, holding her down with ferocious strength, kicking away both Tilotamma and Ikshula who tried to intervene.

"*Release her!*" Atulya's sharp voice cut through her mad haze with the force of a bullwhip. She obeyed, and Tilottamma and Ikshula immediately hauled Urmila out of the pool. "Why, Ishvari?" Atulya cried, his narrow face white with anger. "Nothing justifies the taking of life....are you aware that had Urmila drowned, you'd be on your way to Melukhha to be executed? Never forget that all aspirants belong—body and soul—to our monarch!"

After this incident, Ishvari turned completely away from her co-aspirants. Now she even ate alone, sitting as far as possible from the prattle about beauty unguents, asanas to preserve yonic elasticity, and riotous tales of the sexual peccadilloes of certain noblemen. But the pain of isolation finally broke her will. One night she sought Hariaksa by the river. "From here on, acharya," she whispered, swallowing her pride, "I will speak solely with you."

Hariaksa's face was somber. "You tower over your sisters, Ishvari, and yet you continue to wallow in emotional chaos. Atulya and I are seriously concerned about your lack of humility, in particular, and your hastiness to judge." He shook his head. "Would I not have saved Archini if I could have? Never underestimate the power of karma—invisible laws govern the fates of all those who spin within the wheel of life and death, and no human power can alter certain events."

She averted her eyes, unwilling for the very first time to accept his words as truth.

"You fool!" Hariaksa exclaimed, swinging her back around to face him. "Will you continue to drown in self-pity when your efforts are desperately needed to save our world? The stakes are so high that Inanna herself came here to give you strength and vision!"

Never had she seen Hariaksa so furious. "Demons feed on the dregs that currently run the Council," he said bleakly. "They hover around the weak, waiting to feed on vital energy. And every day they grow more powerful. Takshak must raise the fire again, for only kundalini can burn away his demons. And what do you think will happen if *you* fall into their clutches?" he demanded intensely, looking nothing like the kindly old fellow with whom she'd always felt at ease. "I'll have you know that the peril to Melukhha is so great that Atulya has requested Devadas to re-examine your chart!"

"And what did the stargazer have to say?" Ishvari asked angrily.

"That anger, pride and an immature sense of judgment may well prevent your evolution into a true priestess," Hariaksa retorted. "All these originate in primal fear, Ishvari, which is just another manifestation of the ego. You have a quick mind and powerful tools to dissolve this negativity, yet nothing transmutes your underlying darkness."

The severity of his words re-awakened her fury. "I didn't ask to be dragged here to do your bidding, did I?" she hissed. "And I refuse to bend backwards to gratify cantankerous old men! Choose another if you so despise my nature!"

"Add ingratitude, insolence and the most unruly temper in the history of Rudralaya to your inventory of faults!" Hariaksa bellowed, this time shocking her into silence. "The gods have been gracious to you, Ishvari, and yet the fire tells me just how far you've fallen. Clean your spirit before you leave for Melukhha! Neglect this work, and no one can save you."

"The gods bless and curse in equal measure!" she cried, sobbing. "Those I've loved most I've lost, and now *you* spurn me too." She whirled away from him and fled through the darkness, more scared than angry. As she passed the washroom, she heard the chatter of aspirants. "Poor Ishvari," Kairavi said. "Those darkening half-moons beneath her eyes reveal her utter chaos."

"Why worry about that vile creature?" Dalaja cut in. "Did she even bother to thank us for all we did for her after Archini died? Oh no, she takes it all for granted."

"A maharani, of pariah stock, no less," Charusheela sniggered. "The mother was a witch, did you know? The envoy thought the woman beautiful and took pity on her. That's how our arrogant beauty got to Rudralaya in the first place!"

"Ishvari has a brilliant mind," Gandhali broke in reasonably. "And if she gets her looks from her mother, I'd say the envoy had good reason to be infatuated."

"Hah!" Urmila cut her off. "Brains and beauty alone do not a high tantrika make, dear Gandhali...as Hariaksa never fails to point out, pride inevitably trips over its own tail. Goddess! I pray every day that I'm preserved from such brazen evidence of my *own* disease."

Makshi giggled, patting a curl into place. "You're *so* right, Urmila, I used to take her food every day after Archini died, and not once did she deign to thank me. I wager she'd still be queening it over us all if Archini hadn't preferred death to sleeping with our nobles."

"The Devikotan's out of the running," Urmila drawled. "Did you catch the contempt in Atulya's eyes after she near drowned me?" Her pretty face twisted into a cunning smile. "What odds I'll be chosen high tantrika in her stead, hey?"

Ishvari slipped away in utter despair; she'd grown used to the gossip, but this was the first time they'd brought up Devikota— and how the tale had been distorted! Of course, *she* had made matters much worse by her ingratitude and aloofness. Worse still, her uncouth behavior had cost her the respect of both acharyas. Back in her room, she wept bitterly. Hariaksa was right; no doubt, her head was crammed full of learning but she'd neglected to foster the humility essential to the deepening of esoteric knowledge.

Already leaves were turning brown, orange and gold. When spring came, it would be time to leave Rudralaya. All through that night, she tossed and turned, battling feelings of guilt and inadequacy. Hariaksa had loved her extravagantly—and, ingrate that she was, ever since Archini's death, she had repaid him only with anger, doubt and scorn.

She found Hariaksa alone in the jasmine arbor the next morning. Humbly she begged his forgiveness. Hariaksa's eyes softened; he counseled her on a specific program of cleansing which she added to her practice of asana and meditation. Before long, as if the gods themselves wished to support her, her nightmares ceased and she began to glow again.

At twilight on their final day at the ashram, Atulya summoned them to the great hall. He stood on a podium before them, shrouded in clouds of gray-blue incense. Gold fillets decorated his forehead, his right arm was heavy with ornaments inlaid with carnelian, jade and gold; he wore a horned headdress, and his vermilion cloak was embossed with arcane symbols.

Ishvari gazed at the rows of saffron-robed monks forming a semi-circle around Atulya, dazedly aware that seven years had actually passed. Like the other aspirants, she was garbed in the crimson cotton for which Melukhha was famed, while her throat, ankles and arms were bare of ornament. Atulya gestured for them to sit down before him. She scanned the rows of monks but could not find Hariaksa.

"Greetings in the name of the gods!" Atulya thundered. "Lord Devadas believes the signs to be auspicious—all eleven of you are to leave for Melukhha tomorrow, each a virgin tantrika. We at Rudralaya shall pray daily for your success in raising the sacred fire!"

The women smiled at each other, their eyes sparkling with triumph. A few had worried that Archini's death might have cast a pall on Lord Devadas's decision, but now all was well, at least on the glittering surface of things. Atulya's resonant voice echoed through the hall. "Ishvari of Devikota shall serve Melukhha as high tantrika, consort to Takshak, Maharajah of Melukhha!" He raised his arms skyward as the monks began a slow, sonorous chanting. "May she serve to bring honor and glory to Melukhha!"

Ishvari caught fleeting expressions of envy on some of the women's faces, but none seemed surprised—from the very beginning, she had shone brightest, and even jealous Urmila had come to accept this. Thanks to Hariaksa, she'd survived the only bad phase in her stellar career at Rudralaya, coming out of it stronger than ever. *So why then did she feel so empty?*

"It is customary to tell this story when we graduate tantrikas, so listen well," Atulya said. "When Melukhha first arose along the banks of the Sarasvati, the Wild God began to appear to the sages meditating upon her holy banks. Gratified by the intensity of their devotion, he blessed our civilization and advised our wise men to serve *all* who sought enlightenment. Many great souls would be reborn there, he promised our rishis, but he also warned that many more would go the way of the world.

"One thing profoundly troubled our sages," he continued. "Their meditations had given them extraordinary powers, but not the ability to transform the ignorant. Burning with a higher love for all humanity, they begged the Wild God for help. So Rudra took a solemn oath—*should a soul with great potential stray, he would drive it forward with his psychic whip until it finally fused with the gods—for it is pain alone that we humans can neither ignore nor endure!"*

Atulya's eyes lingered on Ishvari; sorrow flashed across his face. "Inanna risked her life to share her mystical vision with you all," he continued gravely. "Yet most of you preferred to cling to your fantasies. I tell you now—the stakes are much higher than your selfish happiness—we must *all* fight for the survival of our holiest traditions! I bid you dwell tonight on the import of her vision—and allow it to inform your life in Melukhha."

Ishvari could not help shivering. The senior acharya had tried his hardest to keep Inanna from speaking to them that evening; why was he now behaving as if he himself had invited the mesmerizing old priestess to convince the aspirants of the ghastly perils threatening the integrity of Melukhha? Terribly anxious, she once again scanned the hall for Hariaksa, but could not find him—*why was her beloved guru not here to celebrate this most significant of days?*

I am the ritual and the worship,
The medicine and the mantra,
The butter burnt in the fire,
And I am the flames that consume it.
    —*Bhagavad Gita*

MELUKHHA

A barrage of negative thoughts cycled pandemoniously through Ishvari's mind all through the long night that followed. Like wild elephants on the rampage, she muttered out loud, disgusted by her misery at a time that called for jubilance. Outside, jungle winds moaned and howled, causing arka trees to throw monstrous shadows on the dormitory's whitewashed walls. *By Rudra's flaming whip, where was Hariaksa?*

Her thoughts flew to the night before: she had stood in place after the ceremony and Kairavi, Gandhali and Ikshula had come over to touch foreheads with her. Gitali and Dalaja had tossed perfunctory smiles in her direction, while the rest had ignored her—but for Urmila, who'd shot her a look of naked loathing. Makshi, Brijabala, Kairavi and Charusheela had dropped in to her room for a visit later that night—a giggling bunch offering insincere congratulations.

As her mind skittered restlessly over the many attempts made to befriend her after Archini's death; she could no longer hide from the fact that it was *she* who had ignored the girls' overtures, dreading the pain intimacy inevitably brought in its

wake. Now she fought the urge to sneak down to Hariaksa's rooms
to reassure herself that he was all right—by Rudralaya law, not
even a cleaning woman could enter monastic quarters. Getting
caught by Atulya would be like waving a crimson rag at an enraged
bull!

She downed the last of the healer's potion and slept deeply
for a few blessed hours. The sun's probing rays on her face woke
her, and she heard the breakfast gong strike, earlier than usual. She
raced down to the dining hall, hoping to see Hariaksa ambling
down the walkway leading from the jasmine arbor to the hall, but
he was nowhere in sight. Shaken, she entered the hall to find two
monks laying out an array of food on the central table.

The younger monk averted his gaze as he returned quietly to
the kitchen, the other smiled in acknowledgment of the new high
tantrika. Ishvari smiled back, recognizing him as the serene monk
who had recently moved from working in the herb garden to
kitchen duty. Before she could ask him about Hariaksa's
whereabouts, he had placed his left hand on the right side of his
chest in blessing, bowed, and followed his brother out of the dining
hall.

Befriending resident monks was against ashram law;
infractions were punished in accordance with their gravity, serious
ones even leading to expulsion. While some of the women flirted
on the sly with restive novices, to Ishvari's knowledge, only Makshi
had broken this rule. Besides the occasional robed hypocrite who
hid out in Rudralaya, most resident monks appeared to be engaged
in quests to end their egoic suffering. According to Hariaksa, a few
had grown into such intense meditators that they now dwelled in
states of heightened consciousness. The golden aura radiating from
the older monk told Ishvari that Hariaksa had not been
exaggerating.

The monks had set out a lavish farewell meal—in addition to the usual rice gruel served with fruit, honey and yogurt, there were wheat and barley loaves studded with raisins and nuts, butter molded into the shape of flowering lotuses, muskmelon and mango garnished with sprigs of wild mint, and clay pitchers brimming with creamy milk from the ashram's own herd of contented cows. The kitchen crew must have slaved half the night to produce this feast. What a shame worry had robbed her of her usual lusty appetite!

Ishvari watched morosely as other women streamed into the hall, exclaiming in delight as they filled their bowls. Except for a few quick smiles, no one greeted her; nor did she bother to greet any of them. What was the point? With the gods on her side, she would soon be out of their lives forever. She spooned gruel into a bowl, considering briefly whether to join Makshi and Charusheela, chatting exuberantly in a corner. Instead, out of long habit, she walked to the same seat by the eastern window she had occupied since Archini's passing, wondering gloomily where Hariaksa could possibly be on this of all days.

A short while later, Atulya strode into the dining hall in a white, homespun robe and rope sandals, cutting a radically different figure than the resplendent holy man of the night before. Only his eyes had the same intensity as they scanned the room. When they fell on Ishvari, an emotion akin to sympathy flickered in their dark gaze. He spoke as if from a great distance: Hariaksa had tripped over the projecting root of a banyan tree and shattered his right kneecap.

Relief washed over Ishvari—at least her beloved guru was alive!

It was Vikranth who had first noticed Hariaksa's absence, Atulya was now saying. He had scoured the riverside and found him lying unconscious near a cave. Vikranth had carried him directly to the jungle hermitage on his shoulders, praising the gods that the remarkable old monk had not been devoured by prowling carnivores. The healer had prescribed at least thirty days of treatment and rest, which Hariaksa would undergo in the jungle hermitage. Hariaksa's first thought on regaining consciousness had been for his students, Atulya continued tonelessly. He conveyed his apologies for missing the great ceremony, and promised to send each of them light until their own inner fires blazed.

The senior acharya's abnormal pallor did little to comfort Ishvari. She felt curious eyes probing her face, most likely trying to gauge her reaction to the news. Atulya added that Lord Devadas was sending carriages to take each of the women to their different destinations in the sacred city. Then, with a courtly bow, but still no hint of a smile, he turned and left the hall.

Atulya's abrupt exit was followed by exclamations of concern for poor Hariaksa, and praise for Vikram. Still, it was obvious the coming journey to Melukhha was far more important: if they *did* care about the sage who'd served them with such untiring devotion, Ishvari thought, mopping her own tears with the edge of her sleeve, they were experts in concealing their emotions.

Ishvari nursed her gruel until the women ended their feasting and were traipsing out of the hall. Gandhali was raving about how overjoyed her family would be when they heard of her success; which led Ishvari to think of Sumangali—given her isolated existence in Devikota, would her mother even learn she'd been elected high tantrika?

Back at the dormitory, Hariaksa forgotten in the excitement of what was to come, the women gaily packed their meager belongings to the accompaniment of endearments mixed in with tips ranging all the way from lovemaking to tailoring. Ishvari entered the small room that had seemed so perfect to her as a girl of twelve. She shut the door, consoling herself with the thought that the high tantrika lived in splendid isolation. If she succeeded in raising the fire with Takshak tonight, never again would she be forced to swallow the jealousy of these petty women.

She stared bleakly down at the wooden chest containing her few garments, brooding on the mis-timing of Hariaksa's accident. Was it any wonder Atulya was so upset? The two sages were linked by the mysterious fire of kundalini. Together they accomplished the complex task of running Rudralaya in near perfect harmony. Obviously it had shaken Atulya to end the gruelling seven-year training without his cheerful companion by his side.

Well before noon, ten splendid chariots drove up Rudralaya's private lane and raced out again, carrying ten excited priestesses. Ishvari waited impatiently in the banyan grove for her own chariot to arrive, for ancient custom prescribed that the high tantrika should leave last of all. Hariaksa's mishap continued to weigh heavily on her mind: old bones took a long time to heal, and unless the healer coaxed him to change his mind, she knew the sage would avoid pain-killing herbs on the principle that enduring one's suffering melted residual negative karma. It saddened her to think of him in so much agony on the day her own greatest test loomed large.

Then Makshi's lustful monk was striding toward her, his eyes shamelessly admiring. Atulya wished to see her immediately. She walked slowly over to Atulya's chamber—ever since the incident by the pool, she'd managed to avoid meeting him in private.

Atulya greeted her with a curt nod from behind his wooden desk. "Your carriage will soon be here, Ishvari, so you'll forgive my directness. We elected you high tantrika for your sure grasp of the teachings, our faith in your potential, and your physical beauty. Certain signs—among them, the nature of your dreams and your mercurial mood swings—have led us to believe that kundalini has begun to stir within you. And yet, until the fire burns away all identification with body and mind, one becomes all the more vulnerable to demonic influence."

Ishvari squirmed, wishing Hariaksa was here to shield her from this icy aristocrat. Atulya nodded dourly, as if reading her thoughts. "At the risk of disturbing you on the day of the Great Rite, I must inform you that of the four who formed the Election Committee—Lords Devadas and Kushal, Hariaksa and myself—it was Hariaksa alone who voted *against* your selection."

She grasped the edge of the table to steady herself. Atulya paused, allowing her to absorb his devastating words. "As Hariaksa may have warned you," he continued coldly, "I've long harbored reservations about your emotional balance. Nonetheless, I cast my vote in your favor for the single reason that none of the other women approach your caliber. As for Hariaksa, he was only trying to protect you from the trials ahead. And yet his motive was wrong," he added coldly, "for he put *your* welfare ahead of Melukhha's." The sage stared directly into her shocked eyes. "Keep that in mind, Ishvari, before your diseased ego blackens his memory."

His forthrightness cut through her fog of pain like a knife. "It's true you grasp concepts as easily as a swamp frog catches flies," Atulya ploughed on. "Yet to those who cannot forgive, intellectual knowledge is a tool that can quickly turn into a weapon—against the true Self." Clearly he was speaking for her good, yet every word he uttered was eroding the remnants of her confidence. "Remember, demons cannot attack when inner light is strong," Atulya added, his eyes betraying his weariness. "Your carelessness could well unravel *all* our collective work."

She lowered her gaze, unwilling to reveal just how cruelly his words stung. The approaching rumble of chariot wheels brought the interview to a close. Atulya rose and came forward to bless her, placing his hands briefly on the crown on her head. As she left his chamber, now truly dreading what lay ahead, another monk—sweet-faced and scarcely more than a boy—rushed forward from the shade of an arka tree and thrust a rolled palm leaf at her. "From Acharya Hariaksa," he stammered, blushing as his eyes absorbed her fresh beauty. "He'll let you know when to read it." The boy turned and raced back towards the jungle hermitage.

Dazed, Ishvari tucked Hariaksa's message into her bosom. Fighting tears, she picked up her bag from where she'd left it under the banyan tree, and walked toward the splendid chariot, drawn by four snorting black horses. The driver leapt to the ground, his eyes appraising her with frank curiosity. Putting his hands together at his heart, he bowed low.

Inside the plush chariot, Ishvari fought the urge to open Hariaksa's missive. He must have had strong reason to cast his vote against her, but what, by the fire of the gods, could it be? Had he glimpsed something so hideous in her nature that he'd recoiled at her mating with Takshak? Or had he tried to protect her *from* Takshak?

The horses carried her swiftly toward the city, the thunderous beat of their hooves blocking out all but the high moan of the wind whistling through the jacaranda trees that lined the royal highway. Ripening wheat swayed in currents of air as sinewy dark-skinned peasants drove herds of cattle along the criss-cross of country roads. She was leaving the environs of Rudralaya after seven years, but Atulya's grim words continued to echo in her head, ruining what should have been an exhilarating experience. As the wind slapped against her flushed cheeks, Ishvari prayed fervently to the gods to relieve her of the bondage of her past.

Not long after, she heard the sound of the rapid gallop of hooves behind her chariot. Then ropes of silver were flying past her window, whipping the wind like enraged serpents. *Inanna!* Her driver had recognized the ex-tantrika and was already slowing down his horses.

Inanna halted her chariot and jumped down, imperiously waving her whip at the gaping charioteer. "Stick your fingers in your ears, my good man," she ordered brusquely. Ishvari could not help but grin when the man obeyed with alacrity. The priestess strode up to her window, breathing heavily. "Almost broke my back trying to catch up with you," she shouted up to her. "Still, I give thanks we can speak before you meet Takshak."

Eagerly, Ishvari opened the door of the chariot and Inanna climbed in to sit beside her. "Be easy, sweetling, the fire has shown me everything," she declared, patting Ishvari's cheek. "Hariaksa had some sort of terrifying vision…he babbled about it to Devadas and Atulya and made the ridiculous proposal that they elect Urmila as high tantrika. Of course, they shot him down. There was a bit of a fight and Hariaksa stormed out of the conclave."

Ishvari let out a low moan—Hariaksa had suggested *Urmila* in her stead?

"I didn't chase after you like a maniac just to make you weep, you know," Inanna was saying wryly. "You're a sparkling gem beside that witch! Hariaksa was only trying to protect you, just as he would his own child—which is why renunciates are advised *not* to breed! In any case, Atulya should never have told you about Hariaksa's negative vote—royal birth is *no* guarantee against acting like a village idiot from time to time. Imagine even *mentioning* such a thing with so much riding on your maithuna tonight!" Her teeth flashed white in her sun-darkened face. "Well, I'm not much better than that gloomy old stick, am I? The difference is that *I'm* here to help you win Takshak's heart."

She laughed at Ishvari's bewildered expression, her amethyst eyes gleaming. "It's up to us to clean up the mess these great men have made, eh? Well, you can start by melting Takshak into a puddle of desire tonight. Now listen to me carefully....never betray fear, nor overly feminine softness—except during maithuna. Takshak despises timid women—he'll rid himself of you faster than you can blink if he thinks you weak.

"Second, learn to accept that his innate nature is both hedonistic and fickle to the extreme. No lover holds his interest for long, yet *you* are that rare being blessed with both skill and the beauty to do so. Your task is simple—first to ignite his holy fire, and then to continuously fan the flames, so it burns away the seeds of his depravity. Do *not* complicate things with emotion and over-analysis!

"And third, your term is but seven years long. Stay calm no matter what, knowing your true self to be immortal and blissful. All events are illusions projected on to the screen of your consciousness—just as they arise, they must disappear."

"You ask too much of me," Ishvari whispered, panicking. How could so much be riding on a novice? "I need time!"

"So you need *time,* eh?" Inanna roared, her great eyes glowing like embers. "D'you realize Takshak could bring Melukhha down within the next twelve moons—*if* you fail to raise the fire with him tonight?"

"Maybe so, but I am still a virgin," Ishvari defended herself stubbornly. "I can only promise to put my training to good use."

Inanna shook her head. "Training can only get you so far, sweetling. It's the *fire* that brings magic, and that you already possess in abundance, which is why your sister aspirants attacked you so viciously."

Those last words stunned her; could her rising fire have excited the women's jealousy? "But Hariaksa says my fire is only just rising," she whispered. "It's yet to reach my third eye—"

"Truth is, sweetling," Inanna retorted as she pointed to the middle of Ishvari's chest with a long finger, "the fire has *almost* reached your heart, but will not rise any higher until it burns away your childhood wounds. You must trust me in this matter…there *is* no other way out, I swear to you. You *must* use every atom of your knowledge to re-ignite the fire within Takshak—the fire that has died due to his disregard for sacred law. What that fool desperately needs is a priestess burning with passion to wake him up. Once lit, his fire will mingle with yours and together you can drive it up to the thousand-petalled lotus and beyond—all the way to moksha."

"But how will I know our union is working in this way?" Ishvari asked.

Inanna scowled. "Sweet Gods! Don't tell me Hariaksa hasn't schooled you in this? You'll know, of course, when the great vision flashes in your third eye during the Great Rite! The instant you 'see' the cosmic lingam, you must instantly use the fire to transmit it to Takshak."

Ishvari gawked at her, more terrified than ever of the looming ordeal. Hariaksa *had* taught the aspirants this vital technique; how could she have forgotten? And what if she forgot other things at the crucial time? She'd heard that even *nobles* quailed in Takshak's presence…

"Stop this unseemly trembling!" Inanna ordered. "Virgins nowhere *near* as skilled as you have raised the fire during their first maithuna. You *can* and *will* reform that reprobate!"

Inanna leapt nimbly to the ground and strode to her own chariot. Turning her horses expertly around to drive back the way she'd come, Inanna placed a finger on her lips as she passed the driver, who nodded conspiratorially. A disconcerting blend of gratitude and envy flooded Ishvari as the flamboyant priestess rode away; Inanna was the cherished child of a high priest and a princess who had reigned for decades as the unofficial maharani of Melukhha. How could she possibly empathize with a village girl who'd successively lost all her moorings?

As her own chariot resumed its race toward the capital, Ishvari replayed Inanna's words over and over again in her mind. How bizarre to think that Melukhha's fate hinged on her prowess! She bit her lip, mulling afresh over her situation. The challenge thrown to her was monumental, but could she really transmute Takshak's energy to benefit Melukhha?

The sky turned from indigo blue to a dusky pink as the horses slowed to a measured trot. Looking out her window, she saw massive gates inscribed with pictographic symbols. The city's gates opened, a host of guardsmen draped in dark green garments and armed with rounded staves saluted her. She smiled tentatively in response, but the chariot was already picking up speed.

Amazed, her eyes took in structures of every size and description—both residential and merchant—set in clean, wide streets. The horses passed a long, rectangular building that she imagined accommodated Melukhha's famed bathhouses. Carts pulled by pairs of hefty bullocks moved aside to make way for her elegant chariot, their occupants straining their necks to catch a glimpse of her face. Overcome by shyness, Ishvari leaned back, covering her face with her shawl but leaving her eyes free to roam.

The horses turned another corner and she gasped at her first sight of the Great Bath—an immense water reservoir connected to a stunning temple dedicated to the river goddess, patroness of arts and learning. Used only for religious festivals, the Great Bath now lay open and serene in the gathering twilight, surrounded on all sides by verandahs and galleries.

Then the horses were drawing the chariot past the jewelers of Melukhha, who lounged beside their wares, wrapped in woolen shawls that protected them from the chill autumn breeze. Arrays of bangles and necklaces, amulets and armlets, finger rings, earrings and bracelets flashed past, making her shiver with excitement.

Ishvari glimpsed shop verandas raised above street level, with no more than the thickness of a tree trunk separating one from the other, where merchants sat cross-legged, bargaining with customers even as they kept wary eyes on squat, wooden barrels of spices and oils that stood on the busy pavement outside. "Chandi, come quick!" a woman cried. "*Look at the street!* It's our new high tantrika! Come quick!" Ishvari looked up to see women and children milling about on curved wooden balconies constructed above the stores, many pointing down to her chariot.

Then they were passing a vast open area which she took for the Quadrangle—forum for promulgations, edicts and formal gatherings. A statue of a three-faced deity sat cross-legged on a throne, encircled by animals and wearing a large, horned headdress. The Wild God, Ishvari acknowledged in awe—Rudra the Howler, Shiva the Destroyer, symbol of pure consciousness in three aspects—maharajah, yogi, and Pashupati, lord of the beasts!

A shout of recognition went up from some workmen buzzing around a new statue as her chariot thundered past. A few rushed forward to catch a glimpse of the new high tantrika, thereby exposing their work-in-progress—a massive statue of Mahadevi in her most terrifying aspect. A priest carved out of stone stood before Mahadevi, the dagger in his right hand aimed at a woman cowering at the feet of the Goddess. The supplicant was dressed in the ancient garb of a tantrika. Ishvari's jaw fell—*had not Inanna persuaded Shaardul to abolish the ritual sacrifice that purported to atone for Melukhha's collective sins?*

The carriage rolled on, revealing even more horror. In a field bordering the Quadrangle, the naked bodies of three grown men had been impaled on wooden stakes. The middle one was still alive; as Ishvari watched, aghast, his head flopped to one side like a limp rag doll. A gaggle of urchins playing with flimsy kites were gathered near the stakes. A wild-eyed girl reached for a stone and sent it flying toward the defenseless face of the dying man. "Mahadevi, protect us!" Ishvari cried, covering her eyes. She tapped urgently on the lacquer wall that separated her from the driver. "Who were those poor men?"

"Not *poor*, mistress," the driver retorted, deliberately misunderstanding her. "Two merchants and one noble."

"Their crime?" she stammered. Despite all the talk of corruption in the sacred city, she shuddered at the thought that a monarch of Melukhha could possibly resort to such primitive punishment. The early sages had mandated that *all* citizens be cared for with respect, thereby rendering the chaotic rash of deception, theft and murder so prevalent in other cultures almost totally absent in Melukhha. *What had gone so terribly wrong?*

"Who knows?" the driver muttered, with a nonchalant shrug. "I say, best to keep your nose clean until things settle down. Or else, sell everything you own and get the seven flaming hells out of here." He chuckled. "Which, by the way, many of our elite have been doing of late—ask the old tantrika if you don't believe me. Fortunately, it's the rich who most displease our maharajah—which means that if hardworking chaps like me stick around, there'll soon be rich pickings."

How could a lowly employee of the maharajah speak with such temerity to the newly elected high tantrika? Did he think she'd keep her mouth shut? Or did he just not give a pipal leaf for his cursed life? The horses were trotting past a sidewalk bordered with flowering trees under which a knot of bullock carts stood idle. Their drivers leaned against their vehicles and chewed lazily on betel nut as they watched a trio of gamblers throwing a noisy game of dice. A couple of gamblers stared up at the chariot, tossing her lecherous smiles and winks.

Breathing deeply to quell her spiraling unease, Ishvari turned her eyes away from them. Ahead of her, she saw grand homes and official buildings emblazoned with the Melukhhan crest—an elephant standing on its hind feet with its trunk raised to the skies, from where the Wild God and Mahadevi smiled benevolently down upon it.

The carriage sped down a private road, heading for another set of high gates carved with immense symbols. Soldiers opened the gates and the horses began to clip down a long lush pathway. The chariot slowed down in front of a dwelling supported by stone columns and polished tree trunks, and engraved with all manner of images of gods and goddesses. From Atulya's description, Ishvari recognized it as the abode built by Takshak's great-grandfather for his first queen—who had thrown herself down from its ramparts in reaction to his callous rejection.

The horses had come to a halt and were restlessly pawing the rich earth. The leader of the guardsmen was advancing with his troop to form an escort. Inhaling deeply of the fragrant air, Ishvari arose from her seat and stepped down on to the moist earth to meet her uncertain fate.

Woman in truth is the sacred fire,
Her lower limbs are the fuel,
The hairs of her body the smoke,
Her vulva itself is the flame,
The act of entering is the kindling,
The blaze of pleasure is the sparks that fly up:
In this fire the gods offer up the seed of humanity.
From this sacred offering man is born.
He lives for as long as he is destined to live.
And then he dies.
　　　—*Brihadaranyaka Upanisad*

MAITHUNA

Three old women garbed in ankle-length white tunics hurried down the stone steps of the imposing mansion to meet Ishvari. They wore no jewelry and their skulls were shaven clean, indicating they were either celibates, or widows, bound in service to the Great Gods. Bowing low in unison, they raised their shrewd eyes to openly scrutinize her from head to toe.

With a satisfied grunt, the leader gestured for Ishvari to follow her back up the steps. The other two moved to flank her, shielding her from the smoldering stares of the guardsmen. Copper rings studding the huge doors glinted in the late afternoon sun, blinding Ishvari momentarily as she climbed upwards. Breathing deep to soothe her nerves, she followed the crone through the doorway, down a passage and into a massive hall lit by hundreds of flickering oil lamps.

Fine bamboo screens threaded with skeins of gold hung over huge windows, creating a surreal glow. A gigantic obsidian statue representing Mahadevi, manifestation of the cosmic feminine force, and her consort Rudra, ruler of earth, space, heaven and the time-bound realms of past, present and future, dominated the hall. Mahadevi stood exultant upon the prone body of Rudra; her left foot set confidently upon his chest, her right foot upon his muscled thigh. Hibiscus blossoms the color of blood were strewn by her toes, while her neck was adorned by a seven-strand necklace of pearls, a collar of stars, and a garland of human heads—all symbols of the ego to be amputated by her wisdom sword during a seeker's turbulent journey towards moksha.

Ishvari gazed up in awe at this rare depiction of the Great Gods—the workmanship was exquisite! Had the sculptor viewed the Wild God as a spark of consciousness arising out of the primordial ground of the Great Mother? Then she let out a frightened yelp—as if hearing the thoughts flitting across her mind, Mahadevi was smiling fiercely down at her!

The leader of the crones stepped forward with a grim smile and motioned Ishvari toward a cushioned seat, its headrest comprising the upright hoods of seven golden serpents. Ishvari sank into its comfort, gazing at the iridescent mother-of pearl center of a table standing beside the chair as she gathered her bearings. *Had Mahadevi really smiled at her?*

"Praise Mahadevi for blessing you on this sacred night!" the woman cried in a quivering tremolo. "I am Ketaki, and we three sisters who serve the Great Gods are here to prepare you for maithuna. My sisters shall then return to our home behind the palace, while I shall continue to guide and serve you with devoted heart and soul." Her sisters hovered behind her like ghosts. "It's a well-kept secret that every high tantrika destined to raise the fire receives Mahadevi's blessing. The Goddess smiled upon you, Ishvari of Devikota, and now you must live up to her favor."

Ketaki stopped abruptly, observing the strain on Ishvari's delicate face. "Forgive a thoughtless old woman," she rasped. "You must be tired and hungry after your journey." She turned to her sisters and delivered rapid instructions. One scurried away and returned with a silver food tray which she placed on the table before Ishvari. The two departed then, leaving Ishvari alone with her eccentric new handmaid.

Ishvari ate well, her appetite surprising her with its ferocity. Ketaki nodded with approval as she finished every morsel of a delicate grain she could not identify, and picked the last flakes of braised fish off the engraved earthenware bowl. Ketaki pointed to a red cushion beside one of the windows, indicating Ishvari should sit. She poured a blood-red liquid into a goblet and handed it to Ishvari. "To lubricate your vaginal sheath and prevent conception. Sip it slowly for utmost benefit." And with another formal little bow, the old woman hurried out of the room.

She settled into the diamond pose, legs tucked beneath her and spine erect to permit the food easy downward passage. Inanna's ebullience had somewhat restored the confidence that Atulya had demolished, and now, as she sipped the brew, her mind ran through the various teachings on the Great Rite like quicksilver, gathering the numinous data needed to redirect the flow of the maharajah's warrior energy into his heart.

Ketaki returned and led Ishvari into a richly furnished sleeping room. "Rest here, my lady," she ordered, pointing at a couch with copper elephant heads for posts. "Use your yogic practice to sleep deeply—the night ahead promises to be a stormy one indeed!"

A mild euphoria flooded her body; the brew was already taking effect. Burrowing beneath a summer-scented quilt, Ishvari sank immediately into the practice of *yoga nidra*, while recalling Atulya's assurance that one such hour of profound relaxation was equivalent to four of ordinary sleep. Then, as if no time had passed at all, Ketaki was rousing her.

She followed the sprightly old woman down a corridor to a bathhouse, her eyes widening at the sight of white jasmine and yellow *champakali* floating upon the surface of a massive lotus-shaped bath. Lacquer trays holding rows of gem-flecked flagons stood on marble slabs that adjoined the bath and, everywhere she saw radiant colors and styles that transformed the ordinary. In the corner, a young woman plucked out a melody on a stringed instrument; the music flowed, sinuous as a snake, inviting the petals of Ishvari's heart chakra to open.

Old hands disrobed her as the music soared and dipped in unusual cadences. Then the naked young priestess was made to lie on her back on a warm slab, while Ketaki and her sisters rubbed an herbal compound onto her skin to dissolve even the finest of hairs from her underarms, limbs and pubis. Finally they washed her with scented water and toweled her dry.

Entranced by the ethereal melody, Ishvari slid into the bath. Each limb was lathered with a grainy sandalwood paste and her long hair washed clean before she was rolled onto a second slab to be massaged from toe to crown with scented oils. The women began to croon as they applied various oils to specific parts of her body.

"Jasmine perfumes sensitive hands,
Keora scents both neck and cheek.
Hina, harvested in twilight, for two firm breasts,
Spikenard coats each strand of hair.
Musk from shy deer anoints yoni of delight,
Use sandalwood for holy thigh.
And last of all, but far from least,
Let saffron accent delicate feet."

Fingers moved to the base of her spine, tapping and stroking it in concerted motion. Ishvari sent energy up her spinal column until she felt a stirring in her third eye. As the aromas of the oils suffused her nostrils, the musician herself began to sing in a high voice–

Wake up!
O Goddess Kundalini,
Rise up high.
Our high tantrika is ready,
Union is nigh.

In a delightful haze, Ishvari followed the women into an adjoining chamber, where an array of garments in shades of red, gold and violet were laid out on a wooden chest inlaid with ivory figures of playful nymphs. Ketaki dipped her index finger into a clay pot containing vermilion paste and drew a line from Ishvari's pubis, through the cleft between her buttocks, and all the way up her spine to the top of her forehead, indicating the ascending path of the fire goddess. Then she dressed the high tantrika in a scarlet silk tunic embroidered with symbols of the sun and moon, and draped a diaphanous stole woven of gold fibers around her neck.

Ketaki stepped back to study the effect, then applied an unguent to Ishvari's face. The second sister applied red salve to her lips and enhanced her cheekbones with gold dust. Then the third stepped in to darken the almond eyes of the young tantrika with Egyptian kohl. "Bend low, my lady," Ketaki ordered in her harsh rasp, and placed a vermilion dot between her eyebrows. *"Here will your third eye open, and open it must, or Melukhha will die!"*

Ishvari shivered; did Ketaki fancy herself a prophetess, or were these words ritually used to inspire fear in every virgin high tantrika? She gazed into the gleaming copper mirror that stood in the center of the chamber, amazed at the vibrant beauty who stared back at her with luminous eyes. "I must meditate now," she whispered.

Ketaki led her into a small meditation room, where clay statues of the Great Gods stood on an altar encircled by strings of jasmine. Thin wreaths of smoke swirled upward from sticks of incense inserted into the heart of a fresh lotus. Patchouli, Ishvari guessed, inhaling deeply as she settled onto the cushion placed before the altar. The room was cool, and she shivered, whereupon Ketaki reached for a red woolen shawl lying on a shelf and placed it across her shoulders. Ishvari noticed its motif of elephants embroidered in gold thread—she was now part of the royal elite!

"When you hear temple gongs," Ketaki instructed, pointing to a side door, "you must walk through that door, past the banks of the lake, and down to the jasmine grove dedicated to the gods." The crone prostrated before Ishvari. "May your light, O high tantrika, suffuse the Triple World!" she cried. Rising, she joined her palms at her heart in salute and left the room.

Ishvari forced herself to concentrate on her mantra until she felt the incandescent serpent stirring wildly at the base of her spine. As she looped the sacred fire, she fell into a deep trance. It took fast approaching chariot wheels and the clamor of gongs to bring her back to the present.

Leaping up, she glanced out a window facing the driveway just as Ketaki opened the door. "Maharajah Takshak has arrived!" the crone announced, hauling Ishvari up with surprising strength, and propelling her through the door and onto a winding, lamplit path. "O Ishvari of Devikota!" Ketaki cried in her strange manner. "Walk proud with the Goddess!"

Ishvari set off on the flower-strewn path, praying that the chanting of priests and the hypnotic beating of drums would dissolve her spiraling trepidation. Her prayer was answered; soon she began to experience a spaciousness that erased all fear. On turning a final corner, she beheld the lake gleaming in the moonlight, its surface bedecked with hundreds of multi-hued lotuses. Then she entered the jasmine grove, where thousands of delicate ivory blossoms pulsed their distinctive perfume into the cool night air.

In the light of a blazing fire, Ishvari made out the figure of a man seated cross-legged beneath a champakali tree, wearing a woolen robe the color of red hibiscus. She approached him slowly and gracefully, though her heart pounded with all the savagery of a jungle drum.

Takshak rose, his dark eyes glinting. "Welcome to Melukhha," he greeted her warmly. Muscular and strong-featured, Takshak was not handsome in the way she'd often visualized him—and yet his energy was palpable, mesmerizing! A hot wave of feeling rushed up her spine and her knees began to tremble—*what, by the sweet Goddess, was happening to her?*

Firelight threw shadows on his swarthy face as his lips moved in the repetition of mantras. She raised her eyes to meet his, hoping her confusion wouldn't show. "By the grace of the great gods!" he laughed, pulling her down to the kusha matting he had been sitting on. "I must compliment Kushal on his flawless selection!"

On a low stool beside Takshak sat the ingredients of the Great Rite—red wine gleaming like fresh blood in a silver chalice to signify devotion; slices of roasted venison to symbolize the silence of deep love; fish baked in savory leaves to remind them to control their breathing; and a salver of parched grain to represent the special asanas of maithuna. Each ingredient was intended to appease the deities governing the senses, so sexual energy could rise unhindered as they moved into the ritual of Tantric love-making.

Takshak tossed the liquid contents of a jeweled container into the fire. The flames leapt orange, subsiding into an aquamarine glow. He held the chalice of wine to Ishvari's lips and she drank, then watched as he did the same. Selecting a sliver of venison, Takshak leaned forward to slip it into her mouth. Biting into the succulent flesh, Ishvari returned the favor. Thus they partook of each ingredient, interspersing mouthfuls with sips of wine. As the effects of the drink merged with the heavy scent of jasmine, Ishvari found herself hungry for the union to come.

Night flung her cloak over them as Takshak began to utter the seed-syllables leading to one-pointed thought. Gently he helped her remove her garments, leaving them in a lustrous pile at the side of the mat before removing his own robe of crimson cotton. Hariaksa's advice came flooding back to her: *Breathe slow and deep to build sexual energy; rest until the energy floods your heart, then arouse your lover again, circling the energy through yourself, and into his heart and soul. Only then will the Goddess Kundalini blast out from her depths until she fuses with the Wild God, whose essence burns eternally in your third eye!*

She watched her breath, timing each inhalation to be half the length of the exhalation. Years of training coupled with her own unique practice of visualization—which Hariaksa had helped her refine down by the riverside—made the ancient rite seem almost familiar.

"HRIM, may Adya protect my head.
SRIM, may the Goddess protect my face.
KRIM, may the Supreme Shakti protect my heart."

Takshak repeated each mantra three times, touching the respective parts of his body with his thumb, ring and middle fingers as he did so. *"And as for those parts which are not mentioned,"* he concluded, *"may the Primeval Goddess protect all such."*

Drawing her naked body between his thighs, Takshak allowed her to rest for a while against his chest before swinging her around to kiss her deeply on the mouth. Ishvari melted easily into his male strength, enjoying the new and tantalizing sensations that rose up from her lower regions. A thread of breath rose and fell in the pit of her belly as his warrior energy fused with her own. Takshak inserted his finger into a golden container and drew out red sandalwood paste which he rubbed on her yoni. Then he laid his head reverentially at her feet: Ishvari was now his goddess, and he, her divine mate.

They lay face-to-face in the moonlight, drinking in each other's splendor with worshipful eyes. Takshak turned her on to her back before placing his own body over hers. His confident fingers stiffened her nipples then traversed the length of her body even as he explored her mouth with his tongue. The chanting grew louder, rising to meet the harmonies of stringed instruments, flutes and the pulsing rhythm of the drums. Takshak placed his head between her legs and began probing her yoni; pleasure rippled up her body in expanding wavelets. Then he moved upward to cradle her body in his arms. Blood sang in her ears as he lowered his forehead onto hers and sought permission to enter her holy cavern. The words of ancient ritual came easily back to her:

"Now, I command you to sink into me," she whispered.

You are the Wild God and I am your Shakti.

Implant your cosmic lingam in my sacred yoni.

Goddess protects us from negative desires.

May my divine Self shower you with eternal bliss!"

With a groan of delight, Takshak broke through her virgin shield, moving like viscous honey within her roiling vastness. Ishvari poured her spiraling energy into his body, directing her mindstream to merge with his, even as her body absorbed his masculine fire. Galaxies spun as his form rose and fell over her own in cosmic dance. Maintaining their flow of humming energy, they moved together into the position of *padmasana*, then into *janjugmasana*, and finally, vibrating with pleasure, they lay in *samarasa*.

A column of energy shot upwards to penetrate her heart and the cosmic lingam flashed like lightning in her third eye. Instantly she placed her forehead over his to transmit the vision. Takshak shuddered, as if his very existence hinged upon hers, holding her close. The new lovers rested, happy that the goal of maithuna had been achieved.

As dawn tinged the night sky, Ketaki arrived, carrying a ritual drum in her left hand. A jubilant smile crossed her lips at the sight of the striking couple entwined in each other's arms, transfigured by the Great Rite. She beat the drum vigorously three times, communicating their success to the multitudes waiting outside. "Hail Ishvari of Devikota, high tantrika of Melukhha," thousands of voices cheered in exultant response. "Hail Takshak, maharajah of Melukhha! May your joint wisdom, love and compassion expand to nourish the civilized world!"

Joy swelled Ishvari's heart as she heard these thunderous words. Takshak greeted Ketaki with a familiar nod. He turned his gaze back on Ishvari. "Soon we shall meet again, my priestess," he promised, regally confident as he threw on his robe. "I await your pleasure, my lord," she whispered, thrilled that this man would be her lover for at least the next seven years. Was maithuna sexual magic? she wondered, as Ketaki deftly dressed her. Could a single night of Tantric mating transform a cruel debauchee into a man of such masterful tenderness?

Takshak saluted her as Ketaki led her to the mouth of the jasmine grove, where a flower-bedecked chariot awaited her. Elated, she climbed inside as cymbals clashed and the drums started up again—the seven-day marathon of feasting and entertainment had begun in Melukhha!

The horses galloped past cheering throngs. Men and women dressed in finery sprayed the air with rose water and threw handfuls of fresh blossoms at her passing chariot. She lounged contentedly beside Ketaki as serpent fire continued to whirl lazily through her body. So the skinny rebel of Devikota had finally managed to twist the skeins of fate to her advantage! Even if every dirty little story circulating about Takshak's depravity were true, the harmonious ecstasy of their first mating convinced her she could now mold him into a benevolent monarch—just as Inanna had done with his rebellious father.

One must rise by that by which one falls.
    —*Hevajra Tantra*

NARTAKA

Neither Devikota's rustic simplicity, nor the wild beauty of Rudralaya, had prepared Ishvari for the luxury of her Melukhhan home. As she entered the lavish chamber that had sheltered generations of high tantrikas before her, her eyes fell upon a couch placed beside mullioned windows; suddenly she longed to dive into its comfort and hear Mahadevi whisper that the fiery vision she'd transmitted to Takshak had burned her own darkness into ashes.

"Not yet time to sleep, my lady!" Ketaki pronounced dourly from the doorway. "A high tantrika must bathe in Sarasvati water right after maithuna...to purify the six sheaths of body and mind and dispel lurking entities. Mandakini awaits you right now in the bathhouse."

"Tell her I'll bathe later," Ishvari cut her off, irked by such mystical babbling in the aftermath of her success. As if a few pots of river water could heal deep emotional wounds!

Ketaki stepped into her chamber with a grunt, her sharp eyes expressing alarm. Too flushed with success to consider the possible consequences, Ishvari shoved the old woman back outside, shutting and bolting the door. Ignoring the crone's frantic hammering on the heavy door, she stripped and flung herself naked on to the couch, commodious enough to accommodate a lusty couple. This thought led her to relive her night with the maharajah in extravagant detail; as Hariaksa said, no amount of scroll learning could even *begin* to describe the bliss of maithuna!

Ishvari awoke to the soothing music of songbirds from the surrounding gardens. A banyan tree stood sentinel outside her window. Her eyes strayed eagerly beyond it, catching glimpses of yellow amaranth, scarlet trumpet flowers and clusters of ivory lilies in well-tended banks. Laughter bubbled out of her, startling a black bird with a red beak perched on a lower branch of the great tree: if she'd had the faintest notion that her turbulent exit from Devikota would lead to *this*, she'd have *begged* Lord Kushal to take her away!

A copper bell sat on the low table beside her couch. She gave it a long hard ring, and soon Mandakini arrived to escort her to the bathhouse, her manner warm and loving. As she poured buckets of scented water over Ishvari, lathering her with soapy herbs, washing off the residue, then massaging her with a pungent blend of oils, Mandakini spoke of her long experience in caring for women on the spiritual path. She blushed prettily when she spoke of her husband's noble character, adding that while she and Vasudeva had little formal schooling, Ketaki and her sisters came of fine urban stock, and had been trained in Utlaka's famous main temple to support royal women in their higher quests.

Ishvari chose a green silk tunic from the array hanging in the wooden cupboard of the adjoining dressing room, and Mandakini threw a shawl edged in gold thread over her shoulders. Revitalized and glowing, she followed the maid to the spacious dining hall, where a simple repast of rice and greens cooked with red lentils had been laid out for her.

Ketaki arrived, hovering silently as she ate the delicious food. The old woman appeared peaceful, and Ishvari was grateful for her lack of malice; sleep had restored her good sense, and now she regretted her morning's rudeness. "Come, my lady," Ketaki said, when she'd finished. "Let me show you around your new home…serious talk we can save for later."

Did the crone intend to take her to task? Ishvari wondered with a frisson of fear. Should she explain that something awful had come over her—which would be nothing but the truth—and beg the crone's indulgence? But Ketaki was already marching ahead, explaining in her staccato way that Shaardul had hired a master architect from Sumeria to remodel the ancient dwelling to Inanna's taste. The man had done a superb job, Ishvari decided; barring the kitchen, each of the remaining six spacious rooms were embellished with unique artwork and sculpture.

Ketaki concluded her tour with the inner courtyard, dotted with multi-hued flowering bushes. A curved redbrick staircase ran up its northern end, lined with earthenware pots luxuriant with greenery. Hitching up her tunic, Ishvari ran up the staircase and up to a mosaic-tiled rooftop strewn with colorful cushions. Breathing in the warm afternoon air as the panoramic view of the fabled city unfolded before her, she felt like the most privileged woman in Melukhha.

Ishvari returned alone to the library, brimming with esoteric writings accumulated by priestesses over the centuries. A gold-lettered scroll on the death teachings of Egypt translated by a Melukhhan scribe caught her eye. Strolling outdoors to the pretty arbor bordering her chamber intending to savor it in peace, she soon sank into the mysterious inner world of Egypt.

At twilight, Mandakini carried to her a supper of savory vegetable broth and wheat bread on a silver tray. Ketaki joined her after she'd eaten. Old eyes glittering, the crone informed Ishvari that her duty was to guard her like a hawk, and to ensure she did her daily practices—all for the higher good of Melukhha. "And already your defiance this morning has jeopardized your future." Ketaki's eyes blazed. "When a high tantrika turns rebel, my lady, it negatively impacts *all* those who serve her—including her gurus, Melukhha, and most of all, her own higher Self!"

"I…I don't know what came over me.…" Ishvari stammered. "It won't happen.…"

"That first immersion in Sarasvati water is *critical*," Ketaki cut her off fiercely. "Surely a high tantrika should know this? Nor are we ordinary servants you may mistreat…until the fire rises up to the crown and beyond, even a minor infraction can severely affect your primary duty." Her eyes softened at the sight of Ishvari's fear. "You are young and innocent despite your learning, my lady," she added more kindly. "We are here to help you align yourself with higher purpose…treat us as friends, or you might go perilously astray."

This, after Hariaksa's negative vote and Atulya's lecture? Who did this odd creature think she was? And what hideous karma had now dropped her into the hands of a tyrant?

"Be grateful I did not report your mutiny to Lord Devadas," Ketaki added, as if she were aware of Ishvari's belligerent thoughts. "I hesitated only because I suspect kundalini has shot up through *ida*, your right channel, instead of moving up through *sushumna* in the center…which would further unbalance a shaky ego." She shook her head. "D'you know Vasudeva was ready to climb in through your window and carry you by force to the bathhouse? But the god who speaks in my heart said no....so we purchased herbs that remedy serious lapses, and steeped them in your afternoon's bath. Provided you listen to us from hereon, all should be well."

The crone appraised Ishvari's doleful expression with relief. "If the fire has indeed risen up the wrong channel, it must be redirected by strengthening your lower chakras. Disobey me again, and I'll know for sure the fire's gone wrong. Then Lord Devadas will have to judge the matter, and it's likely he will replace you with the other tantrika the Council favors."

Ishvari's spirit sank into her toes—*how could the Council possibly favor Urmila over her?* So much for her fond notion that she would be her own mistress in Melukhha! The nagging question was: how much did the old woman *really* know of such esoteric matters?

"A great pity only a few great ones like your acharyas exist today," the crone muttered. "Most use another's fire to spark their own...and herein lies the problem—if one partner is dis-eased, things can go drastically wrong for *both*." Her voice sank to a whisper. "The old priestess warned you that demons have entered our city in force, did she not?"

Ishvari nodded weakly: *more talk of demons?*

"Our rishis warned that demons would break through Melukhha's portals if we flouted sacred law. This has come to pass, for the demon of insatiability now feeds in Melukhha, its aim being to bring the sacred city crashing down so his minions can gorge as well. The man who shared this terrible news with me has fled Melukha, and the exodus goes on." Ketaki eyed her bleakly. "Your proximity to Takshak makes you a tempting target, my lady; only the proper rising of the fire can repel these cunning beings."

The crone's words were somehow horribly convincing. "Are you sure the herbs you used in my bath will work?" Ishvari asked, swallowing anxiously.

"Our ayurved's the city's best, though he made it clear he cannot undo the consequences of further delinquency." Ketaki's wrinkled face melted into kindness. "Take heart, my lady," she murmured, reaching out to take Ishvari's hand in her own wrinkled one. "You are intelligent and beautiful, inside and out…and we three are aware that much can go awry when the fire begins to rise. And I will be to you as Zakiti was to Inanna—your helpmate and guide."

Mandakini appeared and hovered anxiously. "Go feed that hungry husband of yours," Ketaki ordered her. "I shall take care of our mistress for tonight." As soon as Mandakini left, hoping to divert the conversation, Ishvari asked after Ketaki's sisters.

Now that she'd said her piece, Ketaki seemed more relaxed. "Oh, I sent them home right after you left for maithuna…home being the cottage we've inhabited since we first came to this city fourteen years ago, a stone's throw behind the royal dwelling. We three escorted Takshak's Utlakan bride to Melukhha, you know," she added confidingly. "Our family had served hers for generations, and the *rajkumari* trusted us. When her belly began to swell with child, Takshak coaxed us to remain…and gradually, we three turned Melukhhan."

"Takshak *married*? I didn't know that!" Ishvari blurted, wondering why Charu's father had not passed on this particularly juicy snippet.

"Believe it, my lady," Ketaki said, covering her shaven head with her shawl. "A mere chit she was too, frightened by every little thing. Oh, but our Takshak was so besotted with her. They were married in a stone temple perched on a hilltop in Utlaka's oldest settlement. As soon as the ceremony was over, Takshak raced back to Melukhha to inform his parents, leaving us three to follow on elephant-back with his bride."

"How did his parents react?"

"Oh, Shaardul was relieved...the boy had always been a worry to the old king, he hoped marriage would settle him. Besides, Eshanika came of minor royalty and brought a respectable dowry." Ketaki winked. "Gold tends to smooth rough corners, does it not?"

Ishvari grimaced at the thought of the heavy purse of gold Lord Kushal had handed her mother. "Did Takshak's mother take to his bride?" she asked the old woman.

"Oh, no, not at first...Abhilasha was vexed that her only son had married without her consent. But when Eshanika became pregnant, she softened. You see, the old queen had wanted to bear more children herself, but Shaardul refused to bed her once Inanna entered his life. It was his callous disregard in this matter, we three came to believe, that *really* embittered her." Ketaki's face was somber. "As for Takshak, many speak ill of him, my lady, but once he was soft and big-hearted. I know for sure that he loved Eshanika with all his heart."

"Where is his wife now?" Ishvari asked, her mouth dry with jealousy.

"Oh, the rajkumari died in childbirth, thirteen moons after she arrived in Melukhha. The birth cord strangled the infant and Eshanika died hours later, from heavy loss of blood." Ketaki smiled grimly. "The midwife fled—Takshak swore to kill her with his bare hands."

Ishvari stared at the ground to hide her surging emotions— could she be jealous of a woman Takshak had once loved? Could the living truly envy the dead?

"I still recall that awful day," Ketaki muttered. "Takshak looked like a ghost himself, he did, for Abhilasha too was gravely ill. The old queen had grown cold to the bone over the years, and sweet gods, was she prone to raging envies! And yet mother and son remained strangely close."

A gust of wind blew through the arka trees, shaking a thousand leaves to the ground. Ketaki looked nervously over her shoulder, as if to catch a spy. Then she turned back to Ishvari, her eyes glittering. "Abhilasha simply *hated* Inanna...it was as obvious as a pimple on a newborn's bottom to us all that she'd never win Shaardul back, but the old maharani had gone and convinced herself that he'd return to her—if only Inanna were to vanish. Fortunately Shaardul knew not to take his wife's hatred lightly...he had Inanna guarded at all times." Ketaki chuckled. "Still, she managed to disappear from time to time, once for a very long stretch." She let out a sharp bark of laughter. "Shaardul went berserk, you know...almost wrecked our economy with sheer negligence."

"Where were Inanna's guardsmen? How could she just slip away?"

Ketaki chuckled. "Ah, so you don't know the old priestess too well then...Inanna was up to all sorts of tricks, and still is, clever as a fox intent on surviving a hard winter." She shook her head nostalgically. "The love those two enjoyed—my, my, my, not human, we three used to say, but divine. Inanna was shattered when he passed, but she revived, oh yes, she revived. Some even think her invincible, and perhaps she is, perhaps she is—after all, which ordinary woman could thumb her nose at Takshak and continue to escape retribution?"

"Where did she disappear to during that time, do you know?"

"We never found that out, no. A year or so later, Shaardul woke to find her sitting at the foot of his couch and howled like a wolf during full moon. Inanna stuck to her story...swore she'd been meditating in the mountains with her mother. Shaardul had sent scouts up those mountains, even climbed up himself, and there was no sign of either of those women. Still, he made no fuss, possibly fearing she'd disappear again."

"Where do *you* think she went?" Ishvari asked curiously.

"Back to Sumeria to see her father most likely...Shaardul would never have let her go that far without an army escort, and Inanna hated *that* kind of fuss."

"Did Takshak truly love his mother?" Ishvari asked.

"Oh, he *adored* her, even when she treated him rough," Ketaki replied. "And of course Abhilasha denied him nothing material...after all, he was her *only* child. I happened to be with her the day she passed, not that long after Eshanika and the babe died, may the gods rest their sweet souls. Shaardul was negotiating a treaty with our tribal chiefs, and Inanna was off visiting her mother. I was tempting Abhilasha with a little seaweed broth when Takshak slunk into her chamber, his eyes so swollen with weeping I couldn't bear to look at him."

Ketaki eyes took on an odd look. "Abhilasha lost her mind...begged him to take another wife, a strong woman to bear him lusty children. But Takshak would not make her this one promise...I saw the struggle on his face and wondered. Only much later did I hear that the astrologer—Lord Nirajit's uncle—oh, he was always so accurate—had predicted that any woman our Takshak married would die. He'd paid no heed, and Eshanika *did* die." Ketaki glanced sharply at her. "You see, my lady, why the maharajah has grown so hard?"

Ishvari shivered; so these were some of the tales Hariaksa said she would hear in Melukhha. How many more would tumble out of the royal closets before her term was over? Ketaki shook her head, tut-tutting as she noticed Ishvari's pallor. "Ah, my lady, forgive an old woman for flapping her mouth. Still, if you want to help Takshak fully raise the fire, you must understand him, inside out. He appears smooth on the outside, but trust me, he is tormented within." She lowered her voice. "Say nothing, but our last high tantrika failed miserably."

All Ishvari knew of her predecessor was that she was of the city of Suhma and considered a great beauty. By sacred law, the high tantrika was to be escorted out of the city at the end of her term to a location of her choice and prohibited from returning for another seven years. Inanna had been the only exception— Shaardul had pushed the Council to decree that for as long as he lived, no new high tantrika was to be elected. Now it struck her that if the last high tantrika had failed to ignite the king's fire, then Ketaki and her gurus were right in hounding her to succeed.

Next morning, a seamstress arrived to measure Ishvari for a new wardrobe and returned that same night with a stack of perfectly cut ankle-length tunics in multi-colored cotton and silk. Matching shawls embroidered with lotuses, peacocks and elephants in gold thread completed each ensemble. As Ishvari modeled her new garments before her copper mirror, thrilled with her glamorous appearance, Ketaki and Mandakini carried in a copper chest holding ornaments given to the high tantrika for the length of her term. Breaking into an exultant jig that sent Mandakini into gales of giggles, Ishvari selected a golden rope necklace studded with greenstone, gold and agate, bracelets of carnelian and lapis lazuli, and an ornate gold and steatite brooch, anticipating the admiration she would soon see reflected in Takshak's eyes.

On her third day in Melukhha, messengers arrived with tribute from senior royal officials: Lord Charaka, leader of the Council, sent her a burnished copper container of pure musk; Lord Ashoka, Head of the Royal Libraries, sent her a silver flagon of precious tung oil; from Lord Kushal, she received a delicate parasol painted with luminous portraits of oriental beauties; but from Takshak himself, she noted with mild alarm, there was nothing, not even a simple message. *And why had he not visited her since their lovemaking?*

Every evening she eagerly awaited the maharajah, but a whole moon passed, and then another, and still he did not come. The years of discipline undergone at Rudralaya now came in good stead; aided by Ketaki and Mandakini, she continued to rise with the sun in order to perform a series of shatkarmas that kept her body supple and clean. Before breaking fast, she practiced her asanas and followed them with a breathing meditation that profoundly relaxed her.

Afternoons she spent in the library. In an enameled drawer she found palm leaf writings in the Melukhhan script, so faded she could barely decipher their contents. Other shelves held many of the texts Hariaksa had lent her, along with stacks of writings in unknown scripts. Some day, she vowed, she would learn these alien languages and enjoy the wisdom of foreign scribes.

When still another moon passed with no sign of Takshak, her spirits began to seriously plummet. *Had he glimpsed the awkward peasant beneath her alluring veneer and recoiled?* "Can I not send for him?" she asked Ketaki plaintively during her bath.

"*Send* for him?" Ketaki echoed, her lips twisting wryly. "Takshak has many duties, my lady. It will serve you well to view yourself as *one* of them."

Ishvari burst into tears. "Does Takshak consider maithuna a royal *duty*? With your own eyes you saw how we loved, Ketaki! And yet a hundred suns have risen and set with no sign of him…and meanwhile I'm prohibited from leaving these cursed walls without his permission!"

"Patience, mistress," Mandakini broke in sympathetically. "He'll come when his visitor leaves." A glare from Ketaki shut her up so tight that even after the crone left the bath-house, Mandakini could not be persuaded to say another word on the subject.

Later, as she sat despondently on her terrace in twilight, Ishvari saw the royal chariot speeding past. Rushing to the edge of the terrace, she caught a glimpse of Takshak, his arm wrapped around a laughing woman whose loose hair rippled down to her waist. Angrily she called for Mandakini and this time managed to wring the truth out of her—Takshak was obsessed with a temple dancer from the south, famed for her erotic dancing!

And this was nothing new, Mandakini admitted, after making quite sure that Ketaki was not hovering around—ever since Eshanika's death, Takshak had run through a multitude of scintillating female mercenaries. Ishvari's heart sank to her toes; so the maharaja *was* appallingly fickle. Was she to spend the next seven years confined to her dwelling with only servants for company? What would her gurus think? Only that she'd failed, and failed miserably.

Dejected, she stopped her daily practices, and not even Ketaki's threats to complain to Lord Devadas could persuade her to begin them again. One night, soon after, something hideous flew in through the window and settled heavily on her chest. Forcing her eyes open, Ishvari saw a squat figure crouching on her breasts and leering at her with lidless red eyes, its arrow-tipped tail flicking in horrible anticipation. Paralyzed with terror, she begged the gods for help.

Whether it took a moment, or eons, she couldn't say—for in the thrall of the beast, time itself had come to a standstill. Excruciatingly slowly, the leaden weight lifted off her, and the gremlin, or demon, or whatever the sweet hell it was, flew hissing and cursing right out of the window. Too terrified to reach for the bell which would summon Mandakini, Ishvari spent the rest of the night buried under her covers, stammering the healing mantra Hariaksa had given her.

Although that particular servant of darkness did not return, she began to suffer a recurrent nightmare: she stood naked in the center of a grove of pipal trees, flanked by the other tanrikas. A masked man carrying a bullwhip in his right hand sat on a raised dais. He struck the earth before him and it yawned open to reveal a seething pit. "Jump!" he commanded each of the women in turn, driving them into the pit with the force of his whip. Then it was her turn. "*Jump!*" he ordered, but suddenly she was racing away in the opposite direction.

Hariaksa had taught her to step boldly into a nightmare and reconstruct it so that malevolent forces turned benign. Now she forced herself to apply his technique and somewhat succeeded; instinct warned her, however, that her most crucial battle was yet to come. Aching for the solace only Hariaksa could provide, she wrote to the old sage, describing the demonic visitation and her subsequent nightmares. She sent Vasudeva to Rudralaya with her message. To her relief, he returned with the cheering news that Hariaksa would send help.

That night Mandakini lovingly massaged her scalp in circular motions until she fell asleep. It was still dark when she was shaken awake. "Rise at once, sweetling," a woman urged. "We've little time and far to go." Ishvari sat up with a start—were things so bad Hariaksa had thought fit to solicit the aid of Inanna? Behind the priestess' tall figure, Ketaki hovered.

"Far to go?" she echoed, rubbing the sleep out of her eyes. "What on earth do you mean?"

"I'm here to escort you to my hermitage," Inanna replied, flicking her whip against her thigh. "Hurry…we must leave while it's still dark." Her eyes danced in the flickering golden light thrown by the taper. "All seven hells will break loose if we're seen together…oh, sweetling, can't you almost hear Takshak simply *howling* with rage?"

"He…he could have me killed if he discovers I've left home," Ishvari stammered. "It's against sacred law, as you know. Can't we speak here? Ketaki will make sure.…"

"Speak here indeed!" Inanna snorted. "What use are words, pray tell? You need healing of an unusual kind, and to your extreme good fortune, someone who can help you is right now at my hermitage. Pray do not waste another moment!"

"First tell me why Takshak has abandoned me," Ishvari begged, burrowing even deeper under her quilt. "The fire rose fierce…ask Ketaki.…"

"Such innocence," Inanna murmured, perching on the edge of her couch. "Did you think a single night with the man would melt his stony heart? Maithuna takes place for the eyes of all Melukhha…its success strengthens a monarch's sway over the kingdom. Takshak's a well-trained tantric, and no fool when it comes to affairs of state. What you took for love, sweetling, was merely the superb rendition of a role he chooses to play from time to time." Inanna turned to wink at the old woman. "Ask Ketaki—the rogue's had enough practice, has he not?"

"*But our maithuna was perfect!*" Ishvari howled. "I had the grand vision so rarely given to mortals, which I transmitted it to him in the prescribed way!"

Inanna's silver twists of hair danced about the dark beauty of her face. "It's easy for a novice to mistake light flashing in the third eye for the cosmic vision…yes, you are skilled and lovely, and certainly you deserve the finest, but while Takshak has mastered the techniques of Tantra, subtler aspects elude him." She patted Ishvari's hand. "If that pretty Utlakan had not died along with his firstborn, things might have gone differently for us all. Shaardul and I moved heaven and earth to get him back on track after her passing, but Abhilasha continued to encourage his vices." Her face was sad. "A mother's twisted love is perhaps the worst obstacle to surmount."

"What about his gurus?" Ishvari cried. "Hariaksa said he had the best…."

Inanna nodded. "Shaardul made sure of that…but even the most insightful guru can do only so much. Add a craving for mundane pleasure to a fickle, impatient nature and you have a disaster waiting to happen, especially when a man is king. Takshak judges our love rites too slow—so he settles for the intoxication of the sacred herb, followed by quick gratification, instead of aiming for the upward rising climax that is the priceless reward of maithuna."

Ishvari trembled, hating every word, yet knowing the old priestess would never lie, especially when it concerned the fate of her beloved Melukhha.

"By the gods, sweetling," Inanna exclaimed. "Your lack of guile draws a dangerous flood of words out of me. Will you promise me something in return for my insights? *Yes?* It is just that until the demons have been routed, you must do *exactly* as Ketaki says. Agreed?"

Ishvari nodded miserably.

"So you want to know why our dear king won't touch you, eh?" A sardonic smile lifted the corner of her lips. "Well, first of all, your predecessor was a guttering oil lamp for all her physical perfection. Their maithuna stank of mediocrity and Takshak never bothered to see her again. After a few moans and groans, the insipid creature settled down to enjoying her term. Indeed she became so fat and languid that many sniggered openly when she left Melukhha under royal guard...and now here *you* are, and Takshak senses you could seduce him into loving you even more deeply than he loved Eshanika—who was, after all, a mere child, sorely lacking in fire. Truth is, my lovely, you frighten the fool." She flicked her whip on the floor. "Much safer to fuck pretty mercenaries, easily sated with a smidgen of technique and plenty of gold, than to court a goddess who could break the diamond-hard shield he's grown around his heart, eh?"

"But isn't love the essence of Tantra?" Ishvari whimpered.

"Naïvete does *not* serve a tantrika! Besides, a man must *want* to transform...Takshak's heart center is blocked...he abuses the herb to dull the pain, but it's scarred him, made him brutal and cold. Now the fire has sunk into his muladhara and will not easily rise."

"Then why did you lead me to believe I could transform him?" Ishvari cried furiously.

"*What else could I do?* You needed an infusion of fresh courage after Atulya's tongue-lashing, or you just might have dived into the Sarasvati with rocks on your ankles." Inanna smiled. "And because miracles *do* happen—did *I* myself not draw Shaardul back into my arms?"

Ishvari let out a cry of pure suffering.

"I'd be gentler if we had more time, sweetling," Inanna whispered. "Don't *I*, of all women, know how it is? A cruel knife twists in the heart when the lover dances beyond reach. Still, if you *really* do care for this confused man, come with me!"

The old priestess spoke with compassion, and why would she risk her life again and again if the matter was not critically important? If she refused to go, Ishvari intuited, the demons would attack even more viciously; but to be discovered leaving home would be to court an even quicker death. "Where is your hermitage?" she asked fretfully.

"Hard to give you a precise location, for it does not exist in ordinary time and space. Let me say for now that we who call it home were once expert at the mahavidyas, the great skills given to high mystics. Now we choose to abide simply in the bliss of the Self." Inanna rose and looked down at her with rising impatience. "You feel betrayed, I know, but think for a moment—would either Hariaksa or I harm you in the slightest? Demons are only manifestations of our worst aspects—when they plague a seeker of promise, one must act fast or all is lost."

Ishvari stared at her in utter confusion.

"If a poisoned arrow struck you, would you waste time inquiring into the nature of the poison?" Inanna cracked her whip on the floor. "Enough said! I can't remember a time when our Elders have allowed an outsider to enter our sanctuary! Consider your blessings and *rise!*"

Ketaki handed a white sleeveless tunic to Ishvari and scurried away. Feeling anything but blessed, Ishvari slipped it on; if she was going to fall, it was better to go down fighting.

"Takshak will not learn about this night," Inanna reassured her, throwing a shawl over Ishvari's bare shoulders. "Believe it or not, those idiot guardsmen watch only the front of your home…I sneaked in from the back, and that's how we'll leave."

Ketaki stood by the kitchen entrance holding an oil lamp, worry streaking her tired old face. The crone lit their way across the back garden and through a miniature gate hidden by jasmine shrubs. Inanna's black chariot waited in the shadows, her horses as still as statues. "Get in and catch some sleep if you can," Inanna whispered. "You'll need strength for the healing."

Inanna raced the chariot along dark, winding alleys, avoiding the highway. Ishvari fell into a fitful slumber, awaking with a start when the steeds came to a halt. They must have traveled for hours, she realized, for now they were in thick forest. Inanna leapt down and opened the chariot door, motioning for her to emerge into the moonlit landscape. As if in a dream, she watched Inanna lead the horses to the edge of a stream to drink. "Where are we?" she whispered.

"At my hermitage." Inanna smiled impishly. "Now freshen up at the stream if you please."

Ishvari sat on her haunches and splashed her face and body with the cold water. When she rose, moments later, the old priestess had vanished. "Inanna!" she screamed, frantically scanning her surroundings, but the woman had truly disappeared. Gulping in the cold air to still her panic, Ishvari moved ahead until she found herself on a well-trodden path. The piercing sweetness of a flute came to her ears. She followed the sound, assuring herself that anyone capable of drawing such divine music out of a hollow tube of bamboo could help her through the agony of existence. The melody rose up her chakras, blasting open inner doors until she became one with the song of night birds, crickets and the rhythmic croaking of ten thousand frogs. The humming of honeybees filled the air as she climbed higher and she saw rare species of plants fringing the path. A temple gong rang, accompanied by the deep bass of a horn and an insistent drumming. Ahead a light shone; in dazzled trance, she moved toward it.

A man sitting on the stoop of a stone dwelling beckoned lazily to her. Then she was flying toward him, as if her body had no substance at all. "My wicked Little Goddess," he murmured, rising to his feet. "What monstrous crisis brings you here?"

"My sadhu!" she exclaimed, throwing herself at his feet. "Do you live here now?"

Smiling, he gestured for her to follow him. She obeyed, overcome with emotion, noticing that his lean body was clad only in a lower garment of red cotton. Now she was in a rectangular room whose floors were constructed of a wood shining with natural gloss. Bright cushions were strewn on a kusha mattress that ran all along one side of the unusual space. Jungle orchids on fine green stems, tender faces hued in unearthly shades of indigo, maroon and pink, grew in colorful profusion along the window ledge. A fire blazed in the corner, and against the other wall sat a low couch covered in some shimmering turquoise fabric.

The sadhu motioned for her to lie down on the couch. He sat beside her, his fingers probing her body from her toes and moving upward. He stopped at her heart chakra, increasing the pressure of his thumb until she screamed. "As I suspected," he muttered. "It's here that the demon resides." He struck the center of her forehead and her mind dissolved into cloudy visions: Hiranya's corpse flung on the dung cart, Ghora's pig-eyes glittering as he lunged at Sumangali, Obalesh gurgling on the mud floor, a great python coiled at the base of an arka tree. A scream shot out of her throat as the god of the valley straddled her body, his eyes blazing.

"Let go of these old stories," he ordered. "All we experience is only the result of our own past thought, speech and action, from this and other lives." His thumb pressed down on her third eye, and now she was overcome by flashing memories that did not originate in this lifetime; her spirit spun through space and time as wave after wave struck her, only to dissolve into fountains of rainbow-colored light as they shimmered through her stunned body and mind.

Only the gods knew how long she endured the eerie onslaught, for some witnessing part within her realized this bizarre healing was not occurring in earth time. Memories dwindled to a halt, and then she was hurtling through the vastness of night, minus body, minus mind, in the sheer freedom of spirit. She awoke to dawn's light streaming in through the windows. The sadhu was sitting before her now, gazing at her with such unmistakable love that she began to weep. Suddenly he was everything to her—father, brother, son, friend, counselor, lover. "Did your magic work?" she sobbed, trying to rise, yearning for his embrace, but a force held her down.

"The worst is over," he replied, his clear eyes tinged with sadness. "Yet the Elders say you have more worldly karma to burn. While you slept, Ishvari, I saw thousands of lives you've already lived in quest of peace and happiness. It's your stubborn ego alone that blocks you from knowing that *you* are the Shining One."

"Who are these Elders?" she whispered hoarsely.

"Omniscient beings who see past, present and future. They warn that the time ahead is crucial, and yet there is a way to heal yourself completely, if you are willing."

"I *am* willing," she whispered, swallowing drily.

"Good, for this practice can lead you to unchanging bliss. Begin the moment you return to Melukhha, and do not cease, even after you've recaptured Takshak's heart."

The memory of this man meditating in the hidden valley, leopard at his feet, flashed across her mind. "You are certain he'll return to me?" she asked anxiously.

He nodded gravely. "But whether he'll nurse the fire long enough to burn away his evil will depend greatly on *your* devotion to the dharma, *your* ability to inspire him to transform. Now listen well…from the bliss of the Unmanifest, the One streamed downward to denser regions, dividing itself into a multitude of forms." He held her with his unbroken gaze, his bronzed face bright as the rising sun. "Call this unified source God, or Existence, or whatever you please, but know that even the briefest merging into it evokes a joy unlike any other pleasure derived from the senses. We gnostics call this inner joy *samadhi*. We focus on opening the spiritual heart, and when it begins to open, we know the entire cosmos is contained within."

She drank in his beauty with starved eyes. "How can I too taste samadhi?" she asked.

"Simply add what I'm about to share with you to your current practice." He gestured for her to sit up. Though it pained her to tear her gaze away from his face, she closed her eyes.

"Become aware of the dimensions of your body, bringing to mind that this physical-mental system is only a temporary cage for your immortal spirit." She obeyed. "Now draw up the fire from the base of your spine and feel it rise, like a golden serpent, through each of the main chakras, awakening each one before moving higher, until you reach the thousand-petalled lotus hovering just above your crown." Again she obeyed easily, backed by the ease of long personal practice. "Now expand this golden cord of energy all the way up to the heavens, then down your spine into the center of Earth, and watch as this light spreads, until you—and all beings from past, present and future—are enveloped in its radiance." Ishvari followed him eagerly, marveling at how clearly he taught. "Now fix your gaze through your third eye and plunge into your spiritual heart, two inches away from the breast median and close to your right nipple. You entered your mother's womb as consciousness, you are now consciousness, and you will be consciousness when your body and mind return to the source. Nothing can destroy your true nature, which is the source of all reality, from unmanifest to manifest."

He was silent as she entered the zone he was describing.

"*Who are you really?*" he asked softly. "More than body, mind or emotions, you, and all beings, are of the same essence as the Divine. You are Existence itself, as well as the Consciousness that becomes aware of this, and from this pure knowing erupts a ceaseless fountain of bliss. Plunge into your spiritual heart, Little Goddess, and kiss this joy as it arises. You are this bliss, you are this eternal bliss!"

Ishvari began to feel the ache of something precious opening within the right side of her chest. A strange floating pleasure stopped her thoughts. When reluctantly she opened her eyes—for the sensation was sublime—the sadhu was on his haunches before her, his face shining with love. Shyness overcame her. "What was wrong with me?" she whispered.

"The dark power that rules the mind still besieges you," he replied. "It attacks those destined for liberation most ferociously— as the saying goes, the greater the light, the greater the shadow." She wanted to lay her head on his lap and sleep forever. "All who reside here have won fierce personal battles—and you too shall win," he spoke soothingly. "Fight now and fight hard, Ishvari! Your opponents are cunning, insidious, as old as time, and yet the blazing light of the Unmanifest can dissolve their control over your soul in an instant."

Who was this man under his many masks? Energy stirred fiercely in the region of her yoni. She cried out as it rushed up her spine, driving open the petals of her heart. How savagely she wanted him then, no better than a wild animal in the throes of a driving insane lust. She lapped up his beauty, craving his touch and tender words, reaching out blindly for him—only to be slapped back again by the same unseen force. She whimpered at the humiliating paradox of it all—the high tantrika of Melukhha, envied by every woman in the land, had no power over the maharajah, nor this luminous guru.

"Takshak will return to you," the sadhu repeated calmly. "As for us, we've much to do before we can meet again."

Humbled by her yearning for this stranger, Ishvari could only bow her head.

"No human can manipulate the present, yet tomorrow lies squarely in our hands," he added gently. "How you think, act and speak from hereon, Ishvari, will determine your future."

"Can't I stay here with you?" she begged. "I beg you, let me stay."

The sadhu shook his head as he led her out, then down the path she'd ascended only the night before. Stumbling behind him, she knew her love for this man had existed from beginningless time—*how could she bear to leave him for a capricious and corrupt maharajah?*

"Stay true to your dharma and you will thrive, Little Goddess—the stars foretell your awesome rise, and they do not lie."

"Who *are* you?" she whispered.

"I am Nartaka, heartson of Inanna and Shaardul," he said calmly. His radiance enveloped her like a golden cloak. "You and I have loved for many lifetimes, Little Goddess, and only karma keeps us apart now—karma which can be burnt."

Heartson of Inanna and Shaardul! How had Inanna managed to keep such a brilliant son secret all these years? Weeping softly, she followed him to the edge of the lake. His promises were too ambiguous...how to rely on a sadhu with as much substance as a shadow at noon? Besides, he had been unable to cure her. Worse still, just as Ghora had done so long ago, he too blamed her bad karma for her troubles. She did not care that he could read her thoughts—now she *wanted* him to feel the slap of her skepticism!

"Use the practice I gave you to still your traitorous mind, Ishvari," Nartaka murmured. "Hatha will keep your body supple and fit, but make the direct investigation of your true Self your main practice. Soon, I swear by Rudra's Whip, Takshak will be unable to resist you." He pointed to a rock. "Now sit and turn your attention to the bottom of the lake."

Ishvari glared sullenly into the lake's pebbled bottom, catching glimpses of faces and forms so unutterably lovely that her anger dissolved. Then suddenly she was lying on the couch in her own chamber, hearing the sonorous chants of the priests rising into the morning air. It struck her like a clap of thunder that Nartaka was Takshak's half-brother! Now Ketaki's words about Inanna's long disappearance from Melukhha made perfect sense! Indeed, the naked sadhu loping alongside Lord Kushal's chariot had spoken true—a royal brother *was* deeply concerned about the monarch's fate.

As dust hides the clarity of a mirror,
So the truth is concealed by illusion.
Wisdom is snared among the flames
Of a shape-shifting lust that can never be satisfied.
    —*Bhagavad Gita*

MUSK DEER

"That braised venison was *excellent*, my dear." Lord Kushal emitted a satisfied burp as he patted the slight bulge on his stomach. "And sesame oil *does* add a wonderfully smoky tang to our local wild rice. But don't you think," he continued, as gravely as if he were assessing the current state of the Melukhan government, "the brinjals could have used less turmeric and more roasting?"

"I'll tell Mandakini you said so," Ishvari promised, tickled as always by the envoy's odd habit of dissecting his weekly meal with her.

"So it was Mandakini who conjured up this feast then?"

"Oh no, she's way too busy for that...but I've asked her to give our chef his orders instead of having the old one do it...Ketaki throws a fit if the poor man so much as disagrees with her on the slightest thing." She shook her head in bewilderment. "Never fails to baffle me that a woman of such advanced years and wisdom would choose to quibble over trivialities."

Lord Kushal grinned. "Ah, but I've found wisdom and pettiness to co-exist quite nicely...and Ketaki *does* have her virtues, such as keeping *you* on your spiritual toes."

"Truth be told, I weary of her exhorting me to grow," she complained. "Zakiti is her idol, you know, and from all accounts, *that* woman was a holy terror."

"And are you?" he enquired, inclining his head towards her. "Growing, I mean?"

"Oh, most certainly in girth," Ishvari laughed ruefully, adjusting her scarlet tunic patterned with golden blossoms over her swelling hips.

His sharp but loving eyes scanned her face with paternal concern. "I fear you are none too happy these days, my dear...won't you convince me that I am wrong?"

Ishvari shot him a wary glance from beneath extravagantly long eyelashes. "*Happy?* Ah, but that's a word that carries little meaning for me these days...though I can honestly say I'm grateful for all the gods have given me. My physical needs are well met, after all, and at least a thousand scrolls await my hungry mind." She drummed a tattoo on the wooden table top. "I took your advice, my lord," she blurted. "Asked Takshak to hire me a language tutor for the Sumerian script...."

"And?" Lord Kushal asked, his narrow face tightening.

"Oh, he refused outright. Ranted that an excess of learning dries up a woman's vital juices...that the eyes turn cold and the mind cuts like a sword....swore I'd never be content even if the gods poured every cosmic secret into my brain. Then he stormed away, though stars were just beginning to sprinkle the night sky." A tear rolled down her smooth cheek. "You are our monarch's revered friend and counselor, my lord—pray tell me why a simple request from his own priestess would so enrage him!"

So the worm of discontent was already gnawing at her heart! Dare he risk stirring the pot further? "Don't you know?" he asked, raising an eyebrow. "Takshak tortures you to avenge himself against Inanna, the only woman apart from his long-deceased mother whom he's never been able to oppress or control."

Ishvari nodded, her face pale. "I knew that, of course," she muttered, "in my heart of hearts. Things go badly between us, my lord. I often feel he wants to *break* me, as if I was one of those snorting wild Khotan stallions gifted to him as tribute...."

"The waste of brilliance is most agonizing when it's one's own," the envoy acknowledged quietly. "And yet freedom's a gift we each must earn...why, Inanna fought Shaardul's bullying ways every inch of the way! And going against him, mind you, was a *terrible* risk—our court was brimming with foreign courtesans eager to curry his favor at the time, and Shaardul of course had a murderous temper. But—as you well know, my dear—her courage paid off."

She grimaced; it always stung to hear the envoy praise Inanna.

"Where's the shame in having such a one as your model, Ishvari?" he exclaimed, his narrow brow furrowing with irritation. "Besides, *you* are admired for having drawn Takshak back into your arms, as well for keeping him sated for so long. I urge you now—waste no time repairing your bond. Once Takshak deepens his journey inward, all things will fall into place."

"I've heard that Inanna won her lord back by indulging him to the extreme—as would any skilled courtesan," she said petulantly. "You admire her for *that,* my lord?"

He hid a smile; as long as she continued to react to his needling, there was hope. "Inanna was acting on Zakiti's counsel," he said reasonably. "But don't forget that once she was sure of

Shaardul's love, she clawed like a tigress until she won back *all* her traditional rights."

She threw him a faint smile, aware he was only trying to stir her into fighting for her *own* rights, her *own* dignity as high tantrika. "Is it true Inanna coaxed Shaardul to give up his vices?"

He shook his head. "Not directly, no. Shaardul gave up flesh and alcohol the day Abhilasha passed—the old lion wished to make amends for his callous treatment of his wife, as well as for the random cruelties of his youth….or so Devadas says."

Mandakini emerged from the kitchen, carrying a ceramic dish painted in motifs of blue and gold which she placed on the table between them. "Ah, muskmelon and fresh cream to follow," Lord Kushal murmured, pushing the bowl towards her with a little sigh. "I mustn't have any…as Sarahi says, it's damnably easy to slide from a healthy appetite to gluttony."

"I'm glad your wife is not here to see *me* gorge," Ishvari laughed, spooning a liberal portion into her bowl. "Funny it is, but the worse I feel emotionally, the richer the food I crave."

He eyed her critically: if she did not curb her appetite, she would soon mar her stunning beauty. "Sarahi's been sticking to her greens and grains diet," he said. 'Shun flesh and liquor,' she cries to all and sundry, bringing to mind that crazed hag who sits outside the Great Bath."

She felt a stab of envy for Sarahi's freedom—the freedom enjoyed by the old aristocracy. The envoy and his wife could trace their bloodlines to Melukhha's oldest families, and many such ancient clans, Ketaki had once told her in passing, still practiced austerities to enhance their Tantric practice. As Hariaksa had explained, once the fire reached the third eye, it was best not to ingest the flesh of animals that had died experiencing the agony of slaughter.

Sarahi she had met just once, when the envoy had impulsively brought her along to their weekly meal. A pretty, slender woman with so sly a wit that Lord Kushal had ordered her to use it strictly within a circle of trusted friends, Sarahi had struck Ishvari as an original thinker, unafraid to air her radical views. Nor had she come across as an ascetic, for she had relished the roasted peacock sent over from the royal kitchens. Just as they were hatching a plan to meet again, Lord Kushal had warned them that the high tantrika was forbidden to socialize during her term. Sadly, Sarahi had not come again. "What brought about this change?" she asked, puzzled.

"Oh, it all began when a stranger approached her in the main square—a man so unusual in bearing, Sarahi claims, that she was impelled to speak with him. Oddly enough," he mused, steepling his narrow face in his hands and staring into space, "her description of him brought to mind the ascetic you called the sadhu of the valley."

Ishvari froze—*Nartaka, here in Melukhha?* "How bizarre," she murmured nonchalantly. "What could have triggered so distant a memory?"

"Oh," Lord Kushal laughed, "Sarahi's silver tongue paints such clear pictures that one actually *sees* what she saw. She spoke of this man's radiance and regal bearing, and I saw it all again, that amazing fellow racing alongside my chariot without breaking a sweat!"

"Did he give Sarahi his name?" Ishvari asked, trying to mask her excitement.

"No, though she swears by his demeanor that he is a born royal. He warned her that a string of great disasters would strike Melukhha if we in the Council did not immediately return to the pure way. Sarahi does not suffer fools gladly, and yet his mystical outpouring utterly captivated her. She wished to bring him home to meet with me, but the chariot driver distracted her momentarily, and when she turned back to invite him, he was gone!"

Just as in Devikota, Ishvari thought, her mind spinning.

The envoy frowned. "Why would he approach Sarahi, of all the beauties parading in Central Square? Could he have known she's *my* wife? And that she's been hounding me to stop the rot in government?" He grunted with disgust. "As if I could! One man can do little when surrounded by sycophants and cowards ready to bend over backwards to please our monarch."

Ishvari was shocked—never before had the envoy spoken so openly about the rot in the Council. Her thoughts flew to Takshak, who never consulted her on important matters, treating her no better than a wealthy merchant would his pampered mistress. The only area in which he took care to please her was in his performance of the love rites—and even here he behaved as if there were an invisible audience surrounding their couch, watching and judging. "And how does Sarahi fare in other ways?" she asked, to distract herself.

"Oh, she's been threatening to hunt down a young lover if I don't lose this excess weight…swears to chase me down the royal highway with a riding whip until the fat around my stomach melts. That minx never did mince words." He winked at her. "What say, Ishvari? Dare I seek revenge by shopping for a teen mistress? Charaka swears by his old mother's blood that Sumerian whores are skilled in aiding an aging lion forget both weight and years…I think we can trust the old goat in this matter, don't you?"

Ishvari wiped a smear of cream off her generous mouth and smiled, though she did not bother to answer; Lord Kushal adored his wife, and had done so ever since they had been children squabbling over toys in homes situated on Melukhha's posh northern edge; she was convinced he would rather demolish the Great Bath than wound Sarahi in the slightest.

He brushed crumbs of wheat loaf off his robe and leaned forward. "Now let us speak of *you*, my dear. Ketaki tells me you are assiduous in your holy practices, so I'm not surprised to see you shining like the sun, despite your wearisome little spats with our monarch. Why, just yesterday Devadas said that many envy Takshak his ravishing consort."

"Amazing how mere rumor can enhance reputation," she retorted drily. "But for Takshak and yourself, none of those who praise me have even set eyes on me."

He rocked back in his chair, running slender fingers glinting with diamonds through his silver mane. *How to inspire this child-woman to wake up to the urgency of challenging Takshak before he totally disempowered her?* "But are they not right, my dear?" he probed carefully. "Clearly we've not boasted a high tantrika of such great beauty and skill since Inanna's time!"

Conflicting emotions played across her exquisite face. "As time goes on," he continued, even more determined to boost her flagging self-confidence, "I continue to praise the Wild God for leading me to you. So scrawny and defiant you were then, but those blazing eyes! I knew in a trice that Rudra had marked you for his own." He lowered his voice. "Yet, in your early days here, my dear, I must confess that even *I* believed Takshak had cast you off for good."

Her eyes filled with sudden tears.

"Don't you lose heart, Ishvari," he said softly. "You were born with the fire. I'll never forget the fury on your little face when I said the monks would help you forgive your mother...."

"And I'm angry still," she cut him off, wiping her eyes impatiently. "Such ghastly things happened...and *she* was always too weak to stand up for herself…for us. Did I tell you she's twice asked to visit with Obalesh, and that both times I've refused, without an explanation?"

"*What?*" He glared at her. "Have you stopped to consider your future in that stinking pit? Likely chained to some foul-smelling farmer, slaving from dawn to nightfall to feed a snot-nosed brood! And even if you're foolish enough to resent that poor woman for doing her best, what, pray tell, has your brother done to deserve your scorn? I suggest we waste no more time bringing them both to Melukhha…Devikota's no fit home for the family of our high tantrika."

She swallowed against the painful lump in her throat; no matter what the envoy said, she did not care if she never saw Sumangali again. But Obalesh, the infant she'd carried and fed and bottom-washed? "Have you recent news of Devikota?" she asked abruptly.

Lord Kushal inserted a pinch of snuff in his nose and inhaled elegantly, calm again. "Andhaka continues as headman, supported by Ghora's wily counsel. I can't touch them without evidence of their corruption, and no one dares provide it. Pity Devikota's so insignificant—or I'd plant a mole in their inner circle and catch them red-handed." He cocked his patrician head at her. "Why not get Takshak's approval to bring your mother and brother to Melukhha? The family of the high tantrika is entitled to a generous gratuity if they move to the capital, did you know? It's one of those old and bighearted laws that no one has bothered to change as yet."

A peacock strutted up to their table to pick up a fallen crumb. Ishvari stroked its brilliant tail feathers, hiding her shame that she'd done nothing to free Sumangali and Obalesh from that poisonous environment. "What of the other tantrikas?" she asked abruptly. "Do they thrive?"

Lord Kushal studied her flushed face: it stung him to know that the tormented girl he'd escorted to Rudralaya still lurked beneath her gorgeous façade. Worse still, she was dangerously naïve when it came to comprehending the ugliness of modern Melukhha. The other tantrikas had grown shrewd, having been permitted free movement about the city by their assigned mates. And with the exception of Charaka—a gluttonous man prone to fits of jealous rage—most nobles were liberals. "Well," he said, "Dalaja and Kairavi have wangled positions with Sahadev and Bhima, those handsome twins who manage Takshak's cavalry. And Kairavi has conceived—though she's mighty vexed that the child must be given up for adoption."

"*What are you saying?*" Ishvari cried. "We tantrikas cannot rear our *own* children?"

"Our noblewomen would rise in revolt if their husband's bastards snatched away inheritances from the fruit of their own wombs....in this case, it is Bhima's mother who refuses to welcome a grandchild from a peasant, though Kairavi has honestly earned her title."

Was this inhumane law the reason why Inanna had kept Nartaka's birth a secret even from his own father? "Is gold considered more important than the bond a child creates with its natural mother?" she asked bitterly. "And is Bhima's mother not aware that Melukhhan tantrikas are considered among the world's most cultured women?"

"Melukhha's fast coming to the point where blood and gold count for more than learning," he said shortly, his face morose. "You're lucky to live in solitary peace, Ishvari. *You* don't have to see the rot spreading through Melukhha, staring us in the face with maggoty lips and burning eyes. Our young nobles have less and less respect for tradition...they view our tantrikas as whores, and truth be told, but for you and a few others, our latest crop deserves no better."

"Tell me about the others...." she demanded.

"Well, let's see...Gitali's asked royal permission to enter into a three year meditation retreat on Mahadevi. At my urging, the Council has agreed...."

"Gitali was ever sincere in her love for the gods," Ishvari murmured, pleased. "You must have twisted some arms rather hard, my lord—I've heard the Council doesn't easily part with tantrikas. And what of Makshi? Is her mischief yet undimmed by that bore?"

"Oh, but Haridas is generous and Makshi grows fat on his favor. As for Tilotamma, she now resides with the emissary to Sumeria, while Urmila awaits reassignment to a Councilor. Brijabala dwells with Lord Ashoka, who runs Takshak's libraries, while Ikshula has forged an unlikely alliance with General Tarun." He laughed. "Charusheela mates rather tempestuously with our Treasurer, that old but virile reprobate, and Gandhali fast recovers from the death of her consort and will soon be reassigned appropriately."

She absorbed this information with genuine interest; while Vasudeva brought home snippets gleaned from friends who served important Councilors, and Takshak complained from time to time about the intractability or idiocy of certain nobles, it was the envoy who regularly satisfied her curiosity about the outside world.

"Not to alarm you needlessly, but war may well be in the offing," Lord Kushal broke into her thoughts. "The gods have raised you high, Ishvari, yet the eye of the storm is a perilous home. Opposition against you may mount to such a level you'll give thanks for your seclusion."

"*Opposition?*" she laughed nervously. "*I* have enemies?"

"Come, come," he said brusquely. "I've told you a thousand times that the high tantrika inevitably attracts the worship of commoners and the envy of aristocrats. Most Councilors feel she should remain clearly subordinate to the king—one Inanna's enough for a lifetime—that's the standing joke."

Could war really be looming? The urge to confide her secrets in this caring nobleman stirred. Yet, if by some freak chance the news were to leak—Takshak's wrath, particularly that he had a half-brother through the woman he most hated—could lead to even worse. "No matter your complaints, my lord, I'm relieved to know your voice is still heard loud and clear in Council," she said. "Of that sorry lot, it's you, and a few others, that Takshak respects."

"And yet Takshak is likely to drop me quick as a molten sword if I continue to go against him," he retorted. "Unfortunately, Charaka and his cronies have found a chink in my armor."

She frowned. "A chink, my lord?"

"My bond with *you*! Many are displeased that Takshak's been devoted to you these past thirty-six moons...if your bond with him grows strong again, and he actually begins to *listen* to your counsel, you could hurt them. I presume you know the name of your worst opponent?"

"Charaka?" she asked anxiously.

"So Vasudeva keeps you informed." His eyes were bleak. "Have you heard the latest? Now the beast violates a girl of seven! The girl's mother is a Dom tribal who serves at his residence. Charaka uses the two together, against their will, and while his depravity is common knowledge, this perversion has endangered our goodwill with the tribes. Mating outside the Dom tribe is taboo, and the rogue's a good fifty years older than the child." In the bright afternoon sun, Lord Kushal looked wan. "Takshak's ordered Charaka to restrict himself to mating with a single tantrika from hereon. I'm sorry to inform you, my dear, that he's chosen Urmila."

Urmila? Linked with an influential noble who hated her? The lesser gods themselves couldn't have forged a more lethal alliance! "But she *loathes* me!"

"Hardly surprising, considering you almost drowned her," he retorted with a short laugh. "Of course it's the reason Charaka chose her. Besides, Urmila's close to Makshi, Tilotamma and Gandhali, all of whom have acquired quite a reputation for rowdiness." He sighed. "You must be doubly alert from hereon, Ishvari. As I warned you earlier, should Takshak choose to lead our army, your enemies may attack you in his absence."

Fear gripped her with icy fingers. "Is there a nation foolish enough to take on Melukhha?"

"Did I mention a foreign power? No! It's the Dom mountain tribes of Kumaon and Garhwal, worshippers of old and fierce gods, who've recently grown hostile to us—and with very good reason. Instead of seeking to appease them, Takshak has added fuel to Charaka's fire by plundering their jungles for lumber and killing their big cats for their hides. Devadas and I have warned him they're a tough people and not easily conquered, but to absolutely no avail."

She stared at him, her heart sinking into her toes. "I've little respect for Charaka," she said in a small voice. "But it pains me to learn from you that Takshak is prone to such grave error. Are you sure it's not his subordinates who are acting in vile ways, behind his back?"

"Your lover's the one who gives the orders, woman!" Lord Kushal glared at her. Never had she seen him so furious. "Do you want to know *why* Hariaksa cast his vote against your election?

Because the fire revealed the extent of *Takshak's* malevolence, not yours!"

The blood drained from her face; she could not speak for a while. "Once you loved our king," she managed to whisper. "What has changed your mind?"

"Rather ask *who*," he shot back. "It was the sadhu. Right after I left you at Rudralaya, I began my investigations and found corruption *everywhere*. Worse, it's Takshak who's behind every filthy scheme to extort and cheat. I fear the demons have him firmly in their grip." He raised a hand to stop her from speaking. "Those who misuse the sacred herb stop growing, Ishvari—the drug blasts holes in one's protective sheaths, leaving one prey to dark powers."

Ishvari put a trembling hand to her mouth; recently she'd overheard a clutch of servants gossiping about Takshak's addiction to ganja. She'd brushed their words away uneasily—for not once had Takshak brought the substance to her chamber, nor spoken of his vice to her. "Did you…did you deliver the sadhu's message to him?"

"Oh, indeed I did—repeated it, word for word. He was intrigued by the sadhu's use of the term "royal brother," but when I began to speak of the man's extraordinary powers, he ordered me never to speak of him to anyone else." He grinned wryly. "It didn't strike our great king that *you too* were in the carriage."

She shivered; *why had Lord Kushal kept his silence for so long?* What sword hovered over her head that he should trust her now?

"That sadhu was speaking the truth," he said. "I urge you to be on the alert from here on, Ishvari. Given your isolation, your only true security is to uphold the dharma."

The noonday sun shone over Melukhha; soon winter would be here. She sat before him, regal as a queen. "Come, my lord," she said, summoning up all her courage. "Surely you didn't come here to alternately flatter and frighten me?"

"Drop the act, Ishvari," he ordered bluntly. "You are troubled, and so you should be. And there's worse…last afternoon in Council, Charaka announced that Mahadevi has ordered him to sacrifice a tantrika to appease the gods. I laughed out loud, though fear took strong hold of me. I said Mahadevi must have terrible taste to commune with so base a man. No one laughed at my bitter little joke, not even Devadas, who *always* stands by me. I reminded the Council that Shaardul had permanently outlawed human sacrifice, and that not even his successor could alter this particular aspect of sacred law."

"And?" Ishvari asked, struggling to stay calm.

"Oh, the usual nonsense…claimed Takshak's might could alter the course of the stars themselves, which is nothing short of blasphemy…our monarchs *serve* the gods, they are not gods themselves. But Takshak was beaming! As you must know, our king *loves* to be flattered."

Ishvari opened her mouth to speak, but he stopped her with a raised hand, his eyes softening with compassion when he saw how shaken she was. "I am not done, Ishvari…Charaka has persuaded a Sumerian seductress to sail to Melukhha. He claims this woman's penetration into the mysteries governing the gross realm is so great that kings *beg* her to direct them. She is called Alatu, after the Sumerian goddess of the underworld, and is ravishingly beautiful."

She grasped the sides of the table, unable now to mask her horror. The envoy went on: "This enchantress is here, and already brings out the rutting beast in our Councilors. The Samprati twins have offered her their summer residence, and others are falling over themselves trying to please her." He nodded grimly. "So much for Tantra—her power lies in the black arts."

"Has Takshak met her as yet?" she asked, struggling to keep her voice level.

"He has indeed, and is sorely tempted: Alatu is your physical opposite—streaming golden hair and eyes as blue as the Sarasvati at dawn—and yet I could tell in an instant that she's sold her soul to dark powers. It's difficult to tell her age, for her features are fine and her skin shines like heaven. My spies inform me she's obsessed with gold and power—and that Charaka's promised her a fortune if she wrests Takshak from your arms."

"But he's devoted to *me*!" she protested; yet even as she spoke, she knew she was lying.

Lord Kushal shook his head. "The truth is, my dear, that while you know more of Tantra than any woman but Inanna, you know little of the beast in man."

"Oh, I'm well acquainted with beasts," she cut him off, stung. "Have you forgotten Ghora and Andhaka?"

"There's another kind of beast controlling our city," he countered gloomily. "Far more dangerous that those village rogues."

Terror spiraled upward from the pit of her belly. "What is your advice?"

"Turn Takshak against Charaka while you can," he ordered quietly. "Charaka has bullied our Council for three decades now, but Takshak still rules. Seduce him afresh, Ishvari, just as Inanna did with Shaardul, and do this for Melukhha! Meanwhile I shall get Devadas to urge Takshak to banish this woman—before she brings our city down with her intrigues."

Lord Kushal reached for his cane. A twinge of pain crossed his face. "Indigestion," he muttered. "It's simple food and more rest from hereon, or Sarahi will get her young lover much sooner than she expects."

Ishvari rose, forcing a smile as he placed his perspiring forehead against hers in farewell. The gods had more than compensated for the cruel loss of her father by sending her this loving man. "Take care, Little Goddess," he murmured. He gripped her shoulders, his tired eyes filling with tears. "From the moment I saw you gawking at me in that dusty square, Ishvari, I wanted you to be happy. I beg you now—do *not* be complacent. Village toads cannot compete with the sharks sniffing for blood in Melukhha's waters. Whatever happens, you must somehow thrive."

She sat frozen at the table after he left, trying to make some sense of the disastrous picture he'd painted. She waved Mandakini away, wishing she *had* trusted him with her secrets. He would have been flabbergasted to learn who the sadhu was, and truly delighted to learn that, as a direct result of Nartaka's teaching, she was already experiencing flashes of samadhi.

Yes, despite her inner turmoil at the time, she had practiced Nartaka's meditation every day since. Samadhi had come to her as she sat on the stone bench beneath the great banyan early one morning. It was a feeling so sublime that she had known it could be none other than a beginner's taste of the elusive prize. Now she longed for a time when all separation between seeker and sought had dissolved—just as if a clay pot containing water had cracked open beneath the rushing waters of a mighty river, the lesser merging instantly with the greater.

At Ketaki's urging, early the next morning she had sent Vasudeva to Rudralaya with a sealed missive for Hariaksa detailing her experience. The sage had confirmed her intuition by return message: if she continued to deepen her practice, he promised, her spirit could be freed from the wheel of rebirth in this very lifetime; and Hariaksa never spoke lightly of such matters.

Soon after, Takshak had returned to her. He had offered no apology for his tryst with the southern belle, yet his loving was exhilarating. Gradually Ishvari had come to believe her worst trials were over. *What a joke!* Only thirty-six moons later, war was looming, enemies schemed to drag her down, and, as if all this was not ghastly enough, hanging over her head was the threat of losing her lover to a rival who practiced the black arts. Indeed, the gods were a fickle lot!

By the time Mandakini called her in for her bath, she had managed to breathe herself into calmness. Mandakini lathered her hair with a paste of shikakai berries, then poured pails of river water over her head. Together, the women dried her. As skillful hands massaged fragrant oil into her limbs, she convinced herself that even if Takshak did not love her as she loved him, he would never be foolish enough to give up their sacred coupling for alien dross.

Ishvari rested in her chamber until twilight, gazing up at the painted ceiling where legions of celestial couples were engaged in all the sixty-four positions of lovemaking. It was *here* that her real work had been going on, *here* that she was attempting to heal the wounded spirit of the maharajah, and through him, Melukhha. And no one could deny that the fire had risen in both of them. She refused to entertain the thought that crept furtively along the shadows of her mind—that Takshak had been fooling her, just as he had on their first night of maithuna. So when Mandakini came in to draw the ivory-hued drapes hanging over the windows to block out the fading sunlight, she put her dark imaginings aside and slid into the practice of deep yogic sleep.

How are you, firebrand? Hariaksa inquired. Opening her eyes, she scanned the room. She was alone. Hariaksa laughed in her mind. *I'm always with you, sweetling. Now be quick and read the note I sent you the day you left for Melukhha.*

She leapt off the couch, retrieving his missive from beneath a pile of summer clothes. It was written in Hariaksa's spidery script, the letters dancing in the light of the ivory tapers Mandakini had placed in clay holders beside her couch:

It is sundown, and I lie in our jungle hermitage watching a musk deer race in frantic circles around the devadaru trees, searching for the intoxicating perfume she smells in the air, unaware that it comes from a sac beneath her own abdomen.

I close my eyes and see a little girl from Devikota reach trustingly for my hand. Now she is grown to be high tantrika, and is already experiencing flickers of the highest bliss known to humankind. What saddens me is that—though she has realized that this joy lies within—a willful part of her still begs gratification from the sensual world.

Ishvari, you must know that no human exists who can save you, make you happy, or erase your pain. Yet if you keep your practice strong, no matter what you encounter along the path, Spirit will lead you from darkness to light.

Hari Om Tat Sat.

She read it once, twice, three times, then rolled it up and shoved it under her mattress, her heart thudding. That message had been written almost fifty moons ago, right after the accident that had prevented Hariaksa from attending their graduation! How, by the seven flaming hells, had he known then that someday she would be experiencing the first flickers of samadhi?

Back on the couch, she lay inert, seeing in her mind's eye a musk deer racing in desperate circles, tears streaming down its darkly outlined eyes. Ketaki broke into her misery, carrying in burning sticks of patchouli incense. "Rise, mistress," she ordered briskly, planting the incense in holders on the window ledges. "The maharajah will soon be here." The old woman drew open the curtains and flung wide the large windows of her chamber. Then she helped Ishvari dress in an ankle-length silk tunic decorated with tiny lotuses embroidered in magenta and gold.

At twilight, Takshak raced up the driveway in his black and gold chariot. Striding up to Ishvari as she stood at the entranceway, he enfolded her in muscular arms. She sensed the change in his energy as he steered her through the inner courtyard and into her chamber. "A flagon of Laodicean wine!" he ordered Mandakini.

The maharajah's eyes gleamed in the half-light as he stared out the open window, a sardonic smile playing about his mouth. Reaching into the pocket of his robe, he drew out a conical clay pipe around which was coiled a golden serpent, glittering emeralds for eyes.

"What is that, my lord?" Ishvari whispered, her heart pounding.

Takshak squeezed her right buttock with his free hand, chortling at her gasp of pain. "A chillum—not a device your holier-than-thou gurus spoke of, I'm sure. Tonight we shall employ it to kiss heaven." He grinned, noting the fearful excitement that leapt into her eyes, then drew out a golden container along with a box fashioned out of agate from the same pocket. "And you, my righteous love," he grinned, "are going to enjoy the highest grade of ganja with your monarch."

He sat on the couch, running a finger along the length of the serpentine pipe in a strangely sexual motion. He was already intoxicated, she realized, for the whites of his eyes were streaked with red and his face was ruddy with excitement. "A friend gifted this chillum to me," he drawled, smiling up at her. "A Persian prince, ejected from his clan for some heinous deed. Hysterical fools in the Council swore up and down that the fellow was a spy, but I liked him well enough to give him refuge. Later I even lent him the funds to have his father assassinated—as main heir within his clan, he'd assured me, Persian law could not combat his claim to a vast fortune. Not that long after he left Melukhha, he sent a messenger to me with twice the amount of my loan in gold coins, and this chillum, along with a sack of fragrant hashish."

Ishvari watched transfixed as Takshak stuffed the chillum with a green mixture from the gold receptacle, packing it in with his thumb. Cupping the base of the chillum with both hands, he gestured toward the elegant ivory tapers Mandakini had lit. "Bring me light," he ordered, resting on his haunches beside the open window. Obediently she carried a taper to him. Takshak pointed toward the agate box. "Light one of the splints within," he instructed huskily. Again she obeyed, fighting foreboding. "Now hold the flame to the herb," he said.

The herb caught fire, burning bright orange. Acrid smoke spiraled thick into the air with his first exhale. Suddenly the memory of a chariot speeding toward Rudralaya flashed through her mind: Lord Kushal's magical brew had transformed her fear into expansive delight. Now she wondered, in growing excitement—*would the effects of the smoked herb be the same?*

Takshak inhaled sharply again and the head of the chillum glowed a fiery red. Plumes of pungent smoke left his mouth and nostrils, obscuring his face, escaping through the open window. Again he put his mouth to the stem, inhaling deeply, swelling his warrior's lungs to capacity. He turned to her, eyes cloudy with passion, and offered her the chillum.

To falsely alter the state of your mind is to dance with the darkest of demons, she heard Hariaksa warn, so clearly she thought for a moment that he was standing between them. *But what harm can one single evening of pleasure do?* she argued back silently, even as she drew in the smoke. She coughed, then tried again and again at his insistence, until she could inhale smoothly.

Anxiety vanished as if by magic; she stood beside him as he filled the chillum again, eagerly awaiting her turn. The ganja was potent. Intoxicated, she turned to face him, boldly meeting his heat with her own flaring passion. He placed the smoldering chillum on the broad ledge of the window and propelled her toward the bed, and she fell upon its welcoming softness, moaning as he threw himself lengthwise alongside her.

He reached for the wine and she watched the muscles in his throat bob as the liquid coursed downward. An intense wave of desire flooded her body at his maleness. He held the neck of the bottle to her mouth, laughing throatily as a thin stream trickled down onto her breasts. He kissed her urgently as his warm hands explored her body, then his mouth moved downward to lap up the wine. Her nipples hardened with desire as his lingam rose and swelled against her lower body. *But what of Tantra?* the question floated across her mind. What of the serpent fire that blazed its way up the chakras, connecting female to male, earth to heaven, relative to absolute, fusing two into one single glowing being?

Takshak looked down and saw the hazy fear in her eyes. "Tonight we love like mortals," he declared. His tongue traveled downward, leaving a trail of honey fire until he began lapping at the inner petals of her yoni. The first climax hit her, stilling her mind as it washed over her body in rivulets of amnesiac pleasure. The fire rose into her abdomen the moment he penetrated her—

then stopped, refusing to rise into her heartspace, no matter how skillfully she tried to direct it upward with her breathing.

"My sweet tantrika," Takshak muttered brokenly as he exploded into a series of shudders. Her own body released a second upward flood of nectar as he drew her close, his body melting into hers, his tears wetting her cheek. Night threw her obsidian cloak over Melukhha as she lay quietly in his arms, brooding about the warning message from the serpent fire even as her fingers played with the tight whorls of coarse hair covering his warrior's chest. *Was there a chance Lord Kushal and the other doomsayers were wrong?* Sensing her unrest, Takshak smiled down at her, then reached across her breasts for more wine.

The moon was high when he slipped out of her arms and rose, splendid in his nakedness. He threw on his robe, his expression alarmingly distant. "Tomorrow I leave to wage war against the Doms," he announced, his voice brisk despite the intoxicants. "Light oil lamps for me every day, my priestess, and wish me well! I intend to destroy the serpent as it lies sleeping in the sun."

She wanted to warn him not to add to the grievous wrongs already done to the Doms, and to stay away from the Sumerian for the sake of all Melukhha. All these matters were her right to advise him as high tantrika, and it was his duty to hear her counsel; yet his face was set in granite lines and the drug had weakened her spirit to so cowardly a mush she could not utter a word. Moments later, she heard his chariot speeding away.

Moonlight caught the golden case containing the pain-numbing drug he had left behind. Beside it lay his chillum and the agate box of splints. Had he left them behind to tempt her? She closed her eyes and a vision arose of a glittering sword cleaving her thoughts into two separate streams. She bit down hard on her lower lip, tasting the surge of salty blood as she struggled with her two equally commanding sides: *hedonist or ascetic—which role should she choose?* But the pain was too great...so much easier to dull it with an external substance. In a trance, she crushed a bud between her fingers and brought it to her nose. Its earthy scent filled her nostrils as she sat by the ledge and prepared her first smoke.

Passion springing from aggression is voracious and sinful.
Know that it is hostile to all beings.
     —*Bhagavad Gita*

RAMSES-EM-SETI

Shards of memory from the night before forced Ishvari into wakefulness. She blinked uneasily at the light streaming in through her windows, feeling as vulnerable as a field mouse hiding from predators. Out of the blue, words she'd recently overheard flitted through her disturbed mind.

She had been out in the courtyard perusing a rare and fascinating scroll on the nature of reality while Ketaki and Mandakini strung ivory buds on fine cotton thread in the adjacent jasmine arbor. This fragrant garland would later be laid at the feet of the Great Gods, even as the women prayed for the rising of the high tantrika's fire and the greater good of Melukhha.

Vasudeva had stalked into the arbor then, just back from the city docks where Mandakini had sent him to buy mahaseer fish. The recent midsummer thunderstorms had been particularly hard on the destitute, he'd grumbled, but no one seemed to care—least of all those officially charged with ensuring that cripples, lepers and the insane were to be provided with clean accommodation and nutritious food. In the golden days, he'd added, such officials had had to earn their postings—now all it took was a hefty bribe! As a result, city shelters—once used solely by weary travelers and pilgrims—were overflowing and horribly unsanitary. His voice had dripped contempt as he traced this sorry state of affairs to an increasingly avaricious Council.

Ishvari forced herself to sit up, rubbing her swollen eyes. *How could a man as fabulously wealthy as Takshak was, also be so abominably corrupt?* And what pitiless god had deprived *her* of the skill and brilliance Inanna had shown in reforming his father? It nauseated her to recall just how easily she'd submitted to Takshak's depravity last night…and then, instead of immediately attempting to repair the damage, she'd added to her monstrous sins by smoking even *more* of his cursed ganja. A bitter smile creased her smoke-dry lips: Hariaksa could now safely add hypocrisy and hedonism to her long list of flaws!

And perhaps she was already being flogged for her fall from grace: soon after Takshak's abrupt exit last night, a wraith-like presence had hovered over her sleeping body, transfixing her with its ethereal beauty. Believing Mahadevi herself had come to infuse her with courage, she'd directed her dreaming gaze into the eyes of the wraith—and frozen as red orbs gleamed maliciously down upon her. Mocking laughter had echoed through her chamber as the creature opened her jaws wide, causing Ishvari to recoil at the hellish scenes within.

Fortunately she'd been able to summon up good sense enough to recite Hariaksa's mantra of protection; the sacred syllables had grown in force, creating a lucent auric shield around her, causing the eerie laughter to fade and die. The mantra's power had bolstered her confidence: had it not swiftly dispelled the demons that had tormented her after Archini's death? Gradually, as she observed the rise and fall of her breath, sleep had washed over her.

Now she gazed sadly at the twisted aerial roots of the banyan tree, her perception muddy with lingering smoke and wine. Lord Kushal's string of revelations circled her mind like wicked serpents, his warnings made real by Takshak's misbehavior and reckless talk. Soon an unjust war would erupt in the mountains and forests surrounding the sacred city, bringing in its wake brutal ramifications for all Melukhha. *And what was the high tantrika doing about it?*

A blast of self-loathing catapulted her on to her feet and to the window ledge, where Takshak's chillum and leather pouch of ganja still sat, shaming her with their presence in this sacred chamber. Picking them up as gingerly as if they were live coals, she wondered for a moment if she dared destroy them. The answer was no; unlike Inanna, *she* was too much of a coward to provoke her lover's terrible rage. At the sound of footsteps in the corridor outside, she quickly thrust both deep into a storage chest for winter garments.

Mandakini entered her chamber moments later, her round face merry as always, but Ishvari quickly averted her eyes, unable to face the kindly woman. Mandakini was used to her mistress' moods: humming a gay tune, she replaced the melted tapers and collected dirty garments, giving Ishvari the opportunity to slink out like a bedraggled cur and make her way to the fragrant bathhouse. Before the maid could come looking for her, she scrubbed and cleansed her body ferociously, then threw on loose trousers and a tunic and slipped out into the stone clearing by the jasmine arbor to begin her yogic practice.

Yoga soothed her body, though her lungs still burned and her mind felt dull and heavy. Later, as she walked to the puja room, she bumped into Ketaki and gave her a quick nod instead of her usual morning greeting. Ignoring Ketaki's look of puzzlement, Ishvari shut the door firmly behind her and sat before the altar, begging the Great Gods to forgive her lapse, and vowing to stay true to her practices until the maharajah returned.

The rest of the day passed quietly, but at twilight, her fragile equanimity was assailed yet again when a messenger arrived with a missive imprinted with Lord Kushal's seal: Takshak had ordered him away to negotiate a sensitive trade treaty with Sumeria, the envoy wrote in his fine hand. Meanwhile, he'd managed to persuade Sarahi to remove herself to their ancestral lands, where she would be better protected by those who'd served their clan for generations. War was a volatile time for *all* citizens, he added— discreetly emphasizing his previous warning. He concluded by stating his wish to see her glowing upon his return. And in this troubling way, as if the dark force tormenting her was hard at work, Ishvari lost the support of her one noble friend.

Two moons passed, one succeeding the other in dreary succession. Her isolation, coupled with the void left by Lord Kushal's departure, made the misery of parting from Takshak even deadlier; soon she learned that to be torn away so brutally from a mercurial lover is to plunge a scimitar into a defenseless heart and to keep twisting. And yet the purest agony came *not* from missing their passionate lovemaking, but from the insidious seeds of doubt Takshak had sown within her: *would a true lover have forced her to partake in his addictions?*

At night her anxious thoughts would stray to Nartaka and Inanna. How could she reach them? She considered writing to Hariaksa and asking him to once again send Inanna to her aid, but did not want to trouble the sage, who would be busy with his new batch of aspirants.

Vasudeva brought home ominous news of Takshak and his army: the Dom chieftains were proving wily opponents, their terrain being far more treacherous than anticipated. Trained for the hand-to-hand combat of the plains, Melukhha's troops were at an extreme disadvantage in such dense tracts of jungle. And yet Ishvari steeled herself to maintain her daily routine, knowing inner strength would be all she could count on in the ill-omened days to come.

But the flickerings of samadhi that she had taken for granted now came rarely. Soon, disgusted with the circuitous and vexing thoughts that made meditation sheer misery, she reduced her daily practice to hatha yoga and pranayama. Fear spread its clammy tentacles through mind and body, and, as time dragged on, it took increasing determination to maintain a serene façade. Then, one hazy afternoon as she sat out in her gardens flanked by Ketaki and Mandakini, a guardsman cantered up the drive carrying a missive from the maharajah.

Ishvari's hands trembled with excitement as she unrolled the scroll. *My tantrika*, she read out loud, *the mountains simmer with the heat of battle, and yet I enjoy the role of warrior king—for this cold air intoxicates me with its savage purity and I feel like a man in his element. I write seeking a favor: Ramses-em-Seti, Egypt's Emissary, has arrived in Melukhha and is disappointed to find me gone. As favored uncle of Sargon, God-King and Pharaoh of Egypt, Ramses is vital to our interests. He has asked to meet with you, claiming tales of your beauty and wisdom have traveled far. His race being quick to take offence, I dare not refuse. Besides, his visit will be short—Egyptian royals depend on our pepper, myrrh, cassia and balsams for embalming, so he must soon travel eastward, to*

*negotiate new trade routes. Since our law prohibits you from leaving
your home, I permit Ramses to come to you. I ask that you treat him
with all the considerable grace at your command.* It was signed
simply, *Takshak.*

"So the maharajah intends to relieve my boredom with some
stimulating company!" she cried, even as Ketaki near grabbed the
note from the hands and read it through herself. *Here* was the
evidence she'd begged Mahadevi to provide—that against all her
nagging suspicions, Takshak still cherished her. But Ketaki's face
had frozen into sharp worry lines. "Is not Egypt just as advanced as
we are?" Ishvari asked, wondering what was wrong. "I recall Atulya
quite clearly stating that the striking difference between our two
cultures is that while Egyptian royals focus on their own comfort,
we in Melukhha embrace *all* citizens—or are exhorted to, anyway,"
she added wryly. "At the very least," she added, "entertaining a
high royal will lighten all our spirits. This Ramses-em-Seti must be
a charming fellow...." Her words petered away as the crone's
mouth twisted in distaste. "Sucking lemons again, Ketaki?" she
demanded, annoyed that her crusty handmaid could not rejoice at
this interesting diversion to their routine. "Am I wrong in speaking
as I do?"

"Ramses has plagued Melukhha before," Ketaki said bluntly,
her face flushed with anger. "I happen to know a groom who
attended him during his previous visit. This fellow said that while
Ramses preferred the pleasures of boys, he boasted about seducing
beautiful women. Since Ramses devises cunning strategies that
bring Egypt increasing wealth, the God-King values his counsel.
This fact makes the sick creature even more dangerous to us."

Ishvari laughed nervously; Ketaki's direct and cutting speech
always amused her, and yet she knew the crone never lied or

exaggerated. "Are you sure this is the same man?" she asked. "Is Ramses not a common name among Egyptians royals?"

"Oh, come now, mistress!" Ketaki's face puckered in irritation. "An emissary of Egypt named Ramses-em-Seti who is also uncle to Sargon? No, this is the same brute."

"Ramses was a stripling last he was here, Ketaki," Mandakini interrupted. "And the scandal he was involved in was soon snuffed out. He's older now, possibly more mature. Would he dare mistreat our mistress, particularly with us here to protect her?"

"Such idealism only betrays gullibility," Ketaki retorted sharply. "Humans don't change until the god within emerges, Mandakini, and Ramses has no spiritual life to speak of, though a procession of oily priests trail him everywhere. He plays his diplomatic cards well, no doubt, but as a man he is evil and perverted to the extreme. Takshak should *never* have sent him our way."

Ketaki's grim conviction cast a pall over the beauty of the day. Ishvari did not ask for details of the scandal the emissary had become embroiled in; the less she knew, the more graciously she could behave when he arrived at her home.

But the crone's forehead was creased with worry: why had the maharajah laid such a burden on her old shoulders? Vasudeva was the only male she could count on for intelligent support, for soon after Takshak's departure, her moody and volatile young mistress had insisted on firing many male servants, claiming their flirting with the maids irked her severely. Only a handful of cleaning, garden and kitchen staff remained, but they all returned to their quarters behind the main palace well before sunset. There were guardsmen, of course, armed with swords and whatnot, but not one, in Ketaki's shrewd estimation, could be trusted to shut his mouth in case things went wrong. It was left to Vasudeva and herself to protect their vulnerable mistress.

Ketaki glanced at Ishvari, moved to sudden pity for her innocence. "Be aware that Ramses will care nothing for your rank, mistress," she warned roughly. "I wager that all the vain fool seeks is to boast he dined with a cloistered beauty. But if you keep in mind that he's no more than a strutting peacock, with as many scruples as a starving pig, likely you will be safe."

Ishvari tittered uneasily, both disturbed and tickled by Ketaki's vivid description—like the envoy, the old woman used her tongue freely on those she deemed deserving of contempt.

"No doubt I tend to mix my metaphors and suchlike," Ketaki reacted acidly, "but you would be *very* wrong, mistress, *not* to fear this spoiled creature."

"If this Egyptian's caliber is poor," Ishvari said, keeping her voice calm and reasonable, "why on sweet earth should that worry us beyond the span of his visit? Takshak orders us to treat him with courtesy, and we must obey! And so I declare that we shall ply this naughty man with excellent food and wine, and when we've had a surfeit of his foreign ways, we shall call for his chariot to whisk him away." She patted the old woman's hand affectionately. "And now, Ketaki, will you kindly stop your needless worrying?"

"Naughty man indeed….needless worrying…huh!" Ketaki shook her head in exasperation. "A high tantrika is *never* allowed to entertain a foreign royal without the direct protection of the maharajah or a Councilor! And besides, Ramses knows Takshak will do *anything* to avoid friction with the God-King, which will make him even bolder. Kindly do not forget that you are Takshak's *consort*, mistress, and not his queen. Blood-lines are vital to these Egyptians." Her seamed face tightened with stress. "Ah, if only Lord Kushal were here!"

"I promise to be on guard against this foreign peacock," Ishvari said lightly, though Ketaki's obdurate hatred for Ramses had begun to trouble her. "I *can* take care of myself, you know."

Ketaki raised a bushy eyebrow. "So you think to fend off this beast all on your own, eh?" She did not wait for an answer. "Now this is what we shall do: Vasudeva shall stand guard by your chamber all through the evening. If Ramses pushes you there, Vasudeva shall shove him out, claiming Takshak alone has the right to enter your personal quarters. If Ramses resists, *I* shall emerge, playing the mad old thing I truly am, cursing all who enter the sanctum." Ketaki chuckled drily. "Like all bullies, this Egyptian is bound to dread the curse of the insane."

Ramses-em-Seti arrived the next evening, a sinewy weasel of a man whose clean-shaven face revealed a receding chin. A red linen kilt fell to below his knees, and his narrow feet were shod in high-laced sandals decorated with gold thread. Around his bony neck, a circlet of gold encrusted with emeralds, rubies and diamonds sparkled in the fading evening light, while gold bracelets hung on his wiry arms. Delicately built with a full, fleshy mouth and brows arched over a beak-like nose, the Egyptian appeared to be five decades or more, though his slenderness and grooming did much to hide his age. Having envisioned him with a hanging belly and middle-eastern features, Ishvari almost laughed out loud— *could this modish creature—with eyes so beady he resembled a giant rat fancily attired—truly be the object of Ketaki's fears?*

The Egyptian royal minced toward her, reeking of some alien perfume, a supercilious smile hovering about his wide mouth. "Salutations from Pharaoh Sargon," he said in an incongruously deep voice. He bowed low, then presented her with a woven basket filled with a mound of iridescent feathers. "Plucked from a thousand kingfishers to fashion an ornament for your headdress."

Ishvari struggled not to giggle at his pomposity: his precious gift was useless to her—never once had she worn the formal headdress of Melukhha's early tantrikas. For a shrewd diplomat, Ramses-em-Seti was out of date by several centuries! And yet he proved to be as erudite and charming as she'd hoped; in addition to his own tongue, Ramses claimed knowledge of those of Persia, Assyria and Sumeria.

Speaking cleverly of Egypt's traditions—almost as old as Melukhha's own—his tapestried tales fed her hunger for the esoteric. Soon he had cast a mystical cloak over her fecund imagination, his eloquence conjuring up the massive tombs of Egypt, its river cities and awe-inspiring temples where priests chanted hymns to sulky gods. She shuddered when he described its pantheon of sinister deities, gasped at legends of its wealth, and felt the force of its military might. The complex web Ramses quickly wove almost convinced her that the great arm of Egypt encircled both civilized and savage worlds; it took effort to keep in mind that the territory her own lover ruled over spanned *twice* the area of both Mesopotamia and Egypt.

As Mandakini offered them savories hot from the kitchen, Ramses deepened his seduction. The gigantic structures of Egypt's city states were created by divinely inspired architects to mollify discontented gods, he explained somberly. These gods—much like Melukhha's earliest pantheon—punished sinners with flood, drought, locust and famine. He drew vivid pictures of the immense stone likenesses of the God-Kings, implacable sentinels watching over endless desert sands. Then, slyly aware that his hostess was enmeshed in his masterful narration, he related with ghoulish relish the tale of a thousand female slaves sacrificed to hungry gods before the construction of each royal monument commenced.

This is their custom—you must not take offence, Ishvari warned herself; through the corner of her eye she saw Mandakini, engaged in serving their main meal, turn pale.

Ramses watched her with cunning delight. "The silly things thought they were to be set free after some grand ceremony of liberation! I was there, you know—we of the aristocracy are always given good seats. I watched them dance through the gates of the temple, attired in sheer garments for the first time in their miserable lives, bright with jewels. Little did they know!" Ishvari suppressed a shudder, but Ramses had caught her unease and was grinning wolfishly. "Even as their blood ran into temple gutters," he continued, "their menfolk were bullwhipped into carrying out the architect's orders…it was all part of the rite, you see."

Ishvari nodded calmly, feigning interest, though his narration of this macabre incident spun her from fascination to instant repulsion. Determined not to betray her feelings, she drew the fire up from her lowest chakra to her crown, building up her inner strength. Not an easy task, for right through the elaborate dinner, served on the porch overlooking the gardens, Ramses ogled her, increasing her discomfort till she longed to plead illness and retire.

"Come with me, priestess," Ramses invited, once they were alone again. "Your gardens are famed for their varieties of flowering shrubs. While I myself have no time for landscaping, I fondly dream of overseeing of my own gardens when Egypt no longer needs me."

But Melukhha was *not* famed not for its gardens! It was renowned for originating from the vision of sages who had laid the city's administrative foundations to reflect respect for all beings! Why had Takshak chosen to subject her to this weasel in human guise? But wait a moment…had she not been complaining that her royal lover treated her no better than a mistress? Now, when he had chosen to honor her in this way, she was *still* complaining, just like an ignorant peasant!

Glimpses of guardsmen at the gates reassured her. But why wasn't Vasudeva hovering nearby rather than by her chamber? And where by the high and the holy had Ketaki disappeared to? Weak with fear, Ishvari mumbled an excuse about the wine having made her feel dizzy. Ramses ignored her; gripping her arm, he led her into the garden, past the jasmine arbor and the rose garden, past the grove of arka trees, all the way to the clearing lined with clay tiles where she practiced her yoga. A sheepskin rug she'd used to cover herself during yogic sleep lay beneath the trees— Mandakini had neglected to take it indoors.

Ramses's hold on her arm tightened into a vice, his hot breath fanned her cheek. "Alone at last," he murmured, grasping her chin with his other hand and forcing her to look into his glittering eyes. "I've wanted to say this the instant I saw you, my dear—especially in times like these, a goddess such as you are needs more than one single protector. You must be aware that many of your kind come to cruel ends—murdered as they sleep, poisoned by lovers, reviled to the point of insanity, even stoned to death."

Too vexed to mask her anger, Ishvari twisted out of his grasp and tossed off his arm. Ramses pulled her back to him with amazing strength. "Offended?" he asked, emitting a high-pitched snort. "Perhaps a woman as wise as you are reputed to be can explain to me just why I have this unpleasant effect on all great beauties? Truth be told, I prefer boys: women are too easily spoilt by success. As your own head of Council once advised me, a regular whipping brings the best out of a female!"

Ishvari bit down on her lip; Ramses must never know how utterly he'd shattered her composure by simply mentioning Charaka. *Were the two in league?* As this awful thought flashed through her mind, Ramses lowered his body to the sheepskin rug and pulled her down to sit beside him, his breath burning her cheeks. "Can you believe I sat with one of your predecessors in this very same spot?" He let out a sharp bark of laughter as Ishvari shrank as far as she could away from him. "By the Beard of the Sphinx, now *she* was a woman with rigid ideas about the act of union…I was given to believe I could bed her, but she made no secret of her distaste." Ramses giggled. "Her name escapes me… she was of so little consequence...can you credit it, my dear? Egypt's highest-ranking diplomat spurned by a cocky peasant?" He raked his eyes over her from head to toe with open derision, indicating he thought no better of her.

The same low mocking laughter that had accompanied the vision of the ethereal beauty in her dream the night Takshak left to war with the Doms was echoing through the gardens. A great fear washed over her then, rooting her to the earth. *What in all seven hells was going on here?*

"I bided my time of course, patience being the first virtue of a diplomat," the Egyptian was saying. "But just before the first major trade treaty was to be signed between our countries, I concocted some tale of how this so-called *tantrika* had insulted the integrity of the God-King. I warned your Council that if she were not punished, I would counsel Egypt to withdraw."

Ramses grinned like a wolf. "The helplessness on your king's face delighted me. He hated me in that instant, I could see, but he loved his people more—Melukhha desperately needed that treaty. So he banished the bitch-whore, a penalty which did not satisfy me…what *I* had wanted was to see her being crushed to death by one of his magnificent elephants."

Ishvari stiffened; she recalled Charusheela relating some story about a tantrika banished for causing serious offence to a royal. The woman—reduced to palm-reading in a distant temple city—had eventually lost her mind and killed herself. So it was Ramses who was responsible! Ketaki was right—the man *was* wicked. Sensing the depths to which he would sink, she swiveled away—how could she possibly escape him without angering Takshak?

Seizing the unguarded moment, Ramses threw her down and scrambled on top of her. Clapping a hand over her mouth, he flipped her over, pulling her garment up to her waist. Ishvari struggled fiercely as his erect organ plunged into her anus, the shock of first pain fast turning into a burning agony. Thrashing wildly, she bit down hard on his hand and screamed for help as soon as he pulled it away with a yelp of pain. But still the ugly thrusting continued, accompanied by obscenities she'd never thought to hear. She struck out blindly behind her, raking his face with her nails. He cried out with the pain, then grabbed her head and banged it hard against the tiled ground, again and again and again, until, mercifully, she lost consciousness.

When she came to, she was on her own sleeping couch amid flickering tapers. Ketaki's puckered face hovered over her, gone gray with anxiety. "Is he gone?" Ishvari whispered, pain invading every cell of her body. "Hours ago," Ketaki whispered back, her own eyes red with weeping.

Ishvari tried to rise, but Ketaki held her down. "Peace, mistress, you're safe now," she soothed. "Vasudeva heard your screams and threw the ghastly creature out. His cursed chariot was waiting, and his men spirited him quickly away. Only a few guardsmen saw his humiliation, but Ramses left swearing to see us all finished." Ketaki's face was resolute as stone. "I'll send a message to Takshak tomorrow—our king shall know the truth from someone he trusts."

More than the physical torture of the incident, it was the doubt and mortification Ishvari could not bear. Takshak must have known of the Egyptian's predilections; why had he unleashed Ramses upon her without providing adequate protection? Had he believed Ketaki and Vasudeva would suffice as guards? Or had he underestimated the emissary's daring? All she was sure of was that a man who truly loved her would never have taken such a risk.

"Hold me, Mandakini," she begged. She felt Mandakini's tears falling on her face, while Ketaki knelt beside her, her old face set in terrible lines. "It's over, mistress," Mandakini kept repeating, tenderly stroking her face. "Hush, my mistress, oh my sweet mistress, it's over."

Ishvari awoke with a start some hours later, alone in the light of flickering tapers, hearing again the same low mocking laughter. Fear thickened its coils around her, and grief too, but still she could not cry. The laughter rose to a crescendo, until she was forced to stick her fingers in her ears—she tried, but could not recall Hariaksa's mantra. The laughter ceased, suddenly. In the ensuing silence, she heard a sweet voice calling to her. It came from the trunk of woolens in which she'd hidden the ganja. *Use me*, it invited. *Let me absorb your pain.*

"No!" she resisted, burying herself beneath the covers.

The voice traveled under the covers with her, growing more seductive. *I make the best lover of all, Ishvari*, it promised. *Let me ease your agony.*

"Hush," she groaned, curling into a fetal ball. "Leave me alone." Takshak's abrupt departure had stirred her mind into a restless sludge, spinning her away from her inward journey. Much water had surged across the Saraswati since she had experienced even a *flash* of samadhi. Now she decided she would put the past behind her as a good high tantrika would, and respect Hariaksa's injunction against intoxicants. Yes, she would return immediately to the pure way.

But the pain in her anus flared up again like liquid fire. She heard Ramses's hoarse panting and was enveloped in his fog of hate. "Curse you!" she sobbed helplessly. "May vultures pick your bones clean!" Leaping up, she raced to the copper-studded chest and located the chillum and the ganja which she had hidden there, sobbing as she brought the herb to her nostrils and drank in its earthy smell.

Some had monstrous bellies, hanging breasts,
Projecting teeth, and crooked thighs.
Others were exceedingly beautiful to behold,
And clothed in great splendor.
　　　—Ramayana

ECLIPSE

If you live with the fear of death, Ishvari squinted down at the curling sheet of birch bark in her hand with glazed eyes, *why were you given life?* "Why indeed!" she echoed mockingly. Leaning forward, she flipped the bark right out of her open window, chuckling as it sailed upward on a gust of wind to land precariously on an aerial root of the regal banyan.

The banyan had grown steadily over the past three hundred years, spreading majestically over the inner courtyard, stately witness to the trysting of a succession of high tantrikas with the rulers of Melukhha. Ishvari cocked her head at the giant—why was it rustling its spear-shaped leaves so balefully at her? Did it resent her disrespect for the dharma? *Unthinkable!* No matter its privileged height and position, it was only a *tree,* with no right to eye her so reproachfully. She wagged a stern finger at it, warning its spirit she disliked being made to feel as low as one of the slime-trailing snails currently devouring Vasudeva's summer lilies.

Ishvari lay back again on her soft pillows, thinking it a miracle that the chain of calamities studding her life had not entirely destroyed her mind. Was it just a few moons ago that she'd overheard Vasudeva grumbling to Mandakini about the nefarious activities of one of the two newly hired guardsmen? Though the wily fellow was new to the city, Vasudeva had griped, he'd quickly acquired a network of seamy contacts which he was now using to enrich himself. Mandakini had asked which of the two new guards he was referring to, and Vasudeva had retorted that it was impossible to miss *this* crook—he had the slanting eyes and high cheekbones of a particular clan of mountain folk with a reputation for craftiness.

A desperate idea had leapt into her mind at she had digested his words. She had acted upon it the very next afternoon, tiptoeing toward the main gates in the heat of noon, hoping to find the man nodding away after his afternoon meal. She did not worry about the possibility of other hovering guardsmen—*it was as if an invisible entity had dropped the bold scheme into her head and was now strolling beside her down the winding tree-lined path to ensure it went through!*

Of course she had been aware of the huge risk she was taking—the fellow could quite easily have been a spy in the pay of the Council! Still she had prepared well, garbing herself in a diaphanous violet silk tunic and enhancing her enormous eyes with kohl. And everything had worked out splendidly, had it not? The stocky chap had risen in alarm at the sight of her. But her beauty had trapped him like a fly ensnared in a sticky web, and he'd listened to her whispers with rapt attention. Before he could mull over the consequences of being caught supplying the high tantrika with intoxicants, she had slipped a gold locket studded with gleaming rubies into his sweating palm. This extravagant gesture had won him over with a minimum of fuss.

Overnight he'd begun to pass high-quality intoxicants to her through her window, in exchange for one or more of the priceless jewels entrusted to each successive high tantrika for the length of her term. The barter was executed as she'd requested—with the utmost regard for secrecy. The guardsman was living up to his reputation for having wide-ranging contacts; indeed his latest consignment of ganja was so potent she was enjoying spirited dialogues not just with the banyan, but also with a certain iridescent-feathered bird who hopped perkily about on her window ledge. It was *humans* she wished to avoid, *humans* who'd broken her heart, and *humans* who now threatened the tattered remnants of her sanity.

Her mind whirled to marveling at how quickly the intoxicants eased the knife-edge of anguish she constantly teetered upon. A pity this benefit was so fleeting—every new day she found herself consuming greater quantities to reach the fragile composure she had maintained the day before. It gave her the oddest sensation of running hard to stay in the same place.

Rain blasted the gardens, the hard shower ending almost as soon as it had begun. Good, she thought, the violent thunderstorms Melukhha was experiencing would soon destroy the bark along with its message—ambiguous rubbish that only a dry stick like…like Atulya…could decipher. She visualized the sage's patrician face staring down at her in disbelief. Despite his doubts about her equilibrium—and certainly he had been right about *that*—Atulya had thought well of her in other ways.

So yes, Atulya would have been appalled to see her toss out that teaching. He would refuse to admit that such gibberish would be as valuable to her…as celestial music to a deaf man…or gold to a starving cow. Blindness manifested in a variety of ways, even in so-called sages. Atulya's reverence for the dharma would always come first. "But I am not you, great sage, I am not you," she muttered. Fuzzily she speculated on what Atulya might say were he standing right before her, penetrating her with his needle-sharp gaze. He would remind her that only six moons had passed since Takshak had left to do battle with the Doms, and three moons since the Egyptian had wreaked his own havoc. If one could not endure hard times, Atulya would drone on, how could other virtues be attained? To that rare human whose goal was moksha, was it not best to sink into one's Self and wait for the winds of karma to shift?

Ha! It was obvious that celibates could only *guess* at the pressures faced by an isolated high tantrika under the so-called protection of a capricious king. Ever since the rape, she could honestly inform both the acharyas, hand on heart, that she had not known a moment of peace. And while the physical pain was by now only a degrading memory, even the best ganja could not obliterate the waves of emotional torture that continued to engulf her.

Her eyes moved to the intricately painted ceiling, where a gandharva sported with a goddess, his engorged lingam ready for intimate invasion. The artist was clearly a master of his craft, for the celestial lovers appeared only too real. *And just who did the randy fellow bring to mind?* Takshak, of course, the fickle, feckless, pitiless whoremonger who had cast her into this living hell! Overcome with rage, she grabbed an ebony carving holding down a sheaf of Egyptian papyrus on the bedside table and hurled it upward at the painted couple. "Missed!" she shrieked, as the heavy object came crashing down to crack a floor tile neatly in two. "Perhaps a pail of cold slops will stop your brazen behavior?"

"Mistress!" she heard Mandakini call anxiously. "Did you hurt yourself? Won't you let me in?"

"Can I not converse with my own ceiling without you eavesdropping?" Ishvari retorted. She burst into raucous laughter at hearing her own crazy words. Then anger came again, crashing over her in a crimson wave. "Don't you understand plain talk? I don't want to see *anyone*…leave food outside my door and go. You really *must* stop nagging me, do you hear?"

"Mistress, you must listen, you *must*… Ketaki's physician's here with a message for you." Mandakini's voice broke. "The old one's dying!"

Ishvari sucked in her breath as guilt rose afresh. Truth be told, she sorely missed the feisty old woman. But unlike Mandakini, and Vasudeva—who so far had held firm to his policy of not interfering with her personal business—although the scowl on his sun-darkened face made it clear he resented her disrespect for his wife—Ketaki was a formidable adversary who'd dealt firmly with recalcitrant tantrikas for decades. The old one would have enlisted Vasudeva's aid to break down her door and confiscate her intoxicants. She would have gotten rid of the guardsman instantly, and done whatever it took to prevent her charge from sinking deeper into the abyss.

She reached for the container of bhang and took a long draught—impossible to see a royal physician in this state. "Tell him to leave his message and go!" she shouted. But Mandakini would not go. "Listen to me please!" Ishvari shouted angrily. "Didn't you tell me the old one is in agony? Do you want her to keep suffering? Isn't it best, you blithering idiot, to let her *go*?"

Another draught of bhang blocked out the pathetic cadence of Mandakini's furious sobbing. She was immensely grateful that the guardsman had sneaked in a fresh supply to her just last night.

His goods were always potent, thank the gods, and for this she gave him munificent thanks. Perhaps he was her only true friend in all Melukhha, for he alone risked his life to ease her anguish—which was why she chose to ignore the greed that leapt into his eyes at the sight of the priceless baubles she tossed him, as casually as if they were fashioned of river mud, and the sneaky way he always managed to caress her hand during the exchange.

But what she could no longer ignore was this monstrous sadness growing within her, a sly beast growing obese in the shadows of her mounting darkness. The bitter truth was that Ketaki had cracked her spine in a heroic attempt to stop her leaping off the roof in the aftermath of Ramses's outrage. Ketaki was dying *not* because she was old, but because her attempt to pull her mistress back from the edge had misfired.

Yes, Ketaki had grabbed at her as she stood wavering on the terrace ledge, plucking up her courage to jump. Ishvari had swung around to push her back, whereupon Ketaki had lunged forward with both arms outstretched—as if to embrace and protect her against harm. Instead, the crone had teetered and fallen forward, all the way down to a hardened patch of earth far below.

Before Ishvari could summon up the courage to follow her, Vasudeva had raced up the stairs and caught her firmly from behind. The burly fellow had actually dragged her *all* the way down to her chamber, kicking and shrieking, then had actually *tied* her to the couch with a length of hempen rope Mandakini had magically produced. Since it was twilight, there were no other onlookers at this further degradation of the high tantrika—the other servants had left for the day, and the guardsmen were too far away to have witnessed her flamboyant attempt at suicide.

Vasudeva had rushed off and returned an hour or so later with Ketaki's sisters in an ancient horse-drawn cart once used to carry the royal wounded off the battlefield. Hearing the sisters wailing as if Ketaki were already dead had disturbed Ishvari so terribly that Mandakini had been forced to triple the dose of herbal sedative the palace physician had recommended.

When it became obvious the crone was on her way to some other world and fast, Mandakini had broken down completely. As for her own feelings, Ishvari thought, guilt and regret were so mountainous she had to keep them at bay with constant intoxication, or she'd be forced to find another way to kill herself, this time successfully.

There was no denying the truth, Ishvari thought now; her refusal to accept Ramses's evil had led the old woman to her end. A genuine high tantrika would have used the teachings to quickly heal. How many times had the acharyas drummed it into her head that all that happens to one is solely the result of one's own past karma, whether from this or previous lifetimes? Could she excuse herself on the grounds that too much tragedy had fatally weakened her nerves?

And besides, could guilt grow a single hair on a bald man's head? Besides, who was *she* to decide matters concerning life and death? Ketaki was a dutiful creature, just as she, Ishvari, had once been during her years at Rudralaya and all the way up to the hideous rape. The gods had beckoned, and the old one had obeyed. Emotions only made life worse; far better not to feel. Was it not bizarre how feelings mostly plagued women with grand titles but no real power?

Ishvari rose naked from her couch to prowl aimlessly through the quiet chamber, a jungle cat confined to a cage. She stopped before the massive oval mirror studded with tiny sparkling diamonds on all four of its borders, a priceless gift from Takshak at the time he had returned to her arms, just as Nartaka had prophesied. She gazed at her reflection, trying to recall just how old she was—twelve when Lord Kushal had driven to Rudralaya, nineteen when she had been elected high tantrika, so now she could be no more than twenty-three. Highlighted by the soft gold of morning sun, and despite her state of intoxication, she could not deny her ravishing beauty. And unless another perverted diplomat dropped by to crush her face, or mangle her limbs, she would likely die beautiful, with her exceptionally fine features, taut golden skin unmarred as yet by intoxicants, and hair rippling like black silk to below her swelling hips.

She sighed, staring into her eyes, the weight of every year since Ghora and Andhaka had murdered her father hanging heavy on her shoulders. And here she was, embroiled in another sordid mess—again a victim, not a perpetrator. She stuck her tongue out rudely at her image—just as in Sumangali's case, her good looks had brought her nothing but trouble. And then she gasped—an alien being was peering at her with cunning amusement through her own reflected eyes! Jumping back—as if the mirror itself was alive with malevolence—she blinked several times to clear her vision. Then she dared another look. Now all she could see was an abyss of sadness in the eyes Takshak had so worshipped. Like a wounded animal sensing a lonely death, Ishvari crept back to her couch and wept for the sorry wretch she had become.

Sleep descended briefly upon her though it was only mid-morning. The drugs had dulled her once unerring sense of time and now she behaved like an animal in the wilds—eating when she was hungry, falling into a stupor as intoxicants and corresponding moods dictated. She came to groggily an hour or so later. Before sadness could start hammering at her again, she soothed herself with the promise of sneaking up to the roof at twilight, where she would celebrate moonrise by savoring the spotted mushrooms that were the guardsman's special treat.

Ishvari sat up and lit the half-used chillum hidden under her couch, skillful now after many moons of regular practice, drawing in the acrid smoke even as she anticipated the euphoria to follow. Tomorrow, as the hymns of the priests rose into the air from the Great Bath, she would experiment with fragrant charas mixed with opium. This is how *she* would honor the gods—*she* was forever done with hypocrisy.

"Vasudeva's been to the docks, mistress," she heard Mandakini shout. "There's kingfish and blue-green mussels marinated in lemon juice, turmeric and sea-salt...all you eat are sweets and savories...you'll get so fat we'll have to break down walls to let you out." The frustration in her voice leaked in through the keyhole like a ghostly thing, irritating Ishvari.

"Have you forgotten, O Mandakini," she yelled back imperiously, "that you are speaking to the High Tantrika of Melukhha? I can eat what I want, when I want! And please, if you value your life, never ever again call me fat, do you hear? A well-trained maid does *not* insult her royal mistress!"

A shocked gasp followed her words "I can no longer fight the one who controls you," Mandakini whimpered after a while. "A demon has caught hold of you, a demon you won't admit you serve, despite all your learning." A new note in Mandakini's voice caught Ishvari's attention, evoking the memory of the alien eyes peering mockingly at her through her own that morning. "Vasudeva says abusers of the sacred herb suffer the agonies of the damned, mistress. Opium, he swears, is worse still...."

Mandakini's tremulous voice rose warningly. "Spies are everywhere! Remember, it's the maharajah's gold that pays them. Only Vasudeva and I remain loyal to you, because we both *know* you are possessed. Everywhere there's gossip, from the palace to the alleys, about what you're up to, hidden in your chamber. Our guardsmen sport with palace maids and talk freely. They don't care a fig for you, and scandal spreads like wildfire. It's a matter of time before the maharajah...."

Suddenly Mandakini hammered on the locked door, startling Ishvari into dropping the smoldering chillum. She leapt off the couch and frantically stamped out the glowing clumps of herb burning holes into the costly rug—a gift from the old Queen of Sumeria to Inanna, as Ketaki had once proudly informed her.

"The old one's dying only because she tried to save you," Mandakini sobbed. "All our lives are at risk thanks to your selfishness. It's not our fault the Egyptian hurt you. We tried to protect you...you mustn't blame us for his evil. Can't you see what the drugs are doing? *Can a high tantrika be so blind?* Even Lord Kushal has abandoned you! I beg you, let me send Vasudeva to bring him here, speak to *him* if not to us, but do something or we're all lost...."

Ishvari sat down heavily, frowning. *Possessed?* Did everyone *really* know what she was up to in here? Had the guardsman betrayed her, despite his obvious infatuation for her, and after taking so many of her jewels? And...and could Mandakini possibly be right about Lord Kushal giving her another chance?

Lord Kushal had claimed to love her like a daughter, and *he* was a man of integrity, unlike Takshak and the other rascals in the Council. Surely he must love her still? That is, if his love for her had ever been true—see how Takshak's deceit had her doubting everyone? Or perhaps the envoy would learn to love her all over again, if she begged forgiveness and changed her ways? Oh, there she went again like a blithering idiot.

The envoy had returned from Sumeria and blamed her for allowing Ramses to lead her into the gardens. His scathing words had pierced her like molten knives—at a time she was begging for solace. If even servants could see she was an innocent victim, how could an astute nobleman—who claimed to love her like a father—rip her to bits for no fault of her own?

He had accused *her* of stupidity, blamed *her* for that horror! Then he'd summoned her three stalwarts and torn them apart with his tongue, his rage bringing to mind the royal bulls with inward curved horns that Takshak so enjoyed breeding. She had refused to intervene as he'd castigated the three of them thoroughly—didn't they deserve a tongue-lashing?

Now she shook her head, still unable to comprehend how Lord Kushal could have blamed *her* for Ramses-em-Seti's evil. Had she provoked the Egyptian in the slightest? Was not the emissary's history of perversity common knowledge? Why not hold Takshak to account for sending such a beast to her, instead of damning *her* for being obedient and gracious?

Memories of the mortifying finale to her once close bond with Lord Kushal arose for the thousandth time. The envoy's face had been a mask of frozen shock when she'd asked him to leave her and never return. He had no idea, of course, that she'd smoked a full chillum just before his arrival. She had smoked hard to cover her fear that his sharp eyes would detect just *how* she'd been consoling herself since the Egyptian's desecration.

Yes, she did not deny it—his implying she was a fool for falling for the Egyptian's ruse had provoked her to ask him to leave and never return. The outrage on his aristocratic face had made her giggle. And when she'd seen how her rudeness to the envoy had stunned her servants, she'd started laughing hysterically, at which point Lord Kushal had turned on his elegant heel and stormed away, with Ketaki, Mandakini and Vasudeva looking on, jaws hanging open, just like actors in a bad play staged in the makeshift theatre at Devikota. And still she'd been powerless to control herself, no better than a tavern whore under the influence of a barrel of moonshine. It was only when she had heard the envoy's horses charging away that the flood of tears had come, and never stopped, though now they had turned inward to bury themselves in her heart and swelled into a monstrous ocean.

Lord Kushal had sent her a curt message the next day, asking whether she'd recovered from her folly. *Folly!* Though his use of that word stung afresh, she'd longed to make peace, yearned to confess to him her plunge into depravity, beg for his help. But something stony within would not permit her to respond to his missive. If he returned, it would be a mere matter of time before his clever eyes comprehended the real state of affairs. The guardsman would be exiled and warned to shut his mouth on pain of execution. And with the slant-eyed scoundrel gone, who would help dull her agony? So that was the end of that. *Or was it?*

Not too long afterward, Vasudeva had brought home the shocking news that Lord Kushal had come close to death as a result of excruciating abdominal spasms. The envoy's personal healer suspected the origin of his disease to be minute doses of an exotic nerve poison cautiously administered over an indefinite period of time. At this alarming diagnosis, Lady Sarahi had whisked him away to the family estates to recuperate in safety.

So someone in the Council had tried to kill the incorruptible envoy; was it for his intimacy with both Takshak and herself? Of course only a handful knew just how strained the maharajah's bond with his once favored advisor had grown. *Why was it always the best of men who suffered the most?*

Mandakini and Vasudeva had not informed Lord Kushal of her attempted flight off the terrace. Nor had Vasudeva kept her abreast of the envoy's recovery. Now she hoped the dapper aristocrat was back on his feet, valiantly fighting the worst in the Council so that his beloved city could resurrect itself—just like the Bennu bird of Egypt, whose legend Hariaksa had recounted to her one night long-ago, down by the river.

The red-and-gold feathered bird had exploded out of the heart of a burning tree within the temple precincts of the sun god and was henceforth worshipped as the soul of Ra. The Bennu was honored as a symbol of fresh hope for those who'd tasted the ashes of defeat but still yearned to rise again. Ishvari sighed heavily, loathing herself even more for the weak creature she had so quickly become. Perhaps tomorrow she would send Vasudeva to Lord Kushal with a message begging his forgiveness, asking him humbly to guide her out of this quicksand?

Outside her door, she heard Mandakini muttering away. Ishvari sighed; *this* is what happened when a high tantrika lost authority and dignity. But then, she was no Inanna, was she? She'd allowed Mandakini to treat her like a fragile girl, and this was the pathetic result "What is it now, Mandakini?" she called wearily. "Can you not *please* leave me alone?"

Mandakini uttered a whimper of defeat, then her footsteps faded away down the corridor. Ashamed, Ishvari reached for the scroll she had found in the library last night when the drug had called her out of an uneasy sleep. A faded sheet of papyrus slipped out when she unrolled it, inscribed with a single line—*one must rise by which one falls*. She recognized it as a line from the Hevajra Tantra. Hariaksa had said it meant that one could use worldly things to transcend the world, for the knots of desire and fear that bind one to the world can be loosened by the power of gnosis.

Humans were bound by sensual passion, and ironically enough, only a burning spiritual passion to be free could liberate one.

All very well for a sage to talk such gibberish! Still, she could not forget the simple line. *One must rise by which one falls.* Pondering its meaning, she filled another chillum and walked over to stare out of the window before lighting it. Her mind roiled with a thousand garbled thoughts, her mouth was dry as tinder, and yet she could not deny the demon's insistent demands. *How could she use this teaching to set herself free of this royal mess?* Impossible!

Outside Vasudeva nursed his beloved roses, his back set eloquently to her. These days he would not even greet her with a polite nod. *Everyone* hated her, no one cared how she suffered, or understood that she needed the drugs to keep on living, to stop herself from plunging the rustiest knife she could find into her broken heart.

For the thousandth time since the Egyptian's brutal sodomy, tears of self-pity flowed down her cheeks. *One must rise by which one falls,* she cried out loud, hating herself. She, Ishvari, flower of Devikota, star of Rudralaya, High Tantrika of Melukhha, reduced to slavery. "How does one rise from a bottomless pit?" she screamed at the walls surrounding her like a prison cell. Hearing her shouts, Vasudeva turned towards her. Quickly she ducked from view, scuttling away from the large window like a crab so he would not see her breaking down.

Next morning, Mandakini told her Ketaki was dead: the old one had begun to sink rapidly the moment the physician had reported Ishvari's refusal to accept her message. Mandakini had asked him to leave the note in her hands, but since Ketaki had insisted he deliver it to the high tantrika with his own hands, he had promised to return with it on the morrow. But Ketaki's spirit had chosen to slip away from her broken body before then, and the note had been misplaced in the resulting confusion.

That night, the demon of fear sat jubilantly upon Ishvari's chest, feasting on her outpouring of guilty terror. *Come with me,* it whispered, its foul breath curling against her cheeks like a noxious fog. *Ride me to dark regions where pain fuses into pleasure.*

Ketaki's ravaged face loomed before her and Ishvari saw not accusation in the old eyes, but sad disappointment. Where was Hariaksa? Was he too hiding, ashamed of his firebrand? Atulya walked through blazing desert, turning around to cast upon her a look of such stern reproach she cried out with shame, even as the sand began to swallow up his spare figure.

Pierced by the skewer of sin.
Basted with the butter oil of the five senses.
Grilled on the flames of love and hatred.
So man is devoured by death.
           —*Saktananda-tarangini*

RUDRA'S OWN

The demon grew voracious, compelling her to absorb heavier doses of the drug before permitting her to sink into murky slumber. In her dreams, shadowy monsters chased her through the same dreary labyrinth, confounding her with a thousand twists and turns. She would struggle to find a way out, but always, just on the verge of escape, a masked man would leap up out of nowhere and force her back into the maze with sharp jabs of his spear.

Sometimes Ghora would hover over her, his pig-eyes glittering with malice. *"Be assured, slut,"* he would whine, *"no matter how high you fly, some day I shall expose your base origins!"* Ishvari would jerk upright as his threat penetrated her fogged sleep, quivering like a puppet on the string of his venom. While it troubled her that Ghora's hate could still shake her to the core, what really felt like a kick in the gut was to know that the beleaguered girl of Devikota had shown far more courage in fighting evil than the craven woman she had become.

When the pain of reality grew too intense, dreaming would spin her backward into early childhood, to a time when her grandparents were still alive and her father sober and relaxed. Then she would feel the rock and sway of Sumangali's caring arms, the explosive rumble of Hiranya's laughter, and the chatter of servants from the kitchen. She would trace patterns in the mud surrounding her father's fruit trees, and clamber over rocks that sparkled like gigantic diamonds. Fantastic colors would swirl before her transported eyes, leading her deeper into a nirvana where she felt cherished and protected.

In their aftermath, a benevolent force would embrace her; burying her head in her pillows, she would enjoy a fleeting return to innocence, and wonder vaguely just *why* this force could not simply destroy the demon. It was these joyful reprieves that stopped her from making another dive off the terrace in the dead of night, when she was alone in the brooding house.

Once she dreamed she was seated on her haunches beside Hariaksa, mesmerized by moon rays glinting off the surface of the river. *A tantrika does not attempt to alter a painful situation from the outside,* Hariaksa was saying; *instead she destroys the ingrained habit patterns that cause all her suffering. Life could either make one bitter, or better—why had his gifted firebrand chosen the bitter road?* The dream encounter was so vivid that she'd woken up sobbing; it hurt to admit she no longer had the clarity, nor the energy, to put Hariaksa's wisdom into practice.

Soon she took to sneaking through her gardens in the dead of night, like a thief in her own home. The weird combinations of ganja, charas, opium and speckled mushrooms the stocky guardsman delivered to her were twisting both mind and perception. Panicked, she increased her consumption, but the demon demanded more. "You're a bottomless pit," she accused him with something of her old spirit, and it agreed, even as it seduced her into lighting another chillum.

From Takshak, there had been no word. Ramses has spun intricate lies about me, she told herself, her breath ragged with fear. Or is it the Sumerian witch? How else could he have forgotten I *exist*? If the suspicion that the maharajah had been fooling her with his passion flashed through her mind, she quickly throttled it; were it to flower into loathsome glory, she feared she would disintegrate into a bloody mess.

Such demented thinking drained her spirit. Worse still, but for the first soothing drink of bhang, or smoke of ganja, later attempts to obliterate her fear were futile. These were the diminishing returns Atulya had spoken of in the context of the material world—the more one has, the more one wants, and the more one gets, the less it satisfies.

As her unrest spiraled, Ishvari began to accuse the guard of selling her inferior drugs. He did not deign to reply, but the lust smoldering in his slanted eyes began to mingle with a contempt that made her flinch. "Look well at me, guard," she once teased the bold fellow. "Am I Inanna that you expect high behavior of me? See! I am only Ishvari of Devikota, now the slave of all, even," and here she had tittered, "a man so greedy and stupid he dares to supply drugs to a failed priestess." He had stiffened in anger, whereupon she'd quickly tossed him an uncut emerald—if he too abandoned her, how by the seven flaming hells would she pacify the demon?

When the air turned chilly, her spirits inexplicably rose and she felt ready to battle with the shadow sucking her prana and self-respect. "Tomorrow I shall perform thirty salutes to the sun," she promised herself. "Tomorrow I shall send Lord Kushal a message and he shall come to my aid. All will be well—tomorrow." And as if the gods wished to support her good intentions, she managed to fall into a deep sleep. But toward dawn, she awoke, hankering to sample her new consignment from the guardsman. Slipping into a cotton shift, she stole out into the misty gardens carrying the chillum and the faience container in which she stored her intoxicants. Sighing, she sat on the stone bench beneath the arka trees to smoke a resinous bud.

The first wave of dull pleasure hit her soon after. Ishvari set her instruments down on the window ledge and wove her way between rows of jasmine bushes, inhaling the heady perfume. She stopped at the end of the hedge and shut her eyes, letting morning air wash over her pale cheeks like cool spring water. Then Hariaksa was speaking to her, his voice calm but serious. *It's not too late, firebrand. Return to the pure state and appease Rudra. I swear to you, it's not too late.*

The voices were often so convincing it was growing harder to distinguish between dream and wake states. Hariaksa's words were followed by the unmistakable hissing of serpents from the direction of the banyan tree. The fine hairs on her arms stood erect—could Vasudeva have allowed the dreaded creatures to nest so close to where she slept? Were he and Mandakini hatching some dreadful plot to finish her off in order to save their own skins?

Ishvari spun around toward the massive tree whose entwined aerial roots stretched down to pierce the earth's rough skin, forming a natural interlace of extraordinary beauty. Her astounded eyes took in the figure of a man standing before it, an ash-swathed ascetic wearing curved buffalo horns on his head. Around his blue-throated neck a mass of cobras writhed.

Could the abuse of ganja produce such vivid hallucinations? As she gawked at him, a tiger and an elephant appeared at his right, a rhinoceros and a buffalo to his left. Completing his fantastic animal guard, two superbly antlered antelopes stood before him. The ascetic gestured toward the private path connected to the extensive grounds of Takshak's dwelling and which led past her home. *He will try you to the utmost,* he uttered cryptically, *but you must not succumb.*

What could he possibly mean? Dizzily, Ishvari saw that he held aloft a bowl fashioned from a human skull in his right hand, in his left, a smoldering firebrand. He exuded so macabre a sensuality that suddenly she was raging with desire. He smiled, baring jagged teeth as he held her gaze with the chilling power of his own. Grabbing his erect organ, with a shriek all Melukhha must have heard, he uprooted it and threw it to the earth, where it exploded into a geyser of opalescent fire.

Weak-kneed with alternating waves of desire and disbelief, Ishvari sank to her haunches before him. *You must refrain,* the ascetic spoke clearly and sweetly, his voice like flowing honey. *The tantrika must not defile Rudra's Own.* The tiger yawned, revealing a crimson mouth and yellow teeth. She shut her eyes, overcome by incredulous terror, and when she opened them a moment later, the weird entourage had disappeared. Unsteadily she rose to her feet and made her way over to the window ledge. She grabbed the chillum, stuffed its head with fresh ganja, lit it and dragged the pungent smoke into her lungs, trying to soothe her jangling nerves.

Out of the misty past, she recalled Hariaksa speaking of an elderly monk who had resided at Rudralaya during his twilight years. The monk had killed himself as a direct consequence of abusing the ganja placed in his safekeeping for ceremonial purposes. He had used so much of it, Hariaksa had said, shaking his head sadly, that his mind had shattered. His words had brought back the strange magic of her chariot ride with Lord Kushal. "How could such a happy substance bring tragedy?" she had asked him.

"*Any* substance causes tragedy when abused," Hariaksa had explained. "The road to suffering is often paved with noble intentions. By giving you bhang, Lord Kushal roused a sleeping beast. Now you must be on guard and avoid all intoxicants, except during maithuna, when you are protected by the Great Gods. Without the proper mantras to invoke higher energies, the misuse of ganja can lead to insanity and even death."

What she had just experienced was no doubt a particularly astounding wisp of imagination, Ishvari realized, painted in vivid colors by the effect of the drug on her tired brain. After all, how could an *aghori*—for that is what the man appeared to be—possibly have entered heavily-guarded property accompanied by that string of beasts?

The sound of a bell ringing broke into her trance. Ishvari heard footsteps on the private lane the ascetic had gestured toward. She strode towards it, uncaring of her scanty attire. The guardsmen were nowhere in sight—Takshak's absence had rendered them increasingly lax.

A tall, thin mendicant wearing ocher robes stepped lightly down the path. In his right hand he carried an empty wooden begging bowl, in his left, a copper bell. Such innocence! she thought as he drew nearer, seeing a youth untainted by the muck of the world. Unlatching the wooden gate, she stepped out on to the dirt road, something she had never dared do before. "Namasthe!" she called, not knowing why he attracted her so viscerally. A shield came over his face at the sight of her, but not before she sensed the beginnings of a virgin's lust.

"Come, I've food for you," she beckoned charmingly, slipping back through the open gate and holding it open for him. "Hand me your bowl."

He walked timidly through the gate and stood at a distance from her, clutching his bowl to his chest.

"Follow me," she called, walking toward the kitchens.

"I'll wait here," he said, in a voice deeper than she imagined he would possess.

"As you please," she smiled, marking his reluctance to look at her. She raced down the path, amazed at how fast she could still move. It was good the lad had chosen to pass by this particular gate, far away from the servants' quarters. It would be hours before Mandakini and Vasudeva started their day—the couple performed their morning tantric practice in the privacy of their cottage. And the outside servants arrived much later.

Last night's leftovers, covered with the leaves of jungle palm, had been left on the kitchen table for Mandakini to portion out to the always hungry guardsmen. There was rice pilaf studded with slivered nuts, the remains of a haunch of venison, a portion of grilled river fish and vegetables sautéed with spices. Collecting the rice and vegetables in a clay bowl, she returned to find the mendicant standing where she had left him, his eyes straying around the splendor of her gardens. Fiery energy shot up her spine at the wistful look on his face. She handed him the bowl, but he just stood there, as if immobilized by this unexpected happening.

"This food is unpolluted," she urged, moved almost to tears by his simplicity. He was taller than her, but so thin he looked like he could break. "My cook is ritually correct—better food cannot be found in all of Melukhha."

He held out his bowl, silent but alert. She stepped forward to fill it, her fingers trembling so hard that at least a third of the food slipped to the moist grass. Stooping low, he picked up what he could, returning it to his bowl without disgust, as would a true renunciate. Holding it close to his chest, like a child with a treasured belonging, he bowed, ready to depart.

"Stay, mendicant," she whispered impulsively. "Speak to me."

He looked hesitant. "What could I say to interest a high priestess?"

"Ah, so you *do* know who I am," she murmured, pleased. It had been ages since she had truly conversed with another human, and this handsome lad with his compassionate eyes she was finding increasingly attractive. He nodded, averting his gaze as if she were a forbidden piece of goods. "So tell me," she demanded, taking a tiny step forward, "what is my full title?"

He shifted restlessly, turning his gaze downward, refusing to speak.

"What is my title?" she repeated, irked by his bashfulness.

"High tantrika," he blurted. "But to many you are the…the…the whore of Melukhha."

Ishvari drew back, appalled. "Who would *dare*?"

He shrugged bony shoulders, staring down at the dark earth.

"*I am high tantrika in more than name, mendicant!*" she contradicted fiercely, wrapping her arms tight around her shivering body. "My duties are sacred!"

"They say you neglect them," he said, raising his eyes to absorb afresh the vision of her lush body. "They say you spread your legs for the Egyptian, so our maharajah finds comfort with the foreign witch."

Did this lad not care a pipal leaf for his miserable life? Or was he a spy sent by Charaka to trap her in some devious way? Tears stung her eyes and rolled down her cheeks as she studied him. He was genuine, she decided, communicating his private thoughts in the juvenile hope that he could transform her. "The Egyptian violated me in these very gardens, with Takshak's guardsmen standing less than a thousand paces away!" she cried, even as mocking laugher pealed through the misty gardens. "Pray provide these details to your friends, so they may better grasp just *how* Takshak protects his high tantrika! Come, now, mendicant, you pique me with your snippets…what else do *they* say?"

The lad was staring at her, as if hypnotized. "That the maharajah has no more use for you," he said in a monotone, "that the Sumerian witch accompanies him everywhere, even to the forested mountains where he wages war against the tribes. People are saying he listens to her counsel over that of his own generals, and that without her magic, he'd be lost in that tricky terrain."

Ishvari stamped her bare foot hard on the earth—something she had not done since childhood. *Had Takshak really taken the strumpet with him?* If so, why had Mandakini not given her this news, along with all the other nonsense she screamed through her keyhole?"

"What else?" she demanded, determined to suffer the full extent of pain.

"That your abuse of sacred bhang attracts demons that spread their wings over your roof, spewing venom over our sacred city." He was silent for a moment, then spoke with a candor that hurt even more. "We *all* suffer because you've renounced purity, my lady."

"You don't understand!" she cried, devastated by her show of weakness before this lowly stranger. Again she wanted him to know how the world had conspired to ruin her, as if he were the most important being in the universe. "Listen to me now!"

"I'm only a simple renunciate who overhears rumors," he cut her off. "Daily I beg a meal at the royal kitchens where there's endless talk about your doings. Even servants of bad habits revile you. You *must* return to the pure way!"

She was trembling now, realizing that the voice of Hariaksa had uttered those same words not an hour ago. She opened her mouth but no words emerged.

"I must go," he muttered, possibly alarmed by his temerity in speaking so boldly. "To the Great Bath for purification. A high tantrika is forbidden to leave her home even for an instant, forbidden to speak to strangers. What we're doing is against sacred law!"

"And after you purify yourself," she said, ignoring his chastising words, "would you roam Melukhha, observing from your spiritual tower those still bound by material cords?"

"There are mendicants who may deserve such rebuke," he replied with quiet dignity. "But I, my lady, am not one of them. I was on my way to fast and meditate in the jungle for the duration of three moons when you called me in." A shy smile hovered about his lips. "If even *I* can experience bliss in my heart, my lady," he added impulsively, "what could a *priestess* accomplish? Why not cultivate the heart practices again, stop this vile gossip, and bring new glory to our city? This is the promise of the sages, is it not?"

Wish it were as easy as he described! She gazed at him with cloudy eyes—*had the gods sent him to help her out of this mess?* The lad's smile widened. "My guru said that if I held true to my practice, Rudra would dissolve my body and mind into light," he was saying now. "And through my intention to serve, I would bring peace to those whose only crime is ignorance."

"And just how did your guru define ignorance?" she asked, genuinely curious.

"As being unaware that every thought, word and act has a corresponding effect," he said earnestly. "I speak of karmic law, which applies only when one accepts that the spirit transmigrates. It's clear the consequences of our actions cannot manifest in one single lifetime."

The mendicant's response was rooted in authentic dharma, and yet he was *wrong*, for he believed he'd been chosen for a sacred mission, just as she once had. Now he was studying her with a gentle pity that stung. "If you speak the truth about the Egyptian, my lady," he said, "it's not right that commoners revile you." A martyr's light transfigured his face. "Today, before I leave for the jungle, I shall stand right in the center of the quadrangle and proclaim to all that our high tantrika is indeed a pure soul."

His kind words drove her into a frenzy. "What good would a mendicant's utterances do for me?" she cried. "Who whispers brazen lies in the king's ear? Who plans my death?" Aghast at her own behavior, she threw herself at his bare feet and looked up into his startled eyes. "I'm not much older than you, mendicant," she sobbed, "but already I am broken, *broken!* Comfort me!" She touched his bony ankles with the crown of her head. "Come with me, pour your energy...."

"Madness!" he whispered, staring down at her body, overwhelmed by the realization of her desire for him. "I am Rudra's Own and *you*, of all beings, should respect such a vow!"

In the branches above his head a nightingale sang, the music traveling sweetly to her ears. *Rudra's Own!* The ascetic had warned her against Rudra's Own! In that instant, she recalled the statue she had spied in the quadrangle, of the Wild God in the guise of Pashupati, lord of the beasts. *So Rudra, master of disguise, had himself come to warn her against seducing this lad!*

Even more excited, she drank in the lad's freshness. Idealistic he most certainly was, but also appealing, and so committed to the gods, just as she herself had been. It would be so easy to fall in love with him. But how to inspire this innocent to provide her with the tenderness she craved? Rising to her feet, she brushed her tears away with a careless hand, then grasped his bony shoulders. "Can I share a precious secret with you?" she asked, as the demon took charge.

He nodded warily, though she could see he longed to escape. Two aspects of her being began to do serious battle: the pure one ashamed of her behavior, the other, controlled by the demon and *much* stronger. The pure one sighed, giving up the fight, even as the other spoke seductively: "Did you know Rudra ordered me to wait here for you this morning?" Tenderly she touched his cheek. "He instructed me to dissolve forever the paradox of your disbelief, to remind you that he is both ascetic and lover. You are now free to follow his divine ways."

The lad stood before her, aching with desire, but resisting. "I...I...I harbor no disbelief," he stammered. "My guru taught me how to merge with the divine and I trust him completely."

Ishvari leaned forward and pressed her hardening nipples against his chest. "Be honest now," she murmured beguilingly. "Why are you in robes? Did Rudra himself seduce you with his harsh magic and unearthly visions into worshipping him?"

"I've not been so blessed," he said curtly, brushing her hands off his shoulders. "I forsook the world to fulfill my father's dying wish. He sent me to a guru who, after training me, ordered me to begin my practice. I was happy to comply."

She drew into her nostrils his sweet-sour wanderer's breath. Such a pity the lad was so much stronger than he appeared. *"Happy to comply?"* she echoed sweetly, cocking her head prettily at him. "Ah, but that was only because you didn't know your own mind! I've bared my soul to you, mendicant," she added softly, reaching out to stroke his cold cheek. "Now you must tell me—have you ever tasted the honey of a woman?"

"I've told you I'm virgin and belong to Rudra!" he retorted, turning on his heel.

She stepped forward to block him. "Your words are poison-tipped arrows, yet still I behave with grace." She smiled, ready to attack his weakest spot—his awakening lust. "Answer me now!" she demanded. "Have you dreamed beneath sandalwood-scented sheets, bathed in perfumed waters, been driven wild by the beat of drums, drunk the nectar of the gods, smoked the magical bud of the ganja plant?"

"Why this madness?" he cried, pulling away from her and raising fearful eyes to meet hers. "Rudra *whips* those who break their vows...don't you fear his wrath?"

The pure one within warned her sharply against corrupting his spirit, yet the call of the demon was louder. She stared down at her naked feet, at the nails Mandakini had stained vermilion with the thickened juice of jungle berries. "See, mendicant?" she whispered, pointing downward. "Blood on my toes." She touched her heart. "Blood in my heart, and soon, soon, blood on my hands." Her hand flew to her mouth in shock. *Where had those words come from?* Why did they echo like hammer blows, shattering the morning's loveliness? Then, absurdly, she grew amused by the magnitude of her fall from grace. If even *servants* believed she'd willfully tossed the keys of heaven into a stinking gutter, what more did she have to lose?

Ishvari tossed her head back and silky hair slipped out of its topknot and cascaded down the length of her back. She tossed it again, and it fell over her breasts, a curtain of shimmering night. The mendicant stared at her as the beast took over. Mesmerizing him with her sultry beauty, she slipped out of her shift to reveal her naked body, plumper now—she had not practiced asana for too long—but still stunning. "O mendicant," she whispered huskily, "you and I belong to earth. Let the gods find pleasure in heaven while we make love in my chamber."

"Unholy!" the mendicant gasped. "The servants are right— you *are* possessed!"

An instant, and he is ours, the demon promised, reaching out to envelop him. When his eyes glazed over, she motioned him toward her even as he backed away. He reached the gate, but made the mistake of looking back, right into her liquid eyes. *Get the fool now!* the demon ordered abruptly. *Get him while his knees still quake with the shock of your beauty!*

The lad halted, fluttering with panic, the judgment in his eyes melting into inky pools of desire. In that moment, Ishvari knew she had him. Employing every atom of her loveliness, she drew him closer, forcing his sleeping lower centers wide open. She heard his breath quicken, and slowly, like a sleepwalker, he followed her down the long path and into the quiet house, to her chamber and her rumpled couch, mumbling words of denial that clashed with his rising hunger.

The next few hours passed in a blur of passion. The lad was designed for pleasure, and Ishvari told him so, as with timorous fingers and wondering eyes he awakened her body, kissed her lips, and entered her with incredulous delight. Dropping a thousand little kisses on her belly, he worked his way downward, and she began to shudder with tiny explosions of delirium.

Ishvari drew him up until his eyes gazed into her own. Cupping his besotted face with slender fingers, she pressed her love-swollen lips against the wide shape of his. Sensing his unrest, she sucked him into the hurricane once more, tutoring him in the arts of kissing, stroking, licking and nipping until both were faint with ecstasy. When the first rays of the sun lit the sharp angles of his face, Mandakini knocked on the door, softly first, then louder, when she did not answer. He sat up, blinking in confusion, but Ishvari pulled him down and placed a warning finger on her lips. "Later, Mandakini," she called. "I'll rise later."

As Mandakini walked away, two thoughts struck Ishvari with equal force: one, that she had stopped drinking the anti-conception potion that Ketaki used to administer to her, and, two, that if the mendicant was discovered in her chamber, and the news reached Takshak, they would both be sentenced to a ghastly death. Truly, she breathed as the lad's tongue traveled wild and sweet over her body, what more could existence offer but the twin raptures of sex and death?

Languorous as a jungle cat, she sported with his body that was once again taut as a bow. Expertly, she relaxed his nerves so she could flood his eager body with the erotic pleasure that could enslave him forever. In his embrace, she found herself as free as the wind in the jungle, whistling with abandon, unafraid that she would repulse or shock him with all the art at her command. One day, she resolved, she would teach him to loop the serpent fire. *But not now, silly child,* the demon whispered. *Simply suck the prana out of him and forget your cursed philosophy. Ganja will relax him enough to ride you to heaven.*

So she prepared a chillum and showed him how to draw in the herb, secretly aghast at how cleverly the demon had guided her to trap him in this lethal web of deception. She watched his eyes glaze over, then loved him again as the demon instructed her to do, sucking the prana out of the quivering length of his body. They smoked more ganja, letting their passion swell until she felt her body vibrating with a bliss she'd almost forgotten.

The sun rose higher in an aquamarine sky. Soon Vasudeva would start work in the gardens, and the insolent guardsmen return from their nightly romps. She leapt off the bed, body gleaming with sweat, and rummaged through her chest of jewels. "Here, sweetling," she said, handing him a ruby ring set in gold. "Take this to Jewelers Row and make sure you get a good price. Find travelers' lodgings and sleep the day away—I want you fresh tonight. Be careful when you return—my guards will kill you if they find you in my gardens." She flashed him a smile. "Eat nourishing food as well, my love—goat's milk and almonds feed sexual fire."

Shy as a village bridegroom, he drew her to him, kissing her with exquisite surprise. It took great effort to push him away. "You must leave now."

His eyes were troubled again as he slipped into his orange robe.

"What worries you?" she murmured, caressing his thin arm.

He shook his head bravely, but his expression was sad.

"Oh, but you must tell me!" she insisted softly, suppressing her rising guilt.

The words spilled out of his mouth in a childlike rush. "With you I feel rapture, but my heart pounds with fear when I think of the Wild God."

"My love!" she cried, horrified again at her corruption of this gentle lad. Yet, if she listened to her pure self and set him free, she'd be alone and miserable all over again. Alarmed by her thoughts, the demon was already whispering advice in her ear. "A little reflection and you'll see as I do," Ishvari found herself saying. "Did Rudra himself condemn you to trudge dusty roads with a bowl and a bell that serves only to warn misers to keep their doors locked? Or was it your father, hoping to suck merit out of his son's piety?"

She tensed as she awaited his reaction. Fortunately his face relaxed into a hesitant smile. Yet she feared that his doubts would return with a vengeance. The lad had a fine mind, though he lacked guile. She would do everything possible to keep him. Without his love-juices, needed to replace the prana the demon was sucking out of her, she suspected she would die.

And of course, she would have no choice but to continue to fuddle him with intoxicants. Drugs would shatter his defenses, kill his dreams of moksha, just as they had hers. She wound her arms around his neck, laying her cheek on his shoulder: *how had she fallen so low?* "It's late," she whispered. "Take the back way and beware my gardener. He's the sharpest of them all." She drew him close one last time. "Return tonight," she begged. "I'll be waiting."

He leapt through the window, light as a peacock feather, picked up his half-full bowl, and turned toward the back of the house. Her heart swelled with something precious—the demon was resting, and momentarily she felt like her old self. Certainly the lad had transferred his goodness to her through the essences of love. She lay still, considering her protective feelings for the mendicant. Was this love, this aching tenderness mixed with longing? Yet, at the thought of Takshak, she still felt a heavy craving. Which, then, was true love? *Neither*, she heard clearly. *When you do not love yourself, how can you love another?*

Shocked, she realized the voice belonged not to the addled slave she'd become, nor to the demon, but to the unsullied spirit within. The benevolent presence she had sensed after her few happy dreams was no external force, but her own higher Self! What had Inanna said about demons? That they were only manifestations of one's lower consciousness! Hope flashed like a gold vein in black rock—had Inanna been right, as she usually was? If so, surely if she raised the fire again, drawing it upward to her heartspace, the demon would be incinerated in the process?

A wave of despair followed this flaring optimism—how to raise the fire again without the support of a guru, or a handmaid to guide her? The demon had taken on enough shape to control her higher impulses, and his crafty advice had led her to alienate *everyone*, so he alone could suck the prana out of her, so he alone could rule. She heard the foul bastard chuckling.

The rest of the day passed slowly; lack of sleep combined with the excitement of her encounter had drained her. She resisted using the drugs, relying instead on the memory of the morning's ecstatic lovemaking to keep up her spirits. And every time fear rose, the possessed part of her pushed it fiercely down.

At moonrise she called out to Mandakini and courteously requested a tub of warm river water scented with the oil of roses. Mandakini was unable to hide her joy at her change in mood. She buzzed around as Ishvari soaked in the fragrant water, yammering nonstop about Vasudeva's plans to build a rock garden through which a stream bearing pure Sarasvati water would flow.

Ishvari smiled indulgently at Mandakini's friendly chatter, even as she worried whether the mendicant would return tonight. In her chamber again, she lay down and shut her eyes, summoning up the memory of the lad's sensitive face. Would he return, knowing the danger?

The tantrika has tainted Rudra's Own! boomed the voice of the ascetic.

Shocked, she glanced out of the window. Yes, there beneath the banyan tree stood the Wild God, this time minus his beastly escort! In the corridor outside her chamber, Mandakini hummed to herself, oblivious to his divine presence. Rudra appraised her coolly, his body covered with ashes and his dark glowing features stern as granite. *I offer you another chance to redeem yourself, tantrika,* he said sternly. *Release the mendicant, and I shall destroy the demon that seeks your destruction!*

Ishvari gazed at the Wild God, speechless with awe—Rudra *himself* was offering her redemption—which she had always sought above all material things, had she not? She blinked, and when she opened her eyes a shimmering golden mist filled the space where he had just stood. Grief knifed through her heart and she doubled up, howling like an abandoned child. *What to do? What to do?* If she gave up the mendicant and returned to her holy practices, what was the guarantee she'd ever know peace? Could she trust the gods *this* time? The inner struggle was so hideous she howled and whimpered, thinking she might die.

Outside Mandakini began hammering on her door. "It's all right, Mandakini," she managed to squeak. "I pricked my finger with a pin, and that is all."

But Mandakini did not leave, and, for the first time in ages, Ishvari wondered whether she should let her in, confide in her. Both Mandakini and Vasudeva were rare jewels, just as Ketaki had been. Three heads would be better than one in figuring out a solution to her terrible problems. She had not the hairbreadth of a doubt that they would do everything they could to help resurrect the tantrika within, to make her whole again. But once she confessed her sins, Vasudeva would have the guardsman fired, and Mandakini would sit on her back, close as the shell on a tortoise, making sure she meditated and flexed her body in yoga every single day. Once again she would be a slave in her own home.

The mendicant returned to her in the dead of night, stealing past the guards who were sleeping off the effects of the palm wine easily available right outside the palace walls. She had been waiting impatiently for him right outside her chamber, and when she first glimpsed his tall figure slipping through the trees, her heart had leapt like a hungry fish. With a finger to her lips and a tantalizing smile, she led him to the arka grove and showed him the secret path that Ketaki had once pointed out to Inanna and herself. While sections of it were exceedingly narrow, it wound all the way into the heart of the city. "Use only this way from here onward, sweet love," she whispered, taking his return to mean they were meant to be with each other. "Come after the moon has risen, and enter and leave solely through my garden window."

He nodded his solemn agreement even as he scrutinized her beautiful face in the silvery light of the crescent moon. His own thin face reflected mingled doubt and yearning. She stiffened with sudden terror—would he change his mind and leave?

Why wait? the demon hissed. *Hesitate and he will run!* Summoning up all her female power, she gazed directly into his grave eyes until they melted into pools of passion. Then she drew his trembling body into the curve of her arms and stroked his shaven head, as if he were her beloved child instead of her new lover.

To the earth she fell with one incessant scream,
As she understood what end was near.
Mocking the gods, the enemy who once loved her,
Led the rite of death and fell first upon her.
      —*The Bacchae, Euripides*

CIRCLE OF WORSHIP

In the tumultuous sweetness of loving the mendicant, and the mind-numbing pleasure of the drugs she continued to abuse, Ishvari eased the pain of Takshak's desertion and somewhat pacified the insatiable demon who now ruled her.

The mendicant's birth name was Pundalik. Shyly, he confided that his guru had encouraged him to retain it even after he'd taken vows—for Pundalik meant 'lotus', and his guru believed the name would be a constant reminder of his highest goal as a seeker; just as the lotus was famed for blossoming into extravagant splendor in the worst of swamps, his guru had said, so too should Pundalik, no matter the awful nature of the material conditions he might encounter.

On his death bed, the holy man had advised Pundalik that if he kept firmly to the heartpath in which he'd been instructed, he could dissolve all material chains and achieve moksha in this very lifetime. What his guru had *not* known, Pundalik had added with a sweet blush, was that Rudra had not intended for him to remain a lonely celibate.

Guided by the crafty fiend, Ishvari promised Pundalik that, at the conclusion of her term, the two of them could disappear down to the deepest south. Together they would locate a home where ocean met shore, and pursue liberation in the way of a Tantric couple. She did not need to lie, for she'd grown immensely fond of the trusting lad. But there were moments when she saw fear cloud his eyes and knew that *he* still harbored grave doubts about their forbidden coupling.

It was the honey of their mating that had seduced Pundalik into believing her most outrageous deception—that Rudra *himself* had commanded her to teach him the arts of love. The lad swallowed her lies in order to hold guilt at bay, but Ishvari knew it was the sexual fire she'd ignited within him that kept him coming back, night after stormy night. Only the drugs kept her from worrying about the possibility that one night he might leave, and decide never to return.

Pundalik's outpouring of love seemed to be organically healing old wounds in the fabric of her inner being. Often, when she was alone, and the demon quiet, Ishvari felt a calm that persisted beyond the dull pleasure she derived from the intoxicants. To her secret delight, it appeared that the demon had sorely underrated Pundalik's caliber—the lad had quickly cut his own consumption of the drugs down to the barest minimum, and when he did imbibe, he claimed it was only to please her. Drugs sickened him in ways he could not express, he artlessly explained; nor could he comprehend why Rudra would send him down so murky a path, for drugs disturbed the mind, while it was serenity that allowed a seeker to dive into the heart.

She made peace with his decision, relieved he'd given up cajoling her to stop their use. Besides, the less he consumed, the more there was for herself. But his discriminating use of the drugs infuriated the demon, who cursed Pundalik the moment he slipped out of her chamber.

By now, Ishvari had grown certain that the single deadly aim of the demon was to feed off her prana. *Could it really be a split-off from her own lowest consciousness?* Even if so, she knew the only way to rid herself of the parasitical monster was to cease her abuse of the herb. As for Pundalik, the demon loathed him because the lad truly cared little for the external world. Pundalik lived in his heartspace, which was why the fiend could not twist his perceptions as it had hers; with such an egoless being, she realized with wonder, the demon's range of powers was drastically limited.

As Pundalik's purity began to radiate into her own being, Ishvari reverted to former courtesies. As a result, Mandakini returned to her cheerful ways, putting aside her misery over Ketaki's death, while Vasudeva now treated her as if she'd never misbehaved.

It was the gardener's forgiveness that most pleased Ishvari, for she sensed that nothing would stop Mandakini from caring for her. Over the past three and a half years, she had come to know Vasudeva as a sincere meditator and practicing tantric. Coaxing the earth to produce her finest was his way of worshipping Mahadevi, and yet he was no ordinary gardener—just as Mandakini was far from the average servant.

Roughly three moons after she'd begun her illicit liaison with Pundalik, Mandakini shook her urgently awake. Ishvari came to, startled to see Vasudeva scowling down at her, his broad face creased into furrows of worry. Ishvari silently berated herself for forgetting to lock her chamber door from the inside—*what if they'd barged in while Pundalik was still with her?*

Mandakini's usually bright face looked like an over-ripe mountain pear left too long in the sun, and her stout body quivered like a puppet manipulated by invisible threads. "What is it?" Ishvari demanded, sitting bolt upright, her mouth dry with fear and the after-effects of the drug.

"Takshak's back, mistress," Vasudeva blurted, swiping at his sweating forehead with the back of a calloused hand. He was breathing heavily, his face flushed with exertion, as if he were just back from the city docks where he went every morning. "It's victory he's won for Melukhha, along with eight thousand prisoners of war, but little else. My cousin says the Doms care nothing for gold or precious stones—their passion is for the old gods who cause their jungles to thrive."

Vasudeva's voice was ragged with pain; like the peace-loving monks of Rudralaya, he too shrank from violence of any kind, finding repugnant even necessary tasks such as wiping out the snails, aphids and velvet-skinned red-and-black caterpillars that devoured his precious jungle orchids and bright patches of star lilies. "The prisoners start work tomorrow. Takshak means to get his sewage undertaking completed, one way or another. He plans to bleed them dry for the gold he's spent hunting and killing them." Vasudeva shook his head in disbelief.

The wheels of her brain began to slowly turn: so Takshak was back, and wilier than ever! The underground network of sewage channels linking the southern part of the city to its humming center was a task that had bedeviled him since early kingship. Melukhhans refused to work underground, for they loved fresh air and the light of the sun. Despite the absolute power of their monarch, the working classes still clung fiercely to their rights. Two birds with one stone would now be his—public admiration for conquering the defiant tribes, and completion of a work so enormous that he would be honored forever in the annals of the city. *But why was Vasudeva so disturbed?* Other monarchs too had committed atrocities before settling down to a wise reign. There had to be more, Ishvari knew, seeing the pain growing in the gardener's eyes. "Please tell me everything," she whispered.

"Takshak raced his war chariot around the quadrangle to signal the start of the victory celebrations, mistress," he obliged her hoarsely. "The foreign witch sat beside him, gloating. All Melukhha's buzzing—they say Takshak's rejected you for her, and not just for the pleasure she gives him. The rumor's spreading that it was this foreigner who led us to victory."

"A Sumerian steering Melukhhans against our tribals?" Ishvari cried. "What has fuddled their wits?"

"Believe it, mistress," Vasudeva said gravely. "The Sumerian uses a crystal that reveals secrets hidden to others. If not for her black arts, my cousin swears, Takshak would have been forced to retreat from the territory of the Doms, tail between his legs."

"What else?" Ishvari demanded, gripped by terror.

"There's bad news concerning Lord Devadas," Vasudeva muttered.

"Don't keep me waiting," she begged, for the royal astrologer was Lord Kushal's closest friend and one of the few remaining good men in the Council.

"His attendant found him hanging from the rafters of his chamber early this morning. Lord Devadas left a suicide message...."

"But this makes no sense!" Ishvari cut him off, shivering despite the warm quilt. "Why would he kill himself *after* we've won this hideous war? Are you sure he wasn't *murdered*?"

Mandakini wrung her hands in agitation while Vasudeva cleared his throat. "It was bhang that warped his mind, mistress. He was a sensitive man who detested the greed of certain Councilors. But unlike Lord Kushal who spoke his mind fearlessly, the astrologer was timid. He'd grown desperately sad over the years, his attendant says...."

"What did his message say?" Ishvari interrupted, her voice breaking with fear.

"That his abuse of bhang had led him to err gravely. The single mistake he could not forgive himself for was his wrong selection of the aspirant Archini."

"*Archini?*" Ishvari echoed shrilly. "But she was my closest friend!"

Vasudeva nodded. "This too is known. Lord Devadas claims he was intoxicated when the vision leading him to seek her out arose within his third eye—a great serpent twined around the girl's body, and this he mistook for a sign of rising kundalini. Only when the acharyas began to report on the girl's lack of progress did he realize his error. He was just about to admit his mistake to the Council when she died. Since then, he claims, he could find no peace."

So here, after all these years, was the answer to her nagging questions about Archini! She stared at Vasudeva, struggling with a mixture of emotions. "Did Devadas mention making a mistake about choosing *me,* perchance?"

"Not to my knowledge." Vasudeva stared at her, as if assessing her ability to digest more bad news. "My cousin's captain of the guard and a man of integrity," he continued staunchly. "Urged on by the Sumerian, he says Takshak ordered fugitives to be weighted down with boulders and thrown into swamps. He's razed Dom temples, desecrated sacred images and set vast tracts of forest on fire." Now Vasudeva was tripping over his words in his haste to finish. "Our maharajah's *lost*, mistress, *lost!* He's burnt alive every chieftain he could lay hands on and spurred his men to violate not just women, but *children* as well. He even ordered the eyelids of the head chieftain's wife sliced off before forcing her to watch soldiers rape her daughters...."

A low, hellish scream was rising up Ishvari's belly. This *had* to be a nightmare...she would awaken, the sun would be rising and birds singing sweetly, just like every other day. She blinked, warily, but her servants still stood before her, larger than life.

"On guard, mistress," Vasudeva counseled somberly. "Takshak's sunk into his lowest nature and cannot be reached, neither by love nor logic—the Sumerian's trapped him tight within her claws. Look to yourself—return to your sacred practices and seek the forgiveness of the gods. The gossip will soon die down, as it always does. Meanwhile, we must all be careful—many are predicting the Sumerian has her evil eye on you, and on those still loyal to you."

Ishvari struggled against the encroaching madness; a host of questions jammed the pathways of her mind. Did this devoted couple know about her own drug abuse, as well as her affair with the mendicant? Could Takshak have encouraged such atrocities, or lust for an alien capable of offering him only a smidgen of the joy that she, Ishvari, had been trained to evoke? Had Ramses poisoned Takshak's mind against her as he'd sworn to do? Or was the Sumerian truly a sorceress, capable of twisting men to her diabolic will?

With a rustle of wings, more demons—of fear, doubt and jealousy—sank their talons into her being, feeding on her diminishing prana. She lay back weakly against her pillows, hearing the victory frenzy building in Melukhha. Celebrations would be riotous, for Melukhha had not fought a war for a whole generation. Vasudeva's stolid face reflected great unease. "Be calm, mistress," he advised gruffly. "In times like these our only recourse is to have faith."

"Save some counsel for later, Vasudeva," she whispered, gesturing for them to leave her alone. The drugs had made her both soft and hard; while her emotions surged tempestuously, her spirit was numb. Last night, she'd overridden Pundalik's protests that the herb was stirring up awful fears within him. She had coaxed him to smoke more than the puff or two of ganja he usually inhaled, just to please her. Later he'd admitted that the drug *had* indeed pacified his mind—for a palace guard had caught him skulking around the backwoods of her dwelling and had given him chase. He'd escaped by the skin of his teeth. This news had strained her fragile peace; but later, when their bodies had fused, she had felt much stronger.

Mandakini brought her rice porridge and muskmelon juice. Ishvari drank the juice but refused the porridge, unable to stomach food. She fell back on her couch listlessly, refusing Mandakini's suggestion that she bathe and refresh herself, trying to steer her foggy mind into some form of clarity. Shortly thereafter, a royal messenger cantered up the path connecting her home to the palace. Vasudeva ran outside to receive him and returned to her chamber with a scroll stamped with the royal seal. Mandakini followed anxiously. Clearing her throat, hoarse with the lingering effects of last night's smoke, she read Takshak's missive out loud:

To honor the gods who led us to victory against the Doms, tonight the Council hosts an official chakra puja. You are hereby ordered to attend the ritual at the burning ghats. We meet at twilight. Takshak, Maharajah of Melukhha

"Sweet Mahadevi!" Mandakini cried. "But the maharajah sounds so *hard*! And it's been ages since that rite was performed! The last chakra puja was performed during Shaardul's reign, well before Inanna entered his life...as I recall, it took place in the temple caves below the royal dwelling...why the ghats this time, I wonder?" She studied Ishvari's pallor with concern. "This is *most* unusual, mistress—by sacred law, a high tantrika *never* joins in group worship!"

Takshak's tone *was* frosty. Was this an order that she participate in group mating? The very idea was *preposterous*! A high tantrika was meant to serve the maharajah, or, in rare cases, for an eminent individual honored by him. *Did he intend to publicly degrade her?* Turning her face into the pillows, Ishvari broke into a tempest of tears, aching for the dour wisdom of Ketaki.

But then, if Ketaki *were* alive, would she even be in such a ghastly mess? All her mentors' warnings had been based in love and truth, but she had defied them all. And now her insane rebellion meant she'd be forced to confront her Sumerian adversary in this awful state, in the presence of many who sought her destruction. If only she'd stayed true to her practices, she'd now be glowing and strong, supported by the gods themselves. Tonight, Ishvari suspected, the remnants of her pride would have to be abandoned, like dusty sandals at a temple door.

Vasudeva left, his face dark with trouble. Mandakini followed him out, muttering agitatedly that she had to prepare the ingredients for Ishvari's elaborate ritual bath. Alone again, Ishvari locked her door and prepared a chillum with trembling hands, taking care to blow the telltale smoke out the eastern window and lighting incense to mask the lingering odor. Tears rolled down her cheeks as she realized just how intensely she would miss Pundalik's loving. True, Takshak had melted her into a quivering puddle with his skill, but when she fused with Pundalik, the inchoate poetry of his words, coupled with his tender explorations of her body, all suffused with a childlike wonder, had resurrected her own lost innocence.

In a rare burst of trust, Takshak had long ago confirmed Inanna's words: while his mother had always indulged him materially, he'd said, she'd grown bitter and hard after Shaardul had tossed her aside for Inanna. Kings were intended to raise fire with their tantrikas, Abhilasha had sullenly averred to her impressionable son, not to fall crazily in love with the rutting whores.

For sure, she thought now, shivering despite the afternoon sun filtering in, Abhilasha had set her devil's mark on her son. Takshak was incapable of seeing a woman as fully human; what pleasure he gave stemmed solely from his massive ego. Love to him was no more than a ravening lust, something that flared and died. The idea of aging alongside a lover, of watching wrinkles line a beloved face, only nauseated him. So he'd chosen to flit from flower to exotic flower, to sip the nectar of the new rather than to savor the mature wine that alone evokes bliss.

Ishvari smoked another chillum, unable to stop the flood of insights she'd suppressed in her juvenile yearning for the perfect lover. She'd wanted to believe Takshak had hungered for her, just as much as she had for him, that he took infinite delight in her loveliness and skill, seeing in her the essence of Mahadevi herself. But if he had, how could he have abandoned her so easily for that temple dancer right after their first maithuna, or fallen so easily into the Sumerian's net?

In contrast, Pundalik worshipped her. With only her own fervent tutoring, he was the finer lover and the better man. Yet the fire had not blessed them with mystical insights. *Had Rudra shut the door of their third eyes to punish her?*

With an effort, she brought to mind Hariaksa's few words about the group rite. Chakra puja had fallen into disuse, so the sage had said little about it. All she knew was that it comprised a circle of worship formed by couples engaged in ritual lovemaking to honor the gods. Women participants were to be pious and sweet, male adepts devoted to the gods, free of envy, greed and lust. Grimly she considered the petty arrogance of her co-aspirants and the foibles of Melukhha's aristocrats: *with such participants, could Takshak's great puja be anything but a farce?*

The ringing of the bathhouse gong roused her from a nightmarish doze. She walked down the corridor to the bathing room where Mandakini was stoking the fire with sandalwood. Drifting past the subdued housekeeper, Ishvari lay down wearily on the marble slab. A breeze fluttered the curtains as Mandakini performed the bathing ritual: Ketaki had schooled her well.

Mandakini's powerful love somewhat restored her courage. Dining lightly on vegetable broth, she resisted the urge to indulge in another chillum, and by the time a chariot thundered down the drive to carry her to the ghats, she felt much calmer. Were her fears unfounded? Given his fickle nature, she could accept that Takshak had taken a beguiling woman along to alleviate the tedium of war. But to permanently choose an alien lover over his own high tantrika? *Absurd!* As soon as this night was over, Ishvari resolved, she'd stop abusing intoxicants and delve into inner work. Putting Pundalik resolutely out of mind, she would use all of her resources to lure Takshak back into the cocoon of their worship. All would soon be well again.

The horses raced alongside the river's winding edge, revealing to Ishvari for the first time the northern view of the luminous city, surrounded by shrines, hermitages and pavilions. A sculpture of the Wild God as Pashupati, lord of the beasts, rose majestic on the high riverbank, casting its giant reflection upon the lapping moonlit waters of the Sarasvati. The beasts cantered down the path to the ghats, and stopped beside a flight of stone steps leading down to the river.

A throng of chariots marked with the colors of the Melukhhan elite stood waiting. Ishvari heard the lukewarm cheer of welcome from the assembled aristocrats and tantrikas—etiquette demanded they honor the high tantrika. Peeping warily out of the window with pounding heart, she glimpsed Takshak standing majestically beside an arresting beauty with hair of shimmering gold and icy blue eyes. Her heart sank down to her toes—Lord Kushal was right, the woman was a goddess! No wonder Takshak was besotted.

A heavyset noble with an oily smile dressed in ceremonial regalia strode up to her chariot. Greeting her formally, he introduced himself as Charaka, and gave her his arm to guide her down the ancient stone steps. Charaka was beaming, possibly thrilled with the change in the status quo—now that Alatu had won Takshak, no longer did she pose a threat to his personal interests.

Takshak caught her eye and waved languidly, as if she was a mere acquaintance. Stifling her terror, Ishvari returned his greeting as regally as she could. What could have destroyed their bond? And had *she* ever truly loved him? She tried to read his expression in the moonlight, but all she could discern was that the Sumerian had usurped her position, for Takshak's right arm encircled her slim waist, while her golden head lay possessively against his chest.

Charaka led her down the shallow stone stairs and the crowd followed, with Takshak and Alatu in the lead, figures in wildly hued silks that gleamed in the light of thousands of oil lamps illuminating the ghats. The ground for the chakra puja—an enormous circle inscribed in white chalk to delineate the outward form of the ritual worship—had been prepared in the center of the main ghat. Priests dressed in dazzling white, their sacred strings glowing eerily in the firelight, arranged their seating. She was placed beside a burly stranger in the scarlet robe of a barbarian. Shaken, despite her tranquil facade, Ishvari did not return his confident smile.

On the opposite side of the circle she saw Dalaja glancing furtively at her, then whispering into the ear of her escort. Kairavi, more somber, sat beside a man who strongly resembled Dalaja's lover. These were the Lords Sahadev and Bhima, scions of one of Melukhha's wealthiest families. Makshi sat nearest to Ishvari, clasping the hand of the corpulent Haridas, whose vessels plied the seas carrying southern spices to every corner of the civilized world. Brijabala and Lord Ashoka, the royal librarian, sat to her right, while Ikshula and General Tarun with the glass eye—implanted by Melukhha's most famous surgeon after the general had lost it battling against a frontier tribe—were on her left. Lakshman, the royal treasurer, sat beside Kairavi, ravishing in green and gold, while Charusheela, in rare good spirits, sat beside a stout man with a sulky expression. Finally, Gandhali, her face pinched and worn despite skillful make-up, was paired with a squat, serious-looking aristocrat with bushy eyebrows.

Not one of them smiled or even greeted her with a simple nod and Ishvari's trepidation boiled over into a simmering panic. Her eyes surreptitiously sought out Takshak, noting that the maharajah was more attractive than ever, his complexion burnt a dark gold. He was murmuring into the Sumerian's ear. Beside him sat Urmila, holding Charaka's fleshy hand. Charaka's other hand lay in Tilotamma's lap. A glance at the cousins told Ishvari they were still lovers.

No private discourse was permitted during sacred rites, so, mercifully, Ishvari could pretend to ignore the other tantrikas. Under cover of the dim light, she continued to study Takshak and Alatu, obsessed with her cruel fall from grace. The critical question was *not* whether she could win him back, but whether the witch would urge Takshak to eliminate her.

Chanting signaled the performance of bhuta-suddhi, the ceremonial worship of the elements that preceded maithuna. A priest garbed in crimson cotton put the worshippers into meditation. Beginning with a visualization of the earth element within each of their bodies, he had them dissolve it into water, then into fire, followed by air, and finally into the mysterious ether itself. In the silence that followed, Charaka rose to consecrate the ingredients of Red Tantra—wine, meat, fish and parched grain. The fifth and most crucial element would be the ritual mating itself.

The chanting grew louder, mesmerizing, accompanied as it was by frenetic drumming and flowing shehnais, the wail of stringed instruments and the haunting melodies of flutes, all emanating from the other side of the ghats, where Melukhha's best musicians sat blindfolded, lest they spy the forbidden. Ishvari looked around for Lord Kushal, but he was not present. She shivered, frightened afresh by the envoy's absence. Had Takshak finished the job of the unknown poisoner by killing his incorruptible counselor? Or, even more alarming, *had the king himself been behind the foiled poisoning?*

Charaka rose to address the Circle. "To celebrate our great victory, our maharajah has decreed that bhang distilled from ganja grown on the slopes of the northwestern mountains be served within the circle." He paused, scanning the circle with his crafty eyes. "Remember, my friends—during this coming union of the gods, even *thinking* of sin is to sin!"

Ishvari slumped with relief; the effects of the chillum she'd smoked earlier had worn off and her nerves were screaming for relief. Drugs would relax her, blur the edges of her growing humiliation. Anxiously, she watched Charaka pour bhang into a massive golden chalice studded with rubies, then gesture toward a boy priest to carry it to her.

Every eye in the group focused on Ishvari as she accepted the cup and drank deeply. As she passed it to her swarthy neighbor, Takshak's hard gaze fell on her. The Sumerian was watching Takshak watch Ishvari. Alatu was gloating. Smiling faintly, Takshak stroked the bare arm of his new mistress. Ishvari shivered as she sensed the hatching of some diabolical scheme.

To think she had loved this man for over a thousand nights! Hariaksa was right—change was the only constant in the realm of maya. Her body trembled like a river reed caught in a cross current of winds. Before Takshak had left for war, she'd been considered the highest ranking woman in Melukhha. Tonight, she was but one of many. What fresh horrors did her future hold?

But as the refilled cup of bhang passed from mouth to mouth and returned to her, her terror began to dissipate. She cast happier eyes around the circle as the drug began to do its work. Against the distant backdrop of the Sarasvati, she caught glimpses of smoldering corpses and meditating aghoris. The sky above her was vast. Drowning in the sweetness of the chanting, she recalled that the main aim of the ritual was to dissolve external personality. After close to four years of near solitude, to participate in a group rite of this intensity was—despite the background note of terror— exhilarating in some bizarre way.

The bhang erased her paranoia, allowing positive thoughts to filter through. Perhaps Takshak would grant her more freedom now that he had the Sumerian? As Hariaksa used to say with his lopsided smile, everything always happens for the best. When the cup came around again, she drank greedily before passing it on to the barbarian. Odd, but now she found herself excited by his brooding eyes. Behind her, the waters of the Sarasvati lapped hungrily.

A barge floated to the edge of the ghats. Its passenger, a petite woman carrying a stringed instrument, jumped to shore. As the musician tripped lightly across the sand and cut through the circle to enter its center, Ishvari recognized her as the girl musician who'd performed so sublimely as Ketaki and her sisters had prepared her for her first night with Takshak. Seating herself on a mat of kusha grass, the musician strummed her instrument and began to sing:

From the cellar of the muladhara,
The wine is taken up to the brahmarandhara—
Anything else is mere alcohol.

Her voice was a stream of silver entering the group consciousness—even the most stern-faced men were listening intently to the girl's exquisite rendition of the ancient words.

To slaughter the beasts of praise and blame with the sword of knowledge,
And merge one's consciousness with the absolute:
This is 'real meat-eating.'

Who controls the senses with the mind,
And yokes them to the imperishable is a 'real fish-eater.'
All others are merely killers of creatures."

The musician raised soulful eyes to the night sky, her throat trembling.

In men of animal-nature, Shakti sleeps.
He who honors Shakti is the 'real sexual worshiper.'
Who knows the rapture of the soul's union with the Ultimate
Is a 'real adept of lovemaking.'
All others are merely enjoyers of women.

As the haunting voice faded into silence, a masked man wearing the ritual headdress of a tantric priest leapt from the shadows into the center of the circle. *Who are you?* he demanded, whirling around to point at the maharajah. Then he was pointing at Alatu, and shouting the same question. Leaping and twirling into the air, the priest questioned each of the adepts in the circle. When he hurled his question at Ishvari, the bhang had so intoxicated her that she almost screamed back that while she no longer knew who she was, she'd be most gratified if he'd investigate the question on her behalf.

The agile priest vanished, and three new priests carried an engraved copper chest into the center of the circle. "Tantrikas of Melukhha!" the leader addressed the women. "Remove your garments and toss them into this chest. By doing so, release your relative identities!" The women enthusiastically complied, and the priest made a big show of mixing them up and tossing them into the air in a blaze of color. Beginning with Takshak, the priest instructed each man to choose a blouse, for pairing in the circle had to be indiscriminate. To her dismay, Ishvari saw Gandhali's staid escort selecting her blouse. Then the men were asked to remove their personal clothing, and instructed to wear identical woolen robes the shade of red hibiscus, the symbolic color of Tantra.

Directed by the priests, the men sought the owners of the blouses they had picked. Some of the celebrants were sleek as panthers, their bodies taut and well-muscled. Others had soft bellies and fleshy buttocks. Still, in the dim radiance of the lamp-lit ghats, every celebrant appeared strangely attractive to Ishvari in her rising state of intoxication. Dazed, she saw Takshak grab Urmila and pull her to his seat. The barbarian beside her moved away to claim Dalaja, and then the aristocrat who'd selected her blouse grabbed her by the hand and led her back to his seat, evidently thrilled by the prize he'd won. By the time Ishvari got to her new place, many others were already in position.

The men began to repeat their personal mantras a hundred and eight times, reaching across to position their bodies against their mates, heart against heart, lingam to yoni. The men offered honey to their mates, sprinkled water over their shining faces, symbolically charging the different bodily organs through their practiced touch. Then they shared portions of consecrated meat, fish and parched grain in between sips of wine.

Priests carrying silver jugs poured green streams of bhang into the mouth of each celebrant. Ishvari drank longer than most, convinced that surviving the night hinged on maintaining her state of intoxication. And true enough, the liquor and herbs soon transformed her disappointing mate into a virile god. She looked around, seeing couples engaged in variants of maithuna, just as her partner lifted her right off the ground with amazing strength and positioned her right over his erect lingam. Before he could go any further, even stronger hands were drawing her away from him. She swiveled around to see a tall stranger, with a golden mask covering his forehead and eyes, indicating that she should rise. Baffled by the magnificent mask, her partner offered no resistance. Ishvari looked askance at the watching priests, but they too made no move to stop her.

Rising unsteadily she stood beside the stranger. Behind him was Dalaja, her sinuous body swaying like a lily on a broken stem.

Had the barbarian abandoned her for one of the more adventurous groups forming and dissolving in the chakra? Dalaja took Ishvari's place, and the stranger led Ishvari swiftly away, guiding her along the shadowy inner rim of the circle.

Ishvari floated dreamily alongside, wondering why he felt so deeply familiar. *Who would dare wear a mask of gold—the highest distinction of Tantra—when even Takshak's face was bare?* But all personal talk was forbidden during the rite, so Ishvari kept her silence, intensely happy just to be with him. The stranger stopped behind a knot of lovers and looked directly into her eyes, forcing her into sharp awareness. "Be ready to escape with me," he whispered.

"Who are you?" she whispered back, drowning under the impact of his energy.

His lips curved behind the mask. "Ah, Little Goddess, have you forgotten me?"

"Nartaka!" she breathed, her eyes widening with startled joy.

The sadhu placed a finger on her lips. "Guardsmen are heading our way," he warned. "I'll distract them while you walk quickly past the circle. Run to the bottom of the ghats and look for my chariot. If the gods are still with us, we'll be back at my hermitage to watch sunrise."

Guardsmen encircled them from behind. "The maharajah wishes to know by whose invite you are here tonight, my lord," the head guard addressed Nartaka with forceful authority.

"Tell Takshak I am his royal brother, come to warn him he's chosen a treacherous path," Nartaka spoke coolly. "The gods are angry, their patience is short." Ishvari took a step forward, knowing this was her signal to escape. But the drugs had befuddled her senses and too much was happening too quickly. She thought she heard someone shout her name, and turned to look. In that second of hesitation, a wiry guardsman grabbed her arm. Nartaka turned and saw her struggling. Ishvari saw him hesitate, even as a small army of fierce guardsmen began to race towards them. Then, with a muttered curse, he cut through the circle and simply disappeared.

Desperate now, she tried to slip out of her captor's grasp, but he was holding her arm in a vice. Soon every participant in the circle was aware of the drama being enacted around them. A guard charged back towards them from the darkness beyond the circle. "He just *melted* into the ghats!" he exclaimed, bewildered. "One moment I had him, the next I was holding thin air!"

"Our Maharajah will be livid," the leader of the guardsmen muttered. "The intruder wore the ancient mask of the priest-king, which disappeared during Shaardul's reign...not even *Lord Charaka* knows who he is, or how he got here." He turned to Ishvari, numb with the shock of her most recent failure. "The intruder asked you to follow him, my lady. Surely *you* must know who he is...." He stopped at the sight of Takshak striding across the circle, followed by the Sumerian. Ishvari took an involuntary step backward as her captor released her arm. Takshak strode right up to her, looking *nothing* like the great lover she'd known so intimately.

"Who *is* this cursed fellow?" Takshak bellowed. Alatu stood beside him, a crooked smile hovering about her red lips, her eyes gleaming maliciously. Even in her despair, Ishvari quailed before her overpowering sensuality. And why did she bring Inanna so strongly to mind? Inanna exuded light, this woman spread darkness! "Come, admit it," Takshak insisted. "You *know* him!"

"I've never seen him before," Ishvari lied. "Ask your men— he led me away from the partner assigned to me. I thought he was part of this group."

Takshak hawked crudely and spat at her feet. He turned to the head guardsman. "The man had a message for me you say? Well?"

"Said he was your royal brother, sire," the guard replied, his voice trembling with fear. "Come to warn you of the dangers of your chosen path."

"But I *have* no brother," Takshak muttered. "Who is this scurrilous pest?" He wheeled back on Ishvari. "Why did he come first to you? And why did you leave your partner for him?"

Ishvari stared at Takshak, struggling for coherent thought. Above all he must not know that Nartaka was his own half-brother by Inanna. "The nobleman gestured for me to rise and I obeyed, thinking it part of the rite. The priests were watching. They did nothing to stop him."

Takshak slapped her with such brutal force that she staggered backward. "*Nobleman,* you say?" he hissed. "To a slut who begs a foreign emissary to pleasure her, *any* man would fit that description!"

"Ramses abused *me*, and in the vilest possible manner!" Ishvari shouted, regaining her physical balance. Suddenly her mind was sharp and clear—she was fighting for her life, and it was crucial that everyone in the circle hear the truth of the Egyptian's brutal assault from her own lips. "Have you forgotten sacred law, my lord?" she demanded with genuine rage. "A just monarch investigates *both* sides of a matter before hurling accusations at any citizen of Melukhha, let alone the high tantrika. Certainly, the Takshak with whom I raised the fire would never have set a depraved royal loose upon his own high tantrika!"

Takshak assessed her coolly despite the quantities of intoxicants he'd consumed. "Ah, my dear Ishvari, you sadden me in more ways than one," he murmured, shaking his head in mock sorrow. "How like a rustic to blame a man for *her* crimes. Never mind, we'll deal with the matter of the Egyptian tomorrow." He made as if to turn away, then, changing his mind, whirled back around to face her. "Now speak! Or I'll personally cut out your tongue and feed it to the fish, sacred law be damned!" he thundered. "This stranger's name if you please!"

Ishvari looked into his pitiless eyes and shivered. Ramses had done his work well, but only because Takshak had been primed to turn against her. Why precisely, she might never live to find out. Death breathed icily down the back of her neck. In that instant, she accepted full responsibility for her gruesome situation; against all counsel, she'd tried to escape her pain—first by abusing the sacred herb, then by seducing Pundalik. And now the pain was back with a vengeance. Ironically, she'd die in reprisal for an atrocity against *her*, while her *real* transgressions would likely go undetected.

The Sumerian nuzzled against Takshak's shoulder, whispering into his ear, her eyes penetrating Ishvari with a dreadful black light. Takshak exchanged low words with her, nodding as he came to some decision, then clapped his hands sharply for attention. "Since our beauty here appears to have lost the power of speech, we shall reserve our interrogation for later," he shouted. "And now," he added, a cruel glee animating his swarthy face, "to further honor the union of the gods, I offer to every man here the dubious pleasures of Ishvari of Devikota! Keep in mind—within the circle, forbidden becomes sacred! Do what you will with her!"

Takshak beckoned to a hulking aristocrat. "Come, these village wenches are insatiable. What say we give the flower of Devikota a treat she'll never forget?" He slapped his thigh, sniggering at the varied reactions of the nobles swarming about him. "Why, just look at you...bashful as virgins...intimidated by our delectable whore, eh? Can't you see how she hungers for you?"

Some of the men loped forward eagerly. Ishvari heard a woman cry out sharply. General Tarun and Lord Ashoka rushed forward with worried faces, as if to dissuade Takshak. Haridas, triple chins wobbling, hurried to join them. Alatu whispered calmly into Takshak's ear. Insolently, the maharajah gestured them away. Throwing her roughly to the earth, Takshak straddled her prone body. Like the orchestrator of some horrible drama, even as he grinned ferally up at Alatu, who watched admiringly, slender arms on hips, he positioned several men around Ishvari. Behind these, a second group of aristocrats—eyes wild like animals in heat—formed a second ring. Charaka's pudgy face, flushed with victory, stared down at her. Then Ishvari caught a glimpse of the barbarian towering over the others in his striking red robe.

"Behold the high tantrika of Melukhha!" Takshak shouted, his massive body pinning her down. "And enjoy her charms—she's worked long and hard for them." The maharaja lunged at her as the onlookers howled like a pack of wolves, just as Ishvari thought she heard the faint whinny of horses and the receding wheels of a fast chariot.

Even the heartless criminal,
If he loves me with all his heart,
Will certainly grow into sainthood
As he moves towards me on this path.
                              —*Bhagavad Gita*

FLIGHT

A woman was shrieking right outside her window—and no, this was no drug-induced nightmare. Ishvari shot upright on her couch as the awful keening rose and fell, drowning her in waves of liquid sorrow. A dull pain coursed through her body, from skull to foot. She touched her face with trembling fingers, shuddering as memory returned, then grabbed the oval copper mirror lying beside her couch and stared at her reflection in horror—coagulated blood covered parts of her face, her right eye was hugely swollen, and her lower body burned, as if engulfed in flames.

Vaguely she recalled being flung naked onto her couch like a sack of barley by a couple of Takshak's guardsmen. Other hideous images of the night before began to form in her mind's eye, but the shrieking called for immediate attention. Uncaring of her nakedness, she scrambled out the open window and landed with a painful thud on the moist grass.

Mandakini stood at the edge of the lotus pool beyond the great banyan, wails pouring out of her open mouth as she stared up at the tree. Vasudeva stood a short distance away from her, his face pale. Ishvari looked too, and saw Pundalik hanging from a branch of the banyan by a noose fashioned out of his own orange robes—over the very spot Rudra had appeared barely three moons past! As she too stared upward in shock, a baleful crow defecated on Pundalik's shaven head, and gray-white feces leaked down into the corners of his bulging eyes. She fainted then, crushing Vasudeva's prized trumpet flowers.

"Hush!" Vasudeva commanded Mandakini. "Remember the guards!" But Mandakini was beyond reason, her eyes now leaping from Ishvari's prone body to the swaying corpse, an endless scream shooting up her throat. Vasudeva looked wildly around—fortunately no guards were in sight. Sprinting across to Mandakini, he clapped a hand over her mouth.

But it was too late—someone had neglected to draw the iron bolt across the main gate, and a fierce gust of wind swung it half open—just as two men garbed in the green of royal servants passed by, balancing on their shoulders reed baskets linked by supple wooden rods. Alerted by Mandakini's screams, the men halted, gawking at the sight of the high tantrika's stylish dwelling. With a grunt of fear, Vasudeva shot forward and slammed the gate shut in their faces. Quickly he drew the heavy bolt, then raced back towards his wife, a finger held warningly to his lips. Outside the servants lingered, their voices carrying clearly over the high wall.

"Sweet gods, man, did you...did you see what I saw?" one stammered excitedly.

"With *my* stinking karma?" the other grumbled. "Not a chance. That son-of-a-whore almost broke my nose the way he slammed that gate shut...and hey, that was some godawful caterwauling, I tell you, put the fear of the gods into me."

"Careful, idiot! Drop those swans' eggs and we're in trouble. Now shut your mouth and listen. Remember the monk who used to beg at the royal kitchens? Stop scratching your head like a monkey...I'm talking about the scrawny fellow the serving maids always squabbled over—though what they saw in him *I* never could understand."

"The stripling who called himself 'Rudra's Own'? What's *he* got to do with this?"

"Only that he's hanging from a tree in our high tantrika's garden, dead as a hung pig!"

"By the gods, Satpal," the second man sniggered. "Your woman's right—your brain's pickled in moonshine! See any flute-playing gandharvas hovering over the fellow perchance? All right, that's enough...if that bully cuts our wages for being late, I'll knock your...."

"*You're* the fool. Didn't you hear those screams? It was her maid, I tell you, the curvy one with the big smile. Must have walked right into the lad's icy feet and got the fright of her life—"

"God's balls! So the rumors buzzing around the city are true—our high tantrika's nothing but a whore! The lad was love-struck, I'm sure, or why off himself right in her home? She must have been fucking him good and hard, making up for losing our king to the foreign wench. If you're right, that damned gardener's made me miss the best scene of my miserable life...."

"Ah, so *now* you believe me...I'll wager she promised the lad moksha if he did a good job of pleasuring her. These tantrikas can be mighty tricky, I've heard, what with their silver tongues and holier-than-thou attitudes. Bet you my last copper that pitiful creature never had a chance resisting her—the Devikotan's supposed to be fabulously beautiful. D'you know it's a horrible sin for a sadhu to take his own life? Most likely he did it on account of what happened at the ghats last night...."

"Enough talk...let's get the hell out of here...I'll take the eggs to the main kitchen while you find the chief guardsman and tell him *exactly* what you saw. I'll join you as soon as I can, back you *right* up...play this right, Satpal, and I wager we'll soon see the shine of gold...."

As their voices faded into the distance, Vasudeva propelled Mandakini toward Ishvari's fallen body. "Oh my poor mistress," Mandakini whimpered, sinking on to her haunches.

Vasudeva dragged her up with a muttered curse. "Didn't I warn you a thousand times it would come to this?" he hissed. "But no, you felt sorry for her, covered up for her, disobeyed *me*, your own husband!" Groaning, he pointed at the corpse swaying in the brisk morning breeze. "That oaf spouting hot air outside might have been right about one thing at least—the boy likely lost his mind when he heard—" He shook his head in confusion. "Last night down by the docks I passed a bunch of intoxicated guardsmen. They'd stolen a cask of bhang intended for the chakra puja and were talking wildly...all sorts of awful rumors were already spreading through the city by then...this wretch must have heard the worst of them, and thought she'd been killed—on account of *him*!" Vasudeva struck his forehead sharply. "Why he returned *here* to finish himself off, only the dark gods know...should've jumped into the Sarasvati and saved us this stinking mess. If only we'd both knocked some sense into her." He cuffed Mandakini hard on the side of her head. "And I into *yours*, you brainless woman!"

Mandakini's hand flew up in shock. She backed fearfully away from him—never before had Vasudeva raised a hand to strike her.

"Forgive me," Vasudeva whispered, pulling her close and hugging her against his pounding chest. "I'm losing my mind. What are we going to do?"

Mandakini looked up at him with petrified eyes, wiping them with the edge of her sleeve. She squeezed his hand fervently. "It's *you* who should forgive me," she whispered. "Now tell me what to do and I'll do it."

"Best to leave her right here and get out while we can, but neither of us could live with ourselves then, I know." Vasudeva looked down at Ishvari's motionless body splayed by their feet and sighed. "Truth be told, I felt an awful pity for her after that devil of an Egyptian...."

The deadly consequences of the situation struck Mandakini afresh. "Shut up!" Vasudeva ordered, clamping his hand over her mouth again. "Beg gods or demons, but be strong!" His sharpness cut through Mandakini's daze. He pointed at Ishvari. "Help me get her inside."

Together they hefted Ishvari's dead weight through the house and into her chamber, setting her on the couch. "Throw a bucket of cold water on her, two if necessary," Vasudeva ordered, looking away from Ishvari's spread-eagled body. "If she doesn't come to, slap her hard. Show no mercy or I'll do it myself." He jumped out of the window and back into the gardens.

Ishvari stirred as fragments of Vasudeva's speech entered her consciousness to the accompaniment of the demon's jubilant howls. Her eyes fluttered open, and she reached out for Mandakini, whimpering like a child. Outside, Vasudeva, scythe in hand, shot up a branch of the banyan and swiftly cut the twirled robe holding the mendicant. Pundalik's body fell with a thud to the ground. Vasudeva scrambled back down and pushed the corpse into a freshly dug flowerbed he'd spent hours digging the previous afternoon. "Garb her in your oldest clothes," he ordered Mandakini through the open window as he threw spadefuls of earth into the pit to cover the body. "Then pack food and water. We must move fast, though how we're going to get …."

"Hey Vasudeva!" a hoarse voice called plaintively from the direction of the tradesman's entrance. "O lazybones, where are you hiding? My husband's shaking with fever and sent me in his stead. Come, help me unload this manure you ordered last week…."

"Hush!" Vasudeva warned Mandakini, placing a finger to his lips. "Act like all's well. I'll get rid of this pest fast, but then we must flee. Once the other servants arrive, we'll be in *real* boiling water. It's best we take the jungle route *now*, and hope the gods protect us. If we can get to my cousin's place, he should know what to do."

Mandakini rushed off to follow Vasudeva's directions. Weighed down by dread, Ishvari heard Vasudeva's voice rising and falling, followed by a low voice responding. The door opened and a tall figure entered her chamber. "By all the gods!" Inanna exclaimed. "Wonder he didn't kill her, the monster!" She rushed over and sat beside Ishvari, removing the worn hood she'd used as a disguise. Through a haze, Ishvari saw the fire swirling lightly around her third eye. Inanna placed her hands on the spot between Ishvari's eyebrows, moving them lightly over her wounded face. Warmth flooded her battered body and she moaned.

A pale and frightened Mandakini had slipped in and was standing by her couch, holding a faded blue garment and an old white shawl in trembling hands. Vasudeva burst in. "We've no time for fancy healing, mistress," he said urgently. "Already…."

"I know, Vasudeva, I know," Inanna murmured, stroking Ishvari's arm. "And it gets worse: the Sumerian's persuaded Takshak to sacrifice your mistress at the burning ghats tonight." She snorted drily. "To appease the gods, the bloodthirsty whore claims…that's why *I* came, risking my life more than once, let me assure you—those cursed guards are *everywhere*! If we don't get her to safety immediately, she'll die tonight. The scoundrel swears he won't even give her the drug which reduces the agony of burning." Inanna let out a harsh bark of laughter. "Alatu's done her work well, brought out the full beast in our wonderful king."

Ishvari sat up with a jerk, letting out a cry of terror. The Sumerian was truly a witch! She would be burnt alive at the ghats while all of Melukhha celebrated the great sacrifice! Worse still, Mandakini and Vasudeva would likely be stoned to death as well. *What had she done?*

Inanna's face softened at she turned her gaze back on Ishvari. "There's no changing Takshak's mind, sweetling. I talked sternly to him this morning, but, for the first time, he ordered his guards to throw me out. The beast has taken him over and he's stronger than ever, no thanks to his new mistress." She hesitated briefly. "You should know that, like me, Alatu too is kin to Magi priests." She paused to let her news sink in. "The critical difference is that I honor the gods of light, while Alatu is in thrall to dark powers.

Dully, Ishvari realized why the Sumerian brought Inanna so strongly to mind.

"What now?" Vasudeva demanded, glaring down at Ishvari. "Must we all die, for *her*?"

"Not if you listen to me carefully," Inanna retorted. "I parked my chariot at the back entrance. Throw mud over the gold work and make your way carefully through the city—all the paths leading through the jungle swarm with soldiers. You know how to get to Rudralaya, don't you? First deliver your mistress safely to Hariaksa, then allow him to direct you onward." Inanna nodded, her dragon eyes glinting fire. "My chariot's yours now, Vasudeva. Take care of my horses, please, or I shall be forced to come after you with my whip!"

Vasudeva grinned nervously, then turned and left. "Put these on, mistress," Mandakini said, tossing the coarse garments to Ishvari before rushing after her husband.

"Won't you come with us?" Ishvari begged the old priestess, swallowing dryly. "Takshak will surely kill you if you remain here!"

"He won't dare touch me. Many Melukhhans are *still* grateful for what Shaardul and I set in motion for the common good—another reason the petty fellow hates me. As for Alatu, she's too smart to ever meddle with me—even the dark gods quail before *my* protectors." She stroked Ishvari's cheek. "Calm yourself, sweetling, or you'll die tonight, and your servants with you. The fire has revealed much to your acharyas. The aspirants have already been packed off to their villages, poor bewildered creatures, and Atulya's right now heading for the mountain hermitage with his monks. It's safe up there, hidden up in the clouds as it is. Only Hariaksa awaits you, so you will have to move fast."

"But Takshak will kill you for helping us!" Ishvari whimpered. "Come with us, I beg you…I can't bear yet another life on my conscience…."

"Guilt's a weapon of the lower mind, sweetling; the entity that rules it wants to keep you whirling in maya. Waste no time fretting about my skin—I promise to survive both Takshak and that incredibly heedless woman. And if you wish to please me, simply resolve to shine again."

Vasudeva rushed into the room. "Hear that?" he cried hoarsely, putting a hand to his ear. "They're heading our way...." He motioned furiously to Ishvari. "Let them drag you away to the ghats, let fire eat your shameless body...Mandakini and I are leaving right now!"

"Stop, Vasudeva, can't you see she's suffered enough?" Inanna scolded. "Now take her to Hariaksa while I hold Takshak off. I'll convince him you've escaped southward, throw him off the scent...." She winked at the overwrought gardener. "Do not fear, I'll make sure Alatu won't be able to use her fabled crystal to detect your location. Now pack up and go!"

A bruised peasant girl garbed in a coarse blue robe stared back at Ishvari from the copper mirror. Mandakini rushed in hefting a large cloth bag over her shoulder, followed by Vasudeva, hefting an even bigger sack. "The chariot's waiting," he announced tersely. He turned to Inanna. "We'll owe you our lives if we survive this hellish day, priestess. Farewell, and may the gods preserve you from that ugly pair."

Ishvari huddled beside Mandakini at the back of the elegant chariot. Vasudeva had tied bundles of straw to the roof to disguise its sleek design, and the bales reeked of the manure beside which they'd been stored. As their fetid stink assailed her nostrils, Ishvari gagged, spewing vomit over the side. "Good, mistress," Mandakini whispered, patting her on the back as lovingly as ever. "Better out than in."

Vasudeva leapt onto the driver's seat, grabbed the reins and smacked a horse with an open palm. The chariot leapt forward, barely making it through the side entrance and on to the narrow road leading into the heart of the city. Ishvari shut her eyes, fighting the sour taste of vomit in her mouth, the coarse garments scraping her skin like iron filings. Three years ago she had entered

Melukhha covered in glory; now she was sneaking away in a chariot reeking of dung. In an agony of self-hatred, she rocked back and forth on the cushioned seat like an inconsolable child. Mandakini reached for her hand and squeezed it comfortingly. "Control yourself, mistress," she warned. "Remember what Hariaksa always said? This lifetime is but a dream, only a dream."

Within Ishvari, the demon struggled to emerge. The memory of that dawn when the mendicant had walked lightly down the path flashed before her eyes. Seduced by the demon, she had in turn seduced the lad away from his simple path, metamorphosing into a predatory spider in order to extract every drop of pleasure his chaste body could produce.

One must rise by that by which one falls. The words rang through her cloudy head like sun slicing through fog. In a burst of clarity, she understood their full meaning: brutish energy had led her to commit an atrocity, and yet that same energy, purified by wisdom, could have been used to slice to ribbons the compulsion to self-destruct. In a sword-thrust of impeccable insight untainted by even a sliver of doubt, she finally saw the demon for exactly what it was.

Suddenly she was desperate to be free of its control. *I am more than body, more than mind, more than emotion,* she whispered fervently as the chariot raced through the city she'd once hoped to rule. *I am spirit! My true nature is existence, consciousness and bliss.* Salvation lay in knowing that buried in her heart burned a deathless flame. Holding Mandakini's hand tightly, she called upon the gods to evict the demon, all the while ferociously chanting Nartaka's mantra.

"Keep your head down, mistress," Mandakini warned. "Soldiers on the main road, hundreds of them, dragging prisoners…they're far from done with the madness…."

Ishvari heard the cries of prisoners of war, interspersed with barks of laughter from their guards. The demon stirred violently. "By Rudra's whip!" she screamed silently, unable to bear its din. "Leave me alone!" Still the inner struggle did not cease. Her eyes fluttered open just as Vasudeva maneuvered the chariot into the commercial area, away from the soldiers.

Crowds lined the sidewalks: Melukhhans, traders and sailors, bargaining keenly with local jewelers. Even in her state of disorientation, Ishvari recognized the white cotton of a family of Nubians, and the speckled robes of a dignified group of Egyptians, their swarthy complexions and hawkish eyes standing out amidst the jostling crowds. At the street corner stood a cluster of Sumerian merchants garbed in multi-colored cloaks, gesturing excitedly towards an ebony-skinned eunuch with pendulous lips and golden ear hoops. With zealous blows of his staff, the eunuch was clearing the way ahead for the personage hidden behind the diaphanous curtains of the palanquin following right behind him.

Vasudeva steered the chariot onto a side road, hiding behind a trio of lumbering elephants. Vendors stood on street corners, selling charms against plague, leprosy and the evil eye. A blind girl with opaque eyes begged for alms, while the monotonous chanting of sadhus blended with the roar of the crowd, the anxious bleating of sheep and the lowing of cattle. Every now and then she spied an urchin weaving through the multitude, bent on snatching a purse or two.

A skinny acrobat unfurled a threadbare carpet upon the ground and began to wriggle and twist his body before a circle of drunken admirers. Closer to their carriage, a snake charmer uncoiled the cobra draped around his neck. The snake's hood flared as the gray-haired charmer spun in a hypnotically slow circle for his audience to admire its unusual markings. The serpent rose high into the air, then lunged forward like lightning, almost striking Ishvari as she sat cowering at the back of the carriage. As people shrieked in terror, Ishvari clutched at Mandakini, recoiling from the flickering pink tongue that had come so very close to her face.

It took her a while to recover from the shock; soon the mingling of perfumes, the pungent smoke of vendors frying bajjias of onions and mountain squash and the earthy odors of straw baskets carried aloft by dry fruit merchants from the mountainous lands bordering Melukhha, all began to suffocate her. A hermit sporting a long white beard that straggled down onto his concave chest stood in the midst of crouching listeners, detailing punishments that would fall upon all those who displeased the Wild God. As the chariot drove past a tavern, Ishvari caught sight of men reclining upon divans, calling out for more arrak, more wine, more dancing girls.

A dancer—with painted eyes and naked breasts whose nipples alone were painted with gold—performed on the sidewalk to the lascivious cheers of onlookers, diaphanous skirts twirling around her lithe body. Lured by the excitement, the demon leapt into the space between Ishvari's eyes with an ecstatic howl. *"Leave!"* she screamed, slamming her head against the side of the chariot. *"In the name of the Wild God, get out!"*

Mandakini seemed equally stupefied by the surrounding chaos. At Ishvari's scream, the housekeeper placed her arms comfortingly about her mistress. Ishvari closed her eyes; humbly, she begged the gods to destroy the demon. Sweat trickled down her forehead as she fell against Mandakini's perspiring body, praying to be released from her compulsion to self-destruct.

It happened when she had almost given up hope—a ghastly energy tore itself off the base of her spine and shot upward through her open mouth. The agony was so great her hand flew to her mouth to stifle her cries. As the pain receded, she fell into a trance, feeling a benevolent force usurping her body and flooding it with energy. Then it was over. She slumped weakly against Mandakini, free after many moons of possession.

"Halt!" an insolent voice shouted. "No one leaves the city today!" Mandakini placed a warning arm around Ishvari—they had reached Melukhha's famous carved gateway. They heard Vasudeva's voice, deliberately weak and whining, as they sat petrified at the back of the carriage. "Sire, I carry womenfolk infected with disease."

"Disease?" the guard demanded. "*What* disease?"

"The kind that eats up skin and bone leaving stumps. A contagion that spreads through air quicker than breath." Vasudeva's deep voice rose in a plaintive singsong. "Already one's badly infected the other and now I've begun to fear for my own—"

"And these women are right now in your filthy chariot?" the guard demanded incredulously.

"That's what I said, sire, erupting in evil sores, shaking with chills and stinking to the lowest hell," Vasudeva moaned. "I beg you, sire, may we rest a while in your guardhouse? My elder sister's deathly ill and...."

"Witless son-of-a-stinking-syphilitic-whore! Must we all die with you?" A whip cracked through the air, followed by Vasudeva's genuine howl of pain. It cracked again and Mandakini burst out into piercing wails, while Ishvari shrank back as far as she could, cringing as if the whip was lashing at her own face. "Get out, you ignorant oaf!" the guard shrieked, whipping Vasudeva again. "Take your diseased women and get out of here! The side road, d'you hear? The side road! This section's reserved for important citizens."

Ishvari clung to Mandakini, who was now sobbing wildly. The gates swung open and the chariot moved through. Her mind flashed back to her first sight of the guards in their splendid uniforms, recalling their admiring looks—then she'd vowed to have nothing but success.

Outside the gates snaked the main highway, an endless, stone-paved thoroughfare, empty but for a few corpses, heaved like offal to its edges—staring, bloodless, violated tribals wearing the crude leather ornaments of the Doms. She threw up again, barely missing Mandakini.

"Husband!" Mandakini cried, poking her distressed face out. "Are you hurt?"

"What d'you think? Was it a feather he used on me?" Vasudeva cursed through clenched teeth. "Now be quiet and let me concentrate. Must get off the highway at the third fork."

Ishvari closed her eyes and resolutely began to chant Hariaksa's healing mantra until it grew into a mighty roar. She did not stop until the chariot swerved sharply into the jungle fringing the highway and they were bathed in its pale green light. Clinging to Mandakini, she felt soothed by a world where time itself had stopped. Cool breezes whirled through the branches of ancient trees as she filled her injured lungs with fresh sweet air. The chariot rumbled on, past a grove of mimosa trees full of humming bees. A flock of bright green parrots flew up into the air at their approach; Ishvari watched them rise into the sky in unison, determinedly pushing away all thoughts of what had happened, of what might yet happen.

"Look, husband!" Mandakini called as the horses maneuvered onto another rough pathway lined with thousands of delicately hued trumpet flowers raising innocent faces to catch stray rays of sun. "A stream, there, beside that grove of pipal trees...this must be the right trail for it widens further down the path." The horses came to a halt. Mandakini opened the door of the chariot and leapt down to rush to Vasudeva, whose cheek had been slashed open. A trickle of blood leaked onto his sodden tunic and his face was white—the thongs of the whip had been finished with steel. "I need your help, mistress," Mandakini called out to Ishvari.

Together they moved Vasudeva to the ground. Ishvari deftly fashioned a pillow out of fallen leaves and placed his head gently upon it. "Don't fuss!" Vasudeva rasped, but his eyes were grateful as Mandakini dipped the edge of her garment in water from the gurgling stream and mopped his face clean of blood. "He needs a healer," Mandakini whispered to Ishvari, wringing her hands. "Is Rudralaya far from here do you know? How will we get there?"

"Just tear up my tunic and bandage my face, will you?" Vasudeva groaned. "Stem the blood and let me rest a while. Takshak's guards won't think to seek us here for a long while at least—that soldier won't dare confess he allowed a man and two women in a chariot to leave the city." He laughed, a short bark that turned into a wince. "Word we're on the run should've reached him by now...he'll have figured out who we are, but I'll wager the swine will keep his mouth shut. We'll leave when the moon's high and reach Rudralaya well before daybreak."

Mandakini's face crumpled, and Ishvari realized the housekeeper was a hair's breadth away from complete breakdown—*and this was all her fault!* "We mustn't dally here," she said, amazed by her growing clarity. She tore strips of cloth from the bottom of her garment to make bandages, then knelt down beside Vasudeva. As Mandakini stared, baffled by her competence, Ishvari mopped up the blood, then knotted the bandages over the wounds to prevent infection. "There's no question of you driving us onward, Vasudeva," she said firmly. "It's no great task for me to steer these obedient beasts. Rest a bit, and then we must leave."

Vasudeva made a strangled sound, but Ishvari hushed him. She brought water to his parched lips, then drank some herself, watching as Mandakini packed pieces of braised venison into cracked wheat bread with shaking fingers and handed her a portion. Ishvari accepted the food, leaning against a tree to eat, while Mandakini fed her husband, stopping every now and then to wipe her flowing tears with the edge of her garment.

Mandakini huddled beside her husband beneath the rustling trees, her eyes swollen with weeping. Amazed at her own calm, Ishvari walked the magnificent steeds down to the rushing stream to drink their fill of water before feeding them with the remaining bread. The only sounds were those of the wind circling the trees like a phantom and the mournful notes of water birds.

When Vasudeva stirred a short while later, the women helped him rise and enter the chariot. Repeating her mantra for strength, Ishvari hoisted herself onto the driver's seat, holding the reins with firm hands. Then she guided the horses in the direction Vasudeva had pointed to. As the jungle light dimmed to an emerald glow, she slipped into a dreamlike state where the horrific events leading to their escape seemed to have happened only in imagination. Images of the chakra puja mingled with visions of Pundalik's innocent face, but she snuffed them out with a zealot's determination: to wallow in guilt would mean the absolute end for them all.

The horses moved steadily past dense thickets of *bakula*, past voluptuous *karnikara* trees in full bloom, and groves of ripening purple *jumlums*. The southern breeze blew the mixed scent of the jungle's bounty to her nostrils and she soaked it in ravenously. The first echoes of freedom lapped around her in such honeyed waves that even the incessant pounding in her head—the consequence of depriving herself of the drug—became a bearable penance.

Gradually she became aware of a vast emptiness within her, the space vacated by the demon. *How would Hariaksa react to seeing her again?* Would he forgive her? Comfort her? Help her escape Takshak's wrath? The thought of seeing his beloved face again made her want to increase the speed of the chariot, but she had no whip to urge the horses on, and no magic words to inspire obedience. From within the chariot she heard Mandakini's occasional murmurs.

Exhausted, she secured her upper body to the sides of the chariot with her shawl lest she fall off the seat. Soon she sank into a heavy doze. Then she was running naked through the forbidden valley, racing towards the hill on which the sadhu practiced his rituals with steady, flawless rhythm, the leopard running alongside with consummate grace. She looked down to see her body begin to break up and fall away, arms and legs first, followed by her head. Then, with an explosion that rocked the basin, her chest broke open and her heart leapt out, perfectly red, soaring upward, alone.

Wake and behold me! she heard a great female voice boom. Stunned, she awoke to see the jungle ablaze with unearthly luminosity. A form was taking shape in the center of the light, a luminous goddess with thighs as great as mountains and breasts ample enough to suckle the universe, ascending and spreading outward at the same time until she spanned heaven and earth. "Mahadevi!" Ishvari whispered brokenly, shielding her eyes from the full glory of the vision.

O Beloved! By willfully stealing from Rudra, you have strayed into a savage domain. What you have created, only you can destroy.

Yet what lies behind and before cannot compare to what lies within. One impeccable step followed by another will surely lead you away from the abyss, to the ecstatic immortality of your true Self.

Ishvari curled into a ball as the telepathic stream entered her third eye and diffused through her body. She wanted to ask how, what, and why, but the light around her was fast fading and the carriage was moving on, without her guidance. Vasudeva moaned as the horses made a sharp turn on the narrow pathway. She heard Mandakini's reassuring murmur. Had the couple seen the Mother Goddess? Amazed, Ishvari closed her eyes and began to chant her mantra.

"Mistress, can you hear me?" Mandakini's piercing call cut through her daze.

"Lower your voice and tell me what you want!" Ishvari hissed back.

"Stop the beasts," Mandakini whispered. "See, ahead of you, a gate…Vasudeva thinks it might be the back entrance to Rudralaya."

Ishvari realized with surprise that the day had passed. Opalescent moon glow filtered through the trees. Overhead, flocks of birds winged their way homeward. The horses, without too much human help, had brought them to Rudralaya. Incredibly, she recognized the spot—once, long ago, she had sneaked away with Archini to pick the last of summer's mouth-staining purple berries. Pulling up her skirts, she jumped down.

"Welcome, Ishvari," a familiar voice greeted her. She narrowed her eyes to adjust to the gloom, eager to identify its owner. And yes, it was indeed Hariaksa standing at the gate, thinner than ever, old eyes shining. Beside him stood a slim robed figure with bales of yellow hay at his feet and a cloth bag hanging from one arm. From the unusual serenity of his dark face, Ishvari recognized him as the child monk who had carried Hariaksa's missive to her on the day of her departure for Melukhha, almost four years ago.

Mandakini clambered off the chariot and threw herself to the earth before the aged sage. "Rise, faithful one, it is I who am honored," Hariaksa smiled, bowing to the housekeeper. He spoke to the monk, who slipped out the gate and headed toward the horses. Quickly he fed them with the hay he carried. Hariaksa addressed Mandakini. "You must leave right away. Nikunja has instructions to avoid the plains, which we hear are swarming with bandits. He will take you to our hermitage in the mountains, where you will live quietly for as long as Takshak rules."

"Nikunja carries ample provisions for your journey," Hariaksa added. "When you're at a safe distance, eat and rest." The old monk gestured for the gardener to remain in the carriage. "You'll find a salve to heal your wounds inside Nikunja's bag, Vasudeva. The mantra used to prepare it works fast. Soon, I assure you, you will be fit to work again."

Mandakini's eyes filled with tears as she gazed at the old monk. She tried to speak, but Hariaksa stopped her by raising a hand. "Your love touches me deeply," he said, beaming at her. "Be at peace—you won't be wearing widow's white for decades to come."

Ishvari struggled to balance the joy of seeing Hariaksa again against the disgraceful events that had driven her back to him. Mandakini knelt and made to kiss her feet, but Ishvari pulled her up and drew her close. "It's *I* who should fall at your feet," she whispered into her ear. "Can you ever forgive me?"

"Those who truly love easily forgive," Mandakini whispered back, gazing at her with unaltered devotion. "Find the joy within your heart, mistress, and I will be happy."

"Time to leave, Mandakini," Hariaksa broke in, gesturing toward the chariot.

Nikunja leapt into the driver's seat and took hold of the reins. Mandakini walked to the chariot, tossing them loving looks. When Ishvari made to follow, intending to properly thank Vasudeva for his amazing courage in saving their lives, Hariaksa restrained her with a firm hand on her arm. "Mandakini will convey your gratitude," he said, reading her mind as usual. "Now, my spark of light, you and I are walking down to the river."

As a man abandons worn out garments and takes new ones,
So does the soul quit worn-out bodies and enter new ones.
Weapons cannot cleave it, fire cannot burn it,
nor water wet it, nor wind dry it.
It is said to be invisible, incomprehensible, immutable.
        —*Bhagavad Gita*

JEWEL IN THE LOTUS

"See that?" Hariaksa said, pointing to the moon's reflection on the river's twilit surface. "Now wrap your stubborn mind around this truth once and for all, Ishvari—no matter your predilection for drama, that golden stillness is, and always will be, your true nature." Picking up a flat stone, he spun it neatly into the heart of the reflected orb, generating a swirl of glittering dots. "Look again, and look well," he ordered. "This is how intoxicants inevitably shatter one's peace."

A shooting star flashed across the sky. "A lad came to Rudralaya shortly before Takshak left to wage war with the Doms," Hariaksa said softly. "His mother's sudden death had unhinged him, we were told, and soon after he fell into dissolute company. His father is a wealthy gnostic who sent him to us as a last resort, hoping Atulya and I could somehow redirect his energies. But the boy was fiercely resentful of being caged in what he called the 'backwoods'—he broke every rule he could and disturbed our novices to the point that we had to expel him."

Why was Hariaksa telling her this *now*? "I had faith in the young man's potential," he continued, reaching for her cold hand. "The morning of his departure, I warned him that unbridled sensuality inevitably spirals into misery. I invited him to return to Rudralaya when he was ready to learn a better way. His wild eyes mocked me—all he saw was an old fool with an axe to grind. A few days later he was bludgeoned to death during an orgiastic revelry." Hariaksa paused. "Takshak *himself* struck the death blow, Ishvari. Later we heard that Alatu had urged him to punish the lad for misbehaving with her, though witnesses swear she'd led him on. Needless to say, all the players in this drama—but for the Sumerian witch—were heavily intoxicated."

Ishvari let out a low moan, and Hariaksa threw a comforting arm across her shoulders. "Our monarchs swear before the old gods to protect us, Ishvari. When this oath is broken, the entire kingdom rapidly degenerates. Takshak's brutal murder of this misguided lad convinced Atulya and I that our fiery visions of Melukhha's coming desolation were accurate."

After her own experience at the ghats, Hariaksa's gruesome tale did not surprise her. Besides, had she too not caused the death of a young man? Worse still, Pundalik had been pure and innocent, until she had trapped him in her selfish web with duplicity and intoxicants.

Exhausted, she lay her head against Hariaksa's chest. The sound of his old heart beating made her want to weep, but tears would not flow. "The pleasures of this world are like licking the honey off a razor's edge," he murmured, stroking her hair. "Sooner or later, sweetling, we all feel the pain. But *you* must never give up, for you were born to dive into the heart of reality. Samadhi will come again, I promise—the seeds of inner radiance can never be destroyed."

Far from comforting her, his words made her hate herself even more. She drew away from him suddenly, pulling the coarse shawl tight around her body and hunkering down low. "It happened so quickly," she muttered. "Takshak abandoned me, and the demon was waiting."

"You've whipped yourself enough," Hariaksa scolded tenderly. "And Tantra is far more than the trysting you experienced with either our confused king or that foolish mendicant—used well, it heals the deadly schism that blocks us from knowing that we ourselves are divine."

Now his gentle words evoked the image of Pundalik's tender face hovering over her body, crow feces streaking the corners of his eyes. All around, Rudralaya mocked her with its natural splendor. Self-hatred grew into a venomous torrent, making her feel like an abomination in this sanctuary. "Only fools take the short view of existence." Hariaksa chided. "Pundalik died in the flesh, it is true, but his spirit is immortal—it is existence, consciousness and bliss itself. Already it has taken another form and will surely find moksha in this lifetime."

"The fire showed you this?" she cried, amazed that Hariaksa knew even little details such as the name of her dead lover.

"No, but it revealed to me the causes for the tragedies that erupted that black night. Had you stayed firm and used the teachings well, Ishvari, the chain of events that drove you back here tonight would not have occurred. But then again, pain is often how Rudra whips us forward."

"So what happened at the ghats happened for a reason?" she asked skeptically.

"The answer to that lies in the teachings on karma," he replied. "As for Pundalik, what stopped him from leaving you and returning to his own practices? You are to blame *only* for willfully misleading him—and for that you've already paid a terrible price."

This time his loving words penetrated through her fog of self-hatred. A great relief washed over her; she felt as if a venomous serpent bent on crushing her spirit had fallen away from her troubled heart. Wrapping her arms around her knees, she gazed blindly at the river. "Mahadevi appeared to me in the jungle, acharya," she whispered. "She bade me take heart...."

"You see? No matter what you do, you are treasured," Hariaksa cut in, so kindly that bitter tears, dammed up for too long, started flowing again. River reeds swayed in the breeze, brushing against her wet cheeks. An owl hooted from a karnikara tree even as the death cries of an animal echoed through the jungle. She was but one minuscule cog in the large wheel that was Melukhha—one single cog, yet in so pivotal a position that the wheel would grind to a halt until she was dragged back to burn for the gods.

Panic flooded her again; she struggled against the urge to dive into the river and smash her head bloody on underwater rocks. Hariaksa chuckled drily. "Really, sweetling, such a brazen lack of faith...would the gods bring you this far to abandon you now?" White birds winged overhead in the dusky sky; she wished she too could rise into the air and vanish. "Escape is never a solution," Hariaksa laughed. "We're whipped forward by our own karma, into dazzling light."

Tears came again, but now they were tears of gratitude—at least Hariaksa still loved her. The old monk set his hands on the crown of her head, then shook them into the water, as if ridding himself of pollution. "Soon you'll heal from the abuse of the drug. A true tantrika never grovels in the mud, so long as a single star shines."

A chill crept up her spine as she realized that a juggernaut of evil was hurtling toward them; there was nothing she could do to stop it. She clutched at her hurting stomach. "Why don't we leave for the mountains right now?" she asked him desperately. Hariaksa shook his head, his eyes brimming with compassion. "Listen!" he said, putting a hand to his ear. "Takshak's here."

Chariots thundered up Rudralaya's drive. Moments later she heard a single voice, cold and determined. Whimpering, she clutched at the old monk. "Time to disappear, sweetling," he said calmly. "Whatever happens, you *must* keep the faith. Everything will come out all right in the end."

"Won't you come with me?" she begged, grabbing his arm.

"I shall always be with you, sweetling," Hariaksa replied solemnly. "Now go, I've given clear instructions to Maruti…allow him to guide you to safety."

"*Maruti?*" she cried, aghast. "What can a monkey do? *You* must come with me, I won't leave you to that…!" But a cacophony of male voices, furious to find no sign of human life in the main buildings of Rudralaya, drowned her last words. Ishvari threw herself at Hariaksa, sobbing wildly. "Come, please, run away with me!"

"Where were you when I was bride-hunting?" he teased, though his eyes were sad. "No, sweetling, it's destined I remain to face the king. The time has come to pay my final dues."

"Takshak will *kill* you! See what he did to me…to that wild lad of yours…to the Doms…."

Hariaksa's face tightened. "Disobedient to the last! D'you think a petty and corrupt king worries *me*? My body's run its course, but yours you still need…."

The rest of his words were drowned out by the roar of crashing timber. The odors of burning wood assailed her nostrils and the night sky began to glow with an eerie orange and purple light. Takshak was setting Rudralaya on fire! Hariaksa placed two fingers in his mouth and let out a piercing whistle. The branches above their heads rustled and a langur peered down at them, tail arching overhead like a curved spear. It was Maruti, but much bigger after all these years! "Hide her until the soldiers leave, Maruti." Hariaksa ordered. "Then follow my earlier instructions."

Branches slapped at Ishvari's bruised face as sinewy arms hauled her up into the treetops. Then she was in a green world right below the twilit sky. "My spark of light, I'm always with you!" Hariaksa bellowed from down below. A furry hand clamped over her mouth and she was thrust into the center of high trees above the river, guarded by stern, silent, alert langurs.

To the right, she saw flames devouring Rudralaya. The peaked roof of the kitchen collapsed, followed by the meditation hall which came crashing down, pillars and all. Horses whinnied in tremulous bursts that made her hair stand on end. Staccato galloping brought the soldiers to the edge of the river. She looked down to see Hariaksa standing placidly by the water. Maruti faced her, seated on the opposite branch, finger to his mouth. Shamed by his compliance to Hariaksa's wishes, despite his own unease, she subsided into quiet. Way below her, through the filtering smoke, she saw soldiers surrounding Hariaksa. Takshak stood a short distance away. "You, Daruka," she heard the king say. "Strip this fellow naked!"

Daruka again! The same guard who'd stood by Lord Kushal's side in Devikota!

The man hesitated. "He's a sage, sire! The gods punish—"

"Perish the gods and obey your maharajah!" Takshak roared. "Strip the old man and be done with it!"

Daruka approached Hariaksa cautiously.

"I'll undress myself, my good man," Hariaksa assured the massive soldier, pulling his homespun orange robe up and over his head. "Our maharajah has every right to see this old body in all its glory." Hariaksa folded his orange robe neatly and placed it on the ground beside him.

Takshak raked scornful eyes over the monk's flaccid belly, narrow shoulders and skinny, blue-veined bowlegs. Drawing his sword out of its jeweled scabbard, he aimed it at Hariaksa's organ, nesting in gray curls. "Ah, an unused weapon." The king's eyes blazed yellow. "Now tell me—where is she?" he demanded, the tip of his sword meeting the shriveled head of the lingam.

Pain flashed across Hariaksa's face. "In care of the gods you've spurned."

Takshak shook his head indulgently. "None of that mystical babble, if you please. I'm not one of your peasant girls, hanging on to your every word…where have you hidden her?"

Overhead the sky was orange, the air hot and hazy with destruction. "Where you'll never find her," Ishvari heard Hariaksa's calm reply, even as her heart thumped wildly in her chest.

"Is that how you answer your sovereign?" Takshak queried coldly. He shot the sword back into its sheath and swung around to the guardsman hovering nervously beside Hariaksa. "Pick up his robe," he directed. The man obeyed. "Fashion it into a noose." Again the man obeyed, though he'd begun to tremble. "Excellent! Now, if you please, place it around this traitor's neck."

The guard hesitated, but Hariaksa stepped forward and bent his head, inviting the guard to place the noose around his neck. Takshak raised an amused eyebrow, his lips twisting sardonically. "How I love to see a pliant prisoner…now drag him to the river and drown him. I want to see his gods save him—I need a miracle to restore my flagging faith." He folded his arms and glared at Hariaksa. "Nothing to say, you old fake? You'd give your life for a slut?"

Hariaksa's lips twitched with amusement. "Not for a slut, no. But for a high tantrika destined for moksha? Of course I would."

"*High tantrika?*" Takshak echoed in disgust. "*Moksha?* Are you insane? Why, *everyone* knows the Devikotan's a brazen whore!" The king moved forward as if to strike Hariaksa, but the sage held him back effortlessly, using a force radiating from the center of his upraised palm.

"Once you were a fine student, Takshak," Hariaksa spoke calmly. "But you've reached a point that no human crosses without meeting the hammer of the gods. Be wise and hold back—walk toward the light, and many will assist you in restoring Melukhha to her old glory."

Hariaksa dropped his hand, and Takshak came back to life, released by the bizarre force. The king gathered his wits, pulling his shoulders together and looking around in embarrassment—*an old man effortlessly repelling a warrior half his age and twice his size?* He stared at Hariaksa with grudging admiration...so the old chap *did* have a few tricks up his sleeve. He swung around on Daruka. "Nice way of bargaining, eh?" he shot a crooked grin at the burly guardsman. "My redemption for his life, mixed in with some minor sorcery. What say, Daruka, should I consider his offer?" Without waiting for an answer, Takshak gestured to a group of guardsmen. "Enough talk," he barked. "Drown this traitor and be quick about it!"

Two of the guardsmen approached Hariaksa and walked him right to the river's edge. Hands on hips, Takshak followed them with his glittering eyes. "All right, now, immerse him until he stops breathing—and next we'll hunt down the whore."

Aghast, Ishvari tried to rise, ready to surrender in exchange for Hariaksa's life, but Maruti held her down while another langur covered her mouth. *Please,* she begged Maruti with her eyes, but Maruti held fast. Looking down, she saw the gleam of Hariaksa's shaven skull bobbing on the surface of the water before it was gone. The guardsmen were as restless as their sensitive horses, in the grip of supernatural fear. Ishvari saw Takshak's face grow pale. "Pull him out," he ordered after what seemed like an eon. "An *elephant* would drown in that time."

The guardsmen dragged Hariaksa's body out of the water. *"He's alive!"* she heard Takshak's shocked whisper. "Alatu's right— these monks practice sorcery!"

"If that were so," Hariaksa replied serenely, his naked body dripping water, "I'd vanish and leave you to amuse yourself. I'm merely giving myself time to recite my last prayers."

"If the gods—" Takshak began angrily, then stopped— something way beyond the ordinary was happening here. He coughed, nervously. "Don't force me to finish you in this ignominious way, old man," he pleaded. "I bear you no personal animosity. You're a great monk, a *sage.* Remember you've sworn allegiance to Melukhha."

Hariaksa smiled. "To Melukhha, yes. Not to those who seek to destroy her."

Ishvari saw the flash of Takshak's teeth. "You wound me, holy man," he said. "Please note that it was the Devikotan who brought out the beast in me. Perverted as she is, she dazzled me for a while." Takshak laughed, confidingly. "Holy man, a lover learns more in an hour about a woman than a sage learns in a lifetime. Under that exquisite facade, the Devikotan's still the pariah whelp of a profligate sot and a rustic witch. Let me list her crimes…first, she seduced the emissary of Egypt, threatening Melukhhan interests. Then she threw priceless jewels away to buy intoxicants, and used illiterate guardsmen to satiate her lust. Most recently she fucked a mendicant, a fool who hung himself right outside her window! A cuckold she's made of me in the eyes of my people!" Takshak eyes gleamed. "Now, old man, point me in her direction, and I swear by the high and the holy that Atulya and all your monks shall go free!"

Hariaksa chuckled. "So a king who burns good men alive and urges his men to rape and torture defenseless women and children—*he* finds time to worship the holy ones, eh?

Takshak's face twisted in ugly reaction.

"Would *you* trust a man besotted by a sorceress?" Hariaksa continued reasonably. "You should know that the gods Alatu worships are a ravenous lot. They wait patiently to destroy the sacred city, once *she* has sufficiently weakened *you*."

Horror flashed across Takshak's face; he pulled himself together with visible effort. The guardsmen stepped back from the sage's dripping figure, equally shocked. Hariaksa spoke again: "Melukhha was born to flood the three worlds with light, Takshak. Our old kings strove to be fine men, but you were born under a bad star." Hariaksa sighed. "Once many hoped you'd return to your senses, as your father did, but here you are, threatening a sage with physical death when you've been taught that the Self is immortal." Hariaksa patted his flaccid abdomen, a rueful expression on his wizened face. Ignoring Takshak, he turned to the guardsmen. "Your king has passed the pale of all counsel. Shall I permit him to do as he wills with this body?"

"Seal your sanctimonious mouth!" Takshak screeched. "And die, knowing you are an abomination in the eyes of your monarch!" He turned on Daruka. "Drown him this time, or take his place!"

Ishvari began chanting the healing mantra. "Let him go quickly, Mahadevi," she prayed. "Let this be the end, I beseech you!" But the same unbelievable scene took place again. It struck her then that if he so wished, Hariaksa could easily hold his own—not just against Takshak, but against *all* his men; such was his awesome hidden power, the fruit of long dedication to the gods and the sacred fire. Hariaksa's lips were moving now. Light streamed upward from the crown of his head to form a shimmering circle around his body—the sage was practicing a high form of pranayama. Takshak began to shake in earnest. He gestured to the terrified guardsmen to submerge Hariaksa again. This time the men pulled a corpse out of the river.

Slowly her mind began to work again: *what had Hariaksa just said about paying his final dues?* Still, it was *she* who'd led him to this end. This thought made her cry out in pure misery.

"I knew it! The whore's here!" Takshak cried, gazing upward. *"Get her!"*

Ishvari shrank back against the tree trunk as eyes scoured the branches around her, but another little moan escaped her. Takshak swung back. "There!" he cried, pointing to her hiding place, roughly thirty feet above his head. "Right there, hiding in the trees, like the monkey she is. Check this bakula tree in particular—and remember, I want her alive! Tonight a pyre shall burn at the ghats." He laughed, a harsh bark. "Alatu shall have her heart's desire after all."

A soldier was scaling the tree. Simultaneously a langur moaned, mimicking Ishvari's voice. Then another, and another, and another. Even as she understood that they were seeking to confound her pursuers, sinewy arms were lifting her up through the leafy curtain and she was dropped into a dark space cushioned by nutty-smelling leaves. A chattering filled the air as the entire langur clan came alive. Through a hole in the trunk, she saw Maruti leading the mad chorus, exhorting his comrades like the drunken conductor of Devikota's motley village band. Hysteria welled up within her.

"Monkeys, sire, hundreds of them, carrying on like anything. The tantrika's not there—I looked well. Langurs are sensitive beasts—it's the smoke that's disturbed them, I'll wager."

"Are you sure? I could swear I heard a woman's cry!" Takshak's words were drowned by a series of rumbles followed by a thunderous crash—the beams of Rudralaya's main building were falling, sending a gigantic pillar of flame into the air. The dormitory caught fire with an explosive roar. Takshak's voice came to her ears again. "I'll wager she's hiding in the bowels of the city…her gardener knows the area down by the docks like the back of his hand. And if perchance she's escaped Melukhha, she's likely to head for that godforsaken village of hers."

"The ground's shaking, sire. Best get out while we can. Burning down these trees would be quickest…just in case she's hiding up in one of them."

Takshak considered the soldier's suggestion, stamping his feet impatiently on the hot earth. Ishvari almost choked on her fear. "Looks like a small earthquake." The king paused. "What do your hunter's instincts say, Daruka? Is the whore still here?"

"If she reached here at all, sire, the sage would immediately have sent her to safety."

"Right, then, we've wasted enough time. And Daruka, if you please, never again refer to the old fellow as a sage—black magician would suit him better." Takshak thumped the tree trunk closest to him. "I've burnt enough of these beauties for a lifetime…arrange to have these cut and transported to Melukhha and instruct the royal architect to use the wood for my mistress's new home." Takshak's strength was returning. "Come on, ride!" he cried. "I'll wager the Devikotan's still in the city. Let's smoke her out!"

Takshak aimed a vicious kick at Hariaksa's body. "You there!" he shouted, beckoning to a hefty soldier. "Carry this wretched thing with you and make sure it is publicly displayed at the quadrangle. Nail its extremities to wood for all to see—the corpse of a so-called sage is an effective deterrent to treason." He turned to another guard. "*And you!* Lead a thousand soldiers into the center of the city with instructions to spread the word of the whore's flight. Offer a gold reward—get the exact amount from Charaka. We must finish her fast, before the contagion of rebellion spreads."

"Through the woods, sire," a man yelled. "The front of the ashram's in flames."

"The jungle route it is," Takshak said. "But where's this damned light coming from?"

Ishvari peered out of the hole and down through thick branches. A mantle of shimmering light was spreading everywhere, dimming even the flames from the raging fire. And it was rising up from the river, originating from where Hariaksa had been drowned!

"The black rites have surely been practiced here," Takshak announced, unable to disguise his mounting fear. He swung around to face Daruka. "Take three men and go through the jungle to the whore's village. You know where it lies? Tell the village elders *everything*! Warn them she's been marked a criminal pariah by my personal order, and order them on pain of death to inform me immediately if she's sighted."

Takshak covered his eyes with his hands as if exhausted. Ishvari held her breath. "Hey Daruka, the whore's mother and brother still live there," he said, in a casual afterthought. "Hang the boy, and blind the mother right after—make sure she never forgets her last sight." He turned on Daruka with a muttered curse. "Why so pale, fool? Is this so terrible after what you've already done for me?" He shook his head. "Damn this mist, it's blinding me."

A buzz broke out as Daruka sped away, his giant frame dwarfing his thoroughbred. Ishvari saw others in the eerie, light-streaked fog mounting their horses and heading out, circling the lake, and moving through the trees into thicker jungle. *Was it just hours ago that Mandakini, Vasudeva and herself had taken that same route?*

Maruti reached into the hole and drew her out gently. His small eyes were blinking furiously—the smoke was aggravating the monkeys, and her own lungs gasped for air. Ishvari looked at him, tears streaming down her cheeks. Despite the coils of sorrow wrapping themselves around her heart, she would never forget his quick-thinking support.

Ishvari bowed her head, fighting for clarity; another death on her head, this time Obalesh, the infant with the rosebud mouth she'd adored. *And Sumangali to be blinded?* It would take Daruka time to assemble his men. If she could get to the jungle hermitage where Rudralaya's monks made their long meditation retreats, she could beg the guru to help her rescue them. Even if it meant sacrificing her own life, she would lead her mother and brother to the mountain sanctuary. As she stepped out of the hole and onto the fork of the tree, she saw the dusty imprint of the soldier's sandals. "O Mahadevi!" she gasped, "grant me awareness of the reason I still live!"

Body juddering with aftershock, she joined Maruti, waiting impatiently for her on the ground below. Together they found the exact spot where Hariaksa had been drowned. Hundreds of langurs let out a low keening sound as she stood on the banks that had served as her real classroom in utter despair—many who had loved her were gone, and all because of her.

Really, Ishvari, she heard Hariaksa chuckle. *As if one soul holds such great power over the fates of others! You are only responsible for the waste of your own great potential.*

"Where are you, acharya?" she cried, hoping to see him hobbling out from behind a tree with a mischievous grin on his face. *Everywhere!* his disembodied voice teased her. *In earth, water, fire and wind. This is your time to grow, my firebrand. Aim for the stars, aim for the stars.*

Maruti tugged at her hand and pointed towards the jungle. She had no choice but to follow his agile body, one tired step at a time, until the darkening jungle swallowed them.

Be bold and wise.
Give thyself to the field with me.
Arise!
> —*Bhagavad Gita*

BLIND

Fatigue shrouded Ishvari like an iron cloak, but Maruti pulled her along, refusing to let her rest. Nagging pains slashed through her stomach at intervals, accompanied by waves of nausea; something was very wrong with her body, but even in her dazed conditions she knew Maruti was right to push her forward—survival, not just her own, but that of Sumangali's and Obalesh's—hinged on persuading the hermitage monks to rescue her family before Daruka and his men executed Takshak's inhuman orders.

Maruti gave her a nudge and Ishvari raised her head, gasping at the sight of the colossal banyan tree Hariaksa had said was barely a stone's throw from the hermitage. Over a thousand years old and likely to last twice as long, the spreading giant possessed unimaginable beauty in the silver of moonlight. Hariaksa claimed a band of tantrics still performed rites of love beneath its aerial canopy on full moon nights. Roots from sky to earth, she thought fuzzily, noting that part of its primary trunk had been stripped of bark so initiates could inscribe upon it a thousand names of the gods as part of their ritual worship. Grateful their journey was at an end, at least for this insane night, she stumbled forward and bent low to place her cracked lips on the base of its trunk. Then, forcing herself to rise, she lurched forward.

Hariaksa had praised the jungle hermits for their resourcefulness. Their leader, a friend of Atulya and Hariaksa, was himself a renowned healer. Perhaps her pitiful condition would persuade him to help her despite her fugitive status? Devikota was not far, and at least one of the monks would know the shortest path that led to that rustic hellhole. Once the monks left for Devikota, she'd beseech the healer for a sleeping potion. Sleep would temporarily erase her fearsome situation and infuse her with strength. Tomorrow she would beg the patriarch for provisions, and for a sturdy monk or two to guide the three of them to the mountain sanctuary.

Then Maruti raised his face skyward and began to dart back and forth, sniffing the air. He rushed to her side and pulled her back, yammering urgently. "What's wrong?" she asked, her neck muscles tightening. He reached forward and placed a finger on her lips, then fell back to all fours and patted her feet, indicating she should stand still.

Ishvari watched him shoot up an upper branch of the banyan tree and peer into the distance, sniffing and wrinkling his nose. Then she smelled it too—burning wood! The langur leapt down and shoved her urgently back along the path they'd just trod. "What did you see, Maruti?" she whispered, her heart thudding again. He spun around, pointing toward the jungle ashram, rolling his eyes and mimicking the motion of flames. She understood him—Takshak and his men had burned the hermitage to the ground—her rescue plans were literally dissolving into smoke! And here she was, still alive, the criminal at the source of this spiraling misery, sick and exhausted, trapped in thick jungle with only a monkey to aid her.

Escape took on an even greater momentum, her body moving without regard to her crazy mind. Now they were entering denser jungle, where the trees grew so thick no moonlight could penetrate. Parallel to them, a beast dragged something across tangled undergrowth. Glimpses of gold and black stripes told her it was a tiger. Maruti threw her into the tall grass, and they heard the animal growling softly as it fed. The beast lifted his tawny head, sniffed the air, then returned to tearing off chunks of flesh. After an eon, they watched it drag away the remains of his feast.

Soon they were on their way again. Darkness brought the sounds of predators and their prey roaming the wilderness into frightening proximity—without Maruti, Ishvari knew she'd be long dead. Her stomach rumbled, and her mouth felt thick and woolly, bedeviled by thirst and the bristly dread that festered within. Incapable of taking another step, she crouched at the base of a tree so tall she could not see where crown met sky.

Maruti loped away and returned with a bunch of wild mangoes, their ripe odor making her want to retch despite her empty stomach. Peeling the biggest one, he offered her the naked orange orb. She held the fruit over her tongue, allowing its juice to dribble into her parched mouth. Her teeth sank into the flesh, eating around the stone inside; then, almost deliriously, she was recalling happy evenings with Archini, gorging on wild mangoes as they lay beside the river, spinning the hairy denuded seeds in wide arcs into the febrile depths of the jungle.

The langur ate too, all the while keeping a sharp eye on her. When she was done, he peeled another for her, but she pushed it away, too tired to exercise her jaws. The langur gobbled it up himself, then smashed a mango between his hard palms, made a hole at one end with a fingernail, and handed it to her, indicating she should drink the pulp. Tears flooded her eyes—on her second day at Rudralaya, as she'd lain homesick in her little room, Hariaksa had dropped by, jiggling a ripe bunch of jungle mangoes, and fed her in just this way. At that precise moment it struck her that both the earthquake as well as the luminous mist had been signs that Hariaksa had achieved the grand enlightenment at the moment of death.

"Why did you save me, Maruti?" she burst out angrily. "How can I get them out of Devikota all on my own? Better if you'd saved Hariaksa instead!"

Maruti hung his silver head in empathy. Weary beyond belief, Ishvari laid her head on a tree stump and covered her eyes with the back of a grimy hand. It wasn't long before Maruti was yammering insistently again, skipping around her in circles until she simply had to rise and follow him. High in the sky above stars winked like tiny diamonds. All around the jungle stirred, crawling with the unseen. A jackal howled, long and low. Slowly, the urge to live reasserted itself; Hariaksa had sacrificed his life for hers; the least she could do was to fight for her own. Silently chanting the healing mantra, she followed Maruti into sparser jungle, lit by moon rays.

A herd of chital slipped through the trees ahead. Maruti had brought her to the edge of the jungle, but where in all seven hells was she? She took a step forward, then another, until the langur stopped her with a tug at her garment and drew her down to his level, warning her to hide. Looking ahead, she saw why—they had reached human habitation.

As her eyes adjusted to the stronger light, she saw fields of wheat quivering in moon glow and the contours of a dwelling built on a slope. With a shock, she realized that Maruti had led her to the outskirts of Devikota! In fact, the rambling house on the hill belonged to Andhaka! Torches flickered in the fields behind it and she heard the buzz of voices, followed by the rhythm of hoofbeats. Soldiers were not arriving, she realized with a shock, but leaving, the hard gallop of their horses receding into the night.

The village square where Takshak had ordered Daruka to carry out his inhuman sentence lay a stone's throw from Andhaka's home. She crawled forward, inch by inch along the boundary of the fields, then cut through them, thanking Mandakini for the protection afforded by her rough garb. A dog barked, the sound grating fiercely on her nerves. Behind her an owl hooted. Crouching behind a clump of shade trees, she peered down into the torch-lit square.

Andhaka stood on the earthen dais, beside him was the unmistakable figure of Ghora, plumper, with shaven head and white robes. In the center of the square she saw figures moving around a child's sturdy body swinging from a wooden pole fixed in the earth. A woman knelt at the base of the stand, so still she might have been stone. Pain hit Ishvari like a murderer's blow to her throat—she knew without a doubt that the dead child was Obalesh, the kneeling figure her mother. Her heart pounded so hard she feared it would fly right out of her chest. Meanwhile, Maruti had disappeared.

"So it's done then." Andhaka's bullying voice came to her ears. "People of Devikota, we're lucky the soldiers left us alive! Give thanks to the gods, and to Ghora, who collaborated with the guardsmen in executing these punishments. He's pledged Devikota's cooperation in apprehending Ishvari, ex-High Tantrika of Melukhha. Now I ask him to address you."

Ghora's jarring treble cut through the air. "Close to thirteen years ago in *this* very square, I warned the envoy the girl Ishvari was possessed by a demon. He scorned me, that great noble, though I served merely as a humble mouthpiece of Mahadevi. Indeed, Sumangali herself spoke of the odd meeting of sun and moon at the time of her daughter's birth, so grave a portent I quailed at her admission. And yet the envoy seemed excited by her words." Ghora shook his head in disbelief. "My people, the demon was awake even then, hoodwinking that astute man!"

"God's balls! What pretty stories you spin!" a slurred voice shouted. "As I recall it, the little shrew told the envoy you were fucking her mother, whereupon you ran and hid behind Aboli's skirts." The man guffawed. "Now do finish up glorifying yourself and let us go, oh great priest—it's wickedly hard to digest your lies in the middle of the night."

"Shut your mouth, Kutsa!" Andhaka roared. "Or I'll do it for you, permanently this time!" The headman raked his eyes over the excited crowd, reiterating his warning to all present. Ghora turned to Andhaka and bowed, an oily smile on his porcine face, before turning back to the now quiet crowd. "Tonight the maharajah's own guardsmen confirmed my suspicions," he continued, unfazed. "Under the influence of the sacred herb, the false tantrika offered her body to an Egyptian royal before seducing a mendicant and driving him to suicide. Only the gods know how many other good men she'd already victimized!" Ghora inclined his chin toward the inert figure. "There lies Sumangali, mother of this evil woman and a sorceress in her own right. In just retribution, you witnessed her blinded by order of the maharajah, at the precise moment following her son's death!"

"Why not finish her off right *now*?" a woman hissed. "We could stone her to death and no one would be the wiser...their entire bloodline's damned!"

"You speak truth, Jhumari," an older woman's voice cut in tremulously. "The moment the witch came to Devikota, I sensed her evil....her beauty was the sort a demoness conjures up when she enters the human realm. Our husbands began to stray only after she arrived here, do you recall, sisters? Even our pious priest, loyal to the high ones since his auspicious birth, was once caught in her snare." Angry muttering rose and fell around the speaker. The woman raised a hand for silence and got it. "That same year, mere moons after Hiranya married her, the rains began to fail," she continued in a tremolo. "The drought worsened when the girl Ishvari was born, though oddly enough, Hiranya's own orchards continued to produce rich crops."

The speaker paused, allowing a new round of ominous rumbling to rise and fade before resuming. "Think you it was an accident that Hiranya's parents *both* died, one after the other, leaving Sumangali solely in charge of that prosperous household? Ha! Or that heavy rains finally blessed our region again the year *after* the envoy took the girl away? Ha! Sinful things were *always* happening in that house! I'd say it was when the girl was too young to defend herself that Sumangali sent the demon into her—for some nefarious reason we virtuous folk cannot comprehend. This, I am told, is the particular skill of a witch. Now I urge even the softest hearts among you—do not feel a flash of misguided pity for this blind wretch moaning before us!"

Ishvari identified the voice as belonging to Andhaka's first wife, mother of Labuki—which was why the Devikotans were listening to her false diatribe so intently. Wind rustled the branches of arka trees. Another woman wailed, "Mahadevi knows I'm heavy with child! The shadow of this accursed family must no longer fall upon our people. I say stone the sorceress to death as she lies in the dust!"

"*Shut up!* All of you *shut up!*" Andhaka shouted fiercely, slamming his fist into his palm. "The maharajah's orders were clear—the woman was to be *blinded*, not killed. Takshak wished for her to feel pain for the length of her life."

"The king can afford to be generous," another woman sniffed resentfully. "*He* doesn't have to suffer her foul presence. Throw her back into her hovel, I say—she'll either starve to death, or a beast from that haunted wilderness will get her. One way or another, we'll be rid of her."

As if aware of the malignance concentrated on her person, Sumangali groaned and keeled over. Ishvari sucked in her breath, hugging the tree to stop from falling as pain cut through her lower body. She stuffed a fist into her mouth to stop from moaning just as something tore itself loose inside her womb. Clots of blood accompanied by chunks of a translucent substance slipped out of her yoni to splatter on to the earth. Matter resembling the spongy goats' liver the butcher in Devikota used to display in his shop window followed, slipping down the cliffs and on to the rocky fringes of Devikota. Blood streamed out of her, staining the moonlit soil crimson.

Fighting a flood of pain and dizziness, Ishvari clung desperately to the tree, numb with disbelief—*had she actually lost a fetus without even knowing she was pregnant?* The last few moons had passed in such a blur of intoxicated passion, she hadn't even noticed that her red flow had ceased. The violent group rape she'd survived had likely sparked the miscarriage.

She forced herself to look down at the square again, identifying Ghora through a haze of loathing. Arms on hips, the priest gazed down at Sumangali's crumpled figure, a mocking smile on his lips. "Where's Shani?" he called. A broad-shouldered man she recognized as Devikota's blacksmith came to the front of the crowd. "Hoi, Shani! Pick a comrade and cart the witch to her hovel. Take the boy's corpse with you too, and toss it into the jungle along the way—that'll save us the fuel of burning the cursed thing. Do not fear—I'll be chanting a mantra to protect you from all witchery." Ghora shut his eyes and his lips moved. Then he addressed the crowd again.

"People of Devikota! Should the fugitive Ishvari attempt to hide somewhere in our village, we must capture her *instantly*! Be warned—the chief guardsman informed me her indwelling demon assumes fantastic shapes! I exhort you for the sake of Devikota—light specially prepared incense for protection before you sleep. My good wife Labuki holds a supply you may purchase before you disperse. And chant the old hymns at the break of dawn to protect your children from her spells. The sins of this sorceress must not further taint the innocent lives of our offspring!"

So Ghora had married Labuki! And now the priest had finally avenged the insults Sumangali had hurled at him that distant morning. Incense or not, Ghora would sleep well tonight, the sadistic fraud. Ishvari struggled with rage and terror as Ghora's voice continued to flow, unctuous as sesame oil. "People of Devikota! I beg you not to treat this matter lightly—a fortune in gold hangs upon its tail! Let each of us cooperate in trapping the whore. As your priest, I assure you it is an honorable way to assure our future."

Weak with the continuing loss of blood, Ishvari watched impotently as the men tossed her mother's limp body on to the cart like a sack of goat droppings and moved in the direction of her cottage, to the accompaniment of the crowd's hoots and jeers. Help her, Mahadevi! she cried silently, sinking on to her haunches as she mourned for Obalesh, Sumangali, and the scraps of matter lying on the rocks of Devikota; if a wild animal missed the aborted fetus tonight, she thought with a shudder, the vultures would feast tomorrow.

Winds howled as a shadow formed on the earth beside her. Paralyzed with fear, she saw a great beast lower its body before her. Maruti darted from behind a pile of rocks to leap upon its neck, then gesticulated for her to join him. Rising with difficulty, she grabbed the langur's shoulders and sank down behind him, on to the powerful satiny back of the leopard.

The big cat stood, carrying his double burden with ease. Then they were hurtling across rustling wheat fields, past silent homes, barking dogs and ghostly herds of cattle in Devikota's dry pastures, before climbing higher and higher and higher, right into the aromatic womb of the forbidden valley.

And all things hang on me as precious gems upon a string.
    —*Bhagavad Gita*

AND THE RIVER LAUGHED

The springy kusha matting beneath her battered body felt so wonderful when she awoke the next morning that Ishvari burst into a torrent of grateful tears. No, she had not dreamed the ghastly events of last night—death had been staring her in the face when the leopard had arrived in a blur of speed, to transport Maruti and herself from the dreary fringes of Devikota to the airy stone temple she'd first set eyes upon as a pariah child.

She lay still for long moments, mentally confronting the horrors of her recent past; only the gods could explain why *she* had been brought back to her earliest sanctuary when so many better souls had passed on. A vivid image of the big cat resting his head on the sadhu's lap arose—was he the same beast she'd glimpsed as a child? Then Nartaka's handsome face flashed across her mind, followed by images of the ash-swathed hermit of the valley, the dissenter at Devikota's square, the gnostic healer, and the masked tantric who'd come so close to rescuing her at the ghats: *could all these extraordinary men possibly be one and the same?*

The mere thought of the sadhu's possible proximity made her strangely happy. She gazed out the open window toward the stretch of the valley below, shimmering with the rainbow colors of autumn. It amazed her that after the monstrous events that had swept her through death, degradation, flight and murder, she was back in the comfort of a beautiful day.

In the distance, a herd of deer slipped gracefully through a grove of shade trees. Hariaksa had compared her crude search for happiness to the antics of the musk deer. *One must go within when there's trouble without*, he'd advised, for the entire cosmos was contained within the microcosm of the body, hidden within the spiritual heart. If she explored this truth with faith, she wondered now, would it lead her again to samadhi, and to the permanent end of suffering? In Hariaksa's memory, and in honor of the unseen powers that had returned her to this haven, she solemnly resolved to follow this sacred path.

Sitting up, she wiggled her toes and moved her legs. The intense fatigue of the day before was gone, but she was still weak with loss of blood, and drained by her crazed flight. Yet she felt so feather-light that she imagined that the breeze wafting in through the windows could sweep her up and out into the halcyon skies. In the distance, she saw Maruti scrambling down a slope.

Ishvari stood, noting that only one of her sandals sat by the door; the other must have fallen off during her astounding ride up to the valley. On a ledge on the other side of the sunny room sat a bowl of ripe mangoes and a clay vessel of clear water. Miniature bananas, the honey sweet jungle variety hinting of cinnamon, hung from a wooden hook hammered into the wall. Her tummy rumbled; she was coming to life again.

Breaking a banana off the stem, she stepped outdoors, noticing that the temple's slate roof had been cleverly sloped so rain would not flood the interior. On a nearby rock, a cobra wriggled out of its skin and slithered away, leaving its transparent casing behind. She ate the sweet fruit, blinking happily in the pale gold of sunshine as she absorbed the breathtaking loveliness of the valley. Color dotted every angle and nook, foliage clustered and spilled in shades of green, red, gold and brown, and the surrounding ring of mountains gleamed silver. Something timeless and divine enshrouded her then, seeping in through her pores.

All is god, a sure voice within her whispered. *Every blade of grass, every clod of earth, every petal of every wild flower, every drop of water in the river, every breath of air, even the droppings of birds winging across the sky.*

"What of Takshak?" she asked the Self, sitting on the edge of the rock where the serpent had shed its skin. "Can a murderer be divine?"

How can he not? it said calmly. *We all manifest from one single source, and it's to this same source that we all return when bodies and minds dissolve.*

"What of Ghora and Andhaka?" she asked, her voice trembling.

There are no exceptions, was the reply. *God seeds lie within their hearts too.*

"Why such a brazen lie?" she cried furiously. "Can murderer and sage be equal?"

Equal no, for one has transcended lower nature, while the other drowns in it, the Self clarified. *Still, their ultimate destination is the same.*

"If you're so damnably wise," she cried through clenched teeth, "explain to me why one saves and the other destroys!"

Did you not hear Hariaksa speaking to Takshak by the river? Self chuckled. *Only ignorance separates sage and criminal, though this ignorance does form a ghastly divide.*

Morning blazed into afternoon which faded into twilight. When stars emerged, winking like diamonds in the vastness of the sky, Ishvari realized she'd spent the day contemplating the wisdom of the Self. No longer muffled by the demon of illusion, the inner voice was sure, though it expressed the bizarre and the indigestible. And yet she could not doubt it any more; instead she doubted the warped thinking of the hedonist she'd become, and the narcissism that had prevented her from using the jewels of wisdom strewn in her path. When the sun began its blazing descent, she had not stirred, but towers of doubt had melted into fields of wonder.

Who am I? she asked the trees and the murmuring river, shivering with both fear and delight. Not the miserable village girl who'd quailed at the sight of Lord Kushal, nor the brightest student at Rudralaya, nor the celebrated high tantrika, nor the intoxicated whore of Melukhha. *What was my original face before I was born?* In the stillness of that moment, the world around her opened wide, as if she stood on the highest peak of the Triple World.

Listen to me from hereon! promised the Self, echoing across the valley like divine thunder. *You are that which has always existed, exists now, and will exist forever. Sink deeply into this truth and enjoy the bliss that is your true nature.*

"Why didn't you tell me this before?" she asked tenderly.

I tried, countless times. But you, stubborn child of the stars, did you listen?

Ishvari sat by the river until the sun tumbled behind the mountain range in a crashing blaze of colors, allowing twilight to shadow the valley. She saw Maruti running up the slope, gesticulating wildly. An old woman blundered up the valley's steep sides behind him. Ishvari stood up, ready to flee. *"Wait!"* the intruder yelled imperiously, raising a withered hand. Ishvari stayed her ground, watching the woman reach the far edge of the lake and drop with a curse to its moist banks. With excruciating slowness, she cupped water in her hand and brought it to her mouth, slurping crudely as she fixed bloodshot eyes on Ishvari. "Food!" she ordered curtly. "Food, girl, and fast!"

The hag was filthy, garbed in soiled rags—and yet the rags were silken and their hems shimmered with dirt-encrusted goldwork! Was she an exiled aristocrat fallen on hard times? A witch who'd lost her customers, daring to traverse a region forsaken by ordinary humans? "There's...there's food in the hut," Ishvari stammered. She clambered up the slope, aware of sharp eyes boring into her back. Grabbing the bananas, she flew back down to find her unwelcome guest lying on her back, staring up at the darkening sky. Even prone, she intimidated Ishvari. Timidly, Ishvari placed the fruit by her side.

"Takes off like a terrified ass and returns with a sorry bunch of bananas," the hag snorted. "And I thought she meant *real* food! Come on, feed me," she ordered insolently, making no attempt to rise. Quivering with dread, Ishvari felt again the terror of the ghats, the ravages of flight, the mindless cruelty inflicted on so many, all topped by the loss of the fetus. Guilt and grief hammered at her hard. Would this creature leave if she obeyed her without a fuss?

Kneeling beside the hag, Ishvari peeled a banana and held it out to her. "I said *feed me!*" she shrieked, opening her mouth wide to reveal rotting teeth. Ishvari recoiled with the putrid stench of her. She swallowed the banana whole, like a python swallowing prey. "More!" she ordered, placing her hands beneath her head to gaze up at the sky. She let out a coarse guffaw as Ishvari peeled another banana. "First she brings me bananas, saving the mangos for herself," she grumbled to an invisible audience. "And now she's doling out these cheap fruit as if they were gold...what's the world come to, may I ask, when a guest of my standing is treated so poorly?"

How had the hag known about the mangos? A goggle-eyed Maruti watched them from the highest branch of a fig tree. Ishvari glanced imploringly up at him, but the brave beast who had saved her life against fearsome odds was now paralyzed with terror. She turned back to find the hag leaning on a grubby elbow and smiling maliciously. "Resurrected by the inferior victuals of a defiled tantrika," she announced to the valley at large. Ishvari stared at the crone in horror. "Oh my stars, my writhing serpents, what a frightful ninny the girl is," she cackled. "To think Takshak hunts a wretched chit! Oh, oh, oh, what a howling, hysterical laugh!"

"Who *are* you?" Ishvari quavered.

"All in good time, my holy harlot," the hag rasped, squinting evilly at Ishvari as she rubbed at the grime embedded in the pores of her face with broken and dirty nails. She hawked up a blood-streaked ball of phlegm and spat it upward towards Maruti, who shrank back into the tree, but made no move to flee. "Now tell me," the intruder giggled obscenely, "have you been making plans for your future?" She glanced at the river and waggled her bushy gray eyebrows. "Will I see your corpse floating down this river on my next visit perchance? Or will you sacrifice yourself to the fire in Melukhha's noble tradition, gathering wood for your own pyre, tears pouring down your silly face as you bemoan your fate?"

The witch chuckled, hugely entertained by her own words. "Know what I know?" she shouted up at a cowering Maruti. "If the stupid slut didn't have *one* single enemy," she roared, obsidian slits of eyes glinting. "If the entire universe simply *adored* her! If rocks and flowers and curs and serpents all bowed and licked and kissed her pampered bottom—she'd *still* do a superb job of destroying herself! That's our shining star of Devikota!"

"Who *are* you?" Ishvari cried again, her mind running feverishly over recent events—not even Mandakini nor Vasudeva could have discovered where she was! She turned away to hide the rush of tears. Should she beg the crone for mercy? Convince her how genuinely sorry she was for her crimes? That she wished to spend the rest of her life making amends? A soft laugh floated into the air and Ishvari whirled around. The hag was gone; in her place was a delicate yogini gleaming like a crescent moon in pure sky, naked except for a garland of munja grass around her swelling hips.

Who am I? the yogini smiled. *One of the sixty-four yoginis of this sacred valley. I came to you in disguise to ascertain that you are ready to transform—and you are, for I see that your heart has been cleansed of all demonic influence.*

The sixty-four yoginis! Seekers who, after eons of fierce practice, had won their way into the inner circle of Mahadevi, the Great Goddess!

The Melukhhan debacle has revealed to you that all hedonism is fueled by illusion, the sparkling yogini cut wordlessly into her thoughts. *You created an awful mess despite your great gifts and many blessings, Ishvari, but now you must firmly shut the door on the past and turn your attention to your mother, who suffers horribly as the direct result of your fall.*

Ishvari sank down in worship, stunned by her unearthly beauty.

The time has come to make your amends, the yogini transmitted. *Be swift and decisive and win the battle against your lower nature forever! Start by bringing Sumangali here. Care for her, even as you begin your true inner work. The highway to enlightenment opens rarely, and those who miss the critical turn are lost.*

"Bring my mother to this valley?" Ishvari quavered.

The yogini inclined her glorious head. *Agitated by the false priest, the villagers plan to burn Sumangali to death in her cottage before the moon is full again. Tonight you may rest, but tomorrow you must go to Devikota and bring your mother back with you.*

"You are powerful," Ishvari whispered. "Can't *you* bring her here? I swear to make her happy, to care for her like a loving daughter should."

The yogini's eyes shone with compassion. *This valley is charged by the enlightenment of many beings, beloved, which is why your body has healed so quickly. And though it may appear to be that way from time to time, you are never ever alone.* Her exquisite hands fluttered like silver moths in the fading light. *We shall help you in other ways, but this one task you must do yourself. We bid you use your time here well: shine light on hidden faults and let go of bitterness. Confront all you find repulsive and help the helpless. Tread boldly on both holy and unholy ground, and keep in mind that a yogini seeks balance. Do these things well, and by the crescent on your palm, you will know your true self to be as limitless and pure as the sky.*

A breeze swirled across the valley, cooling Ishvari's cheeks as she blinked back tears of gratitude. Musk and the fragrance of sandalwood filled the air. Then she was alone again. In a trance, she entered the hut and fell asleep. At some point in the night she awoke and saw the leopard pacing up and down outside the hut. As Hariaksa had taught her, she sent him vibrations of kinship. To her joy, the beast turned and stared at her through the window, yellow eyes glowing. Now she felt certain this was the same leopard she'd glimpsed as a child.

"Vegavat!" she cried. The word rose spontaneously to her lips and it meant 'swift'. Over a decade had elapsed since she'd seen him racing up the slope of the valley, and last night he'd carried Maruti and herself here in an effortless burst of sustained speed. Yes, she would name him Vegavat and love him as if he were the respected senior male member of her new family.

The big cat halted briefly in the moonlight, as if hearing her thoughts. Turning towards her, he padded lightly to the open window, his rosette-patterned tail flicking slowly from side to side. Now he was so close Ishvari could see the golden hue of his eyes, and yet she felt not the slightest spark of fear. The possibility that Nartaka had sent him to rescue her from almost certain death, and to be her protector in this magnificent valley, exhilarated her. She sat up, gazing deeply into Vegavat's unblinking eyes, and he gazed steadily back, as if affirming their bond. Then, with a majestic swing of his tail, he resumed pacing. Profoundly comforted, Ishvari sank back into sleep. When dawn broke, she found Maruti seated beside her, holding a bright yellow pumpkin in his arms.

"O Maruti, my precious friend," she cried, flinging her arms around him. He wriggled free, holding the pumpkin above his head and darting over to the fireplace, above which rose the chimney. The fireplace was stocked with wood. She found a wooden board and a knife, skinned and chopped the vegetable, and tossed the pieces into a clay pot containing spring water.

Maruti pointed her toward two stones and made as if to strike them one against the other. Laughing at how well he communicated with her, she did so. As sparks flew, she held the driest twig she could find to them, watching it flare into light. She threw the burning twig into the pile of wood and hung the pot on the copper beam above the fire to cook. Getting down on her haunches, she reached for Maruti and held him tight. "If not for you and Vegavat, my wonderful friend," she whispered, "vultures would be feasting on my corpse right now."

Mashing the pumpkin into a fragrant mush, she poured it into three clay bowls and carried them out to the wooden stoop, placing the third on the side of the cottage for Vegavat. The last time she'd eaten pumpkin mush was the day before Lord Kushal had come to Devikota. She shut her eyes and saw her mother's burnt out sockets staring emptily into a merciless future. "How to get her out of there, Maruti?" she asked bleakly, shuddering at the thought.

Maruti spun around until he was facing the overgrown trail that led past her old cottage to the village of Devikota, nodding his head and gibbering earnestly. Did she dare return? If caught, she'd be dragged back to Melukhha to face an excruciating death. But darkness would shield her as she traversed the craggy path that led through the hills and directly down to the orchard, avoiding village homes and vicious guard dogs. And the yogini had promised her protection, had she not? Whatever happened, Ishvari decided, she would attempt to rescue Sumangali tonight. Had not both Ketaki and Hariaksa given their lives to save hers?

Ishvari found a grassy spot to sit in vajrasana, the pose of the diamond, digesting her meal as the sun kissed her body with welcome warmth. Maruti wandered off without a backward look, but she knew he would return. Walking down to the gurgling river, she stripped down to her bare skin and slapped the handwoven cotton garments against river rocks to loosen the dirt. Then she rinsed them clean under the clear water, praising all the gods that Mandakini had garbed her thus.

Draping the wet clothes on sun-warmed rocks to dry, she slipped into the water, mountain cold and clear as diamond, washing the muck off her body and streaming hair. Tomorrow, if all went well with her plan to rescue Sumangali, she'd forage for herbs and edible wild flowers, berries and nuts, perhaps even find shikakai berries, and prepare the soapy cleansing paste that keeps hair thick and black.

She walked naked up to the cottage and rested, her body still weak. To think she'd been ignorant of the life sprouting within her own womb! But here, in the brazen splendor of the valley, she knew she could stop mourning the fetus she'd miscarried, as well as all the others who'd died on her account. Tonight, before determination waned, she'd rescue her mother and begin the process of burning the mountains of bad karma she had so carelessly accumulated. But what if blind Sumangali took her for a ghost and roused the village with her screams? *What ifs*—there were always too many. If she gave in to doubt, fear would mushroom and sap her will.

The sun was setting when she awoke. She carried the dirty vessels down to the river and scrubbed them with handfuls of river mud before rinsing them off. Setting them on a sunny rock, she collected her dry clothes. Then she fashioned a rough broom out of the fronds of a shade tree, and with hands that had not done menial work for too long, set about sweeping the cottage.

She restocked the fireplace with fresh twigs and used the bundle of fresh kusha matting she'd found in the alcove to create a second sleeping area for herself—Sumangali could sleep on the thicker matting. In another corner, she found a pouch containing two loincloths and a pair of rope sandals. She slipped her feet into the sandals, finding them loose but wearable. It made her ridiculously happy to think they most likely belonged to Nartaka. She would wear them tonight, to protect her from thorns and other spiny creatures that lay in ambush for naked feet.

For the first time in moons, she meditated, choosing to sit by the banks of the river. As her concentration deepened, the trees spoke to her and she understood their timeless, symbiotic dance with earth, wind and water, their submission to the changing seasons, to death, decay, and to the resurgence of life. An eagle soared high overhead and she flew with it, feeling her wings beating against the wind in the cool rays of the emergent moon. When she returned to the river, her inner ear opened, and she heard it laughing at her in a thousand voices.

Was it laughing because she'd been reduced to nothing? At the insidious desires that drove men and women crazy, stealing them away from the sunlight of their spirits, blinding them with ephemeral sense pleasures? Yet, listening with her heart, she understood its laughter to be compassionate, not vicious nor destructive.

When the moon rose high, she returned to the hut to dress. Leaving the mangos for Sumangali, she placed the rest of the bananas and a leather water pouch into a woven bag she slung over her shoulder. Since it would take much longer to traverse the winding, pebble strewn trail leading to her old home in darkness, she raced down to the river, filled the pouch with water and headed for the edge of the jungle. But where was Maruti?

The moon was kind, beaming softly to light her way. Silently she chanted the healing mantra which soon began to vibrate within her, keeping lurking spirits at bay. A shadow joined her soon after—Maruti had arrived. Relieved, she reached down to pat his furry head. Together they moved forward, bypassing clumps of thorn trees and rocks, Maruti taking the lead, turning around frequently to ensure she was all right.

Through the darkness, she glimpsed the old cottage. The thought of her blind mother alone in that grimy stone hut gripped her with such intense sorrow that she came to an abrupt halt. Motioning to Maruti to wait for her, she walked stealthily to the window. In the dim light, she made out a woman sitting hunched on the sleeping mat in the corner. Assailed by grief, Ishvari called out softly: "Maa, it's me!"

The figure shifted into a band of moonlight. "Obalesh?" her mother cried hoarsely. "Obalesh, my son, is it you?" There was such incredulous hope in her voice Ishvari was struck dumb. "Answer me!" Sumangali urged. "Even if you're a ghost, you're still my beloved son, always my Obalesh...."

But Ishvari could not speak, and the excitement in her mother's pinched face guttered, like the flame of an oil lamp in gusty wind. "I'm imagining things again," Sumangali muttered. "Yesterday it was Hiranya calling for his dinner, and now it's Obalesh. Of course I'm mad! Is there a woman born who could lose husband, daughter and son and not go utterly insane?"

Sumangali rocked back and forth inconsolably, uttering harsh sobs that made Ishvari wince. "How could it be *you* calling me, son? Before my eyes they strung you up and snuffed the prana out of you—can humans hang a five-year-old boy? No, those men were demons in disguise! Then Ghora said Takshak had burned my daughter alive, and flames began to lick my own body, devouring *me*...." Sumangali's voice dropped to a whisper. "No one but the gods know how much I loved that child. She was the brightest spark with the rudest mouth and the sharpest mind. When she laughed, the sun came out, and when she cried, one yearned to comfort her, if only to see her smile again." Sumangali sighed. "Even her father knew she was special. We both agreed the gods had entered us the night she was conceived."

Lost in a world of shadows, Sumangali was talking wildly to herself. "I sprang at Ghora then, wanted to tear him to shreds. But a guardsman knocked me down, laughing. Which human mocks a mother's agony? Ghora and the devil held me down then, and another devil shoved that molten rod right into my eyes. I lost my mind with the pain." Suddenly she spat on the earthen floor. "May the gods have mercy on Ghora's soul...*I* can never forgive him!"

Ishvari walked around the cottage, her nostrils assaulted by the smell of rotting fruit from the neglected orchard. Fallen leaves lay thick around the periphery of the house and the door creaked on its hinges; that her mother cared so little for her safety hurt grievously. A vision arose of herself sitting on that very stoop, vomiting into the bushes, her mother rushing out, scolding away, Obalesh's plaintive wailing. She entered the cottage, her feet sinking into dust and dry leaves—the place had not been swept in days. She placed one hand on Sumangali's shoulder, the other over her mouth to muffle a possible scream. "Maa, it's me," she whispered.

Sumangali reared as violently as a wild stallion. "Who dares calls me maa?" she cried. "If you're an evil spirit, begone! Nothing frightens me any more. Hey Death! I've seen your cursed face and you're just another pitiless scoundrel! Come in another guise next time, fool! You've already taken my husband and children, and I care nothing—"

Her mother sounded insane, delirious, and why not? "It's Ishvari, maa, here to take you to safety," she whispered, struggling against tears. In the dim glow of moonlight, she saw that Sumangali's empty eye sockets actually appeared to be healing.

"My daughter? Ishvari?" her mother cried, turning her body toward her as if she could see. "Can it be you? Oh my precious, did you *really* manage to escape the maharajah?"

Ishvari flung her arms around her mother and held her close for long moments. "I did, with a lot of help. But we must be quiet now—noise travels far in this wilderness. Will you come with me now?"

Her mother's hands rose into the air, her fingers alighting on Ishvari's lips. Wonderingly, she traced the oval of Ishvari's face, the slant of her cheekbones and her almond eyes, traveling up to the parting of her hair, then back down to her fine, flaring nostrils. "It *is* you, and how you've grown, my darling!" she exclaimed. "How I longed to see you again, though I knew you hated me…don't deny it, a mother *knows*. After a while, I gave up hope. Then the maharajah's men—"

"Hush, maa, hush, I know about Obalesh," Ishvari said, voice breaking.

Sumangali was silent, her head bowed in despair.

"I'd give my own life a thousand times over to save the two of you," Ishvari moaned, crushing her mother in her arms. "If only they'd killed me instead!"

"Hush child, hush," Sumangali murmured, stroking her hair. "I was broken by your rejection. I'm no fool, despite your low opinion of me. A high tantrika is powerful—she can do as she pleases in certain ways. Many's the night I sat on that stoop, longing for you to call for us, hating you, wishing you'd never been born to cause me this unrelenting pain." She sighed. "But now I shall try to accept that everything has been the working of karma."

She sighed, holding Ishvari's hands tight. "That horrid necromancer in Parushni was right, you know. My beauty *did* cause men to go mad, and their lust awakened a beast within me. This demon moved into you while you were in my womb, preferring a home in a defenseless child." Her face cracked into new lines of anguish. Ishvari did not have the heart to stop her rush of words, though her own panic was rising. "When the envoy took you away," Sumangali went on, gripping Ishvari's hands fiercely, "I couldn't sleep for missing you. I begged the healer for herbs to drown the pain, neglected Obalesh, couldn't eat…even thought about escaping to Melukhha with Obalesh and living quietly with the envoy's gold. But I lacked the courage to start again." She sighed. "My father-in-law used to say humans prefer a known demon to an unknown angel. Life could not possibly have been worse for us in the city, and yet I couldn't leave this haunted wilderness."

Sumangali twisted her hands nervously in her lap. "After you became high tantrika, I swallowed my pride and begged that vile Ghora to arrange a visit to you. He agreed, but only because he was frightened the envoy had planted a spy in Devikota. I wanted Obalesh to fall in love with his brilliant sister—living alone with a sad mother was not good for that bright lad." Sumangali sighed again, and the mournful sound of it was awful to Ishvari's ears. "But you couldn't forgive me, could you?" she said, sobbing now. "Were you worried we'd shame you with our peasant ways?"

Then Sumangali was shouting, alarming Ishvari with her bitter rage. "Did those monks do *nothing* for you then?" she screamed, flailing wildly. "Can a poor widow refuse a maharajah's order and live to tell the tale? I had no choice *but* to let you go, you willful child!" Her mother's shoulders slumped. "What good are words anyway?" She paused, sunk in despair. Then, as swiftly as the anger had struck, she began to soften, and Ishvari caught a glimpse of her old beauty. Sumangali smiled and took hold of Ishvari's hands again. "Forgive me for ranting, sweet child. I'm mostly mad by now. Still, I must have done some good to have you back with me."

"We must go *now*, maa, while it's still dark," Ishvari coaxed. "Once we're safe we can talk forever." Without giving Sumangali a chance to answer, Ishvari went to her clothes chest and emptied its contents on to a cotton sheet. Tying the corners of the sheet, she fashioned a crude bundle she could heft on her shoulders. "Is there anything in particular you want to take, maa?"

"Where are we going?" Suspicion crept back into Sumangali's voice. "Are you *really* my daughter, or some Devikotan wretch, mocking me before leading me to my execution? *Speak!* In the name of Mahadevi, reveal yourself! If it's to my death we go, then do me the honor of letting me know so I can go happily! Don't you understand? I don't *want* to live!"

"Hush, maa, hush," Ishvari begged, tears streaming down her cheeks. "I *am* Ishvari, I swear to you by Mahadevi, and we're going to a sacred place where no human can hurt us." She stroked her mother's quivering back. Mentioning the valley would only increase Sumangali's disquiet. "Where we are going, maa," she murmured soothingly, "there's fruit and sweet water, and birds and beasts live together in harmony. You and I will be the only humans there." Tears stung her eyes. "I promise to make you happy again."

"You were always ready to spring to my defense," Sumangali's face crumpled into regret. "I longed to comfort you after your father died, but I myself was dead inside. Ghora and Andhaka broke me with their evil, and I quickly lost faith in the gods. What little love I could muster, I gave to your brother." Then she cried—"The statue of Mahadevi! And my linga! Hand them to me! And don't forget the incense in the corner shelf above the clothes chest." She got to her feet with difficulty and groped around on the floor. "Where are my sandals?"

"Here, maa," Ishvari said, locating the leather sandals cracked by hard use. She'd find a way to make new footwear for both of them. Hefting the bundle of clothes across her left shoulder, she took hold of Sumangali's hand and led her out of the cottage. Sumangali clasped the statue of the goddess tight in her other hand, her lips moving incessantly in prayer.

The moon lit their slow ascent, highlighting banks of trees and helping Ishvari to avoid rocks and other obstacles. Maruti shot into the path mid-way. Gibbering to frighten away lurking predators, the langur guided them forward, allowing Ishvari to concentrate on supporting Sumangali. Ishvari looked up and saw the sky lightening; soon the sun would rise above Devikota and the farmers would begin their daily work. Just then, Sumangali staggered to a stop.

"What's wrong, maa?" Ishvari whispered, worried.

"A moment, child, just a moment," Sumangali muttered. She looked so frail Ishvari feared she would not have the strength to make it up the final slope.

"Have you eaten?" Ishvari asked anxiously.

"Not since Obalesh was killed," Sumangali confessed weakly.

"Three whole days without food?" Ishvari scolded, ashamed for not guessing. Carefully she tilted the mouth of the water pouch into her mother's mouth, then peeled a banana and slowly fed her. They walked forward in silence, Ishvari supporting Sumangali, Maruti guiding them surely. Much later, Ishvari saw the upper curve of the sun rising over the hills and smiled with relief—now they were safe from the brooding menace of Devikota.

Moments later, Sumangali halted, squeezing Ishvari's hand in a panic. "I forget to collect the rest of the envoy's gold, my darling," she muttered weakly, her gaunt face pale with strain. "I moved most of it out of the cottage…hid it under a pile of rocks in the orchard soon after you left us…will we be needing it now, do you think? For food and suchlike?"

Ishvari fought a surge of tears. "No, maa," she whispered hoarsely. "By the grace of the gods, I promise you that from hereon we shall live happy and free."

When they reached the top of the slope and could see the stone temple, Ishvari stopped to give silent praise to the yogini for the accomplishment of her first great task. "We're safe now," she cried, hugging Sumangali, grateful for the thousandth time that the villagers so feared the valley's alleged legions of ghosts. Then, amazing herself with her own return to strength, she lifted Sumangali's frail body into her arms, and with Maruti marching triumphantly ahead, carried her mother into their new home.

This thought blasts my mind with the force of a hurricane.
—*Sharma, S.K: Hijras: The Labelled Deviants,*

MY BODY, MY TEMPLE

Ishvari strode, naked and bronzed, past the bakula thickets and the banana groves, past the whispering *tilaka* trees and the golden umbrellas of karnikara swarming with black-and-gold striped honey bees, past the river that gurgled beneath her home on top of the hill, moving indomitably toward the site of greatest heat in the valley. When she reached the concave dip above the mouth of the river, she performed twelve *surya namaskaras* in total surrender, then stood motionless in the pose of the warrior, joining her palms at her heart in profound gratitude

This was the season of relentless heat that fried the brain in its own juices. On the hottest days, her skin would erupt into nasty blisters and she feared her head would explode. Resolutely, she maintained her asana from the height of the searing sun to its flaming fall into some other world. Even as her tongue swelled with thirst, and her eyes traveled wistfully to the river, gurgling riotously at her endurance, she resisted, determined to conquer forever her unruly senses. She performed this feat right through the three sweltering moons of high summer, returning home with tart berries, sun-ripened fruit and spring water, exhausted but content. As her skin tanned into dark gold, her spirit grew increasingly alert and fierce.

Fearing Ishvari would catch fever of the brain, Sumangali begged her to stop. "I want to be strong from the inside out," Ishvari explained, eager to dispel her mother's worry. Dawn was spreading over the valley as she caressed Sumangali's face, now restored to beauty by rest and peace. "What you see as madness is only the way of the aghoris, maa, powerful seekers who sacrifice comfort to break through the thrall of the senses. Hariaksa taught me some of their practices, and now I'm using them to burn off my bad karma."

Sumangali listened, her face reflective. Her daughter was more precious to her than life itself, but then she'd always been a wild creature, not easy to tame.

Ishvari sat on the floor beside her mother. "Sometimes I lie by the river and memories rise up again like poisonous fog. I know I cannot resurrect the dead, but bitter tears flow just the same." She sighed. "Karma doesn't dissolve by itself, you know—it *must* be burned, and *I* must burn it." She encircled Sumangali in strong arms. The indolent fat of her last moons as high tantrika had given way to taut muscle and now she was a radiant yogini of the wilds. "Give me your blessings, maa—this is the only path I know powerful enough to set my spirit free."

Sumangali returned her embrace warmly. "It's so strange," she confided wonderingly. "When I focus on the right side of my chest as you suggested, I *do* see inexplicable things. Just now when you spoke of the aghoris, I had the strong sense that you are destined for much more than this solitary existence. So go, my darling, burn yourself to ashes, if peace is the result."

One day at dusk it struck Ishvari that all through the blistering afternoon, neither heat nor thirst had plagued her. She raised her face to the heavens, a smile of victory cracking her dry lips. The skies opened at that instant, and blinding sheets of rain deluged the valley. Sumangali thrust her head out of the window and shrieked—"I've seen lightning reduce a grown man to ashes! Come in this minute!" But Ishvari only laughed exultantly in response, enjoying the torrential blessing—she had won her first battle against the elements.

Now Ishvari began to rise well before dawn to stretch, flex and twist her body into more difficult asanas, focusing on wringing out the last traces of hedonism from her physical being. The shoulder stand she now maintained until the very earth itself seemed to shift its axis. When she bent into the locust and the bow, she became these things. Time lost meaning except when she tended to Sumangali's needs, bringing her mother tangy borums that thrived in jungle shade, purple jumlums, aromatic plantains, and heaps of the sun-ripened crimson and yellow berries that melted in the mouth.

Once she found a sack of rice and a bag of sea salt, possibly abandoned by a villager who'd stumbled by accident upon the feared valley. Yelping with joy, she raced up to the temple to cook a special porridge for their supper, using a handful of the grain and seasoning it with a pinch of the salt and herbs tasting of sun and earth.

On balmy nights, she spread reed mats in front of the hut and drew her mother out to sleep under a mantle of twinkling stars. As they lay in the grassy space between two massive bakula trees, she described heavenly formations to Sumangali, who was occasionally inspired to speak of Hiranya's own love for the stars. Often, Vegavat padded through the jungle to lie by their feet, keeping watch as they dreamed. Ishvari felt like a cherished child on these special nights, flanked by a loving mother and the protective male presence of Vegavat.

"Sweet Mahadevi! Your hair's grown so long!" Sumangali exclaimed one day as she patiently combed out Ishvari's tangles. "When you rescued me twelve moons ago, it hung down to your waist. Now it falls to below your hips. Why not braid it, sweetness? It's unseemly for a woman of your breeding to wear it loose."

Maruti chattered away in seeming agreement, but Ishvari only giggled and asked her mother where the worthies she was supposed to impress were hiding. Then she worked the silky mass into a coil on the top of her head—she was done with trying to impress the outer world.

Later Ishvari poured sun-warmed river water over Sumangali as her mother sat naked on her haunches beside the lazy river. Rubbing fibrous shikakai pods between her hardened palms, Ishvari massaged her mother's scalp with the soapy paste, with Sumangali uttering little cries of pleasure. Seasons had come and gone, and Mandakini's rough clothes had long since fallen to shreds. Now the erstwhile high tantrika roamed the valley naked, covering only her yoni with the leaves of pliant jungle palm.

Sometimes she explored the surrounding jungle with Maruti. At other times, Vegavat traveled alongside her in a blur of speed, a lethal guardian. So close in energy were they that Vegavat would lower his rosette-patterned body to earth, inviting her to ride on his back. Instead she chose to race beside him, increasing her speed and endurance. Soon she began to feel like an arrow loosed from the bow of a god, effortless, golden, and forever arching toward her goal.

While Sumangali lay dreaming in the warm grass by the banks of the river, Ishvari practiced meditation. Straining her mind to recollect Hariaksa's tales of the wild aghoris, she recalled their dictum: *shigra, ugra, tivra,* meaning fast, terrible and intense. Stirred, she vowed to hone her spirit so that it repelled all demons.

Once she caught a flash of the aggressive carp she'd nicknamed 'Takshak' in the depths of the river. Sinking into its alien consciousness, she sliced through the cool water, feeding on schools of tiny fish and the infinitesimal particles that grew on riverweeds. With the eagle that lived on the highest crag of the valley she soared over thick jungles, over snow-capped mountains, hamlets and towns, felt the single-minded focus of a predator swooping down on prey. And when the eagle was killed by an even larger mountain eagle in the battle for a rodent, Ishvari entered its warm corpse, nestled into its still-beating heart, swelled and rotted with its decay, was dragged away by a hyena into a reeking cave to be devoured, excreted and finally reduced to the dust beneath her human feet.

So she experienced every form of life—from the ants who built intricate hills, to the snakes who usurped these anthills for their cool interiors, and right up to the brazenly striped tiger, undisputed king of the jungle. She mewled with the bloody cubs of a snarling tigress and was present at the birth of ten thousand ant eggs, laid in the heart of their earthy home.

The time had come to practice, she intuited, for being, not doing. Refusing to scrutinize these exhilarating experiences with her intellect, all she sought was proof that her old identity was crumbling. And certainly she would never again be content with ordinary human existence.

Study these men carefully; Self commanded as she lay beneath the bakula trees. A vision of wandering ascetics arose before her mind's eye—thin, worn, ageless men, wearing rags so bleached by the elements it was impossible to know their original color. *Note that they are but shadows in the universe, with nothing to give.* The vision faded. *Punishing body and mind will not do any more, Ishvari. To swing from one extreme to the next is not yoga. Spaciousness and compassion are equally necessary to your growth.*

"What next?" she asked humbly, knowing the Self spoke nothing but the truth.

Cleanse your physical body and the five sheaths surrounding it. Thus will you prepare to reside in ananta-maya-kosha, the seat of bliss in the spiritual heart.

Next morning, Ishvari flushed out her intestines with salt water warmed in the copper pail she'd found in the recess behind the temple. This she did below river ground, so her wastes would not pollute the rushing waters. The liquid flushed through her digestive system, leaving her feeling as light as a feather. Next she cleaned the sack of her stomach with more salt water, drunk and regurgitated. She completed her three-part cleansing by flushing her nostrils with salty water, ejecting every particle of moisture through the vigorous practice of skull breathing.

She returned to the hut and guided Sumangali back down to the western edge of the river, where the cries of birds and animals mingled in pleasing harmonies. While her mother rested, Ishvari meditated by the mouth of the river. This became a daily practice and soon brought her to a stillness in which she blossomed afresh, like an orchid in a desert blessed by a fickle rain god.

In the sixth year of their life in the valley, Sumangali took ill, managing only to take tiny sips of spring water. Not even the fragrant pumpkin mush Ishvari stirred up over the wood fire could tempt her. For seven days Ishvari nursed her, massaging her feet and arms, stroking her head for hours. Her only practice was morning meditation, for without it she knew she'd be of less use. "Are you happy here with me, maa?" she asked Sumangali one night.

Sumangali turned her face toward the lushness of the valley. "Happiness I experienced often in your father's arms," she whispered with a faint smile, "but you, my darling, have given me the rare gift of peace."

Flooded with joy, Ishvari placed her head in Sumangali's lap and wept, noticing that her mother's face was more lined and delicate than ever—Sumangali could not have passed her forty-fifth year, yet the unrelenting string of tragedies had aged her rapidly. "Are you hungry, maa?" Ishvari whispered uneasily. "Will you eat a spoonful of pumpkin broth?"

Sumangali patted her hand weakly. "I don't think I shall ever eat again." Her lovely face creased into amusement. "You'll think me mad, but Hiranya and Obalesh have been visiting me. They are the best of friends, and Hiranya is most proud of our son. They visit me when you're off, practicing your strange rites. Your brother stands by the bakula trees, playing the flute I bought for him when you were elected high tantrika." She giggled like a child. "Where he gets his talent from I don't know—neither his father nor I could hold a true note."

Her mother spoke of Hiranya and Obalesh as if they'd simply moved on whole to a parallel realm of eternal bliss and brilliant sunshine. Was she hallucinating? Perhaps, and yet all things were possible in this magical valley. "Don't leave me, maa," Ishvari begged, for she'd grown to deeply love her guileless mother.

"Don't you worry, darling." Sumangali laughed. "The three of us plan to keep an eye on you—you're still way too wild to be left to your own devices. Obalesh intends to soothe you with his flute-playing." She nodded wisely. "In any event, you won't be alone for too long."

"What d'you mean?" Ishvari asked curiously.

Sumangali touched her third eye as a smile of incandescent beauty spread over her wan face. "Your spirit is luminous, Ishvari. I sense it even when you're far away. Soon you'll enjoy the love of many."

Again, Ishvari did not know what to make of her mother's cryptic words. Was Sumangali imagining a grand future for her so she could die in peace? "Is there anything you wish to tell me, maa?" she whispered. "Anything at all I can do for you?"

"I want you to forgive me for hurting you so terribly after your father was murdered," her mother whispered, squeezing her hand. "I'm sorry too about Ghora." Sumangali smiled. "I was so ashamed when you blurted out his sins in public, but also thrilled to know that *you* were the monkey who'd almost split his fat bottom in two." Sumangali giggled. "Such aim you had, my darling, such perfect aim! Oh, how I loved you for defending me before that ugly crowd! I wanted to tell you just why I'd let Ghora use me so crudely before you left Devikota, but you were so angry, so fierce...." She paused for breath. "Truth is, my darling, I feared all three of us would starve to death if he did not bring us food. Besides, he was always threatening...."

"You did your best, maa," Ishvari interrupted her gently.

"Did you know your father was planning to go to the Melukhhan Council with evidence of Andhaka and Ghora's corruption? That's why they killed him, Ghora told me everything."

"Hush, maa, don't trouble yourself now," Ishvari said, her own sadness rising.

Sumangali drew a shuddering breath. "Better to know the truth, my darling," she said hoarsely. "It was Andhaka who decided to kill your father, but Ghora who worked out the details. They hit your father from behind as he was coming out of the tavern, dragged him to the Field of Cobras and poured arrak over him. Ghora forced me to listen to every sickening detail, to make sure I knew how easy it would be for them to finish us off too. He told me a thousand times that many would have praised him for ridding Devikota of a sorceress and her spawn."

Her mother's voice sank to a whisper. "I wanted to die after I lost my Hiranya, but every time the thought crossed my mind, there you'd be, smiling up at me so trustingly, and Obalesh would be crying for his milk." She sighed. "And now I never ever want to think of Devikota again." She was quiet for a while. "But there *is* something I want very much from you...."

"Ask, and you shall have it," Ishvari said, moved deeply by Sumangali's honesty. "I would do *anything* for you, maa."

Sumangali smiled. "I want to *see* you, child, with my inner eye. You've your father's way with words, so draw me a portrait of yourself." She tightened her grasp on Ishvari's hand and waited for her to speak.

Ishvari swallowed, the lump in her throat growing larger. "When I leave this dwelling," she began, "I have to bend low. I'm taller than my father was, by at least half a head, and much taller than any woman in Devikota."

"Yes, yes, yes," Sumangali gasped impatiently. "Things like that I knew right from your birth, for your feet were narrow and long. But whose look do you have, your father's or mine?"

"Most certainly yours, maa, but the sun has burnt my skin to near ebony, while yours is still the color of buttermilk." She stopped, fighting tears.

"Go on, child, go on," Sumangali urged weakly.

Ishvari struggled to keep her voice steady. "I'm thinner than you ever were—indeed I'd suffer if there was famine. As for my face and hair, you know them well."

Sumangali nodded, and gestured for Ishvari to move her to a more comfortable position. "A woman must have curves, indentations and hollows to entrance a worthy man," she spoke firmly. "You're too thin, darling. I want you to eat more, understand? I want you full woman."

"Why? Where is this great lover you speak of?" Ishvari teased softly, even as Nartaka's face flashed across her mind. Why had the sadhu not visited her even once in all these years? "You keep hinting at a companion for me, maa. You must have good reason." But Sumangali only sank back on to the mat with one of her mysterious smiles and would say no more.

One morning Sumangali began to complain of a thirst no amount of water could slake. The night before, she'd shouted that the valley was ablaze. It had taken Ishvari a long time to calm her down. Also, she was increasingly unable to hold her urine. Ishvari padded the matting with layers of kusha grass, which could be easily removed, layer after sodden layer.

"Obalesh!" her mother gasped at the darkest point of night. "Stop playing that flute and tell your father to make ready for me!" Weeping, Ishvari held water to Sumangali's parched lips, but she was too weak to drink.

Next morning, when she rushed back with fresh water from the mountain spring, Ishvari found her mother's lifeless body in the moist emerald grass that thrived beneath the shade of the bakula trees her mother had so loved. Soon after she had left, Sumangali had staggered outside to die in her favorite spot. Staring down at the bow lips curved into a final faint smile, Ishvari felt an ache that pierced her soul.

Enchantress of the world,
Slender as a lotus stem,
Bright as a lightning-flash,
Lies sleeping, breathing softly out and in,
Murmuring poems in sweetest meters,
Humming like a drunken bee in the petals of the muladhara lotus,
How brightly her light shines!
    —*Satcakra-nirupana Tantra*

SERPENT FIRE

Stoically, Ishvari hefted her mother's stiffening body on to her back and carried it to higher ground. Then she slipped into the jungle to collect dry branches, returning to pick up driftwood from the river's undulating banks. She built a pyre around Sumangali's corpse, setting the wood on fire, and throwing herbs into the crackling flames to sweeten the smell of burning flesh.

Exhausted, she watched as orange, blue and gold flames consumed her mother's body. Only when the last cinder died did her tears come gushing forth, blinding her with their ferocity. Brushing them away impatiently, she used a sun-whitened skull to scoop up the ashes and scattered them into the river, watching the gray flecks bobbing on its surface before sinking slowly to its bottom. "Body to earth," she repeated the ritual words somberly. "Spirit beyond all fear and desire. Thus does death set all beings free."

She sat quietly on the twilit river bank, praying Sumangali's horrific series of trials had burned away her bad karma, clearing the way to a precious rebirth. As a cold wind whirled through the valley, the fact of her isolation set her heart beating with an alien terror. Reluctant to enter the temple home they had shared, she remained by the river, visualizing her seventh chakra as a scarlet lotus with a thousand petals in whose core quivered a rod of gold. As twilight darkened into night, she fell into so severe a thrall that all she knew was the glow behind her eyes.

With the force of an assassin's blow, her head began to spin. Buzzing assailed her ears as a column of fire mounted up her spine, shooting tongues of flame in every direction. She dragged herself home, grateful that Vegavat had finally arrived. The leopard waited until she crawled on to her sleeping mat, taking his usual place by her window, turning to look at her frequently with anxious yellow eyes. Ishvari wondered dully whether the big cat knew that Sumangali was gone forever, even as she faded into a restless sleep.

When she awoke it was dusk and Maruti was sitting on the mat beside her, holding three large ripe mangos. Did the langur know that never again would Sumangali comb out the tangles in his silver fur, or feed him choice morsels from her own hands? How did rare animals such as Maruti and Vegavat process loss? Maruti fed her mango pulp, and when she made to rise afterward, he pushed her gently back down. She struggled half-heartedly, but Maruti was persistent and she soon gave up the battle and fell back into a dreamless sleep.

Ishvari stayed indoors for most of the next day, too fatigued to do anything but gaze out at the rolling sweep of the valley. Later, she walked slowly down to the river to bathe. Vegavat crouched nearby, his rosette-patterned tail swinging in slow arcs, and Maruti brought lichees and miniature bananas, which she forced herself to eat. Relief sprang into his intelligent eyes as she cuddled up beside him on the sun-warmed grass—his mistress was going to be all right.

Longing for Sumangali swept over her; she did not grieve for her mother, who had been so eager to reunite with her beloved men. Instead she wept for the void looming in her own strange existence. Hoping to calm herself, she staggered across to her favored spot for meditation, but could not concentrate—a stream of radiant essence moved lazily up her spine, unnerving her with its sinister influence. Moments later, she was teetering on the edge of a precipice that plunged into the shadow world of insanity.

She motioned frantically to Maruti to pour water over her head—the fire of meditation had literally scorched her brain! Chattering madly, the langur filled the clay pot and doused her with cold water. She crouched at the mouth of the river, shivering violently, unable to even glance at the brooding menace of the valley. When Maruti led her back to the hut, she went docilely, though she flinched at every bird cry and every movement in the surrounding jungle.

Night spread across the rolling hills as she huddled on the kusha matting, shivering with a nameless dread that she intuited sprang from a cause greater than the death of her mother. The moment she closed her eyes, a stream of light shot up her spinal cord into her skull, gathering speed and volume. Then she knew what it was—*kundalini*! Yes, the serpent had fully awakened!

Red-gold energy shot up her spine, crashing against her third eye in a crystalline deluge of light. The lucent halo surrounding her now stretched out on every side in rolling waves, as if her mind was communicating with an unseen power. A roaring began in her ears, lights shot across her body like shooting stars. "Mahadevi, Goddess Mother!" she cried, as the sense of calamity grew stronger. In rising desperation, she cried out to the yoginis of the valley for help, as Maruti watched helplessly. Eventually she drifted into a state bordering sleep.

Maruti was at her side with a bunch of purple jumlums when she awoke. Once again she allowed him to feed her, but the delicate fruit tasted bitter. She tottered down to the river, each step crushing tender shoots of grass and the speckled mushrooms that cried out in agony as they gave up their lives. The river laughed when she used its surface as a mirror, cringing at the reflection of her bloodshot eyes and haggard face.

With a supreme effort of will, she tried to recall everything Hariaksa had revealed about the phenomenon of kundalini: the fiery energy shot up the central channel of the spine from the region below the genitals, on her journey toward the Wild God, residing in the seventh center of the body. In the course of this ascent, the embodied self was freed of the ego defilements of anger, desire and ignorance, passing finally into the ecstasy of immortality. Awakening kundalini radically altered mind and body; in certain cases, Hariaksa had warned, the rising fire could lead to insanity and death. *Had Hariaksa known what she would endure here alone in this valley?*

For weeks on end the divine snake allowed her no respite. Swaying bakula trees appeared like threatening monsters, preventing her from leaving the temple. She curled into a fetal ball as shadows fell upon the walls at night, praying for death. But when she saw Pundalik swinging before her, his feces-streaked eyes accusing her of a murderous lust, she knew she was teetering on the brink of complete insanity.

Jumping up, she fled towards the jungle, Maruti chasing after her. "Get away from me!" she shrieked, hurling a rock at the bewildered langur. Vegavat dashed toward her and she offered him her throat. "Go on, kill me, put an end to my misery," she taunted the beast, who backed away in alarm as she took off again.

The cool darkness of the jungle did not soothe her nerves as she'd hoped. The night sky loomed over her as she raced back home, distant stars appearing like an array of diamonds set in vast obsidian emptiness. Maruti appeared, gibbering as she raced along the river's banks. With a burst of maniacal strength, she grabbed him and hurled him into the water. The langur's skull hit the side of a rock and he howled, disbelievingly, his furry hands covering his head as he stared at her in shock. She ran towards him, appalled, but now Maruti held back, his mouth opening in a snarl to keep her at bay—no longer could he trust his mad mistress.

Back in the temple, Ishvari fell into a nightmarish sleep as winds screamed across the valley. In the middle of the night, she rolled off the mat and on to the floor with a start. Something gleamed in the corner—a knife she'd lost a long while ago. She seized it, slit first her right wrist, then her left, then crawled outside, heading for the river. The water guffawed heartily as she plunged into it. "I'll drown in you," she moaned furiously. "Defile your sacredness!"

"Think I'd let you?" the river retorted, refusing to absorb her blood into its clear waters. Looking down in disbelief, she saw her wrist wounds healing, leaving faint white scars. "Please," she begged, bobbing on its surface, for it would not let her sink. "Be kind, my friend of so many years, let me die."

Choose carefully, Ishvari, the river replied. *Friend or murderer—what shall I be? A coward's death now will mean you'll have to return to repeat your role in this ridiculous drama—until you get it right.*

"Then I'll go without your help," she muttered, knowing her heart could not stand the strain for much longer. Her body bobbed in the water as the sun rose and fell and the sky turned from blue to gray. Was she doomed to die without a human friend to mourn her passage? Vegavat's eyes gleamed at her from the river bank, and in the background she heard Maruti's chatter. The animals moved closer to the river, communicating with it in their wordless way. Maruti gesticulated wildly, as if directing the big cat, and the river gurgled, as if giving guidance.

The waters began to rise, carrying her emaciated body upward, higher and still higher. With a mighty roar that shook the valley, the river hurled her forward like a sodden toy, to land squarely on the back of the big cat. With a regal nod in Maruti's direction, Vegavat took off down the hill, so fast she could barely hang on. Dimly, she was aware of streaking past village houses, tracts of thick jungle and isolated hamlets. Then Vegavat was swimming across a narrow band of water with mighty strokes and she lost consciousness.

Wise men who have abandoned all thought of the fruit of action
Are freed from the chains of birth in this world
And go to regions of eternal happiness.
     —Bhagavad Gita

KHARANSHU

"Come, you must drink this," a gravelly voice ordered. Ishvari's eyes fluttered open to see a man garbed in a white loincloth proffering to her a clay bowl brimming with a milky-green concoction. His narrow chest was bare, and his skull shaven clean, but for a tuft of gray hair erupting from just behind its centre. So immense was her relief at seeing another human that she obeyed him, then fell back on to the matting as radiance suffused her.

He placed the empty bowl on the window ledge, then sat beside her on the kusha matting. She stared up at him, dazed: was this man *real*? It was the concern growing on his face as he studied her that assured her she was not hallucinating. Panic struck then, and suddenly she was gasping for air, clawing wildly at the cotton quilt he'd thrown over her skeletal frame.

Cool fingers stroked her skull. "Try not to move," he suggested. "Jumping around like a flea only agitates the fire. Now describe everything you see and feel." She squinted up at him—had he really used the word *fire*? "Tell me why you are in this state," he said, enunciating every word. "I want every fact, and sequentially. And hold nothing back, no matter how trivial."

Laboriously, she related her bizarre story, from the protracted meditation following Sumangali's cremation, to the ghastly ensuing weeks. He listened intently, his eyes widening from time to time, even twinkling with delight when she related how the river had healed her wrist wounds and colluded with Maruti and Vegavat to bring her to him.

"Remarkable!" he observed amiably. "I *knew* I was in for something extraordinary when that magnificent beast bounded right up to my doorstep to deliver an unconscious yogini." He laughed out loud, his compact body shaking with mirth. "I've yet to hear a more incredible tale about the rising of the fire, dear one. You've been greatly blessed to have survived such trials."

His humorous yet caring words pacified her. She studied him with increasing fascination—the hooked nose and wide lips, crooked teeth and intelligent eyes, the high forehead, all combining to form an ugly-attractive portrait. Amused by her blatant scrutiny, he continued his own inspection of her emaciated body, moving from her sun-burnt feet to her drawn face with probing concern. "It appears you are well schooled in the vagaries of the fire," he remarked. "A good thing—for knowledge always renders the healing process smoother."

"So you can heal me?" she cried hoarsely, half sitting up in her excitement.

A stream of light pulsed from the center of his upraised palm to push her back down. "Why else would the gods have sent you to *me*?" he asked, chuckling at her astonishment. "Really, my dear," he added, "it's unwise to agitate the fire with jerky movements.

From here on kindly obey me without question. I find speech enervating unless it concerns essentials."

A memory of Hariaksa effortlessly repelling Takshak by Rudralaya's river in similar fashion flashed through her mind; intuitively she knew she could completely trust this man. His forehead creased into deep grooves. "The burning you describe indicates that the fire rose through the nerve of the sun, the *pingala* channel," he stated. "To awaken the goddess with respect, she must rise through sushumna, the central channel. But I suspect you know this already, eh?" Gently he drew the lower lid of her right eye down to study its condition. "Fire is disturbed by serious transgressions or by unnaturally stringent practices," he remarked without judgment. "When it rises up the right side of the spine—as seems to be your case—one can even burn to death."

Appreciation for his knowledge clashed with shame for her sordid past. This commanding stranger had surely awakened the fire himself, or he could not speak with such clear authority. And yes, her suffering was plainly her fault. Afraid to meet his penetrating gaze, she glanced out of the window. Water gleamed barely a hundred feet away—they were on an island surrounded by the lapping waters of the Sarasvati!

Her host rose and walked into the kitchen area. As she stared at his retreating back, she recalled Vasudeva speaking of a Councilor named Kharanshu, who'd vanished overnight from Melukhha several moons before Takshak had left to fight the Doms. "Why do you revere him?" she'd asked her gardener. "Can he be much better than the rest of those thieves?"

Vasudeva had friends who served Councilors, and who did not think twice about spilling their masters' dirtiest secrets into his trustworthy ears. Over time, he had come to loathe all those who scorned the body of law crafted by Melukhha's earliest rishis.

Besides, although both he and Mandakini lacked higher schooling, the gods had blessed him with a powerful thirst for spiritual knowledge and a gift for verbal expression. Ishvari had always enjoyed hearing his views.

"Ah, but Kharanshu *is* different," Vasudeva had replied. "Incorruptible, for one thing, and also expert in the art of inner investigation."

"*Inner investigation?*" she'd repeated, amazed he would use such a lofty term.

Vasudeva had nodded. "Kharanshu guides all those who wish to experience samadhi, regardless of status or gender. He helped me through much inner turmoil when no other high-born scholar would even hear me out." His steady defense of Kharanshu had surprised her.

"If he's so perfect, why did he run when things got bad in the Council?" she'd scoffed. "Isn't it in our worst times that we most need nobles of his caliber?"

"He had no option but to flee," Vasudeva had retorted dourly. "One night after a fierce quarrel with Charaka, he was taking his usual stroll by the Great Bath when thugs set upon him. Fortunately he was rescued in the nick of time by a friend. Kharanshu vanished that very night." Vasudeva had chuckled. "Soon after, the Council received a message from him: a good man outnumbered by scoundrels must run, it read, just so he can continue to fight corruption."

"And where is your hero now?" she had asked, intrigued.

"Some say he fled to Sumeria, others claim he now coaches princelings in Egypt, but a personal attendant who served him until he fled whispered to me that he lives disguised as a ferryman on the lower banks of the Sarasvati, close to Vallabhi." Vasudeva had smiled grimly. "I believe him, because neither fame nor riches could have lured away the sage I knew. And mistress, I beg you to strictly keep my confidences—there is a gold price on Kharanshu's head."

"Kharanshu?" she called out now.

He turned to her with a quizzical smile. "And who are *you*?" he asked.

"Ishvari, ex-high tantrika of Melukhha, and now a fugitive, like you."

A smile flickered on his interesting face. "So I thought…but how did you recognize *me*?"

Ishvari shrugged. "My gardener in Melukhha spoke highly of you. Once long ago you guided him in the art of inner investigation. Not many would fit his glowing description of you."

Kharanshu laughed. "Ah! Of course I remember him now…a serious fellow who sought advice on inner states of consciousness—and surprised me by understanding every word I said!" He grinned at her. "So I'm that easy to spot, am I, young lady?"

"Hariaksa and Atulya themselves honed my powers of observation. Once," she whispered, as tears rolled down her cheeks, "I was their brightest star."

Her words sounded pompous to her own ears, but Kharanshu nodded gravely. "Yes, now it all becomes clear," he said. "And I shall do my utmost to heal you, Ishvari of Devikota, but only if you promise to leave as soon as you are better. An ugly ferryman can escape detection, you see, but never a lovely yogini." He grinned. "It's so nice to know the rumors of your beauty are true! Even in this state, dear one, you're way too striking *not* to draw attention…and I've no great wish for Takshak's thugs to interrupt my work."

"*Work?*" she echoed, disappointed that he was already speaking of her leaving. It had been too long since she'd spoken to an intelligent human of his standing.

Kharanshu's eyes gleamed. "I belong to a community of mystics engaged in ushering in a new age. Each of us has raised the sacred fire, and now we support others in the same quest." He stroked her burning hand with cool fingers, causing embers of serpent fire to glow at the base of her spine. "The desert will bloom again, dear one, never fear."

"Can you cure me?" she asked again, even more anxiously.

Kharanshu scrutinized her for a long moment. "I believe so…re-channeling your fire should be a simple matter—*if* you follow my directions and surrender to the One, who both transcends and *is* the source of all duality." His eyes gleamed. "But first you must accept that your suffering is the result of abuse of body, mind and spirit. Can you do that, dear one?"

She nodded fervently, a lump growing in her throat.

Kharanshu's eyes pierced her. "You've accomplished no small feat by raising the fire to this height. Still, the delicate fabric of your nervous system is scorched. More than a steady nerve will be needed to repair the damage. Give thanks for your training—it will come in handy."

"So you *can* cure me?" she asked, desperately eager to be done with the torture.

"If the gods conspired to get you here," he replied, a crooked smile softening his angular face, "I'd say they're firmly on our side. The liquid you drank contained herbs to stop the energy from moving. You'll sleep well tonight, and tomorrow at dawn I'll wake you and together we shall redirect the fire up the central pathway. Good thing my boat's right now in Kusala for mending—for the moment we're safe from pilgrims clamoring for rides."

Kharanshu pointed to a stone statue garlanded with fresh jasmine set in a niche in the wall. At the foot of the altar sat a single red lotus. "When I wake you tomorrow, follow me down to the river and bathe in silence. Then return here and sit before that statue. Study it carefully now—observe how Rudra lies prone, inviting Mahadevi to dance upon his form. In the same way, Ishvari, you must surrender your ego to Mahadevi. As you must know, she is the mother of not just the fire goddess, but of all gods and goddesses, indeed of the entire manifest world. Let the goddess dance within your body, and she will reward you with the boon of transcendental wisdom."

Turning her over, he probed her lower spine with gentle finger strokes before moving her on to her back again. Ishvari gazed up at him with gratitude; Kharanshu's wry sense of humor, coupled with his brightness, infused her with the same confidence Hariaksa had evoked. "Now listen carefully," he said, sitting before her. "When you come before this statue tomorrow, become aware of your body as a field of energy. Direct your focus to the left side of your spine, and visualize a cold current shooting up the middle of your spinal cord. Since the fire has risen through the right, you must force the energy through the left, to neutralize the burning and re-channel the fire—does this make sense?" He paused to study her expression, stroking her hand comfortingly. "Don't worry…if anyone can follow these instructions, it is *you!* Keep in mind that I shall be with you from start to finish, sending a concentrated flow of energy to assist you."

Outside a goat bleated. Kharanshu left, and soon she heard the spit and hiss of milk hitting the base of a clay bowl. He returned with a foaming cup of milk, which she drank eagerly—it had been years since she'd tasted this delicacy. Then she lay back, watching him prepare a meal of rice and greens. When he was done, Kharanshu sat down to meditate on a kusha mat in the corner. After a while, he rose and prostrated before the gods. He served them both in earthenware bowls. "Eat," he invited. "The fire sleeps." Chewing each mouthful as finely as she could, she finished the small serving, finding it delicious.

Ishvari lay quietly as sparks exploded along her spine; the feeling was not unpleasant, and languor deepened into the first natural sleep she'd known in weeks. Then Kharanshu was rousing her. Rising, she followed him down to the water. He pointed to a shallow spot surrounded by flat black rocks. Pulling off the robe he'd given her, she tossed it over a rock and sank into the Sarasvati, rinsing her hair and body, noting that when she closed her eyes, her own internal landscape glowed like an alien sun.

Kharanshu held out a white tunic for her when she emerged. She accepted it even as she wrung out her hair and coiled it around her head. Slipping on the garment, she followed him inside, prayer welling up from her depths, and took her seat before the gods. Kharanshu sat beside her, his energy radiating outward to envelope her body. The fire leapt up her spine, blazing up and into her brain. In that elongated state of consciousness, she reached within and unerringly located the nerve, consciously diverting its flow into the central channel.

It felt like an eon before a sound—like the loosing of an arrow—struck her ears. Light zigzagged through her spinal cord, filling her head with blissful luster. The almost immediate cessation of pain filled her with awe. Much later, she sensed Kharanshu moving about behind her. When she turned, she saw a halo of light pulsing around his head. Rising unsteadily, she walked to the mat and collapsed.

Dusk was painting the walls of the hut with fingers of gold when she awoke. A stream of luster was still pouring into her head, yet her brain was clear and bright. "Time to eat," Kharanshu smiled, bringing her a bowl of cracked wheat sweetened with honey and a cup of goats' milk. A tongue of golden flame probed her stomach as she ate, and each morsel and drop tasted like nectar. "And now you must walk a little," Kharanshu suggested.

Ishvari followed his tall figure into the fading light, enjoying the sun's rays reflecting in the lapping waters. At the back of the cottage, she saw a vegetable garden and jasmine bushes growing beside a heart-shaped pond. Three red lotuses, their petals glistening with drops of water, floated on its surface. Not too far from the built-up banks of the river stood a bo tree, its trunk leaning towards the water. A woven hammock swung between its two largest boughs. Kharanshu loped ahead, beckoning to her to follow. When she reached his side, he picked her up as if she were a feather, and placed her on the hammock. "Enjoy the splendor," he said, patting her cheek affectionately. She lay quietly in the hammock, eyes closed, watching the living radiance dancing through the emaciated length of her body and feeling a boundless joy.

Three days and nights passed in silence. As her vitality grew, she yearned to speak to him, but did not wish to break the silence he so relished. On the third night, a boat came for him. Kharanshu returned alone at dawn with the boat. "My friend had news of Melukhha," he said, sitting cross-legged opposite her, his face alight with amusement. "Takshak values you at ten thousand gold pieces alive, dear one, but oh, so sad, only *half* that amount if you're delivered to him dead." He guffawed. "That's more than even *my* head commands. Count yourself honored!"

His expression turned serious. "Tomorrow pilgrims will once again demand passage across the Sarasvati. Neither of us can risk discovery. Sad as I am to see you go, dear one, you must leave

at dawn. Tonight, I'll use the fire to summon your magical beast."
He smiled. "I know you reside in the valley where Nartaka
performed great austerities."

Her eyes lit up instantly. "You know Nartaka?"

Kharanshu nodded. "We belong to the same community. He
saved my life in Melukhha and spirited me here, even purchased
my boat for me. Having no sense of commerce, I tend to attract
cheats—villains *smell* out their next victim, you know. Nartaka,
however, is at home everywhere and with everyone." He grinned.
"He even taught me how to row properly, to make sure my disguise
as a boatman would work. I haven't seen him since—the fellow's a
mystery even to his closest friends."

Hearing him speak of Nartaka with such affectionate
familiarity made her wonder again why the sadhu had never visited
her in the valley. *Had the debacle at the ghats repelled him?*

"You're wrong, my dear," the sage said gruffly, confirming
her suspicion that he could read minds as easily as her gurus.
"Some travel this path alone, others seek good company as they
move into the heart. In both cases, one must reach the inner
orgasm alone—by learning to dissolve the limiting sense of 'I' that
is the root of all our dysfunction. Nartaka gave you the freedom to
become whole within yourself, and not to rely on another for your
joy."

She digested his unusual manner of relaying this age-old
wisdom. "See how solitude forced you to deepen the tools you were
given in Rudralaya?" Kharanshu continued. "Had you not inflicted
such awful damage on yourself, I suspect you might already have
experienced the great orgasm. Odd, isn't it? Entering one's own
spiritual heart is the only permanent solution to the sorrow that
drives us into the arms of unsuitable lovers, and other such forms
of foolishness."

Did he know about Pundalik?

Kharanshu nodded matter-of-factly. "All humans make serious errors of judgment. We believe our own lies—which is why Maya is able to blind us all so cleverly. I myself encountered the demon that held you in thrall, dear one, and he's a wicked one. In any case, *real* enjoyment begins after romantic fantasies die—for that's when human love is kissed by grace."

She smiled shyly at her eccentric savior, wordlessly expressing her gratitude for his many kindnesses. The gods had saved her yet again by sending her to this luminous and engaging sage. "How does one go beyond delusion?" she asked. "In Melukhha, despite everything I knew...."

"The meditation Nartaka shared with you is a sure means of fusing finite with infinite," Kharanshu said. "Moreover, it's a safe one for fragile seekers, since it avoids messy emotional entanglements. Now that the fire has risen properly, it will be even easier for you to use. And once your ego dissolves *completely* back into your Self, all forms of relationship will flow smoothly, for there will be no sensitive individual left to become upset."

Ishvari gazed at him in wonder, amazed by all that he knew of her past.

"Ah, but it's no mystery, dear one," Kharanshu smiled mischievously. "While you slept last night, the fire revealed your history to me in order to assist your healing. Quite a tale, I must say, quite a tale." He gestured dismissively with his hands. "Never mind all that now...what's important is that you extract the wisdom from even your worst experiences and keep the fire of wisdom burning within."

"I'm curious to know more about the demon that possessed me, Kharanshu. How did he come to gain such power in Melukhha?"

Kharanshu tapped blunt fingers on the earthen floor. "What do you know of Soma?"

"Very little," she replied, wondering what the nectar of the gods had to do with demons. "I found references to it in Hariaksa's scrolls, but didn't ask for his views on it—he rarely spoke to me of herbs that could alter the state of the mind."

"But Soma's no ordinary mind-altering herb, dear one. Our ancient Melukhhans called this nectar 'a god for gods', for Soma is a trinity—it's name, the drink, and the divinity it contains together form a godly unity. It was prepared by extracting the juice of a certain plant, but that plant itself has disappeared."

"Can you describe it to me? Perhaps it grows wild in the valley...."

"Even so, why hunt for it now? Our ancients drank it for immortality and other gifts, but when the fire rises within, even *Soma* becomes irrelevant."

"Have you imbibed it?" she asked curiously.

"Soma vanished before my time. However my maternal grandfather described it as being tinted with green and shining like the sun. It had long stalks and was golden in color. Priests gathered it at special times and pounded it to gather the juice, which was then filtered through lamb's wool and blended with cow's milk. The old man claimed the 'roar' emitted by Soma was so powerful it could call the gods down from heaven."

"Was it used solely for mystical insight?"

"Priests valued it for the wisdom it conferred," Kharanshu explained. "But warriors imbibed it for speed and strength." He smiled at her intent expression. "We meet at strange times in our lives, dear one. Once my store of knowledge was vast and I enjoyed sharing it with all seekers; now I believe it has matured into the sort of wisdom that relishes silence."

"Oh, *please* don't be silent with me today, Kharanshu," she begged. "There's so much I'd like to know before I return to the valley."

"Ask freely then," Kharanshu said, beaming. "And please know that in different circumstances, you could have stayed on here for as long as you liked. Of course, I'd have put you to work right away, planting that herb garden, of which I've been fondly dreaming."

Ishvari's heart beat softly with happiness; it was abundantly clear that Kharanshu liked her for herself. "Did we lose Soma because we abused her?" she asked, not wanting to waste another moment. "And what has it got to do with demons?"

"Soma left us because we lost our honor. In the ensuing void our people turned to ganja, bhang and other intoxicants for solace. But all these drugs so popular in Melukhha today are poor substitutes for the god of gods, which brings only light." He paused. "Indeed, our abuse of these substances has led to the fall of our civilization—the lower grade of intoxicants excite the lower chakras and deaden higher ones." He shook his head sadly. "Just look what happened to you...not to mention our poor Devadas."

She nodded, enjoying his esoteric slant on the subject. "So *that's* why the demon could warp and twist me as it did."

"Correct." Kharanshu nodded. "Yet what are demons but the ego itself, splitting off into separate entities? We humans are a collective organism; pure consciousness only *appears* to be divided. In the relative realm, however, these malicious energies can move about freely—*if* the victim's protective sheaths have been weakened by fear, anger, jealousy, revenge, and so forth. Demons feed off the prana of humans, bringing evolution to a halt by accelerating destruction."

"Good and evil exist only as long as we identify with our minds and bodies," Kharanshu murmured, smiling his crooked smile. "To the sage who transcends duality, nothing in this gross realm is real, by which I mean that nothing in samsara is permanent and lasting."

"The night I went to rescue my mother—" Ishvari paused, her face growing sad. "Are you aware of the ugly sequence of events that led to her blinding?"

Kharanshu nodded, his face expressing sympathy.

"She said a demon had possessed her when she was a girl, and that this same fiend had moved into me when I was a defenseless child. Could she have been right?"

"We inhabit a mysterious reality," Kharanshu said with a shrug. "All things are surely possible, but once the fire rises strongly, demons lose all power, for no darkness can survive light." He grinned. "Did you know it was Rudra himself who spawned demons?" Seeing her surprise, he added: "You see, demons stir ugly predilections into full flower, and the humans they possess go insane, or even die—the agony's that bad, as you well know. But once the filth's burned off, the strong survive and grow into spiritual giants. Which is why, in his paradoxical wisdom, our God created demons to drive old souls to seek moksha. Take your own case," he added. "Had that demon not harassed you, would you be here now?" He beamed as comprehension lit her thin face. "Nothing like the slash and burn of emotional agony to drive one into the light, eh?"

"Was it the demon invasion that forced you to leave Melukhha in such haste?"

Kharanshu nodded. "After Nartaka saved me that dreadful night by the Great Bath, when I truly thought my end had come, he warned me a powerful fiend had usurped Takshak's spirit. The entire Council, he confided, with the notable exception of Kushal, whose inner light was always strong, had been infected. I knew then that I could do no more to save our city."

"Inanna too spoke of these evil creatures," Ishvari said. "By her description...."

"Oh, how I relished battling with that woman," he said, his face melting into fondness. "Before you ask, she's safe and in silent retreat somewhere up in the mountains. I do know how she viewed demons, and a myriad other things...but from hereon, Ishvari, I want you to focus on the simplest truths: there is the blissful and immortal Self, and then there is the ego, the identity we begin to fabricate the moment we are born. Once a seeker learns to cultivate samadhi, the fire burns the chains that keep us whirling in delusion. At this point, a seer is born."

Ishvari bowed her head. "Can I not stay with you for a few days? I promise...."

"Ah, dear one, now that the fire has risen properly, *she* will reveal all you need to know. Nor is it your destiny to remain alone. Trust me. I have seen great things in your future."

Before she could ask for more, he'd walked towards the kitchen and was already preparing a meal of wheat bread and spiced lentils simmered with green beans. In the midst of his work, he swung around to ask her: "Have you a goat?"

Giggling at his strange ways, Ishvari shook her head, thinking she would love to have one.

"Goats' milk is the best food for your condition," he announced briskly. "Can't you stun some ignorant shepherd with your beauty, and spirit away one of his flock while the poor fellow wonders whether you're an *apsara* or a devi?" He chuckled at her wry expression. "Of course, if you prefer an honest exchange, I could spare you a few pieces of gold...."

Still giggling, she shook her head—it would be too dangerous to expose herself, especially in this delicate stage of her recovery.

"Don't worry about anything now," Kharanshu said, flashing his crooked smile. "The fire helps unravel the riddle of existence, you know, and more will gradually be revealed to you. Eat well and rest as much as you can when you get back home, and, as I said before, allow the goddess to play freely within your body. Kundalini is a great queen and must be treated as such. Also, you must learn to constantly surrender your will to the One."

"Can I meditate again?" she asked.

"No need to loop the fire from here on, of course," he replied. "Instead, focus solely on the practice Nartaka gave you."

At sunset, Ishvari strolled by the Sarasvati. Gazing at her reflection in the calm waters, she beheld a weakened countenance. Nevertheless, other signs of rising health were reassuring. She returned to the cottage when the moon was high, finding Kharanshu in meditation. She lay down, noticing that the current of fire was now rejuvenating her body.

It was pre-dawn when she awoke. Yellow eyes stared at her through the window of the hut—Vegavat was waiting, and Kharanshu already meditating. On the mat beside her sat a small bundle—the kind sage had packed some garments, a sack of rice and fresh vegetables for her.

Heaving it over her shoulder, Ishvari stepped into the yard. Astride Vegavat, she stroked his gleaming coat, and the leopard sprang into motion, racing along the sides of the river. When the river narrowed, the big cat leapt into the water and swam strongly across. She leaned forward to cling to his neck, enjoying the speed of his sleek body and the splash of water on her skin.

Then they were on land again, shooting across jungle and climbing rapidly. A jet of brilliant substance rose up her spine and spread outward. Vegavat halted at the stoop of her temple home. She leapt off, gazing with delight at the richness of the valley. A happy chattering reached her ears and Maruti bounded toward her—her friend, of course, had forgiven her.

A few days later she awoke to the sound of bleating. Dashing out, she saw not one, but *two* goats, tethered to a bakula tree, chewing on the plentiful grass. She felt a keen disappointment. If only Kharanshu—or his courier—had stayed awhile.

Soon she felt strong enough to enjoy the direct sunshine of the valley. As Maruti plied her with his finest spoils, and the goats poured their bounty into her being, she quickly regained her former strength. One thing she dared not do as yet for fear of rousing the old fierceness was to meditate. Yet she looked forward to the vivid dreams generated by the serpent fire, for the visions were delightfully phosphorescent.

One night she roamed through an alien city where wheeled carriages painted in vivid colors sped past her. Buildings of stone and other shining materials scraped the rim of the sky, while trees stood sentinel on the edges of pathways. Humans jostled past her, some carrying boxes emanating a throbbing music. Women hurried along broad streets, hair in shades from black to gold, skin color ranging from white to brown to black. Through a shop window, she saw spiked, laced, and ankle-high footwear. The images were so strange that she awoke, amazed by the clarity of the dream. From where had it sprung? *Some past life? Or the future?*

She slipped out to watch the sun rising over the mountains, preparing herself for the ravishing beauty of the day. The energy was permanently changing her—every image she saw, inside and out, seemed carved out of living flame, as if the process of thought itself was managed with this lustrous stuff, not merely bright, but capable of perceiving its own brilliance.

When the light in her third eye increased in size or luminosity, the noises in her ears grew more insistent, as if drawing her attention to the unfathomable. She sensed her erotic secretions were being transmuted into a subtle essence for transport to her vital organs, for a pleasant energy suffused her body. Yes, indeed, she'd been usurped by an exultant queen, and yet there was no sign of the much talked of powers associated with it by Melukhhan holy tradition.

Seasons came and seasons passed. One morning Maruti found a gray strand while grooming her hair and waved it before her in grinning silence. Ishvari laughed, pleased to see it—age and the fire had gifted her with a tranquil heart-strength. And yet she remained alone. Why had seers hinted at clairvoyance, of dialogue with the disembodied and other occult gifts as the attributes of an awakened kundalini?

"Evolution represents a rise from earth to sky," Atulya had said, holding aloft a shard of granite. "Eons into the future, even *this* stone is destined to mingle consciousness with cosmic intelligence in a drama only an absolute power can produce. Like frogs at the edge of a swamp," he'd added, "we don't know how small we are next to the colossal forces that encompass us."

Now it struck Ishvari afresh how close these same forces had come to throwing her into the abyss. Only Mahadevi's benevolence had saved her. On wings of gratitude, she strolled out into the midnight loveliness of the valley. The crescent moon shone like soft diamond and her love grew so big that she felt her heart would explode. Vegavat padded over to her from the jungle, and in the throes of torrential love, she bent to kiss him. The big cat backed shyly away, watching his eccentric mistress from afar with yellow, unblinking eyes.

"Come to me if you need love," Ishvari whispered into the rustling jungle. A sound like the rustling of ten thousand trees arose as cobras with upright hoods emerged from their underground homes to pay her homage. Magnetized by her inner fire, these regal broods moved toward her in complex dance, until the earth itself teemed with their hissing presence.

Mahadevi danced upward along her nerves, kissing her spine with gentle fire, and she felt a kinship with these creatures that she'd once feared and loathed. "Come closer," she invited, and the air filled with new sounds as their supple bodies undulated across the edges of the valley, past the riverbed, over rocks and stones, until the earth itself sang with their dance. Serpents surrounded her in writhing circles, their cold passion scenting the shimmering air. Enthralled, she reached for a king cobra and draped it around her neck, where it hung, thick as a man's arm.

Self-possessed, resolute,
Act without any thought of results,
Open to success or failure.
        —*Bhagavad Gita*

GAURIKA

Zaphara arced out of the water to seize an emerald dragonfly, scales flashing copper in the sun as he knifed back into the depths of the river. The ripples created by the giant whiskered fish made concentric circles that diminished in size until the river was again still. Ishvari smiled at this little drama of life and death, recalling the afternoon she'd given the warrior carp his pretty name.

All she saw these days was sheathed in a silvery sheen— which was perhaps why seers were silent in higher states of consciousness; how could words express the subtle wonders revealed by the fire? Often, a golden tongue of flame flickered in the center of her forehead, seat of universal consciousness and abode of Rudra. As Kharanshu had promised, her third eye had blasted wide open, producing indescribable joy and streams of numinous information. The fire had also revealed the immense reservoir of compassion she possessed, but so far its only beneficiaries appeared to be beasts, birds, fish and serpents. Why had she come through such intense suffering to be the lone human inhabitant of this breathtaking valley?

The panicked cries of a child cut through her reverie. Ishvari stood, shading her eyes from the sun, seeing a roiling cloud of dust on the horizon. As it cleared, she saw Vegavat flying upward and towards her, a human form lying horizontal across his back, braids streaming in the wind, thin legs scissoring the air. The big cat had captured an intruder!

Vegavat came to a halt before her, kneeling to display his prize. A teenage girl, her pupils dilated in terror, goggled at Ishvari from the back of the beast. "Don't be afraid," Ishvari spoke in the simple dialect of the village folk. "The leopard won't harm you." She hoisted the frail body off the back of the beast and onto the ground, but the girl shrank away from her, like one of the sky-blue touch-me-nots that grew in profusion all over the valley. Her right leg was deformed and shorter than the left, but her eyes were intelligent, and her face as delicate as a jasmine bud.

The leopard rolled onto his back, the razor-sharp claws on his hunter's paws sheathed. "See?" Ishvari smiled, kneeling before her. "Just like a naughty cat. Now tell me your name."

"Gaurika," the girl stammered, her eyes darting wildly around.

Ishvari visualized the tableau made by Vegavat and herself against the backdrop of the river—how surreal the scene must appear! The fire had brought radiance to her skin, highlighting both the ethereal quality of her features and the eyes that shone in the dark oval of her face. Her hair, made lustrous with shikakai, rippled to her knees like silk, shielding her lean body from the elements. "Your mother must love you dearly to have named you thus," she said, though in truth Gaurika looked miserable and unkempt. The girl stared at her, puzzled. "Don't you know?"

Ishvari asked kindly. "Gaurika was the name of a female sage, a *rishika.*"

"Mama doesn't know I'm here." Anxiety sharpened the girl's high voice. "I slipped away while she was washing clothes down by the river...."

"I didn't tell *my* mother that I came here either," Ishvari retorted with a conspiratorial grin. "You're brave to have walked up here alone, Gaurika. Is this your first time here?"

Gaurika nodded, blinking furiously and licking her dry lips.

"Sit with me," Ishvari invited, patting the space beside her on the river bank. "Devikotans are scared to venture to this valley...what made you come here alone?"

Gaurika ventured a look at Vegavat, who blinked lazily back. Emboldened by Ishvari's kindness, she asked in a rusty squeak: "Are you a devi?"

Ishvari laughed. "Oh no, no...I too am made of flesh and blood, just as you are." Gaurika looked so disappointed that she quickly added. "But celestial beings *do* play freely here, though you may never seen them."

"But can they see *me*?" Gaurika asked anxiously. "And can they hear *my* prayers?"

"What are you praying for?" Ishvari inquired, feeling a rush of love for the girl.

Gaurika struggled for words, then looked down at her foot and back at Ishvari.

"Ah!" Ishvari said. "You hoped to find healing herbs here...and a devi or apsara to cure you with a mantra or two." Gaurika's eyes widened—this naked woman was plucking thoughts right out of her head! "Do boys tease you?" Ishvari asked. "Swear you'll never catch a fine husband?"

"But I don't *want* a husband," Gaurika muttered rebelliously. "Mama says a demon lives in my body. I want to play seven tiles and hide and seek with the other girls. I want to—"

"Do you believe what your mother says about the demon?" Ishvari cut in, recalling how Sumangali's use of the word 'demonspawn' had grievously hurt her.

"My mother *never* lies," Gaurika stated. "She prays to the gods every single day."

"What about your father? What does *he* say?"

Gaurika's lower lip trembled and a tear rolled down her cheek. She swiped it away with the back of a hand, streaking her face with dirt. "A cobra bit him. He's dead."

Ishvari patted her cheek consolingly. "That must have been hard for you to bear." Village life was difficult enough for the poor, but this girl's lack of a father, added to her deformity, must cast an even worse pall on her joy. "If I heal you through the power of the gods," she heard herself say, "will you promise not to tell anyone how it happened?"

Gaurika's eyes flared with hope. "I won't tell a soul, lady! It shall be our secret!"

"Then sit absolutely still," Ishvari instructed, wondering if she'd gone mad. Vegavat rose, eyeing them languidly, causing Gaurika to lean against Ishvari for protection. "Down, Vegavat, you're frightening her," Ishvari murmured. Directing a yawn at the cowering girl, Vegavat rolled on to his back again, paws in the air, an enormous kitten enjoying the sun.

Ishvari felt the energy rising in her spine, serpent fire, sure and fierce. She reached for Gaurika's frail body and drew her closer, lifting the flared tunic to inspect her leg. Shutting her eyes, she felt herself being sucked into the mouth of a swirling mist.

Orange flames snaked from its center and using their heat, she touched the girl's foot with the fingers of her right hand.

Gaurika struggled to draw away, even as Ishvari's fingers held tight, kneading jets of living fire into the dead tissue, massaging away the blocks. Clearly she saw the source of the illness—a clump of nerves, tangled and inert with disuse. With fiery fingers, she massaged the nerves, straightening, then lengthening them, one by one, oblivious to the squirming of the girl. A shining figure loomed over her, holding aloft a trident, serpents writhing about his neck. "By Rudra's whip!" Ishvari heard her own ecstatic cry. "May Gaurika walk free!"

The girl slumped against Ishvari, her body still, only her heart beating. Ishvari held her close until the sun began its flaming descent. Gaurika opened her eyes, squinting at the blaze of colors. "Look down at your foot," Ishvari whispered. "See? If you did have a demon, God Rudra has swallowed it whole."

Gaurika stared down at her healthy foot. She lifted it in utter disbelief, inscribed circles in the air with it as she balanced precariously on the other, placed it on the ground, stood, took tentative steps forward, then raced around Ishvari, not once but three times—probably just to make sure she was not dreaming. She tossed her head incredulously, the ends of her braids dancing on her budding breasts, laughter pouring out of her wide mouth, mingling with the delighted murmuring of the river. "I must go now!" she cried, "I must show my mother!"

"Keep your promise!" Ishvari called after the flying figure. After she'd disappeared into the distance, Ishvari paced back and forth along the riverbank, staggered by this most recent mystery. The fire stirred at the base of her spine, re-energizing her. The healing itself had left her drained, yet she felt transformed. It struck her that both Sumangali and Kharanshu had predicted that her life would expand at some point to include others: *could this sweet child be the herald of a new phase?* Ah, if only Hariaksa or Nartaka were here, guiding her through this unfamiliar terrain! Never had she come this close to apparent sorcery!

Such spectacular healing would be impossible to hide, for villagers were insatiably curious. Talk around evening fires would revolve around the miracle of the healed foot. Inevitably, their minds would stray to the identity of the healer, to what might possibly have driven a beautiful woman to make her home in the forbidden valley. Ghora would wring the truth out of the girl with his nauseating blend of threats and promises. Knowing the scoundrel, he could well proclaim her a sorceress, hunt her down and drag her to Melukhha for punishment. Why hadn't she been clever enough to convince Gaurika that she was indeed a celestial nymph? The superstitious villagers would have swallowed *that* story, and the valley would continue to be the haunt of ghosts, to be avoided at all costs.

Praise Mahadevi, she was no more the drug-sick high tantrika; if necessary, she could live out her life in the jungle. Yet cradling Gaurika's thin body had reminded her of human delights, and given her the satisfaction of using her gifts to ease an innocent child's burden. Escape would be solely the imperative of survival.

Ishvari peered into the surface of the river again, studying her face: far removed from the high tantrika who'd escaped death by the skin of her pearly white teeth. If Devikotans *did* break into her sanctuary, could they possibly link a naked yogini with that glamorous fugitive? No, she was safe, unless Ghora's suspicions had been aroused by Sumangali's disappearance. Should the priest string together certain facts, rumors could spiral toward Melukhha. Still, the balance of power may well have shifted within the civilized world—Takshak could be dead, and Melukhha under kinder reins.

"*Aham Brahmaasmi*," she spoke the ancient words of blessing and acknowledgement Nartaka had given her out loud as she gazed up at the stars studding the vast canopy of night. "I am divine consciousness itself, blissful and immortal."

"Hey, you sweet thing, but that's true for *all* beings," the river chuckled. "If only the poor fools knew it."

When your understanding has passed,
Beyond the thicket of delusions,
There is nothing you need to learn
From even the most sacred scripture.
— *Bhagavad Gita*

HARSHAL

Ishvari woke early to bathe in the river, so swollen with rain it spilled generously over onto banks rich with river reeds and velvety bulrushes. A storm had exploded over the mountains during the night, drawing from the earth green spears of grass and the red and white speckled mushrooms which, when consumed, induced a cascade of mystical visions. Delighted, Ishvari saw that the tiny crimson-breasted birds that nested seasonally in the riverside foliage were back, warbling songs that floated sweetly over the gushing waters.

She gasped at the first shock of the cold water, then swam to a flat rock by the water's edge to scrub her body and hair until she tingled all over. Clambering on to the banks, she wrung her hair dry before letting it hang down the sinuous length of her back. Then rising high on her toes, she prepared for the ancient yogic salutation to the rising sun. Arms overhead, she flexed her spine backwards as the sun began its flaming ascent into the morning sky. Dipping forward from slender hips, she placed brown hands beside her feet, extending her legs far back to form a mountain, buttocks pointing skyward, eyes aimed at earth. Then she arched into the classic cobra, hood upraised, ready to strike, before reversing fluidly back into the first six poses to stand erect again, in the asana of reverential prayer.

Thirty-two times she worshiped the shining orb that kissed the earth with life. Afterward, she lay supine in the corpse position, breathing deeply before moving into the locust, then the bow, rocking on her abdomen with ease. The world turned upside down when she stood on her head, inviting the flow of blood to reverse its direction from feet to skull. She moved into the fish, opening her throat chakra, then sat cross-legged to twist her supple spine in both directions. After sealing in the vibrant energy she'd generated with a special mudra, Ishvari lay on the spongy grass and closed her eyes in readiness for deep relaxation.

Rejuvenated, Ishvari strode to the mouth of the river to meditate. When she opened her eyes much later, Maruti was approaching from the direction of the jungle, dangling a bunch of jumlums. In easy silence they broke fast, listening to the valley come alive with the chirp of crickets and the twittering of birds. Maruti crooned with pleasure as she caressed his gray head, then watched with pert interest as she buried the oval fruit seeds in a hole in the soft banks. The langur headed back towards the jungle, and Ishvari sensed the presence of Vegavat beside her. She stroked the leopard's muscled neck, marvelling anew at the communication that existed between her animal companions— often it happened that as soon as one left, the other arrived.

Vegavat stood, his satin-sheathed body bristling with tension. "Stay!" she ordered, alert for signs of an intruder. Nothing—just the wind in the trees and the musical moan of water birds. But the majestic cat was restless, fixing his impatient, gold-flecked gaze on her and waiting for a signal to investigate. Within her the fire stirred, communicating something. Puzzled, she searched the valley as far as the eye could see. A black dot on the horizon was taking the shape of one man leading another. Rinsing her hands and mouth with river water, she returned to watch the men staggering up the higher slopes like village clowns. Twice, in quick succession, the leader fell, dropping his companion with the weight of his body. Both went tumbling down to the bottom of the winding path, picked themselves up, dusted themselves off, and started upward again. She roared with laughter at the droll sight, startling Vegavat, whose ears fell flat against his skull.

As her laughter pealed across the valley, the leader gazed upward, shading his eyes from the sun and pointing excitedly toward her temple home. *Who were these men?* Intoxicated or insane? Travelers blundering along, oblivious of the tales of the valley's ghosts? Or royal spies, disguised as clumsy peasants? They advanced, undeterred by the steep incline. Such determination, Ishvari thought, moved to admiration. She placed a restraining hand on Vegavat's neck, toying briefly with the idea of hiding. But Gaurika's sweetness had aroused in her a need for human company and these men did not appear to be dangerous. Besides, who would take a naked yogini for a fugitive with a colossal price on her head?

The men made their way up the ribbon of river wending its way from the heart of the valley into the interior of the jungle. "Namaste," she greeted them, arranging her streaming hair to cover her nakedness—the garments Kharanshu had given her were frayed, and often she reverted to her natural state. "Do you come in peace?"

The cripple spluttered with anxious laughter. "Do we look like warriors, Holiness?" he panted. "*I* limp through life, while Harshal here, poor chap, can't see a cursed thing!" He gestured toward Vegavat, whose ears were erect, body poised to spring.

"Could you leash your friend?" he asked plaintively. "I'd so resent being devoured, especially after this hard climb."

It was difficult not to like the voluble cripple. Clearly he was the elder of the two, with a shiny globe of a skull, generous lips curved upward in a round face, and eyes alive with sly amusement. His left leg was deformed, the right overly muscled, his fleshy body showing signs of good living. His companion was thin and much younger, his eyes opaque marbles in a pinched, though attractive face.

"Vegavat won't harm you. Please sit," Ishvari invited. The men collapsed onto the grassy banks, the plump cripple shooting distrustful glances at the giant cat, who blinked coolly back. Ishvari offered them water in her copper container, and they drank thirstily. "Why are you here?" she asked, though she knew the answer.

Beads of sweat rolled down the older man's cheeks. "I'm Skanda of Melukhha, Holiness, and this is Harshal, my only child. By profession, I create erotic friezes for the homes of our nobles, while Harshal lives with his maternal grandmother in Valabhi, carving sandalwood goddesses that people marvel at since he uses only his inner eye." Skanda patted his face with an embroidered handkerchief, breathing heavily. "Harshal lost his sight as a teenager, woke up blind one morning, just like that." His eyes pleaded with her. "You healed Gaurika, Holiness—I'd pay anything you ask to have you restore my son's vision."

Of course Gaurika had talked! "And you, Skanda," she asked, glancing at his deformed leg, "don't you wish to be healed?"

Skanda grinned, quickly regaining his ebullience. "The answer's no, not any more, at least. You see, Holiness, I was born a cripple in Devikota. My parents dragged me from healer to healer, one worse than the other." He patted his shrunken left thigh.

"Mahadevi knows I endured years of kneading and massaging, with rancid tiger fat, bison semen, goats' dung, and what-have-you. Nothing worked. Yet, when I began to sculpt in earnest, my spirit grew. Now I view my imperfection as a tool for growth, and often, I actually find myself grateful for it."

"Acceptance I can understand," she said, "but you are *grateful?*"

Skanda nodded. "An odd thing to say, I know, but I *am* grateful. Let me explain…I've an apprentice with a unique talent for molding clay in just the right proportions. Unfortunately, he's also an expert at rousing my demons. When I long to call him a festering sore on my bum, I look down at my leg—which never fails to remind me that I too am an imperfect creature."

Harshal was listening morosely. Skanda patted his knee affectionately and continued. "Three days ago, we rode to Devikota to attend the marriage of my niece, youngest daughter of Andhaka, headman of the village for over three decades now."

Ishvari stiffened at the mention of Andhaka; so Skanda was the headman's brother? And yet how different they were! She resolved not to be influenced by a biological fact.

"Gaurika danced into the wedding hall and the crowd went crazy. She'd snuck out of the village a cripple, and returned dancing at twilight." Skanda shook his head in wonder. "The elders grilled that child like she was a tough piece of meat, yet she never deviated in the least. Spoke of a big cat and a naked woman pouring cold fire into her leg. Then she dashed off, her mother chasing after her, the priest chasing after them both." Skanda chuckled. "I'll wager no girl's ever given that priest such a headache."

She hid a smile; how could this garrulous sculptor know that the serene healer sitting before him had once given Ghora *much* worse? Skanda continued, grinning. "Ghora threatened to have her flogged to squeeze the truth out of her, and the little shrew swore—before all of Devikota, mind you—that the gods would strike him dead if he so much as *looked* at her cross-eyed!"

Skanda grinned ingratiatingly at her amused smile. "I had to investigate matters for myself, Holiness, and now I know I was right to do so, for light pulses around your head. Apsara or not, I'm convinced you have much power. Won't you heal my son?"

"What inspires your trust?" she asked curiously.

"I had a vision some moons past," Skanda explained. "A luminous female astride a jungle cat appeared and promised to heal Harshal if I took him to Devikota. Today—when I saw the spots on that lethal animal, and against the tide of fear that near swallowed me—I was reassured. Then I saw *you*, and my heart leapt like a hungry fish for bait, for you are *she*."

"I serve the gods, Skanda," she said, marveling at how the fire had evoked his vision. "Alone, I can do nothing. Harshal's vision can be restored only by divine grace."

Skanda shrugged. "Then you must invite the gods to work *through* you, just as our sages do." He added slyly: "I've heard it said on excellent authority that *not* to use one's gifts eventually destroys the gift itself."

Ishvari laughed; it was refreshing to converse with a clever human again. "Let me hear your voice, Harshal," she coaxed, turning to the blind man, liking his quiet nature. "If you had your sight back, what would you most like to see?"

Harshal's voice crackled like withered leaves underfoot. "When I was a boy, gypsy dancers traveled through Valabhi. A girl spun in their midst, light as mountain breeze. I feared that if she stopped, life itself would come to a standstill. Much later, I saw she was an aged woman!" A wondering smile touched his lips. "I'd like to see an artiste hypnotize the world like that again."

Tears stung Ishvari's eyes. Harshal was sensitive, loving and intelligent—no wonder he could create unusual art. Radiant essence streamed upward from her heart and into her third eye as she made her decision. "D'you believe in the gods, Harshal?" she asked, recalling Kharanshu questioning her in much the same way. "Do you have faith?"

"Yes, or I'd have killed myself many years ago," he answered frankly.

"And how are you sure I can heal you?" she asked, touched. "Did you too have a vision?"

"I cannot see the sun," he replied quietly, "and yet it never fails to warm me. Just so, I sense your light." Pain flashed across his face. "My mother dreamed I'd be struck blind for having blinded another in some past life. That came to pass. Recently, she dreamed I'd be made whole again." He shrugged, his shoulder blades jutting through his cotton tunic. "If nothing else, I've faith in my mother's dreams, for she is a pure soul."

"You're blessed to have such parents," Ishvari acknowledged. "So, Harshal, shall we see if the gods will permit us to work a miracle together?"

"I'd do anything to regain my vision," Harshal answered, his voice breaking. "Once, lady, my agony was so great that I tried to fix a noose to the ceiling of my room—but the stool I was standing on toppled over, believe it or not, and I fell heavily and sprained an ankle." He laughed bitterly. "I cursed myself for not even being able to commit *suicide* successfully, but later I felt sure this was a sign that the gods wish for me to continue to work through this terrible karma."

Harshal was a man of depth and caring, and like Gaurika, worthy of receiving the fire. The flame in her third eye shot up into her crown, illuminating the thousand-petalled scarlet lotus of her seventh chakra. "Do you meditate, Harshal?" she asked, in the grip of the unseen power.

Quivering visibly, Harshal nodded. "For twelve years, Holiness, three times a day. It's what nourishes my spirit, apart from my work."

"As though preparing for the fire," she murmured. She turned to Skanda. "Remain quiet while we work, if you please."

"Still as an Egyptian mummy," he replied eagerly, rising and limping toward the nearest bakula tree.

"Now, Harshal," she instructed. "Dive deep into your heart and feel your eyes coming alive." She inhaled deeply and a column of fire shot upward, knocking her backward onto the grass. She forced herself erect. *Why was she playing this dangerous game?* "Harshal," she whispered. "Do you realize my will is nothing before the will of the gods?"

He nodded, warily.

"D'you accept that if the gods wish you to remain sightless, it shall be so?"

The enthusiasm drained from his young face, but he nodded.

Ishvari stoked the flame at the base of her spine, drew the molten thread of energy to her second spinal vertebra, then to her navel, her heart and throat in quick succession. A humming began in her throat, rose into the vastness of her third eye, ascending into her crown, where it turned into a blazing stream that she poured back through the circle of chakras until the fire encircled her body in a vortex of light. Her fingers hovered over his face, aiming surely for the dead centers of his eyes, and the fire shot out, spinning around his sockets, resurrecting dead tissue, linking new and living cells.

Harshal cried out sharply, again and again and again, until the valley resounded with what sounded like the howls of a mortally wounded beast. She shut out his agony as well as her anxiety that villagers would hear and wonder and focused on looping the fire. An age passed and still the fire raged, shooting from her fingers into his awakening eyes. Then she fainted.

Someone was grabbing at her arm. She opened her eyes and saw Harshal standing above her, his face ablaze with excitement. "*I can see!*" he shrieked at the top of his lungs. "Papa, I can see! I can see!" Skanda was moving toward them, so rapidly she thought the fire had healed his limp as well. Skanda prostrated wildly before her. "You *are* a goddess! Don't you dare deny it!" He threw a muscular arm across his son's shoulders, his broad face cracking into a jubilant smile. "By Rudra's silver crescent, your mother will *levitate* when she sees you. Let's surprise her, shall we?" He laughed deliriously, his chins wobbling. "Better not, better not, her heart might not appreciate the shock." Words continued to bubble out of him. "The minute I saw that girl dancing rings around that priest, I *knew* she'd been touched by a goddess. And I was right! I was right! I was right!"

Overhead, a white bird soared, flapping its wings with hypnotic grace. Ishvari felt utterly spent—this healing had taken far more energy than had Gaurika's. Blindness connoted serious past misdeeds, sins fuelled by the extreme of ignorance—which Hariaksa had once told her implied disbelief in the laws of karma and rebirth. Only the gods could safely have burned the effects away. Skanda hovered anxiously about her. "Some water to cool you down? A hand massage, perhaps?"

Harshal was staggering in blissful arcs beneath the bakula trees, gaping at the white and fragrant blossoms, drunk with beauty, heady with color and motion. Could this be the miserable creature who'd groped his way up to her? She glanced up at Skanda and shook her head. "The gods exact a stiff price for the use of the fire, my friend." He looked so guilty that she added quickly: "Ah, but I'd do it all over again just to see the joy on your son's face."

Skanda drew out a leather purse from a pocket. "Holiness, I've gold."

"In your sophisticated circles," she asked wearily, "do goddesses charge a fee?"

"But you've nothing to cover your body!" Skanda protested. "Why not come with me to Melukhha?" he suggested. "It's a crime to hide such savage beauty! I could quite easily set you up in your own salon—I've plenty of gold and many contacts. I wager our physicians will soon be paying witches to curse you—you're bound to steal their clients away...."

She chuckled at his outrageous idea. Skanda slammed a palm against his forehead. "Stupid Skanda," he groaned. "A man famous, not just for his friezes, but for his tiny brain. Why would a *goddess* care for gold and fame?" He mopped his perspiring forehead. "Regardless, you must permit me to return this wondrous favor in some way. I insist, I absolutely insist!"

"There *is* something you may do," she murmured, as a thought took shape.

"Anything!" he cried, striking himself on the chest. Harshal turned away from the bakula trees to eye them both with gratitude. Skanda's eyes filled with happy tears. "If it's in my power, you shall have it. My life, for the sight of my son!"

"Keep your life, Skanda, but here's what you can do." She looked directly at him. "Help Gaurika—remember it was she who led you here. She needs support if she's to rise above the sludge of Devikota."

Skanda leapt up eagerly. "Arrange her mother's re-marriage perhaps? The woman's young and pretty enough, though her expression's way too tragic. I wager nourishing food and good loving could chase away her despondency." A smile crept over his face. "Yes, of course, I could provide dowry enough to attract a man who wouldn't mind marrying a widow, a farmer or tradesman, perhaps himself a widower—"

"Gaurika's intelligent and passionate," she cut him off, disappointed. "Qualities far superior to class, gender and wealth. A tutor could open her inner eye and ear."

"But such tutors are invariably from the upper classes!" Skanda protested. "How could I persuade such a man to educate a peasant *girl*?"

"Reluctance complicates trifles," she said, as an idea flashed. "There's a ferryman who resides on the banks of the Sarasvati tributary close to Valabhi. He teaches the promising regardless of class. Gaurika must request his instruction, and you must keep your negotiations with him private—he's a recluse and does not care for gossip."

Harshal, who'd been listening attentively, nodded. "I know him. He ferries my grandmother and I to the city at the end of every week. An intelligent man, and kind. My grandmother considers him a friend. I shall request her to approach him."

"An excellent idea, Harshal. Kindly tell the boatman that the yogini of the valley sends her warmest greetings." Ishvari turned back to Skanda. "As for Gaurika's mother," she continued, enjoying the sculptor's bafflement at his son's confident intervention, "give her a yearly allowance and find her a decent man if she wants one. Warn her the allowance will instantly dry up should she prevent Gaurika from studying." She paused, overcome by fatigue. "One more thing—should this teacher find Gaurika to be gifted in some area, you must pay for it to be nurtured." She cocked her head at the sculptor, challenging the resentment on his expressive face. "Is that too much to ask?" she asked.

"Not...not too much at all," Skanda stuttered, flapping his handkerchief wildly. "Just *preposterous!*"

Harshal placed a hand on his father's arm. "Look papa, just give the girl's mother enough to escort her daughter to grandma's home in Valabhi. I'll arrange for the girl to be educated, as well as pay her expenses. If her mother's willing, you can help her remarry." He gave his father a stern look from his new eyes. "Keep in mind, papa—you pledged your very life!"

Skanda gestured toward Ishvari. "Yes, but I wanted *this* goddess to benefit, not some chit...look at your healer, Harshal, now that you have eyes, feast them upon her, naked under that curtain of hair, at the mercy of the elements, yet lovelier than any princess I've sculpted!"

"No being is low in the realm of the spirit, Skanda," Ishvari said. "Now keep your word and return quietly to your homes tonight—I do not want my peace disturbed."

"We'll leave the moment after I speak to the girl's mother," Skanda agreed, mopping his perspiring brow. "I'll have Gaurika escorted to Valabhi, by hook or by crook, though my brother's guaranteed to throw a fit to beat all fits. He's strongly opposed to the lower classes acquiring learning—upsets the balance of power, you know."

Ishvari sighed, even more fatigued. For all his sly humor, it was evident that Skanda was just as snobbish as other wealthy Devikotans. "Just throw him a mysterious hint, Skanda—say Mahadevi instructed you to educate the child. No one argues with divine directive, or with influential men." She paused. "So, what passes for news in Melukhha?"

The sulky look slipped off Skanda's face to be replaced by surprise. "So you *are* human after all!" he exclaimed, waggling his eyebrows comically. "A goddess wouldn't give a pisspot for our ugly politics! So what can I share with you, Holiness? There's nothing I *can't* tell you, since my clients seem to have a penchant for spilling secrets." He sniggered. "One fellow said to me the other day that finding trustworthy friends in the city in these troubled days is akin to trying to locate a vegetarian crocodile. And how right he is! Since I don't mix in their circles, and enjoy a good gossip, I make a truly wonderful confidante."

"Start with Takshak," she invited. "What news of our great Maharajah?"

"*Great*?" Skanda inquired wryly, lips twisting in amusement. "Notorious, yes, and perverted, for sure. But *great*? Even I, Skanda, the great exaggerator, wouldn't go that far."

"Why?" she asked. "What has happened?"

"A victim of unbridled excess and ghastly misconduct!" Skanda pronounced. "Our king is dying, and once he's gone, all seven hells will break loose—we've no clear successor, and the Council's weaker than ever. Civil war looms, a prospect that's never before raised its vicious head in our fair city."

"What else?" she asked, fascinated by how much had changed.

Skanda looked around him cautiously, as if spies camouflaged themselves as parts of nature. Harshal laughed. "Come, father," he cried jovially. "Give our Holiness what she wants without all this drama." Skanda jabbed his son affectionately in the ribs. "It's true, Holiness," he said. "Takshak suffers greatly for his sins. In my opinion, his most hellish error was to violate a high tantrika during a love rite. Oddly enough, the woman was born in Devikota. Scandalous tales were circulating at the time about her affair with an Egyptian emissary, but the fellow was known to be so mendacious and cruel that *I*, for one, never could credit the foul talk."

He nodded at the memory. "Many turned against Takshak for his brutal reprisal against the Devikotan. Even if she'd erred, people said, it was because the king had mistreated her." He grinned, happy to share his stories. "Scratch an ordinary Melukhhan, Holiness, and you'll find a thirst for justice in our blood and bones. It's our nobles—spoiled by wealth, privilege and over-indulgent mothers—who set the bad example."

The sculptor sighed and wiped his brow with a kerchief. "Imagine, Takshak was stupid enough to kill a *sage* for protecting this high tantrika. As for Kushal, the one aristocrat who might have been able to extricate him from his troubles, Takshak exiled him— that good fellow died at his ancestral home, or so I've heard."

So Lord Kushal too had suffered on her behalf! She did not dare ask Skanda about the whereabouts of Sarahi lest he get suspicious.

"This high tantrika was *really* born in Devikota, father?" Harshal asked dubiously.

Skanda plopped down on the grass and began to massage his foot. "Yes, my son, and Ishvari was her name, though I too find it mighty hard to believe Devikota's fetid grounds spawned that spectacular beauty. When Kushal selected her, my brother was beside himself with rage. You see, all of Devikota expected his daughter Labuki to be chosen...the idiot *still* hasn't gotten over it." He hooted with laughter, jabbing Harshal in the ribs. "You've heard your uncle mimicking the envoy when he's had too much to drink, haven't you, son? He minces around daintily, purses his lips, and says, in this high-pitched voice—*could you possibly have forgotten whose authority you question?*"

The sculptor shook with laughter, his chins wobbling. "You see, Harshal? Your uncle's a stupid boor. Who else would have defied Lord Kushal, known for his razor-sharp tongue and vast influence? But back to Ishvari." He paused, eyeing them both. "I caught a glimpse of her, you know, when she arrived in Melukhha for her Great Rite." He puffed out his chest self-importantly. "I'm one of a handful who actually *saw* her with my own eyes, believe it or not!"

Ishvari stiffened—*could the sculptor possibly have guessed her identity?*

"That was roughly fifteen years ago," Skanda continued, lost in memory. "I had just delivered a statue to a merchant client and was heading home, on foot, mind you. The sun was so hot, I gave myself a rest under some devadaru trees. A dice game had erupted on the sidewalk, and someone yelled that our new high tantrika was passing. I looked up and actually saw her, face-to-face, glowering away at those crude men."

Skanda uttered a dramatic sigh. "Oh, but she was a cool goddess, so exquisitely featured I recall thinking even *I* couldn't do justice to sculpting her face." His round face gleamed with rapture. "Her eyes, by Rudra! I was drowning in those pools in the space of seconds. Her lips were moist rubies," he continued, licking his own, "red as pomegranate seeds. She was virgin then, but she glowed—" Skanda paused, seeking the right words, "as if she'd fucked a grateful god who'd injected her with the seed of pure gold," he finished in a rush.

He bowed apologetically to Ishvari. "Forgive my description, Holiness, but the woman was mesmerizing. People said Takshak deliberately unhinged her with drugs. One chap even claimed the king believed she'd been conspiring with the old priestess to overthrow him, which is why he was after her blood. By the gods, how he hated, and *still* hates, the imperious Inanna!"

Could Skanda's sources have spoken true? In retrospect, everything he said made sense—Takshak had relied on a vast network of spies and many were jealous of her growing intimacy with the maharajah prior to Alatu's arrival.

"What happened to Ishvari, papa?" Harshal asked.

"Oh, Takshak dashed off to fight those ill-fated Doms, taking that Sumerian witch along to warm his royal balls, and Ishvari went crazy—abused the sacred herb and started pleasuring some half-witted mendicant on the side, curse the lucky fellow." Skanda shrugged. "Which man could blame her for toying with a pretty boy when the king had thrown her away, as if she were no better than a shallow tavern whore? Funny thing is that this mendicant hung himself right outside her window—or he was murdered, no one really knows."

"And then?" Harshal prodded his father.

"Well, Takshak had near killed her at the ghats the night before, during a group rite—in so obscene a way even *I* hesitate to provide details. Before he could try again—Alatu wanted her burned alive, if you can even *imagine* that sort of cruelty from someone who called herself a woman—the girl fled." Skanda stopped to scratch behind his ear. "Nothing so scandalous had happened for eons...the whole city was buzzing with ten thousand rumors for years afterward."

Ishvari managed to keep her expression serene, amazed at how much truth there was to Skanda's gossip. How would he react if she revealed her old identity to him? Instantly she squashed the thought—she'd come too far to take such a silly chance.

Skanda stroked his bald head, mulling over the past. "It was the couple who served the Devikotan who saved her, you know, though people swear up and down that Inanna herself masterminded their escape." He grinned. "Believe it or not, the insane bastard *still* hunts for both those women. Takshak was never able to see his own faults, and he'll likely die that way."

Ishvari's throat was dry, though not with thirst. Within her the fire dipped, as if momentarily in abeyance. "So the maharajah is really ill?"

"*Dying*, as I said Holiness, though the Council tries to hush it up. Many believe Alatu dealt him poison, which is why he's thrown her into his worst dungeon. What fools! If she wanted to kill him, she's had plenty of opportunity." Skanda lowered his voice to a whisper. "What triggered our king's rage is that Alatu hid a note intended for him—a note which claimed Ishvari was innocent of any liaison with the Egyptian. By some strange twist of fate, Takshak happened across it. He fell into such a rage he put Alatu behind bars...and of course, not one of those nobles who panted after her will now lift a finger to free her—they're all still terrified of Takshak, and even more of their own women, most of whom detest the immoral Sumerian."

Skanda laughed and shook his big head. "Just so you know how twisted our maharajah is, he *still* refuses to lift the ransom off Ishvari's head. As for Alatu, he'll kill her, sooner or later, and no one will cry. Which of us can ever forget the horrors she urged Takshak to perpetrate on the Doms? As a result, we've reduced an ancient race, who were once our allies, to slavery."

"And Charaka?" Ishvari asked. "Does he still rule the Council?"

Skanda eyed her suspiciously. "You know a great deal about the city, Holiness...."

"Oh, but the fire throws up snippets from time to time," she cut him off easily, without missing a beat.

He nodded, dubiously; even if he did put things together later, she felt sure he would not share his suspicions; he owed her that much, at least.

"Charaka's currently under house arrest," Skanda went on. "This, after Takshak reprimanded him publicly in the Quadrangle, following exposure of a scandal involving treasury gold. Someone sent damning evidence against him to Takshak, a mysterious fellow who bedevils all efforts to track him down. There's a rumor floating around that he's the bastard son of some aristocrat wronged by Takshak out for revenge. Calls himself Takshak's 'royal brother,' if you please." He tittered. "Must be some truth to it, I say, or why bother to claim blood ties to a monster? Whatever the case, this fellow is making it his business to challenge Takshak. There are those who dare to predict this mystery man may well be our next maharajah."

Ishvari tensed. *Nartaka, maharajah of Melukhha?* If anyone was qualified to rule, it was he, although she couldn't see the near-naked sadhu wanting to hold court.

Skanda mopped his perspiring brow again. "I digress, we were talking about Charaka. Well, he finally went too far—stabbed to death two tantrikas living with him. Caught them in the act of loving each other and went berserk. Imagine that! *Tantrikas,* loving each other like man and woman, and blood cousins too, from what I hear. In certain civilizations such license is permitted, no doubt, but our righteous Charaka certainly didn't appreciate them practicing in his bedroom, though I hear he often used them together for his own pleasure."

He snorted with disgust. "One would imagine *he* was scrupulous in his affairs, that fucker of little girls. The Council jumped right in for a change. Charaka's been under house arrest for a couple of moons now—lost those hideous rolls of fat, and most of his mind too, is what I hear—and Takshak *still* refuses to hear his petitions. If the present Council holds strong, they'll sentence Charaka to death, and rightly so." He grinned maliciously. "You've got to be a maharajah to be able to kill a tantrika and get away with it, I suppose." Skanda sighed. "Filthy politics and filthier politicians! Thank the gods I'm an artist."

Ishvari absorbed this flood of news: the pendulum was hurtling back with all the vengeance of the gods. "And how does ordinary life go in the sacred city, my friend?" she asked.

"Oh, it gets worse every second," Skanda groaned. "Thugs roam the city at night, the government's gone to the dogs. A sick king might as well be a dead king. Our Council promulgates one edict after another regarding security, new taxes, and goddess knows what else. Folks flee the city in droves, heading for the foothills where land's cheap and fertile. Others are moving south, to where earth meets ocean. It's said peace reigns there, and that the natives are cultured and easy." He grinned. "Meanwhile, prices have dropped so low I picked up *three* good homes for the price of one!"

"You've reassured me that life in my valley is far better," Ishvari murmured, staring down at the emerald grass at her feet to hide her sadness; once word of Harshal's restored vision leaked, and leak it would, her private romance with the valley would end forever. Skanda threw himself to the earth before her once more, his lame leg flopping weakly in the air. "Words simply cannot express—", he managed to say, but could not continue for weeping.

Harshal gazed adoringly at her. "If ever you need me, Holiness," he said, "send word to Valabhi. I'm easy to find and yours to command. As for Gaurika, rest easy—I shall protect her."

"We'd better leave before my brother organizes a search party," Skanda said, taking his son's arm and throwing Ishvari a final loving look. "Come now, Harshal, this time *you* shall lead me home."

The sorrow of the worshippers was turned to joy,
For suddenly a light shone in the darkness:
The goddess had risen from the dead.
　　—Goldberg: The Sacred Fire

DELUGE

Harshal's eyes brought the world to Ishvari's feet; by noon the next day, supplicants were wending their way up the verdant slopes of the valley. As they neared the rock on which she sat, Ishvari saw an attractive young woman at the head of the small group, panting with exertion, her eyes red-streaked and puffy. She was draped in a silken sky-blue tunic embroidered in vertical columns of red and gold, and in her arms nestled an infant with deformed limbs.

Right behind her lumbered a grim-faced woman garbed in the green homespun of midwives, her hollow cheeks bearing testament to privation. Stoically she hefted the front poles of a straw pallet, upon which lay an emaciated man with sunken cheeks. A boy held up the back poles of the pallet, his sullen pimpled face glistening with sweat. And straggling way behind was a wisp of a girl of no more than seventeen or eighteen years, her eyes telling a cruel story.

Ishvari watched the motley procession moving up towards her with mixed feelings. The yearning for human company sparked off by her recent encounters now leapt up again, strong as brushfire. So when the supplicants rounded the final curve, she placed a warning palm on the skull of the big cat growling ominously beside her, and prepared to receive them graciously.

Vegavat remained on guard, poised to spring into action at her command, his tail flicking from side to side as he watched the heavyset midwife instruct the boy to place the pallet on the earth; ever since Ishvari had restored Harshal's sight, both animals seemed to have divined that their mistress no longer required careful defense.

The richly clad woman staggered to a halt, clutching the infant to her breast and fixing Ishvari with burning eyes. On an impulse, Ishvari took the child from her arms and held him tenderly against her own breast; as if in some weird recognition of souls, his eyes looked right into hers and his tiny mouth curved into a smile. The woman spoke in an anxious rush. "I must return home before my mother-in-law finds me gone, Holiness...may I speak?" At Ishvari's nod, she began her tale, her gaze dull with pain. "I was married right after my first bleeding, and though my mate is a good and virile man, I could not conceive. My mother-in-law cursed me publicly as a barren woman. Then she ordered my husband to abandon me and remarry."

The woman wiped her mouth with the back of a trembling hand. "My man mustered up the courage to refuse her, but I knew it was only a matter of time before she forced him to obey. You see, Holiness, we are without independent means...." She hung her head, her emotional fatigue apparent. "My mother-in-law is a cruel woman, Holiness, obsessed with the need for male heirs. Ever since her husband's passing, no one in our clan has dared disobey her. I thought of killing myself to put an end to all our suffering, but a passing sadhu gave me his blessing and soon my belly grew big with child. We fed a hundred priests and I began to glow like the sun...and then *this—*" She stared down at her son in Ishvari's arms, her face crumpling.

Ishvari drew the infant still closer, intuiting she could do nothing to make him whole. "My fire only repairs damage, sister— it cannot undo severe karma from past lives." Laying a hand on the infant's forehead, she released a stream of energy into his third eye, receiving, in turn, the information she sought: *the infant possessed extraordinary gifts. He was a sage who had chosen to be reborn in this condition in order to spread great wisdom.* "Care well for your son, my sister. One day, I promise, he will be respected as a wisdom teacher."

"*Such rubbish!*" the woman spat, thrusting out her arms to reclaim her infant. "With three fingers to wash his bottom, and so many useless body parts, you want me to believe he's here to save the world? Why not admit you're just another fraud?"

"*You* shut your cursed mouth!" the midwife yelled, shoving her work-reddened hands right into the mother's face. "Look, you! It was *these* hands that pulled Gaurika out into the world! *I* was first to see her damaged foot...and now that little cripple races around Devikota like a frisky pup!" She glared at the stunned woman. "If you hate your son so much, why not run back to that mansion of yours and beg your husband to plant another baby in your womb? It's all that rotten liquor your in-laws serve that has brought this ill-luck upon your family! You can tell your greedy bitch of a mother-in-law I said so too!" And with a string of curses, the midwife splattered the earth around her with betel-leaf spittle.

So the infant's mother was the daughter-in-law of Vamadeva, Devikota's tavern-keeper and Andhaka's cousin!

Vamadeva was dead then, likely due to consuming too much of his own liquor, leaving his quarrelsome wife to rule their sprawling joint family.

Tears spilled down the mother's cheeks. She stared miserably at Ishvari. "Grief has driven me mad, Holiness, forgive me…I *do* so love this child…he gives out such a calming energy when I lie beside him that joy fills me…even my man's grown to love the little chap and swears to take care of both of us, no matter what." She swallowed drily. "But just yesterday his mother announced she'd found him a second wife with a big dowry. Her face was so black with hate when she saw me rocking this little fellow to sleep that I decided to end both our lives. Moments later, Gaurika flew past our window, chasing a ball that had fallen into our compound." She looked pleadingly up at Ishvari. "I took it as a sign that I should come to you first."

"Only the gods may give and take life, sister," Ishvari said gently, recalling Atulya's icy rage when she'd almost drowned Urmila that hazy afternoon at Rudralaya. "Hold this child a moment," she asked the midwife, who obeyed with alacrity. She placed her humming right palm on the mother's forehead, directing the energy to blast through the crown of her skull so the woman could receive healing wisdom. When she felt the vibrating spirals of energy lessen, she lifted her palm and bid her rise. "The ways of the Divine are mysterious but sure," she said, gesturing for the midwife to return the infant to his mother. "Be brave—life is not easy for *any* of us, and yet we are *always* cherished, especially in our darkest times. Your mother-in-law is powerless before the will of the gods. Love your son with all your heart, for I swear to you—the fire does not lie. One day, this broken child will bring peace to many anguished souls."

The woman gaped at Ishvari, then inclined her head, perhaps realizing that an exalted source was choosing to speak through the beautiful yogini. She drew out a length of white cotton embroidered with golden peacocks from her bag and draped it around Ishvari's neck. Reclaiming her infant, she raised a hand to her heart and walked much more lightly down the hill.

Before she could disappear around the curve, the midwife dragged forward the pallet upon which her husband lay in a stupor, then threw herself at Ishvari's feet. In a flash, Ishvari saw that seven demons inhabited the body of the man, demons of intoxication and degradation. The reek of stale liquor emanated from the man's pores. "In Rudra's name," she addressed the demon leader boldly, "I bid you leave this man free!" Odious whispering ensued, evoking memories of her own ghastly possession. Resolutely, she clung to her center. "*Leave!*" she commanded, as the fire rose to its height. "By the power of the holy beings who rule this valley, I command you to forswear all human homes and to begin your own journey back to the light!"

The demons jostled with each other cantankerously, resisting her and draining her energy. Drastic measures were called for. She beckoned to the boy. "Place your father in the shallow part of the river." Stony with hate, the boy dragged the twitching body of his father to the edge of the river and heaved it into the cold water. The river babbled uproariously as the man came to life, and the demons howled profanities. Ishvari smiled—no evil could survive the pure waters of this river. The man kicked viciously, but the boy held him down determinedly. The midwife ran forward to help her son, tears streaming down her withered cheeks.

"Make sure he can breathe," Ishvari urged the boy—it was clear to her that a part of him longed to drown his father. She battled for the soul of the drunkard till the sun rose high into the noon sky. The third supplicant sat at a distance, her eyes flickering with disbelief as Ishvari cajoled, threatened, and finally drew up the full force of the serpent fire, uttering sacred syllables to eject the demons. Acrid spirals of smoke rose from the man's gaping mouth, turning scarlet as they made contact with the air. "In the name of Rudra," Ishvari commanded, "I bid thee gone!"

A scarlet cloud hovered menacingly over Ishvari. Then, as if struck by a bolt of lightning, it disintegrated and vanished. Instantly the man's rancorous mien altered. He stood awkwardly in the running water, his sun-burnt face growing as innocent as a boy's, his bewildered eyes darting from his wife to his son and then to Ishvari. The midwife threw herself to the earth, bathing Ishvari's feet with tears. Kneeling, she delved into her robe to draw out a coarsely woven woolen shawl and placed it reverentially on the rock beside Ishvari.

The midwife and her son hovered behind him as Ishvari addressed the man. "Returning to your old ways will bring back the demons in force, magnifying your suffering a thousand times." She leaned forward to whisper the healing mantra into his ear. "Repeat this right through the day and chant it until you fall asleep at night, calling upon divine light to flood you from crown to toe. Most importantly, stay away from liquor. Do this, and the demons cannot return."

Ishvari gazed into his eyes with compassion, seeing clearly why he had plunged into the abyss of addiction: survival had been viscerally hard in the aftermath of the drought that had struck Devikota and surrounding regions during her childhood. The demons had struck when he'd been too weak to resist. Kharanshu was right—toxic entities could *not* attack unless the victim had already been weakened by fear. "Most of all," she added, pouring light in through his third eye, "give thanks for your wife's support, and work hard to regain your son's respect—or else, the seeds of *his* dis-ease will germinate and attract new demons, turning him into your enemy."

The farmer glanced fearfully at his glowering son, perhaps realizing for the first time how terribly he had wounded the boy. From behind his mother's broad frame, the boy glared at his newly-born father; Ishvari did not need to delve into his heart to sense his craving for affection beneath the roiling resentment. The three left her then, the midwife shouting her praises all the way down the hillside.

Only then did Ishvari turn to the girl, so thin that her skin wrapped like ivory around her fragile bones. For this timid creature too she raised the fire to its roaring heights, shooting energy into the bony cavity of her chest to dissolve the sorrow encasing her heart. The girl fell to the earth in a faint and Ishvari covered her body with the midwife's shawl, humbly asking Mahadevi for guidance. Probing the girl's consciousness, she saw sexual violation by her father, a widower who'd loved his wife with an insane passion. When his wife had suddenly sickened and died, the man had turned to the fruit of their union for solace. He'd passed away recently, leaving behind his severely disturbed daughter.

Diving deep into akashic realms, Ishvari contacted his morose spirit and ordered him to release his daughter. The obsession was still strong, but her persuasion worked, leaving both spirits free. Ishvari was so drained that she rested while the girl slept beside her, her fragile body so still she might have been taken for a corpse. When she awoke much later, Ishvari stroked her forehead gently, cleaning out residual fear. "Your father regrets the harm he inflicted," she said. "Request the gods to find him suitable human birth so he may quickly incinerate his bad karma."

The girl's eyes grew wide with dread at the mention of her father. Mahadevi alone knew *what* she had endured! Ishvari stroked the girl's spine, infusing her with courage to face the ugly past before letting it go forever. Then she placed her palms on the girl's crown chakra, pouring fresh energy into the emaciated body. Probing further, Ishvari saw she was now living with her maternal grandmother; it was the old woman who'd urged the girl to find the healer of the valley. "Grow strong with the blessings of the gods," Ishvari murmured, sensing she would gradually recover with her grandmother's help. "Sleep well, eat nourishing food and learn asanas to help you relax. It is safe to dream again."

As days and nights melted into each other, supplicants began to travel to her from villages bordering Devikota, then from Melukhha, the prosperous island of Kairavi Yavana, and even from the distant cities of Suhma, Valabhi, Kamarupa, Konkana, Utlaka and Asmaka. Apart from a few hours snatched for sleep, Ishvari shared her fire with rich and poor, aristocrat and farmer.

One night, alone again after hours of healing, she was warming herself at a fire she'd built at the mouth of the river when a woman emerged from the darkness. She was garbed in the elegant manner of a rich courtesan, and cradled a lacquer box containing fireflies in her hands, a device used by the fashionable in lieu of a night-light. In the foreground stood a burly figure armed with a sword and two horses. "May I draw near, holiness?" she inquired courteously.

Ishvari nodded, though she resented this intrusion into her well-deserved rest.

"I bring you a gift," the woman answered. Placing her fire box on the ground, she gestured to the guard, who came forward and handed her a glossy pelt before returning to his post. "I'm told a yogini cannot refuse the skin of a tiger," she said, sinking to her knees to display the striped fur which had been skillfully fashioned into a luxurious cloak.

Ishvari ran her fingers through its plushness, saddened by the thought that one of Vegavat's kin had been killed to clothe her. "Once this skin covered a man-eater killed by our city's most intrepid hunter," the woman explained in a melodious voice. "Badly wounded, the tiger had begun killing the old and very young for food. Taking this beast's life saved many lives, Holiness. See? My own seamstress has sewn his skin into a garment fit for a yogini."

The courtesan's perfume was the same extravagant blend of crocus and spikenard that Ishvari herself had once worn in Melukhha. Consoling herself with the thought that karmic law was unerring—even in the animal realm, killers were eventually killed—Ishvari slipped the garment over her neck. A smile flashed across her visitor's lovely face as it fell in sumptuous folds to cover her lithe body.

"You look exceedingly well," Ishvari remarked, touched by her visitor's warmth. "What brings you here?"

"Appearances deceive, Holiness," the woman murmured, rising to her feet. "If not for my duties to my ancestors, I'd end my miserable life without regret."

"Yet you appear to have much more than most. What sorrow could make such a beautiful and wealthy woman long for death?" Ishvari asked curiously. The fire would not give her information unless it was essential to healing, or her own wellbeing.

"Will you listen to my story, Holiness?"

Ishvari studied her delicate features and hennaed palms, the rippling tresses decorated with jasmine buds. "Speak freely," she invited, seeing her younger self in the exquisite courtesan.

The woman drew closer, speaking in a low tone so her bodyguard could not overhear "I've traveled from afar to see you, Holiness, not daring to move about in daylight for I'm well known in certain circles. My name is Amrita and I was born twenty-one years ago in Kairavi Yavana to a famous courtesan, one of a pair of identical twins. From our fifth year on, Saundharya and I learnt the arts of dance and music. We studied grammar, logic and astronomy, even as retired courtesans instructed us in the arts of love. Our double beauty stunned those privileged to see us, and soon our fame spread." A nostalgic smile curved her bow-shaped lips. "My twin and I grew so close in body and mind we could read each others' thoughts."

Amrita's mouth twisted bitterly as she sank on to her haunches. "My mother groomed us to command the highest fees and warned us never fall in love—love, she said, would waste all the gold she'd poured into our education and shatter our dreams. So you can imagine her rapture when the maharajah of Melukhha invited us to his palace twenty-four moons ago, offering a fortune in gold for our virgin bodies." The box of fireflies glowed, shadowing the planes of Amrita's expressive face. Ishvari stiffened: *did all roads lead back to Takshak?*

"Suffice it to say, Holiness," Amrita continued in her melodic voice, "the maharajah exceeded our expectations. We drank bhang fortified with almonds while hidden musicians played ragas that drove us insane with desire. Takshak broke through my virgin's sheath first, and then, as I watched, senselessly happy in the grip of the drug, he entered my sister. All night long Takshak pleasured us, seducing us with his wit, charming us with jokes, stroking our newly awakened bodies with his sure touch."

The courtesan stared down at her box of dancing fireflies. "I survived that night with my heart intact, but not Saundharya—

Kama, our mischievous god of love, hurled his thunderbolt at her and she was lost. Flattered by her girlish worship, the maharajah encouraged her to remain with him, whispering compliments that made her blush. As soon as we were alone again, I reminded her that his reputation was black with holes. Never had I seen Saundharya so furious! She insinuated my motive was not to protect her, but stemmed from jealousy." The courtesan uttered a harsh sob. "I knew then that the rogue had weaseled his way into the darkest recesses of her heart where neither logic nor loyalty prevail. I could only pray that when the scales fell from her eyes, my beloved twin would return home wiser for the experience. So, wretched and alone for the first time since we were born, I returned alone to our home in Kairavi Yavana."

Amrita wiped her eyes with a scented kerchief. "Soon after, a small bag stamped with the Melukhhan seal was delivered to my mother. Already lost in fantasies of a glorious future for us all, my mother was devastated to find it contained a single tola of gold. Later I learned that even as Takshak had been making extravagant love to us, he'd been plotting Alatu's execution." She paused, her vivid face grave. "I was curious about this foreigner who'd caused such havoc in the great city, Holiness. Alatu was beautiful, intelligent and wild, I'd heard, and once the maharajah had worshiped her, even as our ancestors worshipped the sun and stars. What could provoke a man to destroy such a lover? Truly, Holiness, it made me fear greatly for Saundharya.

"Shortly thereafter, word reached us that Takshak had ordered Alatu to be burned alive in the Quadrangle on a charge of treason. My uncle, a merchant who travels weekly to Melukhha, was appalled by the peoples' joy—he could not believe that *humans* could hate so much. Not long afterward," she continued in a dull monotone, "he came by again, this time to deliver the news that

Saundharya had leapt to her death from the same ramparts as the old queen; even to this day, Holiness, nobody knows exactly why. Today is her third death anniversary."

The courtesan moaned in pure anguish. The box of fireflies fell from her hands, its lid cracking open, and the freed insects rose tentatively into the night air, hovering overhead in phosphorescent knots of green and gold before dispersing over the hushed valley. Ishvari stroked the courtesan's bowed head and murmured: "Now I understand your despair."

Amrita nodded gratefully. "That my mother had been greedy enough to sell her *own* daughters to such a devil wounded me terribly, Holiness. I cut my ties with her and moved to my own home, where I conducted a brisk business to keep from killing myself. Soon I earned a reputation as Kairavi Yavana's most desirable courtesan—but, on those rare nights I slept alone, I could not stop thinking of Saundharya and Alatu, who had both been destroyed by the Melukhhan king. Indeed, my nightmares forced me to seek the advice of a scholarly friend. It was he who assured me Alatu was a sorceress who'd done indefensible evil. He told me Takshak had turned on her only after discovering she'd hidden a message concerning the innocence of the fugitive high tantrika."

Ketaki's missive again! Ishvari kept her expression impassive, fearing to arouse Amrita's suspicions, but the courtesan was too engrossed in her own story to care. "Perhaps my mother is right...and love *is* a dangerous thing," Amrita said, pursing her vermilion-tinted lips. "My friend claims it was only when Alatu fell in love with Takshak that he lost his passion for her. Strange as it sounds, the maharajah desired her most when she flirted with others and treated him lightly...Takshak craves *only* what he cannot fully own, my friend says, like a child who hungers for a new toy and discards it soon after it is acquired."

Amrita smiled wryly, even lovelier in her distress. "There are times I'm overcome by gratitude for my profession, Holiness...allying oneself with a single lover appears to be most perilous—for most men mistake lust for love. And yet, somewhere within me is the hope that real love *does* exist. If I don't believe this, Holiness, I fear I might still kill myself."

A vision of Nartaka flashed through Ishvari's mind; she'd not seen him since that horrible night at the ghats, but her love for him seemed to have blossomed, like a bud unfurling its face towards the sun. "It does exist, Amrita," she murmured. "Believe me, it truly does."

The courtesan fell quiet, her face growing serene in the moonlight.

"How does your friend know Takshak so well?" Ishvari asked.

"Once he was the youngest member of the Melukhhan Council and knew the king intimately. He claims the seeds of Takshak's disease sprouted after his young wife's death; not even his tantric gurus could alter his blasphemous stance that women are mere playthings. Perhaps this was his callow way of striking back at Mahadevi for stealing his bride and unborn child away from him...or at his mother for letting him down in so many little ways...or at Inanna, for winning his mercurial father's love. Like many other nobles who could have kept the sacred city strong, my friend too fled to Kairavi Yavana when Takshak began to attack anyone who dared stand against him."

Ishvari nodded, admiring Amrita's keen mind. "Even privileged men struggle with primal fear, Amrita. A woman's mystery frightens them, for some of us can reduce even a seasoned warrior to pulp. Try to have compassion for such men, for their armor stops them from growing."

Amrita frowned, then, as she digested the words, nodded her lovely head in appreciation.

"And now it is time to extract the wisdom from all these awful experiences and surrender your burdens to the One," Ishvari advised her gently. "When your heart is clean again, Amrita, a man who has shed his own armor will offer you the *real* love you want— the love that survives change and blazes fiercely long after mere physical beauty fades."

Pity swamped Ishvari at the thought of the sick and lonely Takshak—to be given charisma, virility, intelligence, wealth, the admiration of his citizens, as well as the devotion of one splendid woman after the other—and then to spurn it all for the oblivion of animal pleasure!

Amrita cleared her throat nervously. "People say your fingers transmit divine fire, Holiness…I beg you to kill the demon that stirs up such misery that I'd rather be dead."

Ishvari caressed her wet cheek. The bodyguard moved restlessly in the shadows. "It's not a demon that hounds you, Amrita, but a form of despair—the insidious kind that shreds the heart and numbs the soul." She paused, listening to the voice of the fire. "I hear Kairavi Yavana hosts a hospice for the dying. I suggest you prepare delicacies with your own hands and carry them to its most desolate inmates. As you feed them, lend them your ears, and your own sadness will fade into insignificance. The fire has spoken and it never lies."

"Is that your *entire* counsel?" Amrita asked skeptically.

"There's more…pray that your twin finds her way to the light…and keep in mind that Rudra whips those he most loves most cruelly. Treat your pain as a gift intended to help you evolve, and soon you will taste the peace and joy buried in your own heart." Beneath the painted façade, Ishvari saw sensitive intelligence in her liquid eyes. "Pleasing men for gold is unworthy of your gifts, Amrita. You *will* find a worthy mate when you've grown to deserve him." She smiled. "Perhaps it will be this scholar you so respect?" Amrita blushed, and Ishvari knew the courtesan was in love with her friend, but too scared to admit her feelings, even to herself. "Until then, strive towards your spiritual goals and surrender the results to the Divine."

"I treasure your counsel, Holiness," Amrita murmured. "Every time a man appraises my worth in gold, my soul shrinks. I hide my feelings well, but until tonight I haven't been able to forget or forgive. Now I know Takshak is just a weak and frightened man, worse off than a starving urchin in Kairavi Yavana's worst slums—after all, even an urchin can hope for better."

"What news of Takshak's current state?" Ishvari asked.

"I hear that physicians from every corner of the civilized world are baffled by his ailment," Amrita confided. "Takshak lies in a shadow world of oil lamps and servants, shrieking and wailing like a baby at times—as my friend says, quoting some great Melukhhan sage, no living being, high or low, escapes the hammer of the gods. Some say the Sumerian cursed him before she burned to death. If so, the curse of a betrayed lover's a deadly thing, especially given that Alatu was a sorceress. The Council's trying to keep all of this quiet, of course, but word's out and the city's in a panic."

Amrita lowered her voice to a whisper. "I've a confession to make, Holiness...I was on the verge of offering myself to Takshak—just so I could get near enough to kill him with the juice of poisonous mushrooms." Her lips twisted. "Can you believe that despite his sickness he *still* calls women to his private chambers?" She chuckled drily. "Though what he's able to do with them in his state confounds my imagination. I thank the gods I came to you first." She studied Ishvari's face intently in the moonlight, her face melting into admiration. "Many say you're one of the sixty-four yoginis, come to ease the suffering of our people. May I presume to ask your origins?"

The urge to tell Amrita her own incredible story rose fierce. How much more pain, terror, loss and degradation did *she*, Ishvari, have to speak of? But she would not speak, not for lack of trust, but because burdening Amrita with such information could crack her fragile composure. "I came to this valley as a desperate girl," Ishvari murmured, "and my spirit has lived here since. Once I too was rabid with hate, Amrita, but fortunately the gods took pity on me and the fire rose."

I am the heat of the sun.
I hold back the rain and release it.
I am death, and the deathless.
And all that is or is not.
    —Bhagavad Gita

GHORA

One spectacular day towards the end of summer, Maruti and Vegavat disappeared. As Ishvari lay napping under the bakula trees that night, the fire threw up a vision regarding their sudden and inexplicable vanishing. Through intricate details revealed, she received confirmation that their spirits had been close to her in past lives, and that the gods had summoned them to see her through an excruciating rite of passage in this lifetime: now she was to look for them no more.

Ishvari felt neither sadness nor fear to be alone again; what she did feel was a surge of gratitude for their long and magical companionship; had there been humans around to distract her after Sumangali's passing, she realized, she might not have been quite as open to receive the numinous grace of the fire goddess.

As for Nartaka, Kharanshu's words had been on target—by leaving her to flower alone in the valley, the sadhu had shown her true love. Enforced solitude had led her to finally experience wholeness; alone for decades, she had come to realize that while a lover can indeed evoke untrammelled delight, it is the inner beloved that truly brings one to completion.

Every evening after the stream of supplicants headed back home, Ishvari lay on the banks of the wise old river, allowing nuggets thrown up by the fire to mature into living truth.

Once she lapsed into a lingering dream-state in which she glimpsed a mandala of souls set in a dazzling pattern that revealed the unique beauty of every single being. Now she was sure that all beings manifested from a single source and radiated into countless entities.

The human was possibly god's most fantastic creation, a complex sentient instrument designed for divine power to express itself. True evil was a myth; the real culprit was ignorance, reinforced by false notions of separation. Beneath the often hideous veils of ego, spirit shone as the eternal and living substratum, ever lustrous and pure. Even the conscienceless brutes who had taken the lives of so many beloved to her were destined to find their way back to the light; instead of enraging her as it would have done before, this knowing only deepened her peace.

Yes, indeed, this universe was an infinitely mutating dream in which all things—even mud, stones, flowers and water—were composed of light and intelligence. Earth was surrounded by rings of galaxies, and new universes were constantly being created. The source of everything was a thunderous silence, the shining face of God. And ironically, it was her heart that had led her to this enlightenment, not the sharp intellect that had won her the rank of high tantrika.

One evening as she lay beneath the bakula trees gazing up at the stars, Ishvari felt the beginning of a major shift. Close to dawn, her spirit voice awoke her. *Your time in this valley draws to a close,* it said calmly. *Prepare yourself.* "Is that so?" she asked, startled.

"Who will heal the sick if I leave this valley?" *All humans have spirit guides and the fire waiting within. Removing pain also prevents some from growing. By sharing the fire so compassionately, you've burned your bad karma. Now direct your supplicants to find their own paths to freedom.* "How?" she asked. "Most are riddled with superstitious fear and will not listen." *Other high beings will come to their aid. Be calm when you next face your supplicants and the right words will come forth.* "But where would I go?" she asked curiously. "This valley is my home." *Shame on you, Ishvari,* Self chuckled. *The entire cosmos is your home!*

Joyfully she climbed to the highest spot in the valley and sat beneath a flowering arka tree, absorbing the beauty of the sweetest abode she'd known. As the sun rose in the morning sky, she acknowledged the wisdom of her inner voice; in truth, healing no longer fulfilled her. Oh, how wonderful it had been to see Gaurika run, how thrilling to witness Harshal feast his eyes on bakula blossoms. Many Devikotans who'd harassed her family had sought her fire since, and not one had recognized her as the unkempt child chosen by Lord Kushal; never in her wildest dreams could she have foreseen the happiness that healing her erstwhile enemies would bring.

Thirty-six moons had passed by since she had poured fire into Guarika's crippled foot. She had healed with passionate love, treating each patient as she would her own Self. But now, base human nature was turning her work into a farce; decrepit patients were carried to her, and she was expected to restore them to vigor. When she advised some to surrender to death with dignity, they often hurled accusations of fakery at her. Still others came just to gawk at the exotically lovely healer, who performed her incredible miracles with such humble grace.

Recently a pair of rich merchants from Asmaka had approached her: the first brusquely ordered her to trace a lost trading ship, the other offered to move her to lavish city quarters if only she would place a death curse on a business rival! She had sent them off without rebuke, fearing to disturb the fire. It grieved her to note that the number of such supplicants was starting to equal those who came to her to be healed.

Only rarely did a supplicant truly touch her soul. One such had been carried to her on a litter a few moons ago—a giant of a man with skin so yellow she had drawn back, thinking she had been brought a corpse to resurrect. But the man was alive, and when he'd opened his sunken eyes, the depth of his gaze had raised the serpent fire to its roaring heights. The fire had shown her that his blood was toxic due to the ingestion of baneful roots, and she had sent curative heat coursing into his veins. Guarded by his attendants, he had fallen into a deep sleep until dusk, awaking refreshed. She'd sent him away with simple advice on diet and herbal baths.

It was still early when she walked down to the river to bathe in its sunwarmed waters. She returned to her dwelling for a meal of bananas and goats' milk. By the time she was done, villagers were already making their way up the slopes. She waited until they seated themselves before the healing rock, observing both men and women, old and young, and a few children. Throwing the tiger skin over her nakedness, Ishvari walked down to the river bank to meet them.

Bracing herself against their displeasure, she launched into her farewell speech. "People of my heart!" she began. "For thirty-six moons I've used divine fire to heal! But now my spirit asks me to cease. So today I shall repeat what I've said to you many times before—that each of you possesses the same gifts I do. By polishing these tools, I swear to you by the power beyond all earthly powers, you can heal yourselves!"

"Mind you, some of us have to make a living!" a stout woman with an ugly lump on her throat shouted belligerently. "I've no time for your holy practices, and that greedy witch on the other side of the river won't give me the herbs to bring down the swelling on my throat—not unless I give her my last sack of wheat!"

"My healing fire will not rise again," Ishvari spoke tenderly, as empathy surged for the woman's frustration. "I know your story, Kolambi, and I've given you a simple way to heal your sickness," she added, pinning the woman down with her calm gaze. "The gods, it is said, are happy to aid those willing to aid themselves."

"Simple to you may be difficult for me," Kolambi muttered, her jowly face flushing.

"Not if you open your inner ear and truly *listen*," Ishvari retorted. "You're far from stupid, Kolambi, and even children can absorb what I teach, for they are not blocked by rigid beliefs." She looked steadily at the angry woman. "Now listen well: first, you must accept that in our human form we are all imperfect, though the degree and nature of imperfection varies. We all feel angry, bitter, sad, jealous, vindictive, guilty and regretful. We do not forgive even trivial slights." She paused to focus briefly on each of the other supplicants in turn. "Our greatest fault is to mistake the unreal for the real—by giving importance solely to that which is temporary, and ignoring our true nature, which is light and joy itself."

Most were drinking in her words, as if accepting that soon she would be gone. "The emotions that cause our suffering are encouraged by the demon of pain, whose intent is to keep us circling in delusion. Deny its existence and it controls you; watch it with amused curiosity, and it skulks away—for this demon hates to be recognized as the destructive child it truly is.

"Slowly you will become aware of a higher self existing above and beyond all earthly suffering. This is the witness—wise, loving, fearless and connected to all other beings. This witness is your true Self, for it survives the death of body and mind. And when ignorance dissolves, you will be healed by your own divine light." She smiled warmly at Kolambi. "Is that simple enough for you, my sister?"

In response, Kolambi bent her head and muttered angrily. Ishvari turned to the others, seeing doubt battle with faith in her integrity. Three pretty girls were smiling, as if they understood her, and amazingly, some of the adults seemed to have truly listened. The wisdom of the inner voice would take root within those willing to grow; for the rest, she could do no more.

"Won't you use your fire just one more time to burn away the sores on my chest?" a middle-aged fellow with dark circles beneath his eyes begged. "My wife swears she'll never ...."

"Look, maa!" a girl shouted, pointing to the slopes below. "It's our priest!"

Startled, Ishvari turned and saw Ghora, grown bowlegged and desiccated with age, charging up the steep slopes of the valley as if chased by a legion of fiends. Trailing behind him was a plump woman with red-rimmed eyes. Panting heavily, Ghora turned the final curve, a mere fifty human feet from where Ishvari sat by the edge of the river, coming to an abrupt halt before her. Shading his eyes from the sun, he eyed her with beady speculation: *could this sun-burnt woman wrapped in tiger skin possibly be famed for her wisdom and magical powers?*

Ishvari smiled; so not even *Ghora* recognized in her the girl he'd failed to destroy! Memories flashed—Sumangali lying insensible on the packed earth, Obalesh's swaying corpse, the shadowy mass of villagers fired up by this man's shrill exhortations. Once she'd hated this sometime fawning, sometime bullying, but always corrupt and cruel priest of Devikota. Now, as she looked into his piggy eyes, all she saw was a pathetic fellow, blinded by lust and greed.

"Namasthe," Ghora said briskly, joining his hands in greeting. "I am Ghora, priest of Devikota, and this is Labuki, my good wife." Labuki came forward and prostrated before her. Lord Kushal had been right after all, Ishvari thought, amused—Labuki's prettiness *had* faded into plainness. Vexed with Labuki's subservient manner, Ghora hauled her roughly to her feet and raked the supplicants with his cold eyes. "Only Devikotans here, I see. Well," he demanded, "what are you waiting for? Leave! All of you, get out! I'm here to deliver an important message to the healer—in private!"

The group stirred, but no one moved. "Can't we wait until you're done, O Ghora?" the washerwoman asked. "We've trudged all the way...."

"Out of the question!" Ghora barked, wiping the sweat off his brow with a kerchief.

Ishvari watched the supplicants rising reluctantly, unwilling to interfere with Ghora's petty drama—in any event, she'd nothing more to say to the village folk. Grumbling, the group moved reluctantly down the slope. As he passed Labuki, the man with the sores called out: "Has your boy returned yet, O Labuki?" Labuki shook her head, and broke into loud sobs.

"Quiet, wife!" Ghora growled. "Your father's promised to send searchers out for him if he does not return by evening. Don't trouble the healer with this trivial matter."

Labuki glared at him, then rushed forward and knelt before Ishvari. "Find my boy, Holiness," she pleaded. "A willful child he is, with no respect for his elders…slipped out last evening and hasn't returned. Won't you help us find him, *please*?"

Ghora stepped forward and pulled her up angrily. "Don't force me to dismiss *you* as well, woman!" He turned to Ishvari, pendulous lips twitching. "I'm here to inform you that our maharajah orders your immediate presence in Melukhha."

Ishvari fought the urge to giggle at his pomposity. "Isn't it customary for a monarch to send an envoy with so important a message?" she asked coolly.

Ghora frowned. "Envoys attract attention and this is a strictly private matter," he answered stoutly. "Your fame has spread to the sacred city. Takshak orders you to attend him at once."

"I'm done with healing," she said. "My healing fire will rise no more."

"It's the duty of *every* citizen to come to the aid of our maharajah!" Ghora exclaimed, his face reddening. "A chariot awaits you at my home right now to take you straight to our king. Be grateful for the honor and desist from playing your coy game!"

"What ails your king?" she asked, marveling that her loathing for Ghora had simply melted away. She felt no need to toy with him, though she found his melodramatic manner hilarious; karma would take care of him, far better than any human agency could.

"No one can tell," Ghora replied haughtily, drawing himself up to his full height, which was not very impressive. "Healers from Crete, Sumeria and Egypt are just as baffled as our illustrious Susruta himself, who admits he can do nothing more." He shook his head. "Our poor king lies in darkness—even *candlelight* hurts his eyes."

"Convey my apologies to Takshak," she said. "Tell him I'm done with healing."

Ghora snorted in disbelief. "You joke, I am quite sure! Takshak is *your* maharajah as well! Can you be so ignorant you are unaware of the extent of his power?" He glared at her with such indignant ferocity she had to struggle to keep from laughing out loud. "Despite his illness," he continued, oblivious of her amusement, "our king is still as mighty as the gods! Only an idiot bent on suicide would send such a dangerous answer back to him."

"Then inform Takshak the healer of the valley is an ignorant rebel," she retorted lightly.

Changing his tune instantly, the shameless wretch fell to his knees before her. "Surely you're aware that such a message will mean both our deaths?" Ghora whined. "Heal Takshak, and you'll have gold and fame beyond your wildest dreams, servants at your beck and call.…"

Ghora had not changed a bit! Labuki gazed beseechingly at her from behind her groveling husband. Ishvari closed her eyes, asking the gods for news of their son. The fire within burned incandescent before subsiding into a steady hum. A vision of a path to the jungle flashed, against a backdrop of ominous red. Labuki's intuition was right—her son *was* in grave danger.

Ishvari drew her cloak tightly about her body as she slid off the rock. "I'm off to find your boy, Labuki," she said, patting the anxious woman on the back. She turned back to Ghora. "I suggest you run back home as fast as your stumpy legs will carry you, demonspawn. It's risky for criminals to linger here after sundown—the spirits who rule this valley are a rough lot."

Ghora's face turned a dull scarlet. "*Demonspawn?* Why such gross insults?" he hissed. "Come with me now, or you'll regret it forever…perhaps you've not understood the honor…."

The maverick girl who'd thumbed her nose at the priest lived on: grinning at Ghora's astounded expression, and Labuki's delight that she was off to find her son, Ishvari leapt down on to the river bank and kept walking, until she could no longer hear Ghora's frantic shouts. Guided by the fire, she traipsed through ropy tangles of vines and waded across streams made magical by tiny, glittering frogs, persevering for hours until she entered its dark heart.

The leafy green sunlight filtering through the trees was fading when she heard voices. She followed them to the edge of a clearing, shocked to see a naked boy—his face flushed with blood and terror—hanging by his ankles from a flame-of-the-forest tree. A drummer beat a rhythmic tattoo on a gourd instrument as tribesmen, Kirata or Sabara from the look of them, danced around their shivering captive, their bare bodies gleaming with animal fat. The drumming grew faster as the shortest of the tribesmen leapt into the middle of the circle, brandishing a curved hunting knife at the boy. Ishvari moved closer, tripping over a tree stump in her haste. At her cry of pain, the drummer stopped and the men dispersed instantly to seek the intruder. They caught her, semi-collapsed.

"An outlander woman!" a tribal shouted. "Clothed in big cat fur and most beautiful!" He spoke a dialect of Yambu, the language of the far northeast.

"Hey! Get out of the way, let me see," another ordered. The fire flared and Ishvari felt her consciousness dimming; only the thought of the boy kept her aware. "Aiyee! Here's one more gift from Chandika!" the second fellow exclaimed jubilantly.

"Let's sacrifice her along with the boy!" another yelled.

"Yes! Throw them both into the swamps...so we can hunt them down later with our dogs. Chandika will smile upon us!"

The brutality of this suggestion brought Ishvari to full alertness. She tried to sit up, but a midget tribesman jumped on her legs and pinned her down. Two men, by their appearance twins, strode toward the midget. "Wait, Bodhav! All captives must first be taken to Ushana!"

"Well spoken, Kamapala," a man agreed. "We've done much wrong...let Ushana decide."

The boy was cut down from the tree and lifted up by a couple of the men. The midget shouted and gesticulated angrily as a tribesman threw Ishvari across his shoulders, but no one listened to him. They moved into deeper jungle, traveling for perhaps an hour before Ishvari was thrown in a heap on the ground beside a mossy cave. Moments later, the boy's body landed beside hers. She placed her arms around his shivering shoulders, holding him tight.

"Ushana!" she heard the men calling. "O Ushana, come see our fine gifts!"

A stick jabbed at her breast and Ishvari shut her eyes, reluctant to face the man who ruled her bloodthirsty captors. Footsteps approached her. "You, Rana, lift her head up," a sonorous male voice ordered. "And light, more light."

A golden stream of serpent fire buzzed in her third eye as someone crudely prised apart her eyelids. "*You!*" she gasped, recognizing the distinctively tattooed face of the seven-foot giant chieftain who'd been carried to her by a group of his worried tribesmen.

"By the blood of Chandika!" Ushana exclaimed. "Do none of you fools recognize the healer of the valley? Here is the yogini who saved my life!"

"What about the youngling, Ushana?" the midget who'd sat on Ishvari's legs demanded resentfully. "We've not sacrificed for many moons. This is why you sicken! This is why our tribe's been thrown out of our ancestral hills!"

Ignoring the midget, Ushana held out his enormous hands to Ishvari, helping her to rise. Heart pounding with relief, she stood, pulling the boy up with her. "This child is kin to me, Ushana," she announced firmly.

"How so?" the midget challenged, darting a malevolent look at Ishvari.

"Shut your mouth, Bodhav," Ushana ordered coldly. He turned to his tribesmen and pointed to the space between his eyes. "While you were out hunting, I dreamed," he said simply. A hush came over his men. "I dreamed that at the moment of my healing three weeks ago, a sacred fire ignited within me. In its molten center, Chandika took wondrous shape."

An eerie collective moan rose into the still air. "People of my heart," Ushana continued hoarsely, "Chandika came to tell me she no longer thirsts for blood!"

The midget's face warped with hatred. Suddenly he hurled his spear at Ushana. Without thinking, Ishvari threw herself at Ushana. They both fell to the ground as the spear whizzed harmlessly over their heads to pierce the trunk of a tree. Ivory sap flowed from the fresh wound. Only the boy's retching sobs broke the stunned silence.

Leaping to his feet, Ushana seized the midget's neck with one massive hand. "Chandika warned me, Bodhav," he announced, shaking the midget as effortlessly as he might a rag doll. "Twice you've poisoned my dreaming potion." Disgusted, Ushana dropped the fellow to the ground where he lay, stunned and breathing heavily.

A child screamed; Ishvari turned, astonished to see tribeswomen carrying infants, and girls, both prepubescent and teenage, emerging from the cover of the jungle groves. Dark breasts with elongated rosy nipples hung free on sinuous bodies, some heavy with milk, others upturned and ready for motherhood. Sobbing raucously, a big tribal with a heavy face and vacuous eyes threw herself to the ground next to Bodhav. Sighing heavily, Ushana bent low and pulled her up. "Mate of Bodhav," he addressed her. "You know our old ways—your husband must be stoned to death for his sins, but I give you my word that you and your daughter will not be harmed."

Bodhav wriggled like a wounded serpent at Ushana's feet. "Every tribesman sings your praises, mighty Ushana," he whined with sly desperation. "For the sake of our tribe, reveal the extent of your kindness before all...."

Ushana's voice was heavy with sadness. "If you *had* cared for our tribe, Bodhav, you'd never have trod this evil path. Your ingratitude wounds us all. Didn't I hold the elders back from sacrificing you to Chandika because they feared your deformity would bring us misfortune?" He sighed again. "Perhaps I was wrong...what true clansman tries to destroy his benefactor?"

Bodhav's pugnacious face flushed with rage. "My motives are noble!" he roared, leaping to his feet. "I seek the prosperity of our tribe! A return to our old ways of worship! But when blood is to be shed, you hold back. Your eyes are turned so deeply inward we don't exist for you anymore! It's your indifference to our welfare that has incurred the wrath of Chandika!"

Ushana shook his head. "No more lies, Bodhav. Your motives have always been base." He turned to Ishvari, his deep-set eyes melancholy. "Twice you've saved my life, healer. Now guide me in the best way to deal with this ingrate."

"I will indeed," Ishvari agreed, immensely grateful to the fire for transforming the lethal situation. "But first assure me of an escort back to the valley—this poor lad's mother is crazed with worry." Ushana gave her a dignified nod, and she relaxed. "This is my counsel," she said clearly, for all to hear. "Do *not* kill this foolish man, for bad karma will fall upon your own noble head. Instead banish him for life, lest his evil further infects your tribe."

Ushana grew quiet for long moments; then he smiled and nodded his agreement. The midget's jaw fell in disbelief; moments later his face grew ugly with fresh malice. "Mind your back, Ushana!" he spat, arms on his hips. "Bodhav is not finished with you, oh no, he is not!" Several tribesmen moved angrily towards him, but Bodhav scuttled rapidly into the jungle like an enormous, ungainly land crab, and no one cared to pursue him.

The chieftain motioned to the twins. "You, Sumantra, carry the healer on your back. She's hurt her foot, be gentle with her. You, Kamapala, take the boy. Follow the shortest route and leave them safely in the valley."

The ride back was surprisingly swift, for the tribesmen knew secret ways and amazing shortcuts. Before too long the valley stretched before them, surreally beautiful in twilight. She slid down Sumantra's back, and the boy followed suit, dashing behind her to hide; it would be many moons, she thought, before he recovered from his blood-curdling adventure. Raising crossed palms to her heart, Ishvari bowed to the tribesmen. The twins solemnly returned her salute, then turned back, only the rustle of leaves indicating their swift departure.

Ishvari limped alongside the boy until they arrived at the path leading into Devikota. She stopped and fell to her knees then, hugging him close again for long moments as she breathed in the unwashed child smell of him. "Never forget the terror of this day," she whispered into his ear. "The blessings of the gods must be earned, not squandered." He goggled at her, struck dumb by conflicting emotions. How fortunate, she thought wryly, that he resembled not the swinish Ghora, but his once pretty mother. "And be good to your mother," she added. "Mahadevi herself will bless you then."

She gave him a gentle shove homeward; despite his terror, the boy had experienced her love, and hopefully sensed its difference from his mother's cloying attachment, as well as his father's angry affection. Perhaps he would grow up to be the antithesis of Ghora.

The senses are great, and the mind is greater still.
Greater still than that is buddhi, the seat of reason.
But beyond lies the Atman.
Aware of that ultimate self, be steady and at peace.
And strike the enemy, however elusive he may be!
　　—Bhagavad Gita

MAYA

As Ishvari hobbled upward to her dwelling, exhausted by the day's bizarre stream of events, she spied someone sitting on a flat rock beside the river. He came to his feet at the sight of her, a tall, lean man with shaven skull dressed in the white garb of a celibate monk.

"Acharya!" she cried in incredulous recognition, just as someone rushed up behind her to playfully cover her eyes. "And who are *you*?" Ishvari asked, enveloped by the unseen stranger's affection. "Let me see *your* face first," retorted the stranger, removing her hands. Ishvari swung around to see a sturdy white-haired woman whose dark eyes twinkled in a seamed but comely face. "Indeed, it is my mistress!" the woman exclaimed, placing her hands on her hips and grinning at Ishvari's confusion. "*What?* You don't remember your faithful Mandakini?"

"Sweet Mahadevi!" Ishvari cried, her weariness evaporating instantly. "Is Vasudeva with you? How did you know I was here? Have you been waiting long?"

"Ah, it's my mistress all right," Mandakini gurgled with laughter. "Bubbling with a hundred questions and all at the same time." She kissed Ishvari roundly on both cheeks as Atulya approached them, beaming. Physically, the sage looked much the same, but his spirit felt lighter. Despite her swelling foot, Ishvari prostrated before him.

Atulya raised her up, looking at her with such intense love that her eyes filled with tears. "I'd have come earlier," he murmured, brushing the tears off her cheeks with long fingers. "But Kharanshu reported you were thriving. Of course, when Mandakini heard I was traveling to your part of the world, not even her precious husband could prevent her from joining me."

"Come, mistress," Mandakini said, taking her arm. 'Supper's almost ready, and you and I have much to catch up on. We're to leave tomorrow, acharya says, though I'd like to stay longer, or better still, take you back with us." She giggled. "I've learned not to argue with a sage."

"So soon?" Ishvari cried, limping after Mandakini. "Where's Vasudeva?"

"At our ashram school," Atulya explained, following them into the temple. "We've close to ninety students now, boys and girls, all mountain-born. They can be mischievous, even defiant at times, but Vasudeva keeps them in line quite easily. Nevertheless, we must allow him to return to the work he most enjoys, which is growing our food. And besides, Kharanshu's expecting us." Atulya waved off her disappointment. "Rest easy—we'll all be meeting again, and soon."

Mandakini stirred rice broth seasoned with vegetables on the leaping fire, darting adoring looks at Ishvari as she added spices to the contents of the clay pot. The delicious aromas piqued Ishvari's hunger, reminding her she'd not eaten since early that morning.

Mandakini pointed to a corner of the room and Ishvari smiled her thanks when she saw the sack of supplies. "Vasudeva would have sent you entire bags of his best produce," Mandakini said, her eyes twinkling, "except that acharya here said you wouldn't be here too long anyway, and not to bother."

Ishvari sat on the floor and directed fire into her own foot until the swelling visibly eased. Atulya sat close by, watching her work with paternal pride.

"What happened to your foot?" Mandakini asked with concern.

They both listened intently as Ishvari related the weird events of the day. Atulya nodded with satisfaction when she spoke of her meeting with Ghora, his smile widening when she provided dramatic details of how she'd come to rescue his son. "Today, the spirit of Hariaksa dances," he said simply. He inclined his head towards her in an almost formal gesture. "Both Devadas and Hariaksa were right in their high assessment of your worth, my dear. It was *I* who was wrong." He flushed, suddenly looking like a tender boy. "Will you forgive me?"

"You were not altogether wrong, acharya," she said, deeply moved by his humility. "I *did* betray the wisdom you all poured into me." She smiled through her tears. "Was it not you who taught us that karma is judged mainly by intention? Let me assure you that never for a single moment did I doubt *your* good intentions."

Atulya's ascetic face shone with pleasure. Ishvari mopped up her tears and bowed her head in overwhelming gratitude—after teetering on the brink of insanity and death due to her misdeeds, the gods had allowed her to win the praise of the once grim senior acharya himself!

Mandakini killed the fire and produced a stack of leaf bowls to serve the food. They carried their bowls out to the flat rocks by the river, relishing their repast as dusk fell over the valley. "The jungles bordering Devikota teem with seekers, you know," Mandakini announced. "Poor people—if one can ever call aghoris and yogis that, and get away with it...they're exiles now, banished by our new religious laws, forced to make their homes in the wilderness."

"So the madness continues," Ishvari said sadly; with the seers gone, the glory of Melukhha would soon fade and die. A sudden thought struck her. "Perhaps you should carefully spread the word that this valley exists, Mandakini? Here our yogis can worship in peace, for there's good water and food, if one cares to look for it. It would be wonderful to live again in community."

"Only *you* won't be here when they arrive," Atulya cut in. "Things are changing rapidly everywhere in our kingdom, my dear, for only greedy and short-sighted fools remain to serve Takshak. It won't be long before Melukhha stews in utter chaos."

"Someone mentioned Lord Kushal had passed on," Ishvari probed.

Atulya nodded somberly. "Twelve years ago, and three years into exile, deep in the country where his family has estates. I happened to be with him when he took that final journey, Ishvari. He was certain you and I would meet again, and urged me to tell you that had he known you were in the grip of a demon, never ever would he have abandoned you. Indeed, several times before he drew his last breath, he ordered me to give you his deepest love."

"So he knew I was safe...and doing well?"

"I assured him the fire had indicated strongly that you would thrive. He died at peace."

"And Sarahi?" she asked.

"That fearless woman is long back on her feet after her great loss." Atulya smiled. "It's rare indeed to encounter a couple who are the best of spiritual friends. You'll be meeting Sarahi again, Ishvari, and this time you'll be free to forge a strong friendship."

If the sage knew of her disappointment at being denied friendship with Sarahi, did he also know of her wicked seduction of Pundalik? "And Inanna?" she asked, trying not to blush.

"Ah, the fantastic Inanna," Atulya murmured, his eyes twinkling as if he'd read her stream of thought. "Takshak actually threw her into prison after you escaped…apparently Alatu had convinced him that Inanna was out to usurp the throne. There was a huge public outcry…Inanna was greatly loved as you know…but this time Takshak was intent on finishing her off. One night he had her locked up and heavily guarded, and by dawn she'd vanished. But for Nartaka, I fear she'd have been trampled to death by elephant the very next morning."

"Is she still alive?" Ishvari asked, hoping she could meet the fascinating priestess again.

"Death came to her quietly a few years ago, while she was meditating."

"Praise Mahadevi! But tell me—how on earth did Nartaka manage to free her?"

"Ah, but Nartaka never speaks of his exploits, and Inanna vanished for good after that final fiasco. All we have left, my dear, is yet another interesting mystery to baffle us."

"Where is Nartaka now, acharya?" she asked.

"It's safer no one knows his whereabouts, for he has the biggest price on his head. Had Inanna cared for temporal power, Nartaka could easily have been king, and Melukhha would still be thriving. Unfortunately our court was bristling with intrigue at the time he was conceived, so Inanna wisely hid her pregnancy even from Shaardul and vanished until after he was born."

"Did she birth him in Sumeria?" Ishvari asked, eager to know everything she could.

"Oh no...Nartaka was born and raised in our mountains. When he turned twelve, Inanna sent him to study gnosis with Magi priests in Eshnunna. Later, he returned to be schooled by our own sages. The rest is history, for Nartaka is a living legend in gnostic circles." Atulya smiled. "You know, of course, that it was he who first drew you to this valley?"

She nodded; just thinking of the sadhu who'd played such a crucial role in her tempestuous past had set the fire smoldering red-gold at the base of her spine. "Will I see him again, acharya?"

"Patience, Ishvari," Atulya counseled kindly. "Time will reveal all."

"Now listen to how we traced you to this valley," Mandakini cut in cheerfully. "Kharanshu sent a couple to our hermitage—Harshal of Valabhi, and his bride, Gaurika, a native of Devikota."

"*What?*" Ishvari exclaimed, utterly amazed by *this* particular twist of fate.

"Just you be quiet and listen for a change, mistress," Mandakini scolded happily. "Well, this Gaurika spoke to me of a beautiful healer living in a haunted valley. She said this devi had used serpent fire to heal her deformed leg, whereupon Harshal chimed in to say that this same woman had restored *his* sight." Mandakini laughed. "Gaurika had danced for us earlier that evening, you see, bewitching us into silence—not one of us could believe they'd both once been physically impaired. Vasudeva and I reported their tale to Atulya that same night, and we all agreed this healer just had to be *you*."

Ishvari shook her head, astonished—Harshal and Gaurika together, Atulya changed for the better, and Vasudeva and

Mandakini carrying on their lives of service into old age! Truly, the cosmos was governed by a compassionate power.

When the moon rose high in the night sky, Atulya walked further down the riverbank to meditate, but Mandakini urged Ishvari to report all her news since they'd parted company at the back gate of Rudralaya. So Ishvari spoke of the miracle of Hariaksa's death, and of Maruti's clever and heroic guidance through the jungle. When she came to the horrors she'd witnessed in Devikota's square, Mandakini wept, and when Ishvari recounted how Sumangali and she had lived happily together in the valley until her death, Mandakini wept even harder, this time with joy. Ishvari concluded with Kharanshu's masterly guidance in redirecting the fire.

Mandakini was silent for a while, digesting the incredible sequence of events. Then she tenderly pinched Ishvari's cheek. "I've met many other strong women in my long life, beloved mistress, but no other appears to have had so many great souls concerned about her welfare."

They left Atulya seated peacefully beside the river to sleep inside the temple. When they awoke, the sun was rising and Atulya was sitting silently by the window. Struck by his stillness, Ishvari was unable to believe that she'd once feared, even *hated*, this brilliant and wise man. Truly, time and suffering had mined the gold in both of them, for Atulya too had transformed.

Outside, the bakula trees rustled in the morning winds and the river gurgled. Atulya strolled away, and Ishvari and Mandakini sat beneath the trees and drank in the morning splendor of the valley. Pulling a wooden comb out of her bag, Mandakini brushed Ishvari's long hair till her scalp tingled. "Would you happen to know my age, Mandakini?" Ishvari asked curiously.

Mandakini coiled Ishvari's streaming long hair atop her head. "So you haven't marked the years with notches on some helpless tree, eh?"

Ishvari laughed. "As you can see, Mandakini, time does not count for much here."

Putting the comb down, Mandakini began counting the years on her fingers. "Let's see now, twelve when you left Devikota, nineteen when you entered Melukhha. Forty-two moons later—was it that quick?—you were back in this valley, so that's close to twenty-three. Vasudeva and I have lived in the mountains for seventeen years, which would be roughly the time you've presided over this valley." She beamed. "May I inform you that you've reached the ripe old age of forty?"

"Forty?" Ishvari cried in shock. "But I am *old*!"

Mandakini erupted into giggles. "I'm much older, and Vasudeva and I *still* practice maithuna." She cupped Ishvari's chin in her hands. "And if you don't know it already, dearest, you're lovelier than ever—the gods have kissed you with marvelous depth and richness."

Knowing her age affected Ishvari profoundly. Now she truly appreciated her inward progress, though one aspect of her life remained to be explored: a higher love between woman and man. Were her feelings for Nartaka exaggerated by decades of solitude? "Since you are so perceptive, dear Mandakini," she said impulsively, "would you care to throw some light on why Nartaka has not bothered to visit me here?"

"Ah, mistress, from all I've heard, that man is like the wind blowing over the Sarasvati in winter," Mandakini murmured. "Swift and incomprehensible, with no discernible pattern."

"I think I love him, Mandakini," Ishvari whispered, blushing.

"But you hardly *know* him!"

Which remark prompted Ishvari to relate all her experiences with the baffling sadhu. Mandakini listened in wonder, tenderly stroking Ishvari's back. "Now, sweetling," Mandakini said, when she was finally done, "I see why no other man could satisfy you."

As Ishvari strolled with Mandakini along the banks of the river that afternoon, a willowy tongue of fire flickered in her third eye. Suddenly she saw the world of phenomena as a flimsy veil of exceedingly fine vapor. Entranced, she picked up a stone, enjoying the sight of the trillions of dancing particles that composed its solid appearance, then moved her attention to the ceaselessly moving dots in every speck of sand. Now she understood what Hariaksa had divulged to her so long ago—that maya did *not* mean the tricks of illusion performed by traveling magicians; instead, maya meant that what human eyes and senses took for ultimate reality was merely a thin curtain over multitudinous layers of subtle realities that formed so grand a design it staggered ordinary human conception.

When Atulya and Mandakini bade her farewell that evening, Ishvari released them in peace, for the fire was alive within her. That same night, alone under whispering bakula trees and a golden moon, she dreamed of white-complected men in strange garb ordering dark-skinned laborers to move piles of rubble, under which they unearthed skeletons and painted jars, shards of pottery and palm leaves that disintegrated in eager hands, broken childrens' toys and scattered bits and pieces of jewelry. The outlines of the colossal granary of Melukhha hovered before her astounded eyes, and, as the vision continued to unfold, revealing chaos and destruction, she recognized the crumbling brick walls of the Great Bath.

She awoke briefly, aware she was dreaming part of the same dream that Inanna had recounted to the aspirants at Rudralaya. It never failed to astound her how the super-intelligent tentacles of kundalini pervaded all realities, linking past, present and future, fusing unconscious, conscious and superconscious into a detailed network that provided her with the information she received in the form of flashing scenes. Still, she could not decide the time or nature of the fire's revelations—Mahadevi gave her what she *needed*, rarely what she wanted.

As she fell back into sleep, Self propelled her consciousness into a remote future, where she caught glimpses of people in a vast subcontinent with contours that seemed simultaneously familiar and alien. From remote citadels of power, politicians mouthed platitudes, even as they enriched their coffers for generations to come. She saw trembling girls sold to aging lechers and teenage widows thrown on funeral pyres, as drums drowned out their agonized terror.

In ten thousand homes in ten thousand cities and towns, brides served as kindling to the raging fires of inhumanity. Mansions sat smugly hidden from ugly, bursting tenements, where women whored and drunkards reeled through dreary corridors of poverty. Babies' bellies swelled with hunger as screams rent the complex tapestry of this strange, new world.

The enlightened see the same essence
In a wise man, a king, an outcaste, a dog or a crow.
    —Bhagavad Gita

TAKSHAK

Life took on a sharp piquancy after Atulya and Mandakini left: with Maruti and his regular offerings of fruit gone, Mandakini's supplies run dry, and the milk from the aging goats rapidly dwindling, Ishvari could no longer take nourishment for granted. Reluctant to forage in deeper jungle, she managed on the wild fruit and berries she picked on her walks through the valley.

Then, on the twenty-first day following their departure, she found a reed basket sitting on the rock of healing. Inside nestled an abundance of fruit found only in the heart of the jungle, layered with feathery fronds to keep them fresh, and six loaves of unleavened bread. This timely gift, the fire told her, came from Ushana, the tribal chieftain whose life she'd twice saved.

The baskets arrived at regular intervals, the edibles they contained sustaining her until the next one mysteriously turned up. Only once, waking before dawn, she happened to see a lithe near-naked figure depositing a basket on the rock before turning back towards the jungle; so swiftly did he move that she could not rush out in time to thank him.

No longer did supplicants attempt the arduous climb to seek her out—the distressing news that the yogini's fire would rise no more to repair illness had spread. Using her newfound leisure to practice conscious surrender into each moment, she awaited clear signs regarding her future. And while she did, the fire deepened her knowing that all things rise into brilliance before fading away, and that this cycle repeats itself until mortal fuses with godhead.

When dusk shadowed the valley, a bizarre restlessness would occasionally grip her, at times so violently it felt like a strangler's rough hand squeezing her throat. Then her mind would pitch and swell tempestuously into past and future. *With one foot in the past and the other in the future,* Hariaksa used to say as he pounced on a day-dreaming aspirant, *one urinates on the present.* His comical irreverence had never failed to send the girls into infectious giggles. Now, Ishvari used his vivid metaphor to keep her attention focused on the present.

Skilled as she had grown in dissolving emotional darkness by investigating the nature of her true Self, brief cycles of obsessive thinking occasionally plagued her. At these times, she became poignantly aware of another being alive within her, a female yearning to explore the frontiers of sacred relationship. Images of Nartaka would flood her consciousness then, so vividly that she could see the contours of his face and thrill to the resonant cadence of his voice.

Until the full rising of the fire, feelings of abandonment had scourged her. When she'd spoken of her insecurities to Lord Kushal, the astute envoy had said that the only permanent antidote to such pain was to shatter the ego to rubble—a near impossible task for most. And he'd been right: both her past love relationships had been propelled by desire and fear, and both had ended in tragedy. Nartaka alone held the promise of true depth in love, and yet, this unusual man had held himself aloof during her most challenging times in the valley. What tricks fate played!

Early one morning after moving through a satisfying series of asanas, Ishvari lay down on a flat basalt rock beside the river, delighting in the darting of shimmering dragonflies overhead. A carp shot up from the bed of the river like a silver arrow to snap up a dragonfly and dive back into the water with his prize. It was kin to her old friend Zaphara, whose bloated body she'd seen floating belly-up some moons ago. She smiled to think Zaphara had left behind numerous kin to keep memories of his flashing, coppery beauty alive in her heart.

The carp's dive back to the river's depths caused ripples to move across its surface, expanding into wider concentric circles that reached their largest circumference before vanishing. Once again, the water reflected the bakula trees and the splendor of the morning sky.

A flock of bright green parrots with red-ringed throats shot out of a grove of arka trees, and the thunder of elephants stampeding through the jungle came to her ears. On the river bed, she spied round, pastel-hued pebbles resting between emerald tendrils of ferns. Three plump catfish emerged from the mica-flecked mud, stirring silt with their whiskers. In seconds, the water was so muddy the pebbles were lost to her eye. Indeed, she thought wryly, life's ceaseless momentum left in its wake a cloudy string of events only an enlightened eye could unravel.

Out of the blue, a nebulous scene unfolded before her: she saw a cottage form itself against the backdrop of high mountains, its gray stone walls bright with the hardy pink and yellow roses that flourished in high altitudes. Inside the cottage, Vasudeva lay lifeless. Age had shrunk his burly frame, yet his face was tranquil. Beside him sat Mandakini, composed but pale, her hard-working fingers for once still in her lap. Atulya entered the dwelling, his eyes radiating warmth. In the background she heard the happy chatter of children. It was clear that Vasudeva's spirit had passed on, and yet, instead of sorrow, Ishvari felt only gratitude to Mahadevi for transmitting tidings to her of those she loved.

At twilight, roughly two moons later, Ishvari rested beneath the canopy of bakula trees surrounding her dwelling. Boughs heavy with blossoms hung over her head, and she inhaled their fragrance with pleasure. Within her, the fire glowed, artfully governing the systems of her body. It was dark when she rose, driven by the urge to urinate. As she squatted by the river bank, her eyes strayed to a line of advancing lights rising up from the bottom of the valley, and her sharp ears caught the drone of male voices cutting through the silence.

Quickly she splashed cold water on her face, longing suddenly for Vegavat. Should she hide in the jungle until they left? No, escape did not feel right, and yet the fire was alert, pulsing up from her spine, warning her! Throwing the tiger skin around her body, she seated herself on the rock of healing and gauged the distance to the nearest path leading into the jungle—at the slightest threat to her safety, she decided, she would take off like a streak of lightning and hide until the men were gone. Certainly neither a city dweller nor an ordinary villager would dare follow her into the jungle until morning, if at all.

Strong winds blew away the cover of clouds, revealing a crescent moon. In its pale light, she glimpsed men holding aloft a covered palanquin. Relief flooded her: here was just another prosperous supplicant, traveling under cover of night, determined to rouse the recalcitrant healer into service! She turned to the fire within, circulating it in smooth arcs from base to crown. When they turned the final corner, she was prepared.

"Hold the torch steady, Pala," a gruff voice ordered. "*What? Can't* see her? On that rock beside the river, so still you can barely tell her from stone...."

The men approached her with uniformly confident bearing. As they drew nearer, Ishvari saw the palanquin was covered in crimson silk embroidered with gold needlework. Diaphanous curtains hung from a central point, concealing the identity of the personage reclining within. Men garbed in green, crimson and saffron came forward, four carrying the palanquin, the fifth leading the train. The head porter stepped forward and she saw that the insignia decorating his uniform defined an elephant on its hind legs—the royal emblem of Melukhha!

"Takshak of Melukhha honors the healer of this valley!" the man cried.

How foolish she'd been to believe Takshak would forgive the impudence of a rustic healer! Ishvari did not allow her voice to betray her shock. "I am honored," she responded, her words traveling clear and unafraid through the still air.

The guardsmen set the palanquin on the ground before her, arranging it so Takshak was placed slightly above her level—it would not do for a king to raise his eyes to a commoner. Responding to the impatient rustling of the curtains, a guardsman parted them. Takshak lifted a trembling hand and pointed toward the bottom of the valley. "Go down and wait," he commanded feebly. "I'll call when I'm done."

Ishvari's thoughts flew unbidden to those excruciating early days following her escape when she'd conjured up this meeting with a blistering torrent of emotion. Takshak had crept into her dreams, sometimes alone, sometimes with the mendicant, raising bizarre fantasies of passion, arousing her until she wanted him despite his fickleness, against his cold evil. No other man had pulled the strings of her life to more effect—Takshak had sexually shamed and near killed her, drowned her beloved guru, burned down the jungle hermitage, hung her brother, blinded her mother, and capped it all by placing a huge ransom on her head!

She stared at his emaciated figure, stunned by the massive blow time had dealt him—Takshak the magnificent, fueled by cruel caprice and the extremes of sensual indulgence, had shrunk to a pitiful, withered imitation of his once vibrant majesty. Something about his gaunt body, curled to one side like a diseased child, wounded her grievously. His head was propped against cushions marked by spreading yellow stains of fresh vomit. His eyes were tinged with the reddish-yellow of advanced disease, bringing to mind a mortally wounded lion.

The leader of the guardsmen set flaming torches into the river mud, then wheeled around and motioned to his men to follow him down the slope. Ishvari realized that her life had come full circle; now the pathetic sight of the man who'd taken her virginity was almost unbearable!

Fixing her attention on the base of her spine, she vaulted energetically across the space between them to probe his body with the fire, examining its network of nerves. The virulence of his disease was so strong she almost fell off the rock. The fire located the nine-headed demon of insatiability, predator of humans of misdirected passion, the patient evil that bides its time as its victim slips into the bottomless pit of the senses. *This* was the ancient cunning demon Amrita's friend had glimpsed in Takshak—the devil who denies a man intimacy, the comfort of companionship grown rich with time. *This* was the demon who'd driven Takshak to feed on one lover's prana after another, uncaring of the suffering he inflicted. And the awful pity of it all was that Takshak had cravenly obeyed, in a vain and fatal attempt to slake the unquenchable thirst of his shadowy master puppeteer.

Sighing, Ishvari withdrew her probe. Even before the guardsmen had rounded the curve and vanished into the darkness, she knew that, in the space of a single moon, this wretched creature would exhale but be unable to inhale. "O Takshak!" she cried impulsively, overcome by the waste of his enormous potential. "See where your hunt for power and pleasure has ended!"

Takshak stirred, his eyes slits of annoyance. "Who are you, woman?" he demanded. "How dare you address your monarch so insolently?"

Never place your head in the mouth of a tiger, Hariaksa had warned. "Do you recall Ishvari?" she asked cautiously, aware of the enormous risk she was taking—Takshak was just as dangerous ill, perhaps more so, for now he had nothing to lose.

He fell back on the palanquin with a shuddering sigh. "Yes, of course, this fantastic healer just had to be *you*." His lips curled into a bitter smile. "Do I recall Ishvari, she asks," he mocked her in a high falsetto. "*Do I recall Ishvari!*" His eyes radiated malevolence. "Could I possibly forget the rustic bitch who made a laughing stock of me before my own people?"

Takshak cleared his throat. With visible effort, he sat up and shot a wad of phlegm over the side of the palanquin. "So the gods have thrown you back into the wilds, eh? Indeed, it's a *great* pleasure to meet you again, Ishvari, I'd forgotten how touchingly honest and naive you could be, despite years of learning, a low commoner beneath the surface gloss." He laughed, a short bark, provoking her and studying her face for a reaction. She smiled at him coolly, genuinely amused; some things never did change—Takshak would die a condescending snob.

"Did you think your monarch so *witless?*" he demanded hoarsely. "A beautiful yogini living alone in a haunted valley, wasting the sacred fire on mere peasants. Hmm…would an unlearned peasant presume to give lofty advice to both rich and poor? No, she had to be educated. So why not the city, where she could earn a fortune in gold? A fugitive, perhaps? *Even the notorious ex-high tantrika of Melukhha?*"

Shifting his shrunken body, he watched for signs that she was impressed by his logical brilliance. Ishvari gazed tranquilly back at him, revealing nothing. A frog croaked, signaling a raucous chorus. Fish splashed in the river. Fire torches flickered at the base of the valley, indicating the presence of his waiting guardsmen. She relaxed, enjoying the cool whip of river breeze on her face; she was safe until he called to them, if his voice could even carry that far.

"There's pain in your eyes," Takshak muttered, his eyes darting obsessively over her face. "I'm sorry for my harsh words, Ishvari, but as you well know, I've a wicked temper." He attempted a boyish smile. "Can you forgive a fool who regrets letting a jewel of your caliber slip right out of his hands? But who knows…perhaps you too are regretting your loss?"

Now he was slipping back into the past. "It's night in my gardens," he whispered throatily. "Ishvari of Devikota glides toward me, feet like dark arrows, every muscle taut, thighs resembling plantain trees, navel a half-open lotus floating in the river of her belly…those ghastly crones certainly knew how to dress a virgin." He leaned forward, wincing with pain, seeking to convince her. "Raising fire with you was the *most* profound experience of my life, Ishvari. If that Sumerian witch hadn't—" A spasm of coughing cut him off. "Alatu was to blame for *all* your suffering, you know," he continued persuasively. "She *hated* you…*you* were the shining one, and therefore she engineered your fall, with our dear Charaka's help, of course. As your gurus would say, evil always seeks to bring good down to its level."

He sounded like an adolescent trying to soften her with half-baked teachings.

"It was Alatu who coaxed me to send Kushal to Sumeria when I left to fight the Doms...and it was at her urging that I sent that weasel Ramses to you. I *cared* for you, Ishvari, truly I did...our nights of loving had brought you closer to me than my own breath...truth be told, the tumult within my heart as I lay beside you alarmed me. Your trust in me, your honesty, the purity of your gaze—all of this recalled Eshanika, whom I lost when I still believed in love.

"I made the error of telling Alatu I loved you as much as I'd loved my sweet bride. It was *she* who suggested I smoke ganja with you...the whore had tricked Devadas into showing her your astrological chart and learned of your weakness. I capitulated, fearing that if I stayed true to you, the gods would steal you too away from me, just as they had Eshanika." His whole countenance oozed self-pity. "And what would I do *then*? A maharajah cannot just pine away and die of grief, can he? No, no, no, it's simply not done."

Sadness welled up within her as she listened to his string of excuses and justifications; he spoke a mixture of truth and untruth in layers so inextricably enmeshed that he himself, she was sure, could not have told the two apart. The very same words of devotion would have thrilled her as high tantrika; now she was grateful that events had conspired to kick her out of his life.

"You should be flattered," Takshak was saying reproachfully. "Ill as I am, I've traveled far to meet you in person. One word, and my soldiers would have dragged you back to Melukhha in chains.

But I wished to honor you, by speaking to you in the privacy of your own wilderness."

Ishvari gazed at him, tears spilling down her cheeks at his monstrous denial.

"Weeping for what could have been?" Takshak inquired gently. "Oh, sweet one! I can only guess at the pleasurable shock of seeing me again after all these years...."

The lump in her throat grew mountainous. *How to break his narcissistic bubble?* Could he honestly believe she would desire him in his present state? Or that, having escaped his wrath, she'd allow herself to be dragged back to him in chains?

"I've more news for you," Takshak continued, leaning forward. "News to help you absolve me of *any* guilt for trying to destroy you. As you know, Ketaki sent me a message swearing Ramses had violated you against your will. Alatu hid it from me, scheming whore that she was, but I found it...the stupid woman should have burnt it if she meant to survive my wrath." His eyes gleamed like those of a wild animal. "Deep down I always knew that *my* Ishvari would never have succumbed to that unsavory fellow, and yet my lust for Alatu—*lust*, mind you—forced me to please her. Besides, it would have been impolitic to vex our mercurial Sargon, which is why I accepted Ramses's ridiculous tale—that you had *begged* him to satiate you, claiming that *I* had been away for too long, and that your erotic juices were streaming."

He laughed, a pitiful sound. "Alatu rewarded me well for my sins. She had her ways, that witch, oh my, my, my, did she have her little ways. But when I read Ketaki's message so many years later—and no, it wasn't just the news she gave me, but the steady love she held for you that impressed me—the spell lifted, and Alatu had no chance. I finished her brutally, Ishvari, I had her burned alive in the Quadrangle with all of Melukhha celebrating. Yes, Ishvari, it was in *your* memory that I made her suffer for ruining the great passion you and I once shared."

The shadow of a smile crossed his cracked lips. "You'll be pleased to hear that soon after Alatu screamed her way to death— and no, her gods did not save her as she swore they would—I bribed one of Ramses's *own* priests to poison him." He chuckled. "Cost a fortune—that cabal of sanctimonious rogues who surrounded that wily fellow were always an avaricious lot—but worth it to ensure he died in extreme agony." Takshak's skeletal face contorted with fury. "Even *now* the thought of him defiling you enrages me, and Alatu was to blame…it was all her fault.…"

Ishvari stared at him, honestly baffled: did Takshak *really* hold Alatu responsible for his evil? Or was he putting on a desperate act to get her to raise the fire?

"It's your turn to speak, dearest," he said. "What happened with the priest of Devikota?"

"What of him?" she asked, puzzled.

He shook his head indulgently. "Your fire does not give you such tidings?"

Ishvari shook her head, even more puzzled; the fire had revealed nothing, and since she'd stopped healing, no visitors brought such news to her ears.

"Why then, Ghora—wasn't that the fellow's name?—was on his way to Melukhha, with the headman of Devikota and two merchants. They were traveling in the chariot I'd sent to Devikota to carry *you* back to me. Bandits attacked it a short distance from the city, believing it carried royalty." Takshak took a shuddering breath. "The rogues were so infuriated to find mere *villagers* inside that they castrated, and then hung both the priest and the headman. The merchants escaped by handing over their gold. One of them claimed the priest had boasted he was carrying important news about the fake healer—news meant for *my* ears alone."

He licked his cracked lips. "Kushal *hated* that Devikotan priest, you know. Said he was in league with the headman, and that both were crooked beyond belief—as if *I* would give a fig for so insignificant a village." His eyes flickered over her face, trying to gauge her emotions. "I'll wager this news makes you happy, Ishvari. After all, those two scoundrels killed your father, did they not?" He paused for breath. "Do you think Ghora recognized you and sought the reward?"

"Perhaps," she shrugged, feeling a little burst of shock that karma had finally caught up with Ghora and Andhaka. She did not bother asking Takshak why he'd not removed the reward on her head once he was convinced of her innocence; nothing about this dangerously ill man had ever made sense. "Still, what a terrible way to die," she added, almost to herself. "No worse, I suppose, than a man struck unconscious and dragged to a pit of venomous serpents."

"Ah, I see," Takshak said. "You're thinking of how those two killed your father—and matching that up with your phenomenal knowledge of karmic law and suchlike. Well now, let me be frank—there's no need to play the saint with me...those men destroyed your family, and *I* am no village cretin begging for your fire." His eyes narrowed. "That mendicant who hung himself in your gardens—tell me, was he your lover?"

She nodded; why bother to lie to a dying man?

"A wanderer with a begging bowl?" Takshak cried, seemingly more mystified than outraged. "To sink so low after loving *me*?"

"Pundalik was pure," Ishvari replied. "He gave me what you never could."

Takshak sneered. "There's more to that story, of course. Never mind. Did the idiot hang himself, or did the guard supplying you with intoxicants do him in?" He shook his head. "Wouldn't talk, you know, that guardsman—went to his execution with his jaws clamped shut. Possibly because he knew he'd die anyway—we'd already traced your supply of drugs to him."

The past, with all its horrors, was as trivial to her as a distant dream. How could Takshak continue to cling to such pettiness in the face of looming death? Once a young high tantrika had been dazzled by his splendor, swooned at the thunder of his approaching chariot, and craved the sweetness of their coupling. *But had she ever really loved him?* The answer was no—at first, she'd been too enthralled by her own beauty, intellect and powers of seduction to understand *real* love, and later, too beaten down by king and circumstance to fathom its subtle nature. Still, the fire had risen between them, and the gods had blessed them with rare visions. Thanks to Takshak, she'd awakened the sleeping fire goddess, who now guarded her so fiercely; this thought humbled her, and compassion for him rose anew.

The rhythmic music of cicadas cut through the night, frogs croaked at the river's edge. Takshak's eyes glazed with pain. "The mendicant's *nothing!*" he rasped suddenly. "But satisfy me in one thing—who was the masked man at the puja? *Another* secret lover?"

Ishvari shut her eyes, praying for guidance. Should she tell him? No, the pain would be more than Takshak could bear. "He was never my lover," she said truthfully.

"That pleases me," he said. "Just thinking of him agitates me to the core. It was seeing you come alive in his presence that night at the ghats that provoked me...though of course it was *Alatu* who insisted I offer your body to those men. I had to obey the evil creature…I feared her magic." Takshak pinned her with his sickly eyes. "Now, come, my goddess, be kind to your king. You must have known the man. Why else would he have headed directly for you?"

"I *do* know him," she said quietly, giving in to the urge to break through his façade. "He is Nartaka, your father's son through Inanna and your half-brother. That is why, O Takshak, you love, fear and hate him—Nartaka is everything you could so easily have been."

Takshak's head fell back against his pillows in utter shock. Ishvari heard his guttural breathing as he struggled to raise it again. His eyes blazed with loathing, for he had no doubt she was speaking the truth. "*That evil whore!* To hide the existence of a son from my father! To turn my own half-brother into my enemy, to encourage him to block and humiliate me at every turn! Only a practitioner of the black arts could have rescued her from a dungeon encircled by armed guardsmen! *Everyone* knew this man was behind her escape! *Everyone* was laughing at me! That was the beginning of my decline, you know. I blame him for all that went wrong after that…."

"So much becomes clear to me now," Takshak whispered, his voice shaking with rage. "*Now* I understand Inanna's wickedness—she wanted her *own* son to rule!" He pulled himself together with a great effort. "I'll catch this bastard once I'm strong again, teach him a lesson he'll never forget. But now you must raise your fire for me and be quick about it…the pain's unbearable and no herb's potent enough to ease its sting. You *must* help me, Ishvari!" His voice shook with desperation. "We'll rule Melukhha together! I swear to you, we'll make history…."

"I've probed your body with the fire, Takshak, and it's too late for healing. Better to use your remaining time to beg the gods for forgiveness and make whatever amends you can...."

"*Lying whore!*" he cut her off, struggling to sit up. "I *command* you to heal me!"

"The goddess rises at her own will," Ishvari replied, unflustered.

Mating fireflies floated into the air and hovered over Takshak, casting a greenish glow on his pallid features. He sank back, his voice taking on a beggar's whine. "Have mercy on Melukhha, if not on me, Ishvari. I've no heir, only bastards who'll fight each other to death for the throne. The city's bound to fall into the hands of my inept Council. Put aside the past and help me. I swear to crown you maharani of Melukhha!"

"Your sole concern has been your pleasure, Takshak, no matter the cost to others." He opened his mouth to protest, but she held up a warning hand. "Why waste your breath? The fire will *not* rise for you."

Takshak shut his eyes, exhausted. "Say what you will, Ishvari," he muttered. "I *know* you can heal me. Two nights past, she appeared to me and advised me to seek the healer of Devikota. Cruel as she could be, it was never in her nature to taunt, which is why I am here tonight...."

"*Who* appeared to you?" Ishvari asked warily.

"Who else but Inanna? She always had this uncanny knack for making *me* feel like a peasant. I detested her because she turned my father against my mother, who died knowing my besotted father would have died to save a single hair on that whore's infernal head...."

"Inanna loved you enough to want you to evolve," Ishvari said firmly. "Karma throws us obstacle after obstacle so we can grow from our pain, Takshak. Men who destroy life and beauty are feared, never venerated. Take responsibility for your predicament and beseech the force beyond all forces to erase your past."

"Ah, my failed tantrika turned preacher," Takshak sneered. "What amazing faith you still flaunt!" A sly smile curved his dry lips. "I wonder how long it would survive under the threat of an executioner's sword? Would you crumple like Hariaksa, who offered me your life for his own? I refused, of course, swore I'd get you without his help. And I have, haven't I?"

Ishvari's heart swelled with sorrow; Takshak believed his own lies. Suddenly, it was critically important that she battle the demon waiting for him to die in order to drain the last of his once prodigious prana. The fire rumbled, disturbed by her dangerous thoughts, even as the demon stared back at her through Takshak's yellow eyes—voracious, cunning, insidious. She recoiled, coming to her senses—this demon had fed on Takshak from his youth, growing stronger the sicker the maharajah became; it could well destroy her. There was only so much the fire could combat while her spirit was still encased in human flesh.

Though no breath of wind stirred, the torches left behind by the guardsmen flickered and died. In the pale silver of moonlight, an ethereal being appeared before Takshak. Ishvari uttered a cry, for she knew her to be Mahadevi in her guise as goddess of death, immortal consort of Yama, lord of the underworld. The lovely apparition touched Takshak on his third eye and he groaned as he glimpsed the hell realms to which he was bound. Then she was gone, and silence crashed like thunder about Ishvari's ears. She fell to her knees, weeping soundlessly for Takshak. *Leave now*, her soul whispered urgently. *Head for the jungle!*

"Guards!" Takshak screeched weakly, pounding on the sides of his palanquin.

She slid down the rock, racing along the banks of the river. Ahead loomed the dark shape of the jungle. Behind, all she could hear was Takshak's violent retching.

To the pure in heart, everything is pure.
        —*Kaulavali Nirnaya Tantra*

BELOVED

As Ishvari raced past the jagged boulder against which she'd tried to crack her skull open as a child, a flashing vision of the Wild God in all his awesome glory rose up from her third eye. So Rudra's prophetic words had come to pass! Scourged by his divine whip, that anguished girl had evolved into a woman of transcendent light.

Serpent fire streaked up her spine, fueling her flight. As soon as she entered the moist darkness of deeper jungle, she paused to rest against a gnarled banyan trunk, giving thanks for the protection of Amrita's tiger skin garment even as she absorbed the eerie, nocturnal sounds of the jungle. "What now?" she humbly asked Mahadevi, inviting the fire to illumine her third eye. Almost instantly, a vision of a reed basket of fruit swam before her eyes. The message seemed clear—she was to seek Ushana.

Fearlessly she made her way through thickening foliage, avoiding overhanging branches and clumps of spiky thorn bushes by groping ahead with sensitive fingers. A beast roared and she slid into a copse of trees, waiting for the awesome sound reverberating through the still air to cease. Invoking the mantra of protection, she broke cover, grateful that her feet seemed to possess an intelligence all their own and were leading her surely into the heart of the jungle.

Serpents, some as thick as the arms of warriors, hung heavily off ancient trees and slithered across the damp earth. Rather than recoil from them as she would have done in the past, she felt an affinity with their primeval spirit. A wild boar with lethally curved tusks glared at her from across a clearing. She walked lightly past it. After negotiating tracts of dense jungle in darkness, she stumbled upon the same magnificent flame-of-the-forest tree that Ushana's tribals had used to suspend Ghora's terrified son. Now she knew for sure that she was on the right path.

Encouraged, she increased her pace, nursing the fire in the hope that the soft glow emitted by her body would repel hostile attack. Finally she heard the faint throb of drums. Accelerating toward the reassuring sound, she found a group of tribesmen sitting around a fire—one man a whole head and a half taller than the rest.

"Ushana," she called softly. The chieftain turned, and she saw from his tranquil gaze that he'd been restored to his full majesty. "Praise Chandika!" Ushana announced in the rumbling bass that seemed to rise up from his belly. "The healer has arrived!" His companions smiled their greetings, rose in a group and moved to sit a few feet away to give the two of them privacy. Ushana pressed his palms together in solemn greeting, gesturing for her to sit beside him. "Rest for a while, healer, and then you must leave," he said. "I've given Sumantra and Kamapala precise instructions regarding your journey. Right now they are preparing to carry you to safety."

Relieved by the giant's uncanny awareness, Ishvari sank into a cross-legged position beside him, stretching her hands towards the glowing coals with a sigh of pleasure. "Takshak's men may come after me," she said. "Are you armed? Can your men fight trained soldiers?"

Ushana snorted. "City soldiers won't even be able to *pick* up on our scent, healer, let alone defeat us. No doubt, your maharajah is brutish beyond belief—a pure miracle it will be if our Dom brothers ever recover their pride or their numbers. Yet Chandika's burning love constantly embraces my own people, and our particular hardships have made us wily.

He smiled and patted her thigh. "It was Chandika who prophesied your flight while I was dreaming three nights ago. Our goddess instructed me on how to help you, and advised me to lead my people to the other side of the river. Our new home is hidden behind swamps abundant with game and impenetrable to all but such as us." He smiled, revealing upper teeth sharpened to fine points. "And now that your maharajah has killed the sorceress, we shall be safe."

The chieftain placed his massive palm over the right side of his chest. "Chandika kissed my heart to show her pleasure at how things have come to pass, healer. Sadly, Bodhav's evil had infected more men than I ever suspected, but thanks to your timely intervention, our tribe once again lives in harmony." Ushana's deep-set eyes were bright in the firelight. "I've sent most of my men ahead, with all the women and children, to prepare our new home. Their drums tell me shelters have been built, and that there's plentiful food and good water—just in case the king's men dare venture this far. But I think not, given the serious troubles breaking out like a virulent rash in that once splendid city—one more renegade, no matter how beautiful, would not be worth the effort." He smiled grimly, his eyes taking on a faraway look. "No matter what happens to Melukhha, healer, Chandika assures me our people shall prosper in these parts. And *you* shall always have a home with us, should you ever wish it."

He placed his arm around her shoulders and pulled her close against his muscular body. Releasing her, he stared intensely into her eyes with his own deep-set orbs that seemed to see into other worlds. "When the moon rises high again, healer," he rumbled. "I shall drink the dreaming potion in your honor. A song of praise for the yogini who shared her fire with a thousand strangers shall spring forth from the heartspace our goddess kissed." He stroked her face with long fingers, his eyes shining with affection. "It shall be so lyrical a song, I promise, that our people will want to sing your praises forever."

Ishvari bowed her head, overcome with the sweetest of emotions; of all the supplicants she'd healed over the years, it was this man—whom refined urbanites might well hold in contempt for his primitive beliefs—who'd emerged as the most wise and generous. Indeed, once she too might have shuddered at his fierce devotion for Chandika, a goddess notorious for demanding blood sacrifices. But the vision Ushana had shared with his tribe the day she and Ghora's son had been captured proved that Chandika no longer thirsted for the blood of innocents—if she ever truly had. After the awakening of the fire, it had become dazzlingly clear to Ishvari that all deities were just manifestations of one ineffable power.

Ushana handed her a clay amphora half-filled with a greenish liquid, its outsides cleverly delineating a phosphorescent embossed form of the goddess he worshipped. Ishvari held it carefully in both hands, turning it around to study its stunning artwork. Never had she seen anything quite as bizarrely beautiful! Chandika's fearsome jaws were open wide, her bloody tongue hung out of her gaping mouth, and her teeth were sharpened to fine points—just as were Ushana's. The artwork was so vividly real she could almost see the gleam in Chandika's protuberant eyes, and feel the live energy running through the twisting coils of hair that streamed down the amphora's convex sides. "Drink this potion, healer," Ushana said. "The way ahead can be tricky at times. These herbs should help you sleep."

Ishvari hesitated as an image of Lord Kushal handing her a silver cup of bhang arose in her mind's eye. "It's blessed liquid, it can do you no harm," Ushana assured her kindly, plucking the thoughts right out of her mind, just as easily as Hariaksa, Atulya and Kharanshu had. Sensing his pure love, Ishvari raised the amphora and poured its contents down her throat. "Where am I going, my friend?" she asked, as the potion snaked its way down into her abdomen, leaving behind a trail of cold fire. Could Ushana be sending her to the mountain sanctuary where Atulya and Mandakini now thrived?

"All to be revealed in goddess time," Ushana replied nonchalantly, chuckling at her wry expression. "I laugh to see the interconnection of all things, healer—had you not twice saved my life, I'd not be here for you today." He reached forward and ran his fingers through the dark silk of her hair. Clucking with disapproval, he pulled out a gray strand, then another, and tossed them into the fire with a muttered curse. It was as if the giant wished she would remain forever young!

Ishvari smiled up at his strangely attractive face, gleaming in the firelight, feeling like a child embraced by the love of a good brother. Ushana patted her on the back, then beckoned towards the shadows. The twins who'd carried herself and Ghora's son back to the valley emerged from the darkness. "It's time to leave," Ushana informed them. "As always, travel safe and return home in peace. May Chandika grow wings on your feet!"

Euphoric warmth was already spreading through her body—the herbal concoction was potent. Sumantra darted behind a clump of trees and returned with an unusual contraption—a seat woven of river reeds and cushioned with handwoven cloth. Stirrups made for the feet were attached to its bottom. In the flare of torches, Ishvari saw that supple bamboo rods had been inserted through upper loops. Kamapala set the front of the rods carefully on his shoulder and called to his brother to grip the ends, six human feet behind.

Ushana lifted her up and eased her into the chair, bending to insert her bare feet carefully into the stirrups. "I had the seat rewoven and the rods replaced so it's strong and comfortable for you," he said, grinning proudly at her astonishment. "It belonged to my grandmother, first female chief of our tribe—a weighty and belligerent woman who enjoyed eating above all other activities and rarely, if ever, exerted herself. It was she who sent me to your fabled city for my education, and I hated her for it. Fortunately, she passed on before I was forever spoiled by city pleasures, and I returned to guide my tribe. This seat has not been used since her passing."

Ushana's grin turned mischievous. "It's our tradition to honor our ancestors, healer, and yet every day I pray to Chandika that our tribe is never again ruled by such a one. Truth is, most women are not wise as you are. I'm convinced our world will continue to exist only if females focus on bearing children and cooking."

Ishvari laughed, filled with gratitude for Ushana's confident support. Now was not the time to share with him tales of the wisdom and superior love of women such as Inanna, Ketaki and Mandakini, or of the intuitive intelligence that was, for the most part, unique to the female of the species. It was a pity there was no time to get to know Ushana better, and perhaps to discover whether he had good reason for holding such harsh views on women.

As if reading her thoughts again, Ushana winked naughtily, then bent low to place his third eye against her own, in a gesture of spiritual comradeship. "We shall meet again, healer, and you shall have the chance to erase my ignorance. Now go with Chandika!"

Then she was moving into even darker terrain, her body swaying gently in her soft pouch. Sleep came swiftly and she dreamed. Maruti and Vegavat appeared beside her, the monkey juggling lychee shells, the big cat casting his protective golden gaze upon her from time to time. Before long, the spirits of Archini and Sumangali joined them. Then there was Obalesh, playing his flute sweetly as Hiranya looked on with pride. All her spirit companions shone with the same, fiery radiance that she possessed.

Every now and again, an unfamiliar energy stirred in her groin, as if another divine force, too long asleep, was resurrecting itself. Whether she was waking or dreaming she couldn't tell, but once she heard her porters splashing through water and felt moistness seep through her seat.

The patter of rain overhead awoke her from a deep slumber. She was lying alone on spongy kusha matting. Where had the twins brought her? Looking around, she realized she was in a cozy clearing surrounded by colossal banyan trees whose aerial branches formed so tight a canopy that, despite the heavy rain, not a drop fell through. Enthralled, she saw that the whole area was covered with matting, and that the wood of the trees was so old it gleamed golden-brown. On a natural shelf, formed by the plaiting of roots, was a clay bowl piled high with glistening jungle berries and golden-hued mountain pears. A dying sun streamed through the knotted walls of the unusual dwelling, creating a surreal charm.

She pulled the tiger skin close around her, shut her eyes and curled up again, feeling as if she'd traveled to a higher realm.

When she awoke, much later, her eyes fell upon a narrow moonlit path that curved around a rough corner. She followed it and found herself in a cubicle shaped out of twisted aerial roots, ingeniously transformed into a washroom equipped with an enormous green faience water jar, sandalwood cleansing powder, a cloth towel striped in orange and white, and most surprising of all, a flagon of oil hinting of musk and white roses!

Whose home was this? A hermit with a taste for rare comforts? Lest the inhabitant should return and toss her out before she could take advantage of her good fortune, she quickly stripped, and washed the grime off her hair and body. Drying herself vigorously, she moisturized her skin with the scented oil, feeling as pampered as a maharani. Refreshed, she lay down again on the matting, listening to the patter of rain on the trees and the muffled boom of thunder.

Somewhere, the chataka bird who subsisted on raindrops had turned its face to the skies, ecstatically drinking the fluid that gave it life. Sighing with pleasure, Ishvari stretched her body, immensely grateful for her own life. To escape twice from a virulently sick and materially powerful man with no scruples—this was divine protection indeed!

Ishvari considered her situation afresh, her mind skimming over recent events. Soon Takshak would pass away. Who would succeed him? The Melukhhan Council, acting in concert? An ambitious aristocrat ready to seize power at the decisive moment? Her eyelids fluttered with the onset of a new wave of sleep, and the fire settled into a dull glow, as if Madadevi herself desired rest. Tomorrow was time enough to plan for the future.

At some point in that blessed night, a man lay down beside her. Ishvari awoke to the pleasure of strong fingers running through her hair and wandering over the contours of her face, their tips vibrating with energy. Opening her eyes, she gazed with quiet awareness into the face of her beloved. As Nartaka's dark eyes met her own, the divine force already stirring within her exploded into full flower.

Tapers threw flickering shadows on the natural walls of the enclosure even as it struck her that the tribals had carried her back to the gnostic hermitage. Decades ago, it was here that this mystifying man had initiated an unhappy high tantrika into investigating her true nature. Smiling down at her with the assurance of unquestioned love, Nartaka invited her to rest her head against his chest. She nuzzled against him, matching the rhythm of her breath to his as she fused with the energy of his firm body. His eyes narrowed as he trailed his fingers down her spine, and she pressed her lips against his, embracing him with passion. Then he was worshiping her like the goddess she had become, face to face, heart to heart, yoni to lingam.

Fire rose, strong and insistent, enveloping them in a mantle of warmth as it looped and swirled through their bodies. Brilliant energy soared up Ishvari's spine, igniting each chakra along the way. A slender cord of shimmering light connected their bodies, minds and spirits, as if they were ecstatic dancers in faultless synchrony. A high singing rose in her throat and pierced the air, and then she was radiance and bliss, the primal force.

As she entered the vastness of the third eye, Ishvari saw faces and forms melting into one other—Sumangali suckling Obalesh, Hariaksa sitting placidly beside the river, Archini peering down from her perch on the dormitory wall in silvery moonlight, the patterned bulk of a python slithering into the gloom of deep jungle,

Urmila and Tilotamma in hot embrace, Lord Kushal raising an eyebrow as he listened to her with grave interest, wise Ketaki and devoted Mandakini, passionate Vasudeva, Maruti gibbering in fear from a tree as the hag mocked her by the banks of the holy river, Kharanshu gently lifting her emaciated body on to the swaying hammock beside the Sarasvati, Atulya's paternal smile as he bade her farewell in the valley, Takshak's yellow eyes watching her like a predator even as he shifted feebly on his grand palanquin.

Vegavat roamed proudly through emerald jungles gleaming in the shadow of high black mountains. The wildflower face of a girl appeared and faded into the visage of a wrinkled crone who changed into a bearded stranger with the cold eyes of a killer. A middle-aged monk with shaven head burned on a pyre, his eyes raised high in hope. Packs of monstrous beings whose limbs spanned earth and sky raced flying creatures with wingspans of a thousand feet. Jagged teeth ripped burly, ape-faced men apart as huge women whirled around a blazing fire, over which the carcass of a demon roasted.

The moon rose high above the jungle as Ishvari and Nartaka danced in the ancient rhythms of love, its cool light saturating the space between and around them in lucent waves that expanded and contracted with their movements. Nartaka placed his head on her breast, and her breathing deepened as she experienced the wholeness formed by male and female in a state of bliss. Then there was no movement, no sound, only a dreamlike fusion that melted their minds, bodies and spirits into a single luminous unbounded sweep.

The eightfold yoga
The six regions of the body
The five states
They all have left and gone
Totally erased
And in the open
Void
I am left
Amazed
There is but a rounded Moon
A fountain of white milk
For delight
The unobtainable Bliss
Has engulfed me
A precipice
Of light.

Pattinattar, Tamil Tantrik Siddha

GLOSSARY

acharya. Guide or instructor in religious matters; founder, leader of a sect; learned man or title affixed to the names of learned men.

aghora. *one who cannot be shaken or agitated;* extreme path of Tantra, also known as the left-hand path, involving practices of intense ritual worship. See also **Tantra**.

Aham Brahmaasmi. *I Am the Divine Consciousness.*

ahamkara. identification or attachment to one's ego.

ahimsa. to refrain from violence towards all living things, though **self-defense** is considered the sign of a strong spirit. Ahimsa springs from the dual notion that all living beings are connected, and that all forms of violence entail negative karmic consequences.

apsara. celestial nymph.

arak. distilled alcoholic drink made from the fermented sap of coconut flowers, sugarcane, grain or fruit.

arka. *ray of light;* holy tree native to India known for its medicinal properties, with thick, ash-colored branches and a milky sap. Arka flowers cluster into a bunch, and each flower bears five petals with an inner structure resembling a crown.

asanas. Physical postures which have evolved into the vast body of *hatha yoga*, designed to unify body, mind and spirit. See also **yoga**.

ayurveda. System of ancient Indian practices intended to promote physical, mental and spiritual health.

bakula. Sacred evergreen tree that grows throughout India, known for its fragrant white flowers, sweet fruit, and use in Ayurvedic medicine.

bhang, bhanga. Intoxicant prepared from the leaves and flower buds of the female cannabis plant, smoked or consumed as a beverage in the Indian subcontinent. Associated with the God

Shiva, it is used to induce sleep, to relieve anxiety and to whet the appetite. See also **ganja**.

buddhi. Intellect.

chakra. Circle, wheel; used to indicate psychic centers within the human body. See also **kundalini**.

chillum. Conical **pipe** used for smoking marijuana, hashish or tobacco; fashioned out of clay, porcelain, soapstone, glass, wood.

champakali. Bud of the perfumed yellow champaa flower native to India.

devadaru. *wood of the gods*; tall evergreen coniferous tree sacred to God Shiva that thrives in the western Himalayas and has construction, aromatic and medicinal uses; also known as cedar or deodar.

dharma. Spiritual law; one's higher calling or duty.

devi. Goddess, or female aspect of the divine.

ganja. Bud of the *cannabis sativa* (marijuana) plant.

gnosis. Path to self-knowledge leading to enlightenment, designed to relieve one of cultural and religious indoctrination, and to reconcile one to a personal deity; synonym for Sanskrit word *jnana* meaning *path of wisdom*.

guru. Being of knowledge, wisdom, and authority in a certain area, who guides others. A true guru is most often held to be a prerequisite for a seeker to attain self-realization. See also *acharya*.

hatha yoga. *Hatha* combines two Sanskrit words: *ha* meaning sun, and *tha* meaning moon. Thus, Hatha Yoga is known as that branch of Yoga which unites pairs of opposites, referring to the positive (sun) and negative (moon) currents in the system.

ida. Major *nadi* corresponding to the left side of the body and the right hemisphere of the brain; associated with lunar and female energy, and thus thought to produce a cooling effect. See also **nadi**.

jiva. Immortal essence of a living organism which survives physical death.

jnana. Sanskrit word *jnana* meaning *path of wisdom.* See also **gnosis.**

jumlum. Purple fruit with tart-sweet flavor, also known as jambhul.

juttu. Tuft of hair jutting out from a point a little to the back of the top of the skull; wearing a juttu indicates a certain status.

karma. Hindu laws of cause and effect that ensure that every single thought, speech or action—positive, negative or neutral—must inevitably produce a corresponding result. Karmic seeds may ripen immediately or later in the same lifetime, or may be planted in one lifetime and ripen in another, when specific causes and conditions arise. See also **reincarnation.**

karnikara. Deciduous tree up to 15 meters high with bright yellow flowers that grows all over India.

ko. Unit of measurement.

kohl. Eye cosmetic used in India, the Middle East, Africa and South Asia to darken the eyelids; also used as mascara for the eyelashes.

kundalini. Primal energy coiled quiescently at the base of the human spine. When properly awakened, *kundalini* shoots up from the base of the spine toward the highest psychic center or *chakra* positioned at the crown of the skull; also known as *serpent fire* or *sacred fire.*

kusha. Perennial grass used in various traditions as a sacred plant; mentioned in the *Rig Veda* for use in sacred ceremonies and also as a seat for priests and the Gods; specifically recommended by Krishna in the *Bhagavad Gita* as part of the ideal seat for meditation.

linga/m. Male organ of reproduction; often used to symbolize Shiva and male creative energy.

maithuna. Tantric rite of love-making; once the union is consecrated, maithuna becomes a divine channel for the interplay between Lord Shiva and the Goddess Shakti or Mahadevi. See also *Tantra; Tantrik; Tantrika.*

maharani. Queen.

mala. Prayer beads. See also *rudraksha*

mandala. circle; geometric pattern representing the cosmos, metaphysically or symbolically, a microcosm of the Universe from the human perspective.

mantra. Sound, syllable, word, or group of words originating from a rishi or seer in a high state of consciousness and used for spiritual transformation.

maya. illusion, or *that which can be measured.* Indian philosophical concept centered on the notion that one does not experience the environment itself, but rather a projection of it, created by one's unique mind; also refers to the principal deity that manifests, perpetuates and governs the cosmic illusion, and the dream of duality between the world and the Self in the phenomenal *Universe.* See also *samsara.*

moksha. release; liberation from *samsara* and the suffering involved in being subject to the cycle of repeated death and *reincarnation.* See also *reincarnation; sadhu; samsara.*

mudra. Symbolic or ritual gesture, mostly performed with hands and fingers, and often used in conjunction with *pranayama* to stimulate different parts of the body and to affect the flow of *prana.* See also *prana, pranayama.*

nadi. river or *flow.* In traditional Indian medicine and spiritual science, channels or meridians through which the energies or consciousness of the subtle body are said to flow. Nadis connect at special points of intensity called *chakras* and carry a life force energy known as *prana*.

ojas. *vigor;* essential energy of the body equated with the 'fluid of life'; when sufficient, ojas is equated with immunity; when deficient, the result is weakness, fatigue and ultimately disease.

pariah. Person with a social stigma due to alleged criminal behavior or non-acceptance of societal norms.

pingala. Major *nadi* corresponding to the right side of the body and the left hemisphere of the brain; associated with solar and male energy, and thus thought to produce a heating effect. See also **ida, nadi.**

prana. Vital life-sustaining force believed to flow through a network of fine, subtle channels in the body called *nadis*. See also **ida, pingala, nadi.**

pranayama. Extension of *prana*. The word is composed of two Sanskrit words, *prana,* life force, or vital energy, particularly, the breath, and *ayama,* to extend, draw out, restrain, or control. See also **prana.**

puja, pooja. Ritual performed as an offering to a deity to receive blessings.

rajkumari. Princess.

rakshasa. Demon.

rebirth. See **reincarnation.**

Red Tantra. Tantric teachings that pertain specifically to sexual techniques used by couples in order to reach permanent liberation from suffering.

reincarnation. *rebirth;* occurs after physical death when the soul or spirit returns to life in a new form, though bearing the karmic consequences of past lives; since one cannot validly exist without the other, karma and reincarnation are two sides of the same coin. See also **karma.**

rishi. *seer*, to whom truth is revealed in states of higher **consciousness**; a female seer is known as a *rishika*.

rudraksha. Evergreen broad-leaved tree whose seed is traditionally used to make prayer beads or *malas* (garlands/rosaries).

sadhu. Ascetic or wandering monk committed to achieving *moksha* through meditation and contemplation. See also **moksha.**

sacred fire. See **kundalini.**

samadhi. Experience of pure formless consciousness in the spiritual heart.

samsara. *continuous flow*; cycle of **birth**, **life**, **death**, and **reincarnation**; repetitive existence; continuous stream of consciousness, or the continuous but random drift of passions, desires, emotions, and experiences.

serpent fire. See **kundalini.**

shatkarmas. Tantric foundational practices for cleansing the physical body.

siddhi/s. *perfection, attainment, success*; supernatural powers that result from spiritual practice, and include clairvoyance, levitation, bilocation, reducing to the size of an atom, materialization, accessing memories from past lives, etc.

soma. Ritual drink among early Indo-Iranians and subsequent Vedic and greater Persian cultures. The Vedas portray *soma* as a god, and drinking it was said to produce immortality.

Surya Namaskara. Sequence of hatha yoga asanas practiced at different levels of awareness and whose origins lie in the worship of Surya, the Hindu solar deity. Known in English as Sun Salutation.

Sushumna. central *nadi* through which *kundalini* energy should ideally ascend; flanked by *ida* and *pingala*, *sushumna* connects the base *chakra* to the crown *chakra*. See also **chakra; ida, kundalini; pingala, nadi.**

sweetling. small, sweet thing; used as a term of endearment.

Tantra. *loom, reweave;* fusion of two Sanskrit words: *trayati* (explosion) and *tanoti* (consciousness). Tantra encompasses celibate and sexual techniques and holds a radically positive vision of the whole of reality as an expression of a joyous Divine Consciousness, i.e., the divine interplay of Mahadevi/Shakti and Shiva. Tantric practices and rituals aim to bring about an inner realization of this truth, bringing freedom from ignorance and rebirth in the process. See also **maithuna.**

tantric/tantrik. Male adept of *Tantra.* See also **Tantra.**

tantrika. Female adept of *Tantra.* See also **Tantra.**

Triple World. The combined dimensions of the universe; also refers to earth, space and heaven, or past, present and future.

The Two Truths. Truths pertaining to the two main realms of consciousness of Absolute and Relative; also known as nirvana and samsara, unmanifest and manifest; infinite and finite, etc.

vasana. Karmic residues or unconscious propensities; present awareness of past (life) perceptions; compulsions/predilections from past lives.

yoga. Physical, mental and spiritual discipline originating in ancient India, whose goal is the attainment of a state of balanced spiritual insight and tranquility. Literally, *union* of inner male and female, *ida* and *pingala,* yin and yang. See also **ida; pingala.**

yoga nidra. Yogic sleep, or deep relaxation of body and mind leading to inner peace and joy.

yoni. Female genitalia; often considered as a symbol of the Goddess Shakti, and female creative energy.

BIBLIOGRAPHY

Whip of the Wild God was conceived in 1993. Decades before, and up to the date of this novel's publication, however, the author immersed herself in the vast areas of Hatha Yoga, Buddhism, Sufism, Taoism, Advaita-Vedanta and related philosophies. While acknowledging a great debt to the many adepts, scholars and writers by whose work she was inspired, the author is unable to recollect every book she has read in quest of understanding mysticism. What follows is only a partial list of her reading material, and includes sources for citations within the novel.

Auboyer, Jeannine. *Daily Life in Ancient India: From 200 BC to 700 AD.* London: Phoenix Press, 2002.

Avalon, Arthur [Sir John Woodroffe]. *The Serpent Power: The Secrets of Tantric and Shaktic Yoga.*
New York: Dover Publications, Inc., 1974. First published, London: Luzac & Co., 1919.

Euripides. *The Bacchae and Other Plays.* Translated by Philip Vellacott. London: Penguin Classics, 1972.

Feuerstein, Georg, ed. *Enlightened Sexuality: Essays on Body Positive Spirituality.* Freedom, CA: The Crossing Press, 1989.

Holy Madness: The Shock Tactics and Radical Teachings of Crazy-Wise Adepts, Holy Fools, and Rascal Gurus. New York: Paragon House, 1991.

Tantra: The Path of Ecstasy. Boston: Shambala Publications, Inc., 1998.

Feuerstein, Georg, Subhash Kak, and David Frawley. *In Search of the Cradle of Civilization:*
New Light on Ancient India. Wheaton, IL: Quest Books, 1995.

Goldberg, B.Z. *Sacred Fire: The Story of Sex in Religion.* London: Jarrolds, 1937. Facsimile of the first edition. Montana, USA: Kessinger Publishing, 1995.

James, William. *The Varieties of Religious Experience: A Study in Human Nature, Being the Gifford Lectures on Natural Religion Delivered at Edinburgh 1901-02.* London: Longmans, Green & Co., 1902.

Johari, Harish. *Chakras: Energy Centers of Transformation.* Rochester, VT: Inner Traditions–Bear & Company, 1987.

Judge, William Q. *Bhagavad-Gita, Recension, Combined with His Essays on the Gita.* Pasadena, CA: Theosophical University Press, 1978.

Karma-glin-pa. *The Tibetan Book of the Dead.* Edited by W.Y. Evans-Wentz. Delhi: Winsome Books India, 2008.

Kenoyer, Jonathan M. *Ancient Cities of the Indus Valley Civilization.* Karachi: Oxford University Press and American Institute of Pakistan Studies, 1998.

Kramrisch, Stella. *The Presence of Śiva.* Princeton, NJ: Princeton University Press, 1981.

Krishna, Gopi. *Kundalini: The Evolutionary Energy in Man.* Boston: Shambhala Publications, Inc., 1970. First published, New Delhi: Ramadhar & Hopman, 1967.

McArthur, Tom. *Yoga and the Bhagavad-Gita: An introduction to the philosophy of yoga.* London: Thorsons, 1986. Mookerjee, Ajit. *Tantra Asana: A Way to Self-Realization.* New Delhi: Ravi Kumar, 1971.

Morinis, E. Alan. *Pilgrimage in the Hindu Tradition –A Case Study of West Bengal.* New York: Oxford University Press, 1984.

Odier, Daniel. *Tantric Quest: An Encounter with Absolute Love.* Rochester, VT: Inner Traditions – Bear & Company, 1997.

Pagels, Elaine. *The Gnostic Gospels.* New York: Vintage Books, 1979.

Robinson, James M., ed. *The Nag Hammadi Library in English.* Translated by George W. MacRae. San Francisco: Harper and Row, 1977.

Sharma, S.K. *Hijras: The Labelled Deviants.* Delhi: Gyan Books Pvt. Ltd., 2000.

Sinha, Indra, ed. *The Great Book of Tantra: Translations and Images from the Classic Indian Texts.* Rochester, VT: Park Street Press, 1993.

van Buitenen, J.A.B., trans. *The Mahābhārata, Volume 1, Book 1: The Book of the Beginning.* Chicago: University of Chicago Press, 1973.=

—*The Mahābhārata, Volume 2, Book 2: The Book of Assembly; Book 3: The Book of the Forest.* Chicago: University of Chicago Press, 1975.

—*The Mahābhārata, Volume 3, Book 4: The Book of the Virata; Book 5: The Book of the Effort.* Chicago: University of Chicago Press, 1978.

Wasson, Robert G. *Soma: Divine Mushroom of Immortality.* New York: Harcourt, 1972.

Wheeler, Mortimer. *The Indus Civilization; Supplementary Volume to the Cambridge History of India, 3rd ed.* Cambridge: Cambridge University Press, 1968.

ACKNOWLEDGMENTS

The seed of this novel sprouted in the biting Manhattan winter of 1993. Since then, as I traversed the globe in quest of inner peace, it has shaped itself to the twists and turns of my spiritual path.

A multitude of beings inspired me on this journey. I thank my family of origin for imbuing me with a passion for storytelling; Jeff Caughey, who opened my heart to the transforming beauty of tantric philosophy; James Kelleher who informed me with vedic astrological authority that I had best complete this novel; Swami Asokananda, who dazzled me with eastern philosophy; Joneve McCormick, who insisted I keep writing; Alice Tasman, my Manhattan-based literary agent in early and later years, Marcela Landres, who inspired me to create the character of Inanna; Alan Machado-Prabhu, for his penchant for historical detail, Antoinette Botsford, who inspired me to refine this saga; Nandini Rao, who worked enthusiastically with me on a recent major revision; Jo Sgammoto and Jen Wilson, both of whom have been amazingly generous with their praise and support.

To name a few of the thousand other muses who urged me on in no particular order: Michael Roach, Chloe Tartaglia, Mark Kemper, Daniel Reid, Ryan Shaw, Gabriel Carciamaru, Raj Acharya, Deborah Peters, Gabriel Constans, Jürgen Marsiske, Karen Marshall, Christine Stromer, Katherine Lambert, Kathy Braun, Karin Johnson, Vimala Storey, Kalpana Ghai, Putli Bijoor, Stefan Dombrowski, Joseph Goldman, Silvia Gonzalez, Radha Metro, and KB, who supports me steadfastly as I investigate my higher Self.

Finally, immense gratitude to all my gurus from beginningless time, especially to Rudra-Shiva in the form of the sacred hill Arunachala, and the luminous seer Bhagavan Ramana Maharshi, who coax me away from the ravening darkness of egotism, and toward the gnosis that reveals each of us to be the blazing light.

2702451R00251

Made in the USA
San Bernardino, CA
25 May 2013